Edward gave a mental snort. "You continue to disobey orders."

Sophia groaned in frustration, probably suspecting where his statement was leading. "I'm very sorry." She sucked in a breath. "I shan't do it again. As I came out alone, I thought it would be safe." She sent him a sidelong glance. "Is this a punishable offense, my lord?"

Perfect. She knew she was wrong. She saw what was coming. Her side-eyed glance told him she mayhap even invited it. Who was he to refuse a girl a spanking?

He took a deep breath, wishing... *No. She's not mine to covet. But she is mine to punish tonight.*

His eyes shuttered as he considered. Was he taking advantage of her naiveté about Ton rules? He knew she'd enjoyed the last punishment and could not deny either of their desires. He almost heard the turn of the key as his conscience was again locked away.

He pushed, "We have been over this, Sophia. Punishment is an important learning tool. Hopefully, it shall be an incentive for you to obey specific directions in the future."

Frustrated, she crossed her gloved arms. "Darn it. My feet hurt so much. I did not anticipate my bottom becoming sore, too. I shan't be able to sit *or* stand comfortably."

That wasn't a no.

Sophia's Schooling

School of Enlightenment
Book One

by

Maggie Sims

Sophia's Schooling

Cover Art by *Lisa Dawn MacDonald*

The Wild Rose Press, Inc.
PO Box 708
Adams Basin, NY 14410-0708

Publishing History
First Edition, 2022
Trade Paperback ISBN 978-1-5092-4302-0
Digital ISBN 978-1-5092-4303-7

Published in the United States of America

Dedication

To Mum, my first A+ editor
And to my husband, my real life romance hero

Acknowledgments

It takes a village… For this book, it was a virtual village, as I finished the first draft in the height of the shutdown. Despite all conferences being online—or maybe because of it—I met an amazing group of people and this book would not be in your hands without them. My Virtual Critique Partners (VCP) are phenomenal partners in writing, encouragement, and brainstorming, as well as critiques. Special thanks to the OG team who still hang on Zoom with me regularly. In person support from my local RWA chapter was also wonderful.

Michal Scott, Ainsley St. Claire, Annabel Joseph, and others—all multi-published authors—have spent valuable hours mentoring, supporting, and teaching me. The Passionate Ink org, especially the leadership, has also gone above and beyond.

And most of all, first of all, and last of all, my very own real life romance hero, my husband. I would not be able to write romance without you in my life.

Chapter One

Spring 1816

Edward Morduant stood in his friend's front hall, watching the butler walk away, shoulders tight, hands fisted at his side, a letter scrunched in one.

The library door was open a crack, and he saw Nicholas Howard, Earl of Suffolk, raise his head at the knock.

"Sir." His butler, Harris, entered, fingering a calling card with the print crossed out and something scribbled on it. "I beg your pardon, but…" He cleared his throat. "The Earl of Peterborough is here to see you."

Nicholas's head pulled back, and his voice echoed his confusion. "Charles?"

"Ah, no, sir." The butler's lips pressed together for a second. "Edward."

"What?" The earl surged to his feet and strode to the door. "Edward!"

Edward's shoulders dropped a fraction in relief when Nicholas grasped his shoulder and directed him into the library. "Come, I've ordered tea."

After they settled into their usual spots in matching Chippendale armchairs by the unlit fireplace, Nicholas commented, "You look rather grim, my friend. What's happened?"

Edward handed over the note with the seal broken. "Charles is dead—a fever, apparently. You're talking to the new Earl of Peterborough." His voice rose on the title, betraying his tension. He leaned forward, resting his forearms on his thighs, dangling his hands between them.

"Ah, gads. I don't know what to say. I know you and your brother were not close, with the age difference, but I am sorry." Nicholas frowned, as if considering the implications. "I also realize inheriting your brother's responsibilities was the last thing you wanted. How are you feeling?"

Edward sighed. His friend had played a significant part in Edward's successful graduation from Cambridge. Nicholas had seen him struggling with the quantity of reading. Eventually, Edward admitted that words and letters became scrambled, and it took him forever to wade through the literature, to say naught of the Greek and Latin. So Nicholas had read important passages aloud and practiced their arguments for oral exams with him.

After school, Edward was relieved. He was clear of reading more than a newspaper or letter and had a steward to help with the books for the horse training business he wanted to grow. Charles had promised him funding and use of the family seat to start the business if, and only if, he had graduated. Edward had struggled through graduation and spent the last seven years reveling in his freedom and following his dream.

Now, he faced Parliamentary bills to opine on in the House of Lords. While he was glad of Nicholas's help, he resented the need to ask for more assistance. To complicate matters, they were not in Town together that often, necessitating letters. Worst of all, given the various alliances needed to navigate Lords, he risked his secret being exposed again.

"We were not close, but 'tis strange to think he is dead. He and his wife were always going to soirees on new scientific developments and writing to me about them, with sketches." The men exchanged a grin at Charles finding a method of writing that worked best for Edward. "Most of the time, I feel overwhelmed. I don't even know where to begin."

"What needs to be done immediately?"

"That is what I came here to ask you." He ran one work-roughened hand through his dark hair and nodded at the note. "Charles's widow has asked how long she has to vacate the London house. I know she hasn't much family, but she and Charles rarely visited Peterborough, so I had the run of the place…"

Staring into space, he contemplated having his brother's widow on the estate without his brother. "I am not certain I want her in the dower house, and she would likely be bored stiff in the country anyway; they were both city people. I just wish they'd had children. I would have far less to worry about. Hellfire, I shall have to consider marriage and heirs at some point." He stood to pace in front of the fireplace, frustration turning to agitation. He had no interest in the complications or monotony of being tied to one woman forever.

"Hmm, well, not to be callous, but it couldn't have happened at a better time. The Season is about to start. You have plenty of chances to find a wife."

"No, just no." Edward's shoulders tensed, the words forced out between tight lips in immediate reaction. "I don't have time right now, nor the inclination. And now, of all times, I need whatever small liberties I may find from the conformity of an earldom. Never mind the fun of sexual spankings, I cannot envision a marriage without a method to ensure good behavior." He added with a smile, "Blast it, 'tis your fault for dragging me to Cheltie's house party that summer. Although given the excesses I saw there, mayhap I should be thankful that only spanking appealed."

Since then, the two men had shared many evenings at Sarah Potter's Spanking Club before Nicholas ended his membership to marry. Edward ducked his head and mumbled, "And I have no interest in leg-shackling myself to some harpy who will discover my inability to read."

"Edward, I had no trouble finding a wife, and I was with you that night the busybody duke heard us mention the club. As for the other, I wish you could see not all women are like your governess. Others will understand."

"Come now, Nicholas, you know better. The headmaster's assistant at boarding school was the same. I am surprised I didn't have permanent birch stripes before I discovered holding it was the far better option. And the Ton loves nothing better than an excuse to rip someone to shreds. Hellfire and damnation, I never expected to end up as the earl. Charles was married for seven years. He should have had an heir by now, dammit!"

He shook his head. *Of all the members of White's, it had to be one of the biggest gossips. Imagine what would happen if he knew I take hours to get through the front page of the newspaper.*

Nicholas's mouth flattened. "But he didn't. And while I understand your concerns, you'd be surprised at what doors an earldom opens. And what legs…"

The men both snickered before sobering again.

"I am not ready to give up the spice and variety I enjoy at Sarah's." Edward left it at that. He refrained from repeating his fears of discovery regarding his reading affliction, given Nicholas's dismissal of that issue. He supposed, because his friend did not mind, he'd assume others would not as well.

"I don't know that you—" Nicholas began.

A tap on the door preceded Nick's wife Roslynn's entrance.

The men rose, Edward stepping forward to bow and kiss her hand. "Ros, you are breathtaking, as always."

"Edward, lovely to see you. I am very sorry to interrupt. I merely desired to tell Nicholas his cousin and I are stepping out soon. We are off to my modiste in Bloomsbury Square." Her gaze had gone to her husband, but returned to Edward. "We shall see you for dinner on Friday, sir?"

"I would not miss it."

Nicholas tugged her closer and kissed her briefly. "Have fun and be home for dinner."

"Yes, my lord," she replied with a quick, shallow curtsy. Her gaze lowered in deference, an intimate smile for her husband on her lips.

As Ros glided out of the room, Edward remained standing. "I must start thinking through what needs to get done. I shall start a list, then mayhap I could run it by you?"

Nicholas nodded.

"First thing is to write Charles's widow and tell her there is no hurry. I had already rented a house here for my trips into Town. It seems I shall have more need of it than I expected. She can maintain the family residence here while we take time to adjust and consider the future."

Nicholas shrugged. "I am here any time, you know that. Just be careful about letting too much time pass. Begin as you mean to go on. It sets expectations better, in marriage as well as with in-laws."

Edward furrowed a brow at Nicholas's smirk as he headed for the door. *Is he referring to his own marriage? Bah, no matter. I am not about to marry and risk some society miss discovering the fact that I can barely read.*

Too impatient to wait for his gelding to be brought around, Edward turned to the back hall, aiming for the stables. The staff was accustomed enough to his habits that no one paid heed.

****

Edward strode through the stable toward the stall his horse, Ash, was often given. In the stall before Ash's, he noted a new addition to the stable. Stopping at the half door, he looked over what appeared to be a Palomino, with warm tan skin and pale mane and tail. The mare was meticulously groomed and calm but inquisitive, looking at him when he stopped. She wandered over to sniff at him like a puppy looking for treats.

He scratched her nose and grinned. "You're a very pretty girl."

Ash shifted in the next stall at the sound of

Edward's voice, and he heard a whispered oath. He frowned. Was someone in Ash's stall? Nicholas's stable hands had been directed to leave him be.

Edward took the few steps to peer in and saw a figure facing him in a crouch by Ash's front leg, white-blonde hair reminiscent of the Palomino's mane half hanging out of her cap. She shifted to accommodate the horse's sidestep, and her breasts swayed in her simple loose muslin dress. Distracted, Edward watched for further movement of the pale mounds as they pressed against the cotton. His cock stirred in his trousers, jolting him. He'd never had such a visceral reaction to a servant.

Ash's head swung up, then down at him, scenting him, and the gelding pulled out of the girl's grasp to step forward to his beloved owner.

Edward's anger returned, delicious view or not. "What are you doing in there? Come out at once."

Her head snapped up, mouth open in shock.

His gaze ran over her features, eyes the color of a rare clear British sky, skin so pale as to match her hair, and pretty pink lips he wanted to… He refocused on the risks to this tiny creature next to his beast of a horse.

Closing her lips, she frowned. "I was simply treating a small sore on his leg."

Edward noticed the jar of salve in her hand.

"I don't care. Your employer should have told you not to mess with visitors' horses. Not even the stable staff touch my horse." *Certainly not some chit who likely knows nothing about horses, as pretty as she may be.*

He opened the half door and stepped in to check Ash's leg. Wanting to see the salve, he again instructed her, "Give me that and get out of the way."

"Here, then." She thrust the jar into his hand. "But mind you, I want that back. I made it."

His brows rose. Bringing it to his nose, he sniffed it, then stuck a finger in to smear on the back of his other hand. It seemed to have much of the same ingredients to his stablemaster's salve. He watched her through his upper lashes as he squinted and tried to evaluate why a housemaid would be out here in the first place. "Did someone from the stables call for you?"

"No, I was here checking on Nellie and saw this beauty come in." She tilted her head toward the Palomino's stall before doing something that made his heart stop. She patted Ash's ribs, then brushed by Edward to duck around the horse's head, leaving no room for error.

His breath caught. She was still a stranger to Ash, and he typically did not like people in his space.

"*What* in damnation do you think you're doing?!" Edward roared, channeling his fear into anger once she was safely away from his mount's teeth.

"What you said, sir." Her voice was nonchalant. "You asked me to get out of the way."

"Never. Ever. Do. That. Again. With any horse, but especially with one this size that could crush you."

Her laugh tinkled out. "Ah, he won't hurt me. Will you, boy?" She was by Ash's head now, which shook side to side.

Edward was sure there had been a fly bothering the horse. 'Twasn't like the animal understood this curious young woman, after all.

He saw red, his many frustrations catching up to him, and now this *girl* thinking she knew better than he.

Stomping around his horse's muzzle, he shoved the beast back a bit. As the well-mannered horse stepped out of the way, Edward leaned over the chit, a muscle in his clenched jaw ticking. "You don't know this horse. If I ever catch you playing fast and loose with an unknown horse again, I will spank your arse so red you will not sit for a week. Do you understand me?"

Somewhere under the anger, he knew he could not do that in a household not his own. He had never needed to or thought of doing it with his own staff. But this girl's disregard for her own safety provoked him beyond anything in recent memory.

Why do I care about some chit who should not be in the stables anyway? His conscience chose then to weigh in. *Or do I merely want a chance to spank her arse?* He admitted that the glimpse of her creamy breasts and the swish of her muscular arse past him probably contributed to the desire, but so did his experience with training skittish horses.

She gaped at him.

Edward groaned as he led Ash away from the silent girl. *Stupid. To share my hobby with a strange young woman, when I know women are vicious and cannot be trusted. Ugh. This earldom is annoying and distracting. I need to visit Sarah Potter's and take out my frustrations on someone who welcomes it.*

****

Sophia Wilkinson found her hosts in the library, heads leaning toward each other from either side of the desk. She knocked on the open door.

They both looked around, and the man at the desk rose. He was around thirty, with straw-colored hair atop a lean six-foot frame. "Come in, Sophia. How have you fared?"

"Well, thank you, my lord."

"Harris tells me you arrived last night?" Nicholas referred to his butler, who Sophia had met upon her arrival. The earl and countess had been out, not expecting her until the following day.

"Yes. You have a lovely home. Thank you for inviting me." She peered up at him.

His invitation had been more command than request, although she supposed it was necessary. A year ago, her father had died suddenly of a stopped heart, riding home from a veterinary visit. The earl, a distant cousin who owned the country house they managed, had arranged for chaperones. A local baron's sister and her husband stayed with Sophia for her period of mourning, after which Lord Suffolk called her to London.

His notes to her had been kind, offering a Season and a marriage settlement so she would have her choice of futures. Sophia would rather have been riding with her father, helping with animal care, and dismissed it as a courtesy until the last one.

Despite some villagers' and farmers' opinions on women helping with their livestock, her father had often brought her with him. He told her to stay quiet and out of sight when possible, and he would not allow her to help with births or messier visits. Regardless of limitations, she had loved the work and the time with her father. As an only child, she had made friends with the housekeeper's daughter until they moved away for the housekeeper's second marriage. After that, her father and her horse were her only friends and confidants.

Thankfully, the earl had seemed to know that and ensured her beloved Nellie accompanied her. Riding into London, she'd been appalled at the tight confines of the streets, the homes sidling up to one another, and the overwhelming grayness. Everything was gray. The buildings, the street, the sky, her mood…so unlike the lush green hills of the country estate that had been her lifelong home.

Now, she faced the earl and his wife and prepared to learn what her future held.

"Please, call me Nicholas. And may I present my wife, Roslynn. She's been looking forward to having another woman in the house."

Roslynn came to her feet, smoothing her peach skirts, and reached for Sophia's hands. The countess appeared closer in age to her than to the earl. "Welcome, welcome. I hope you slept well. If you've eaten, I thought we'd do a bit of shopping for a new wardrobe for you. The Season is about to start, and there are several soirees we've been invited to."

Sophia tensed, biting her lip and casting her gaze down in discomfort. Why would these people, who were essentially strangers to her, offer her a home and new clothes?

"I thank you, my lord, my la—er, Nicholas and Roslynn." She glanced between them, still holding the countess's hands. "But I do not require a Season, nor do you need to spend your money on new clothes for me."

Although, if she could not stay at her childhood home, she wasn't sure where she'd live or how to secure her future. Marriage would give her a stable home and hopefully children. Ideally more than one, so none would be lonely as she had been. But while she did not desire to be shunted to the first suitor available, a Season seemed excessive and overwhelming.

"Nonsense. 'Tis not a question of need. We are happy to support a family member," Ros said, Nicholas nodding in agreement. "I, for one, am happy to have a partner for shopping."

The earl rolled his eyes at his wife with a smirk and gestured for the ladies to sit before turning back to his chair.

Sophia remained silent, not having expected such a warm welcome or contemporaries. Having assumed an avuncular earl, she had been prepared to negotiate options for her future with him. Their apparent happiness at her presence confused her. She'd need to recalibrate her approach. If only she believed the sentiments were genuine, but why would they care for a stranger simply because they shared blood?

Nicholas propped his elbows on the desk and laced his fingers. "As I wrote, I was shocked and saddened to hear of your father's sudden death. He and I corresponded through the years about his family—you, in particular—and the estate."

Sophia's brows rose. "I was not aware of that, my lord."

Nicholas elaborated. "I actually came to visit once, a few months after my father passed. Your father was very helpful with tips on running a country home. It was a year or two after your mother died, and if I remember correctly, you were in the schoolroom. You insisted on sleeping in the barn with a friend that night, so I missed meeting you."

He smiled, and she returned it tentatively.

"Afterwards, your father and I stayed in touch as

he wanted me to be aware of estate business. Perhaps more importantly, he wished for you to have every opportunity to further your education and experience and make a good marriage. He believed time in London would be essential for you to expand your horizons. Having your choice of gentlemen beyond the young men of your village and neighboring burgs would benefit you in finding an advantageous match."

Sophia mulled this over. "Why did he never tell me this?"

The earl shook his head. "I'm afraid I cannot say, but I believe he would have soon, given your age. We were planning a Season in London for you when we lost him. Do you recall I mentioned it in my first letter to you?"

She glanced away. "Er, yes. I confess I thought they were empty words from a distant relative."

"I understand, but no. I thought it might give you something to look forward to."

Sophia's brows furrowed. "Why would you desire to do this, my lord?" After all, he did not owe her anything.

"You are family, Sophia. Your father helped me well beyond that one visit, and I had agreed to help you. Even if I hadn't discussed it with him, I would anyway. That is how family should be."

Not in my experience. Sophia shook her head infinitesimally. *Family dies, leaving you alone, without a mother or father or even a home.*

Even the villagers married for expediency more often than not. They expected their children to forge their own paths when they were of age. Her mother's family had never visited or even written. While her father's family had apparently stayed in touch, they had only been faceless landlords to her until now. It was hard to reconcile or to want to forge a relationship with them, given that everyone she loved had abandoned her. She realized her parents had not deliberately left her, but being dependent on others' generosity was frightening. She needed to secure a home, just as the villagers did.

"Well, I appreciate your generosity," she said. "I hope to make a match quickly, so I shan't be a burden on you and Roslynn."

Nicholas smiled warmly. "You needn't rush. Ros is excited at the prospect of having you here. I feel as though I know you a bit from your father's letters, but I too am looking forward to getting better acquainted. You are welcome here for as long as you wish."

The ladies rose to leave, and the earl looked up. "Oh, and we are having a friend to dinner on Friday for you to meet. The Earl of Peterborough is one of my closest friends since university. He's agreed to be your escort to the first few balls with us."

Sophia nodded, wondering if he was the ferocious but annoyingly attractive man she had sort of met in the stables, who had thought she was a servant. What would her hosts think of him escorting her if they knew he'd threatened to spank her? Her stomach flipped again, as it had when he'd yelled about her bottom. The sensation felt more like curiosity than nerves—or breakfast.

Chapter Two

By the time he had struggled through more paperwork for the estate and made emotional decisions regarding his brother's arrangements, Edward was exhausted and opted not to go out.

Unable to sleep despite his fatigue, he found the day's events circling his mind and dredging up unwanted memories.

He was eleven, standing rigid by his governess's desk. She was the third governess he'd had since his brother Charles left for boarding school. In her forties, she became more bitter and pinched-looking every year. Charles was ten years older, so they hadn't shared time in the schoolroom. But his school workbooks left behind had provided later governesses with a yardstick for comparison. Charles had been a stellar student, and none of them had let Edward forget how poorly he compared. Especially this old biddy.

Edward had managed to memorize the pages he thought she'd want him to read, but she had guessed his ruse. The tyrant was as observant as she was intolerant. She searched the bookshelves for something less familiar to him. If he was not able to read the page within a reasonable timeframe and with some semblance of clarity, she'd move on to the birch branches tied and sitting in water in the corner. Again.

When Charles was home on a break from

university, Edward had gone to him in desperation, wondering if his older brother might help him, mayhap even tutor him. When Charles saw his struggles, he had quizzed Edward verbally. His brother had talked through new ideas with him, revisiting them a few days later. Edward had almost perfect recall of what he had learned. Charles had hugged him and told him that reading was simply harder for some people than for others. He would need to work harder and study longer. Together, they'd devised learning techniques for Edward to avoid reading and writing when possible.

The governess returned with a book—he could not see the title, and it would have taken him precious minutes to read it anyway—and handed it to him open at the start of a chapter in the middle of the book.

He stared down, the letters and words a jumble, as always. Trying to focus through his growing fear and frustration, he frowned, sounding letters out under his breath.

Her narrow lips pursed, and she stood. "'Tis a very good thing you are a second son. You are not fit to carry the title. Your brother read all these books by the time he was ten. He was working out of your father's library at your age."

Despite the sting to his pride, he rolled his eyes at her oft-repeated mantra. *'Tis not like I disagree. I should hate to be the earl with all that reading for the estates and Parliament.*

"Right, then, Master Edward. You know what to do." Gesturing to him, then the desk, she marched over to the birch.

Shucking his breeches, Edward leaned over the desk, resigned to a sore backside again. The birchings had gotten worse this year as she worried for her job and was running out of time to prepare him for boarding school. He had also begun to fill out in the shoulders and gained height, and he suspected she had begun to enjoy these sessions, based on her breathing. The thought disgusted him and infuriated him further.

He counted through clenched teeth as the supple branches whipped into his arse cheeks. "One."

School had not been much better.

Edward had managed to keep current in most subjects, but there was no way around literature, and as a second son, he did not have the allowance to hire a tutor or, in his case, someone to read to him. His vexation was channeled into outbursts and minor fights with schoolmates, which led to more punishments.

The headmaster used public birchings and delegated them to his assistant, a woman of similar age and demeanor as Edward's governess. He'd often wondered if interview questions were designed to hire women with that attitude.

Boys of that age had all sorts of reactions to being birched. He remembered a few boys whose cocks had grown harder at each stripe earned. Others cried pitifully. The others commented, whispered, and even snickered. Edward stood stiff and silent, refusing to show weakness, directing his rage at the woman wielding the instrument of pain.

When I am done with school, I will never put myself in a position of vulnerability again. No reading or writing around people. Especially women.

Edward shook off the memories and the lingering rage at the women in his life who had hurt him. Perhaps if his mother hadn't died when he was young, he'd have had one positive female influence, but she had.

For a long time, he hadn't understood how people could be sexually aroused by pain. Finally, he'd asked a boy in private. From his responses, Edward understood more how the edges of pain and pleasure came together. While he'd never like that, he was fascinated by the idea of finding that edge and maintaining it for others so that even pain was pleasurable, rather than miserable like in his past. But school, then university, were his priorities.

****

Mrs. Bell, the modiste, welcomed Sophia and Ros with a warm smile, ushering them to the windowless back room. Ros had explained in the carriage on the way over that she had asked the dressmaker to start a few gowns and a riding habit, basing her choices on Nicholas's coloring, hoping she guessed correctly at a familial resemblance.

"Nicholas's hair and skin are only a shade darker than yours, so I think we'll be off to a good start," Ros said.

Sophia doubted gown color would make all that much difference to her, but she did wonder at the riding habit. Hers was terribly worn, and the chocolate brown had faded to a dirt-like tone.

As Mrs. Bell shooed all but one of her assistants out, Sophia's gaze was drawn to the garments hanging on hooks against the far wall. Her eyes went past the perfect butter yellow gown to the astonishingly luxurious undergarments hanging with it. Gossamer sheer drawers and a matching chemise in the palest of creams were of a linen and silk blend, shimmering in the light. Matching, intricately quilted stays with a shocking cut hung with them. She looked at the shallow cups, trying to picture how they would look cupping her breasts rather than covering them.

"Okay, dear. Let's get you out of this, so we may fit everything on you, then we'll make any adjustments and deliver it to you within a day or two."

Sophia stared around at the modiste, her assistant, and Ros, all standing there waiting for her to turn, to help her out of her dress.

"Is—is there somewhere a bit more private?" she stammered, thinking of the cut of the new undergarments. While she was confident and bold in her knowledge of horses, she was used to the country and quiet and only her father nearby. Having these people in her space and asking her to disrobe was disconcerting.

"Come now, Sophia," Ros said gently. "It's just us ladies…"

Bowing her head, Sophia changed out of her clothes and into the new drawers, chemise, and petticoat. The modiste's assistant drew the stays around her and laced them behind her. As she looked up, Ros and Mrs. Bell turned to glance at each other and nod.

"Perfect, thank you," Ros murmured.

"Of course." The modiste made a quick, shallow curtsy.

Sophia frowned at the exchange but lost her train of thought when she caught her reflection in the mirror. Her breasts sat in the quilted demi cups of the stays, nipples barely under the lip of the cup so they looked as though they were being presented in open dishes and quivering like creamy custard. She tugged at the garment, gasping.

"Uh, I think these need more fabric," she near whispered, afraid of sounding ungrateful even while trying to overcome her shock.

"No, they're perfect." Ros pulled her arms away. "Wait until you see it all together."

The assistant carried over the gown and layered it over Sophia as she stood watching in the mirror with wide eyes.

Once the dress was on, the lower-cut stays were not visible, and the cut of the gown's bodice framed her upper body perfectly before draping from below her breasts to the hem line. Then the modiste asked her to walk back and forth so she could judge the fit and the length. From the first step, Sophia felt a jiggle for not having full coverage from her stays. She hoped it was not noticeable to others.

The rest of the day passed in a whirlwind of shops, fabrics, pins, tucks, and decisions that veered between amazing her and feeling excessive. How many dresses did one need? Ros chatted easily, regaling Sophia with stories of her childhood and Season, putting her at ease and giving her more faith in Ros's statement about desiring another woman in the house.

At the dinner table that evening, Ros entertained Nicholas with their accomplishments. His level of interest surprised Sophia.

He listened intently, asking questions, "Hmm, and did you get bonnets and slippers for each of the dresses?" and "Will those be enough for the balls in the next month?" and "What of day dresses?" and finally "And I'm certain there must have been a riding habit in there…"

There were actually two, a fact that astounded her.

One would be ready a mere sennight after the dress for dinner with the earl's friend. Ros had promised her the loan of one for the interim.

"Did you get anything for yourself, Ros?" Nicholas asked.

Roslynn froze for a second before slanting a look at Sophia. "Oh, ah, yes, milord."

Sophia's head came up in surprise, as she had not seen Ros buy anything. In fact, she had felt awkward by the end of the day with so many purchases made solely for her. And why did Ros slur the honorific *milord* as a servant would?

Ros flashed her a pleading look.

Nicholas, having caught Sophia's sudden movement, directed his next question to his young cousin before Ros could continue. "And what did Ros get for herself, Sophia?"

"Er, I'm not certain, my lord," she murmured, dropping her gaze and twisting her napkin in her lap. "I was a bit overwhelmed by it all."

"Mmm. Well, I expect you may show it to me later, dear."

Ros's response was suddenly subdued. "Yes, milord." She lowered her head, but snuck a side glance at her husband.

Watching from the corner of her eye, Sophia swore she saw a glint of challenge in Ros's eyes. She'd used *milord* again, too.

Nicholas frowned back at his wife, and Sophia worried more about the extent of his anger than Ros's form of address. *Did I take too much time deciding on patterns for my gowns? Oh, this is my fault. I knew this friendship would be short-lived.*

Her heart pounding, she needed to escape. As pudding had been served and consumed, she excused herself. She desperately wished to get a book from the library, but she had not asked and daren't return to the dining room with so many unspoken messages flowing.

****

An hour later, Sophia lay staring at the bed canopy, unable to sleep. Did she dare slip downstairs to the library in a virtual stranger's home without permission? Nicholas—*the earl*—had mentioned a desire to see the fictional purchase. Surely, that would occur in their room.

Throwing a wrap on over her nightrail, she crept downstairs on bare feet and crossed the wide hall to the library door. It was cracked open, but as she reached for the handle, she paused, hearing a repeated staccato sound. The muted, sharp beats made her think they came from the far end of the room. She remembered Nicholas's massive desk with large windows behind it facing the gardens.

She frowned, trying to figure out what caused the noise. Her senses went on high alert when she heard a muffled cry, then a deep-voiced murmur. Concerned as to what caused the cry, she edged the door open a few inches, thanking the servants for well-oiled silent hinges. She pushed and walls of books came into view lit with flickering sconces, then a couch, then the edge of the mahogany desk at the end of the room.

Who cried out, and where were they?

She heard thwacks again, several seconds apart, then a groan. Uncertain whether to worry about the person moaning or her own safety, Sophia nudged the door an inch farther, then nearly gasped, swallowing it in time.

Roslynn's thick red-brown hair was up, and she wore her clothes from dinner, although in disarray. She was bent over the desk's end, holding the front and back edge, her bare breasts pressed against the wood, her dress and camisole yanked below them. Another inch of the door, and Sophia stopped blinking, eyes widening. The countess's skirts were tossed up over her back, and Nicholas stood sideways to her, his back to Sophia. His position was just far enough back that Sophia spotted the woman's knickers around her feet, leaving her bare from waist to ankles.

Nicholas's clothes were also mussed, his shirt untucked and loose about his shoulders. He wielded a leather strap the width of Sophia's wrist.

His arm came down again. The leather in his hand curled back at the end from the speed of his downward stroke, then snapped hard against Ros's already-striped curves. Without the door muffling it, the impact sounded much sharper. And more painful.

"Ten. Thank you, milord. I am sorry." Ros's face was wet with tears, but aside from a cringe when the strap hit, her expression was serene.

"Two more. Why do you not listen to me? Stop worrying about spending my money. You are exquisite, and I want to see you in lovely things." Snap!

"Eleven. Thank you, milord. I am sorry."

"I know you are now, love," he purred, smoothing his hand lovingly over her bottom and running a fingernail over one stripe, causing Ros to wince. "But you keep disobeying. Hence the strap." Snap!

"Twelve. Thank you, milord. I'm sorry." Ros sighed.

Sophia thought that was the end and placed a foot behind her to flee. She realized her body had flushed with heat, her pulse elevated, even as she contemplated the passiveness of Ros's acceptance of her punishment.

I would be wailing at the first swing. Does she mayhap like being hit? Did she deliberately not buy something for herself?

She reached for the handle to draw the door closed but noticed the tool drop by Nicholas's side as his hands went to his waist.

Ros slid off the desk, turned to show Sophia her opposite profile, and sank to her knees, letting her skirts fall around her but leaving her breasts bared above her scrunched bodice. As Nicholas had been standing to Ros's left, facing away from Sophia, she could not see what he did. Then he turned to face his wife.

Sophia's eyes went wide. Goodness. He had undone the laces of his breeches and taken out his member.

It was sticking up at an angle...pointing at Ros's face.

Having spent so much of her life around animals, especially horses, she knew the basics of male anatomy, but the size of Nicholas's organ seemed rather disproportionate to his height.

Then Ros licked her lips. Frozen in place, mesmerized, Sophia could not have moved if a fire had broken out.

Nicholas leaned forward, holding his shaft and pointing it toward those wet lips. "It is time to finish your punishment. Although seeing your face, I am not actually sure 'tis punishment." He chuckled. "You know the rules. If you perform well, you get an orgasm.

But only if I am feeling generous."

An orgasm? Sophia did not know what that was. But then Ros's tongue distracted her from the strange word, as it extended to lick the thick red stalk. After she wetted the length, she licked her lips again and sucked the whole thing into her mouth, her nose buried somewhere in Nicholas's breeches.

Horses definitely do not do that. Oh Lud, why does my stomach feel funny? A hot shiver ran down her spine and centered between her legs as she watched. Her nipples poked through her nightrail and wrapper.

Nicholas's fingers speared into his wife's hair and fisted it, forcing her away until he was almost out of her mouth, then drawing her back. She relaxed into his hands, hollowing her cheeks as he pushed, taking a quick breath through her nose, then sliding back down the wet length.

After a minute, he let go and reached one hand back to a bookcase. "Now, we shall see what you can do without me guiding you."

This seemed to surprise Ros as her lashes swept up to glance at him, her lips still around him.

Her hands came to rest on his hips, and she varied the pace, pausing to lick the sac below as one hand came around to grab his wet length. Then her mouth was back up, her head bobbing, cheeks hollowing until he groaned and grabbed her head again. He sped up the thrusting. Sophia wondered if it hurt Ros's hair, but she appeared fine. Her eyes were open and focused on Nicholas's face, and while they teared, her hands stayed lax on his hips, not balling or tensing.

Suddenly, he pulled back all the way with an audible pop as he freed himself from Ros's mouth. He bent to lift and turn her, then practically threw her back into the spanking position on the desk and tossed her skirts up again. Palming her buttocks, he elicited a brief hiss from her, cut off as he stepped forward and slammed into her in one move. Her hiss turned to a moan, sounding more like pleasure than pain.

Despite not being allowed to attend any animal husbandry visits, Sophia had snuck out to the barn once to peer out as several neighbors encouraged a stallion brought in to mount one of their mares. Then a stable hand had walked near her, and she had to duck. Similarly to that quick glimpse of horses mating, Nicholas was bent over Ros, covering her, although horses would not reach around and grab the mare's breasts as he did. And Sophia's skin had not heated, nor had her stomach fluttered when watching the horses, as they did now. Another tremor ran through Sophia, and one hand unconsciously raised to cup a breast.

His hips retreated, then jerked forward.

Nicholas straightened to look down at Ros and ran his fingernails lightly over the stripes on her behind. He reached around to touch a spot out of sight under her belly as his pace quickened.

Ros whined and arched her hips back to meet his thrusts over and over. When his hand moved from her breast down past her belly, she trembled from head to toe and thrust her fist against her mouth, emitting a muffled shriek.

She certainly seems to like this part, punishment or no.

Sophia remained transfixed, torn between a desire to flee, embarrassment at watching such a private event, and imagining what it would feel like to have a man stripe her bottom then shove that *rod* into the part of her that pulsed with heat.

Nicholas's pistoning hips sped even faster. Ros only partially stifled her scream and arched more as he growled long and loud and stilled after a particularly fierce thrust, then bowed over her again and cradled her. They had finished this punishment, mating, or whatever it was.

Realizing they might look around, Sophia pulled the door to, grabbed her candle, and raced on silent feet back to her room.

There, she tossed and turned, trying to process her body's reaction as she replayed what she'd just seen. Her nightrail twisted around her, and her legs shifted against the bedclothes. Thoughts of a book long abandoned, she was obsessed with what Nicholas had done underneath Ros to elicit such sounds of need.

Unable to stand it a moment longer, she explored. Her hand reached down to stroke through curls and pet her nether lips. They were swollen. As her fingers slid over them, she realized wetness seeped from between them, and they had parted. The folds between them were also swollen, and she gasped as her finger brushed a protrusion. Her hips jerked and twisted.

What was that?

Her finger returned, stroking the nub. 'Twas her flesh, but bigger and harder than it had ever been. *And so sensitive.*

She flinched again as fire shot up from the spot to her chest, her nipples hardening and her cheeks flushing. Trying to imagine someone else touching it, she understood why Roslynn had shrieked.

But as she rubbed it again, the friction increased,

and it was not pleasurable. She stopped and lay there panting. Was that what she had seen? Or was there more mayhap? Her thoughts returned to the big dark man who she'd encountered in the stables, and she fell asleep dreaming of him following through on his threat to spank her, in much the same manner as Nicholas had done to Ros tonight. In her dreams, the mysterious man turned her bottom red, stroked that nub, and it was *all* pleasurable. How strange.

Chapter Three

Edward settled into a comfortable chair in the Morning Room at White's. As always, he made sure it was in a quiet corner facing the doorway from the main entrance hall, leaving the coveted window seats for others. He followed his usual habit of picking up one of the newspapers provided for members.

He and several friends who were unencumbered by the responsibilities of titles usually gathered late at night, selecting strategically located tables before Parliament let out. Once the House of Lords released its Peers, they heard the raucous stories of wins and losses from Nicholas and others. He guessed he would be one of the latecomers now.

An older earl scanned the room. Edward nodded to him over the newspaper he held, and the man wound his way through the clusters of furniture to greet him.

"Mordaunt."

"Sir." Edward nodded a greeting before tackling the conversation he was likely to have to repeat often in the coming days. "Unfortunately, I have sad news. My brother fell suddenly ill a month ago, and his fever spiked beyond help. He is no longer with us. You'll see the formal announcement in the papers this sennight."

"I say—Charles?" His gray bushy eyebrows rose in sad surprise. "How terrible. He was so young. I am sorry for your loss." He nodded to Edward. "'Tis

29

Peterborough now, eh? I seem to remember his wife hadn't done her duty by him yet." The earl shook his head, lips pressed together as though he found Charlotte lacking.

"Yes, sir. 'Tis a bit overwhelming, I must admit. I had rather counted on Charles having more time…and heirs. I would appreciate any guidance you can give me, of course."

Long before Charles's death, Edward had started this habit of sitting in a corner of White's with a newspaper before his cronies joined him. Having already trudged through the headlines at home, he came to White's to learn more details of England's happenings. When a peer greeted him, he asked them their opinion on a particular headline he wanted to understand. He could usually extrapolate the underlying bit of news in the exchange. If he had grabbed the *Morning Post* or the prior *Sunday's Observer*, he'd ask if the *Times* had had anything to say on it, and learn the opposing political view of the situation. Now he thought to expand that to Parliamentary news and gossip.

"Any time, any time. Your father was an important ally, as was Charles. I am quite happy to continue that. And speaking of heirs, you should give that some thought. You have been rather brazen with your, ahem, other…choice of clubs, greenhorn. I dare say the young gels will be leery or, at least, their mamas will. That will take some consideration."

Edward gritted his teeth. *D'ya see, Nick? With one strike against me, I can imagine the reaction should anyone in this set discover my reading issues.* Hellfire, he hated the flummery of the Ton. The whole city of

London irked him, the balls more so than any other part. The stilted prescribed movements, the formal requests for introductions, the need to worry about who one danced with or if they were a hair too close. And heaven forbid one stepped out to the gardens for fresh air.

The lord continued, "I see you are reading the news again. I always seem to find you in this corner, paper in hand."

"I suspect 'twill be even more important for me to know it now. By the by, have you seen the article on that steam locomotive they've managed to build up north?" With that question, Edward was able to fill in the blanks in his knowledge without laboring over the newspaper for hours.

****

That evening, Edward made his way to his preferred club in a discreet townhouse on a side street just north of Mayfair. White's was important for political connections and social interactions, but for pleasure, he chose Sarah Potter's Spanking Club.

Several years ago, Nicholas had dragged him to a house party given by the very young Earl of Cheltenham. Cheltie, as he was known, had a reputation for mixing the Ton and the demi-monde, providing risqué revelry at these parties without being ostracized for it. Probably because he made the invitations so coveted and secret that none dared discuss the particulars.

At the event, Edward had seen women tied, spanked, fucked…and, of greatest interest to him, birched. Men were in similar positions, put there by both men and women. But Edward's focus narrowed instantly to where a man birched a woman's buttocks. He was enthralled by the sight, in such contrast to his childhood experiences. He remembered his conversation with his schoolmate about the edge of pain and pleasure and his speculation on how he might enjoy controlling that balance for someone. Opportunity lay before him. His cock rose and stiffened as he watched, and he asked if he might take a turn.

Cheltie sat down with Nicholas and him to establish the rules of engagement. Everyone was there willingly, but not everyone wanted the same thing. Later in the house party, it became more apparent who was into what with whom. But for the first day or two, newcomers observed. Then only pursued interactions with people they had seen in similar roles. Crucial to remember was that either party could put an end to any play by saying "enough."

The host encouraged the men new to the environment to try over-the-lap spankings first and provided two willing and eager participants. The girls had flipped their own dresses up and foregone knickers. When Edward spanked the girl on his lap, introduced only as Fanny, she squirmed and asked for more. Surprised, he paused, and she offered sex instead. She'd been wetter than any woman in his past from the spanking alone. The whole experience had been better than any drug, any drink.

Unused to women being so openly interested in sex, Edward questioned Fanny's motives but wanted to learn more.

Cheltie had directed them to Sarah's in London, where they bought memberships and visited often. He shunned the birch, opting for his hand or, after some thought, his crop. He delighted in applying the tool of his trade to girls' arses. Thus his sexual predilections became honed.

The first time Edward visited, frustrated at a long letter from his solicitor that had taken hours to decode, he had let his anger take control. The woman he'd been spanking called a halt, and Sarah had stepped in to explain that anger had no place in these interactions. Even in a domestic setting, using spanking to correct behavior, anger should be mitigated by offering corporal punishment as a solution. Only when both parties were calm and accepting should that penalty be administered, and then the disagreement should be considered done.

That made sense, and Edward regretted his actions. From then on, his interest in spanking women morphed from retribution against his childhood memories to sexual dominance and control. But he never lost his distrust of women. After all, the women at Sarah's were being paid for their time and willingness. And none of them knew he could not read.

Now, he sat in Sarah's parlor and sipped a brandy, watching the comings and goings. A viscount was directed to a private room, and a marquess emerged from the hallway looking satisfied.

Then it was his turn. The maid assigned to the parlor leaned over him and provided the house's traditional prelude of her breasts within the loose low-cut bodice that fell away as she bent. All the young women employed at Sarah's used corsets rather than stays and no other undergarments, making the most of their assets.

Edward could not help comparing ripe melons to

the peaches he had seen the other morning in Nick's stables. He hurriedly chose a blonde he was familiar with from prior visits and finished his brandy. He refused to consider why he chose a petite woman with blonde hair. Flicking his crop by his side, he was glad that she'd be face down for the interlude.

****

List of tasks, correspondence, and questions in hand, Edward knocked at the front door of Suffolk House.

The butler directed him to the library where Nicholas again worked behind his desk. Ever the host, he rounded the desk to greet Edward and gestured to the seating area by the fireplace, asking the servant for tea as they took their usual chairs.

"How has the transition been going?" Nicholas asked, guessing correctly that he had concerns he desired to voice to a friendly ear.

"I was familiar with the various estates for the most part," he said. "And at least temporarily, I'm going to trust the stewards Charles had in place to continue with minimal guidance."

"Yes, prioritize what needs your attention most."

"My concern is less about what needs my attention. Rather, 'tis what will be most difficult for me to learn, given that I was not trained for this role as Charles was. I did not take part in discussions of Parliamentary proceedings or laws being considered, even when my father was alive. And certainly, I didn't keep abreast in the years since, as Charles was young and seemingly healthy."

"Right, then. Walk through it with me." Nicholas settled back after pouring the tea.

Edward looked at him gratefully. "Thank you, your help is invaluable to me—" Nicholas held up a hand to stop him, and he grimaced. "Rot it, you know what I mean. I have gone by to see Charlotte, and she helped me sort through the more urgent-looking business on his desk. She was remarkably knowledgeable about his affairs, which was a surprise but frankly expedient."

He leaned forward in his chair and sipped his tea. "As for the rest, I have organized papers and thoughts into Parliamentary, the horse business, and various properties. Oh, and there are a few odd investments and other correspondence I don't think are urgent, but I should like to bring them by for you to review."

"Of course," Nicholas said. "You and I were always much closer than either of us was to Charles, but he and I discussed some investment opportunities at White's. I may be familiar with them or can at least direct you to the right person. What of his solicitor—now yours?"

"I meet with him tomorrow." He gave the solicitor's name, asking, "Do you know of him or his reputation?"

Nicholas nodded. "You're in excellent hands. Another thing not requiring immediate action. At least Charles actively managed the earldom, keeping a watchful eye on the family holdings. You could have been in much worse circumstances."

"Nick, d'you think there is any way to delegate enough of my responsibilities as earl to stay involved in the horse training? And how much will I risk if I continue my membership at Sarah's?"

"In answer to your first question—not in the short-term, but once you have gotten over the hump learning it all, there may well be." He grinned, unrepentant. "Particularly if you take a wife." Laughing at Edward's expression, he waved off his retort. "As for Sarah's, you know she demands discretion." Nicholas leaned forward, elbows on knees. "Right, then. What else? What about the horse training? How long can your stablemaster manage in your absence?"

"Actually, that is the responsibility I worry the least about." Edward sat back. "Charles—ah, *I* have a steward to manage bills and correspondence for the business side, and Russell, my stablemaster, knows the horse training side as well as I do. I have the utmost confidence in them moving forward smoothly for several fortnights at a time as needed. Mostly, I miss it," he added with a smile. "But I'd have been here now anyway, as you know, for the Vauxhall event."

"That leaves Parliament. I can help with that. The first several bills to come to us are usually budget related. But last session's Importation Act is likely to be a big topic of discussion. It caused riots last year, and they may well continue."

"That is the one they are calling the Corn Law, no?"

"The very same."

"On the surface, it appears to help domestic farmers by not allowing the importation of grains at lower prices."

"Well, it depends on how you define farmers. Tenant farmers may not see the benefit if landowners do not pass through profits. And what of all the city folks whose income does not change but who also must pay a higher price to put the same amount of food on the table?"

"Hmm. Peterborough is a growing city, but from an overall perspective I think of us as an agrarian society."

"Less so every year. I can set up a meeting with some allies at White's so we can discuss a path forward regarding this." Nicholas made a note. "That brings us to the point you raised last visit." Nicholas smiled tightly. "A wife."

Edward shot him a sharp look. "We've already discussed that. You have my answer."

"First," Nicholas said, "I am not suggesting you give up all your preferred pursuits at once. And whether you need to give them up at all is a separate conversation. But would it hurt to look in the meantime? The Season is starting, and you had promised to help Sophia get established." He paused. "Although given your new role and responsibilities, I should offer you the chance to change your mind, as your time is more limited now?"

"No, of course not. I shan't back out now," Edward replied. "Unless you wish me to?" He shared the conversation he had at White's. "I'll repeat that my reputation—or my preferred pursuit, as you put it—is a bit too widely known for a young lady's best interests, but I defer to your judgment for your cousin's reputation."

"Thank you."

"Has she arrived yet?"

"Yes, actually. She is usually in the stables at this time, though, so you may not see her until Friday dinner."

"The stables?"

"Her father was a vet, and she inherited a passion

for animals. Especially her horse, Nellie."

Edward's breath caught. He had threatened to spank his friend's cousin. Thank heavens he hadn't gone through with it.

****

Sophia skipped once in pleasure at seeing Ash poke his handsome head out over the stable door to whicker at her.

"Hello, my lovely beast. How are you?" She scratched his muzzle.

She conjured a memory of the horse's owner, his hard muscled body and fierce countenance, broad shoulders, dark hair, and equally dark eyes. His actions had told her he cared about animals' safety as much as she did. She recalled his threat and paired it with the library scene she had witnessed the night before.

Hmm.

A spanking sounded less intimidating and more titillating now. Particularly from such a handsome gentleman.

Sophia had only ever kissed one boy, a tenant farmer's son back home whom she had caught bathing in the creek. She'd stopped to admire his pale naked torso, and he had teased her when he caught her spying. They were both fifteen, and his torso was nothing like she suspected Lord Peterborough's to be. His kiss, which had been soft and pleasant but not earth-shattering, was likely equally different.

She greeted Nellie and asked her for patience before nipping into Ash's stall. Patting and petting the massive equine, she ran her hands over him, checking for bumps, sores, and knotted muscles. She turned to his mouth, bringing out some greens the cook had saved her.

After he snacked on a handful, she ran her hand along his lips, the other holding his bridle, unnecessarily so as the horse remained still for her.

As she lifted a lip to check his teeth, a muffled roar came from behind her.

She flinched, barely managing not to leap in the air and spook Ash, and yanked her hands away from his mouth quickly. Ash whinnied at his owner and lifted a hoof to step forward but waited patiently for Sophia to get out of harm's way.

"Get back, you stupid girl! I don't care how well you think you know horses. You should never put your hands near a strange horse's mouth."

He scowled down at her as he held the half door open. His other hand had caught Ash's bridle, holding him to allow her to pass.

"I was admiring this beautiful steed. And we were fine until you scared me by sneaking up on me." Sophia left off the honorific, even suspecting who he was. If he knew who she was, there would be no spanking or pleasure-screams for her. But if they both pled ignorance, she might get a chance to experience whatever it was she'd watched Ros enjoy.

Brushing by him, she turned and looked up, licking her lips as she wished for a kiss.

He glared mutely at her, his gaze flickering down to her lips, then back up.

"Ash is fantastic and a perfect gentleman. Can you say the same? Or are you contemplating my punishment?"

His eyes shuttered momentarily before they burned back at her, hotter than ever. Gripping her arm, he closed the half door and strode down the main stable corridor with her. At the entrance to the back garden, he turned to her, still holding her arm.

Sophia pouted, suspecting she'd missed her opportunity to compare kisses.

"Miss Wilkinson, I presume?" His voice rolled over her, deeper than Nicholas's, sending a lick of heat through her and commanding her response.

How does a voice do that? Oh darn, he knows who I am. "At your service." A small curtsy and a raised eyebrow. "Lord Peterborough, I presume?"

"Lovely to meet you, although I would prefer more auspicious—and less dangerous—circumstances. Please stay out of my horse's stall in future. If you see something that needs my attention, bring it to me."

"And risk a spanking? Hmm."

Edward's cheeks flushed, but he remained firm. "I must apologize for that, Miss Wilkinson. As you might have guessed, I did not know who you were. I understand your father was a veterinarian. You should still use caution with horses you don't know."

Abandoning thoughts of a kiss, anger sparked. "I beg your pardon, Lord Peterborough. I thank you for your direction. I'll be sure to bring any concerns regarding Ash to you." She almost spit the words at him, her spine stiff.

"Miss Wilkinson, I—"

With a sigh, she deflated. "I realize you are trying to ensure my safety, my lord. I wish men would trust me a bit more, but I understand." She dipped a shallow curtsy. "Until Friday, my lord," she said before turning away.

Why did she always have to prove herself when it

came to horse care? Men would talk with other men and take advice without ever checking their stock to see how well-cared-for the horses were.

Nevertheless, her disappointment about that did not dim her wish for a kiss or a spanking.

****

That evening, as they ate, Sophia asked her hosts about their upcoming dinner guest.

"Lord Peterborough?" Ros frowned before understanding dawned. "Oh, Edward. I beg your pardon. I am still adjusting to that. He only recently became the earl. Until now, he's happily rusticated at the family estate in Peterborough, breeding and training horses."

Sophia perked up. "Oh? Ash is adorable, the sweetest tempered gelding I've seen in a long time."

"You saw Ash?"

"And Lord Peterborough. In the stables. Twice."

"Hmm." Ros looked thoughtful, earning a warning look from Nicholas. "What did you talk about?"

"Er, Ash." Sophia wondered how *spanking* would go over. She stifled a snicker. "And, um, Nellie."

"Of course. I can't think of two people who love horses more than you and Edward." Ros slid her gaze toward Nicholas without moving her head.

Sophia watched him for a reaction, but he kept his head down as he sliced a bite of roast, simply giving one negative shake.

Ros smirked and winked at Sophia. "Have you given any thought to what you'd like in a husband?"

Nicholas shot his wife a sharp gaze but said nothing.

Sophia searched for a polite way to answer Ros. "I

am sure London has much to offer, but I confess I miss the open fields of country life. As does Nellie. So a country home would be nice."

This city is so gray and so crowded. I'll have better luck finding a husband or another solution here, but this place is dark and dirty and miserable. How can people live without fields? I can hardly breathe from the odors.

"That sounds fair. What else? Oh, mayhap a list." Ros grinned at her. "Mmm, a Suitable Husband Attributes List."

Her cousin's smile was infectious, and Sophia grinned back. "Er, an affinity for horses?"

"Of course, of course." Ros nodded.

What about Lord Peterborough? And the possibility of being spanked to pleasure-screaming? Gor, he is magnificent...and imposing.

She thought of Ash, who was huge but gentle. She didn't think the new earl was the gentle type.

"Enough, Ros." Nicholas narrowed his eyes at his wife.

Feeling lost in the unspoken conversation flowing around her, Sophia stayed silent as she wondered what she was missing. 'Twould be nice to feel a part of their world...or any world. She was tired of being alone, but everyone she loved either left or died. She rather wondered if she was unlovable or cursed.

Her father had included her in his world, keeping her close, and she had adored her time with him, helping animals and learning of the world through spirited discussions of newspaper articles. When his sudden death left her completely alone, she had resolved to avoid future heartache. Marriage would give her and Nellie a home, but she daren't risk loving someone again.

Before she forgot, Sophia turned to the earl. Remorseful about her library spying, she requested, "My lord, may I borrow a book from your library before I retire?"

"Of course, Sophia, you are welcome to anything here. Mrs. Harris in the kitchen usually leaves snacks on the table when she retires, as I am a night owl. And there is paper and a pen and ink in the desk in your room if you wish to write any letters. Harris would be happy to post them for you."

A blush stained Sophia's fair complexion at the reference to his nocturnal activities, but he either did not notice or chose not to question it.

She changed the subject. Her father had subscribed to both the *Times* and the *Morning Post* to stay abreast of Parliament and hear both the Whigs' and Tories' sides of issues. He had enjoyed debating them with her at dinner most nights, even though by the time the newspapers reached them, the bills were likely past or deferred. "May I ask what newspapers you receive?"

Nicholas chuckled. "Ah, you are your father's daughter. I neglected to mention that yesterday, didn't I? Our correspondence included some more controversial topics in the House of Lords, as he had asked that I keep him informed. Ros enjoys reading and discussing politics sometimes, too. I promise she is not all ribbons and bows." He grinned at his wife before turning back to Sophia. "You'll be happy to know that both the *Times* and the *Post* are delivered every day, and I finish with them before lunch. They're kept in the library."

"Oh, and someone with a newspaper subscription. Add that," Ros said before ducking her head at another glare from Nicholas.

As the servants cleared dessert, Sophia rose. "Thank you, my lord, I shall duck in there now and take a peek."

He nodded, dismissing her.

Determined to ensure she had something that would help her sleep, Sophia deferred delving back into political battles until the next day. She settled on a penny dreadful and a farriery book by Edward Snapes, instead.

After dropping the books in her room, she ran down the back stairs and out through the kitchen to visit with Nellie, pocketing the green carrot tops Mrs. Harris had left out for her. *Nellie is going to get fat soon with all the wonderful treats.* She considered the puddings served every night. *As shall I.*

After confirming with the stable hand, Bobby, that Nellie had been exercised earlier, Sophia grabbed her currying tools and gave her friend a rubdown as she reflected on the day.

"Right, then. I shall see you tomorrow, girl. Ros has offered a ride tomorrow to show me a park. Mayhap that will give us an opportunity for a run, eh?"

Sophia forced herself to go straight upstairs. No checking the library for books or aught else. Her hosts' after-hours activities were their business, not hers.

Chapter Four

Edward stepped into Suffolk House and handed his coat to Harris. A movement on the stairs caught his eye, then a flash of flaxen mane flowing into a dress the same color. As he turned and took in Sophia, he caught a glimpse of an extra bounce of her bodice. He froze with his hat half-extended for a few seconds before resuming the motion to Harris, his gaze lingering on the ice-blue-eyed angel in pale yellow.

Criminy, she's delicious. I regret not spanking her when I had the opportunity, when I thought she was a servant. 'Tis darned inconvenient to have my cock stirred by the chit I have promised to protect. And that shimmy. Is she not wearing undergarments?

Sophia paused a few steps shy of the entryway, locking gazes with him. In that moment, Nicholas and Roslynn emerged from the library, unlocking Edward and Sophia from their motionless tableau.

"Edward, welcome." Nicholas came forward to grasp his friend's hand with both of his.

"Perfect timing, everyone. Let's adjourn to the front parlor for sherry, shall we?" Ros threw open the double doors.

The room had a large window facing the street, framed by peach curtains, and the fire and candles made the room welcoming. Warm browns prevailed, with gold and peach accents, so the decor was neither feminine nor masculine, while remaining formal with gilt-edged furniture.

Nicholas dismissed the servant, preferring to serve his guests.

"Edward, I understand you met informally, but may I present my cousin Sophia, come to us from Stamford, just to the west of your lands." Nicholas introduced them before moving to the decanters.

Edward bowed over her hand as Nicholas added, "Sophia, my best friend Edward Mordaunt, now Earl of Peterborough."

She dipped in a shallow curtsy to him.

Unable to resist the advantage of his height, he followed the swell of décolletage with his eyes. Her downcast gaze missed his lapse, a fact he was grateful for.

Seeing Ros out of the corner of his eye, he recovered quickly. "I understand from Nicholas this is your first time to London. How are you finding it?"

"Strange...but exciting." She darted a furtive glance at Ros that Edward did not understand.

Nicholas handed them all their glasses, and they perched on the settees.

"We of course," Ros said, "had to start clothing Sophia for the Season, and then I showed her Hyde Park."

"Oh, and did you enjoy the park?" Edward asked politely.

"It was lovely, my lord." Sophia's response was less shy. "We rode a loop. I am happy to have an open place close by in which to ride. Nellie loved it."

"Ah, the pretty Nellie." He smiled.

"Sophia is an excellent horsewoman and did a lot

of riding at home," Nicholas interjected.

"Yes, if only I had more time from managing the household here and in Suffolk to ride with her." Ros tightened her mouth into a moue.

Nicholas shot Ros a look, and she rearranged her expression.

Edward found himself saying, "I am sure I can accompany you at least some days." He nodded to Sophia.

What in hellfire? That was a damned fool commitment to make. His lips flattened at his own eagerness. As if he did not have enough to do with his new duties as earl. And while he was attracted to the girl, he did not want to mislead a virginal miss with hopes of marriage.

Ros gave Nicholas what seemed like a smug look, but he chose to ignore it, focusing on Sophia's reply.

"Thank you, my lord. I would enjoy the company when you are free."

A servant entered, indicating dinner was ready, and the group rose to adjourn to the dining room. Ros and Nicholas led the way, so Edward offered Sophia his arm and followed them.

Her hand met his arm, her head only barely above his shoulder, reinforcing exactly how petite she was. She had to reach up even to walk arm in arm with him, their height was so disparate. He suppressed the urge to peek at the neckline of her dress. This was Nicholas's young innocent cousin.

He sighed. *I might need another visit to Sarah's.*

The press of her hand on his arm distracted him, and he inhaled, only to find his head filled with a subtle floral scent mixed with lemon. *I was simply trying to*

47

help Nicholas by offering to ride with her.

At last, they breached the doorway to the dining room. He led her to a seat and held her chair for her, again needing to resist temptation to watch her bosom as she sat.

Damn me. I do not usually have to remind myself not to ogle young misses.

Moving away from her enticing perfume, he sat across the table from her, draping his napkin over his bulging lap. Nicholas sat at the head of the table to his right, Ros on the opposite side with Sophia. He suspected seats were arranged so the men could discuss business by the second course while the women held their own conversation.

As expected, Nicholas turned to him as the soup course was cleared. "How are the horses?"

Sophia's eyes went wide, and she focused intently on the men.

"Expensive and temperamental as always, but doing well."

"Are you buying, selling, or training right now?"

"Mostly buying and training. I hope to have a dozen ready for sale before the auction later this summer." Edward sipped his wine, glancing at Sophia who had stopped eating. Her interest surprised him. *Strange country girl.*

"My lord, if I may ask, what breeds do you focus on? And what other training do you offer?"

Edward's brows raised at the pointed questions. His distraction with her bouncing bust and his resulting barely controlled desire took his mind to training girls to the pleasures of his crop.

He stifled a groan. *This is Nick's ward, for*

heaven's sake.

"Most breeds," he responded, returning to the conversation, "depending on the need. I sell matched sets for carriages and pirogues, riding horses, and a few racehorses for those interested. And I sell workhorses to the hackney companies in town. While those are generally mixed breeds, they have great stamina, are less expensive, and need training as carriage horses do, to handle the noises and crowds on London streets."

"Who trains them for you?"

"That is in question right now." His mouth turned down in memory. "My brother died suddenly a month ago, making me earl. Before then, I owned the horses and trained them myself but used his land, giving him a percentage of my profits. With my new Parliamentary and other responsibilities, I am relying on my stablemaster for now. I need to see how I can balance Town and the business."

"Ah. I am sorry for your loss, my lord."

Edward nodded. "Thank you."

Nicholas cleared his throat and changed the subject, asking Edward, "Are you attending the equine auction at Vauxhall next Friday then?"

Edward affirmed he was before they became engrossed in discussing their estates' farming plans for the spring.

He glanced over several times during the last course, feeling Sophia's gaze on him, but each time he looked, her gaze was on her plate. *I am imagining things, including still smelling that delectable citrusy floral scent. She is not for me. Nicholas would have my head for eyeing her, having spent enough time together spanking girls at the club. I still wonder how he gave that up. I never shall. Marriage is the last thing I want, and Sophia, while lovely, is certainly a girl one marries.*

****

The idea of applying a crop to a willing female arse lingered in Edward's mind after dinner as he made his way to Sarah Potter's club.

Giving the password to the doorman, he entered the parlor with a bar at the far end. He nodded to the other gentlemen in the room, recognizing two but not feeling gregarious.

After pouring a drink, he settled in an armchair. The maid entered as he sipped his brandy, stopping to whisper to a man across the room. The gentleman strode to the hallway door, ostensibly to find the room the maid had designated. She then crossed to Edward's chair. Standing before him, she leaned forward to ask his preference for the evening, giving him the expected peek down her bodice.

After a brief dispassionate perusal of those assets, his gaze rose to hers. "Who is available this evening?"

He was fleetingly surprised at his lack of reaction to the attractive display of young flesh, but dismissed it, choosing another blonde from the names listed. He asked for time to finish his brandy before moving to a private room.

Sipping, he laid his head back against the chair and recalled the many times he and Nicholas had come here. His thoughts turned to the conversation they had when Nicholas met Ros and fell in love.

"Shall we head over to Sarah's, then? We have not been in almost a month," Edward asked one Saturday evening a few years ago as they both finished their drinks at White's.

Nicholas looked uncomfortable. "I've been meaning to talk to you about that. I am done with the Spanking Club, I'm afraid. My focus is on Roslynn. I plan to ask for her hand."

Edward was not shocked but wondered how Nicholas could forego a favorite activity. They had discussed their shared dislike of the approach many noblemen and women took after arranged marriages, continuing liaisons outside of their marriage. Both men were determined to uphold their marriage vows and, until recently, both had eschewed interest in marriage for that reason.

"You are really ready to walk away from women on their knees for you to spank, birch, or cane?"

Nicholas nodded. "If I must. All I know is that I cannot live without Ros. I shall live without the rest if necessary."

Edward could not fathom caring about a woman enough to give up his preferred method of stress relief.

"How would it not be necessary?" Edward asked. "You can't think to teach a noblewoman the joys of spanking. Or of sucking you off?" *And if you did, wouldn't she use it against you, given how vicious women can be?*

Nicholas shrugged, declining to answer, and shortly afterward excused himself from the men's club, indicating an early morning ride with Ros.

Edward hadn't thought about Nicholas's lack of response since that night, but now he contemplated it again. Had Nicholas and Ros reached an understanding on domestic discipline? He did not recall Ros being subservient. On the contrary, she offered unsolicited opinions more than most wives. But mayhap they had a very different private life?

Bah, wishful thinking. He was creating the wife he wanted. Either way, 'twas not worth risking ridicule.

Edward liked nothing better than a crop in his hand and a woman's rosy arse arched and offered up for him. His hand itched to hold a spanking implement. He realized why he had chosen the blonde. He kept imagining Sophia's pale hair swinging as her head bent in supplication, her breasts bouncing like the maid's, then swinging her over his lap... *Would her bottom be as soft and lush as her breasts appeared? Or would it be firm and muscled from riding?* Edward shifted in his chair, his breeches uncomfortably tight.

The maid returned. Leaning over him, she whispered, "She awaits your pleasure in the blue room, milord."

As he looked at her swaying breasts, he demurred, apologizing. He didn't want to be here. These were not the breasts he wished for, and the other girl's hair was the wrong shade of yellow. The person he most wanted to spank was Sophia, as unlikely as that was.

He needed to get his urges in order before he danced with her at a ball. All thoughts of spanking a young lady not even in her first Season yet, much less one related to his best friend, were to be abolished.

But nor would a substitute do.

****

When Edward rode up to the front of Suffolk House, he was surprised to see Sophia leading her own horse around from the stables, rather than waiting at the door for a stable hand to do it like most young ladies of the Ton.

"Good morning." He felt her hand quiver once as he helped her onto the mounting block and wished their gloves away to feel her skin against his. Leaning in to boost her trailing foot, he inhaled the bouquet of flowers of her perfume, and his groin stirred. He shook his head once to clear it and checked that Bobby was ready to accompany them.

"Shall we, then?" he asked, mounting Ash again and leading them along Grosvenor Street toward the park.

"Thank you again for inviting me, my lord. 'Tis such a beautiful day." Sophia practically levitated in her saddle.

"Hmm…" He arched a questioning brow at her before glancing at the gray sky.

She let out a breathy laugh. "Well, 'tis warm at least."

"Yes, indeed. And may I say, Nellie is extraordinarily well-behaved."

He returned her broad grin as they reached the park, and she echoed his phrase back to him, moving Nellie into a smooth trot. "Shall we?"

Flashing a quick smile over her shoulder, she aimed for the main path, as it was early enough that the horse, carriage, and pedestrian traffic did not require a walking pace.

Edward caught up easily on Ash, who stood two hands taller than the Palomino. The four of them made a striking ensemble, a devil and angel comparison doubled by their mounts.

He caught her gaze and smiled. "Tell me how you came to love riding so well."

"My father—Nicholas's father's cousin—trained

as a veterinarian. I learned by watching him and later helping. Given the cost and distance of the physician, tenants even came to my father for medical help or advice for their families, so I've learned some of that as well."

Edward wondered what the extent of that learning was, based on the salve she'd made for Ash's leg. But given the injuries to stable hands he'd seen, he also worried about someone her size working closely with such large animals. "It took me ages to find a good vet, and I was forced to choose between the cost of paying an exorbitant amount to have him on hand solely for the horses I train or share him with the surrounding area and my tenants and worry about availability. Before I became the earl, my plan was to learn more from him as a cost-effective compromise."

Sophia looked thoughtful at that.

Edward changed the subject. "Tell me about Nellie."

Sophia grinned. "I got my first horse when I was twelve," she started. "And I named her Penelope, for my best friend who had moved away."

"So Nellie is short for Penelope?"

"Well, yes, but not the same one. My father had bought me an older mare because she was gentle and a bit smaller given my size at that age. She is retired and a much-loved pet in the Stamford stables now," she explained. "We call her Penny. Nellie is my second mare, also named Penelope. You'll never guess what I called the barn cat." Her smile widened.

His lips curved in return. "Hmm, I'm sensing a theme here. Where did your best friend move to? What does she think of this naming convention?"

Sophia frowned. "I don't know. Her mama was the housekeeper, and we learned side by side in the nursery. But her mother remarried, and they wanted to be closer to her husband's family where there was better work for him. I wrote to her, but I never received a reply, so I do not know if my letters found her or not."

"Ah. I am sorry, Sophia." Edward softened his tone. "How old were you when she left?"

"Twelve." One side of her mouth curled up in a brief smile that fell away quickly.

He snorted. "Ah, so I take it you got your first horse soon after?"

She nodded but remained withdrawn.

"It seems you still miss your friend," Edward ventured.

"The village was spread out, and as my father was caretaker for the estate, we were seen as gentry. It was hard to make new friends. That was why my father allowed me to ride with him and how we became so close."

"Roslynn appears happy to have you here. She'll be a good companion for you." He tried to be positive.

"Yes, my lord," Sophia demurred. She did not appear convinced.

As they rounded the farthest curve on the riding path, Sophia asked, "How are you finding the earldom?"

He snorted again. "Bah. So much reading. And talking. I'd much rather be working with the horses."

"But there are important laws at stake, my lord." She looked shocked, and Edward was taken aback by her attitude. In his experience, young ladies of the Ton did not give a fig about laws.

"Certainly, there are. I am wading through all of that now. 'Tis painful to separate the wheat from the chaff, however."

"I agree, but 'tis so important. My father and I read the papers together every day. Even though they were weeks old, we'd discuss every bit of news. I can't imagine not reading or not taking every opportunity to influence laws before they are finalized."

Of course, I had to befriend a veritable Blue Stocking, who can't imagine not reading. He lowered his head in frustration and stared at his hands gripping Ash's reins, eyes burning.

She continued. "The one I've been most concerned with is the Corn Law from last year. Will Parliament look at revising that, mayhap?"

Edward hid his astonishment. His discomfort was forgotten as his thoughts turned to her reasons for caring. "Hmm. Yes. Nicholas and I have spoken about that. My initial thought was that it seemed designed to help British farmers and the economy. But—"

Sophia jumped in. "Oh, no, my lord. 'Tis designed to help British landowners. Not the people that actually work the land. Nor all the people who do other jobs that are moving our country forward in industries such as textiles, metals, and other goods. That law was written by the titled nabobs to help themselv—" She looked at him sheepishly.

He smiled ruefully. "As I was going to say, Nicholas set me straight. We are meeting with some other members of Lords soon to discuss it."

"I beg your pardon, my lord."

"Ah, Sophia. You forget, I was not a titled nabob until recently. 'Tis quite all right." Fascinated by her knowledge and emboldened by her deference when she'd felt she had overstepped, he dared to tease her. "No punishment was earned for that."

She looked at him in surprise, then smiled slowly, leaving Edward with an uncomfortable seat on his horse due to a hardening cock.

They rode the rest of the way in silence, Edward stealing glances at Sophia with *punishment* reverberating in his head while she appeared contemplative.

When they arrived back at Suffolk House, he helped her alight and handed his reins to a groom.

"I need to speak to Nicholas. May I accompany you in, or are you going to the stables with Nellie?" He offered his arm.

"A gracious offer, my lord, but you guessed correctly. I handle most of Nellie's needs. Shall I take Ash for you as well?" An impertinent smirk.

He narrowed his eyes. "A gracious offer, but no."

She was still grinning as she and the groom walked back toward the stables with their mounts.

Edward made his way to the library, waving his friend back into his desk chair when he would have risen.

As he closed the door, his host asked, "How was the ride with my cousin?"

Edward smiled, replying diplomatically, "She is an expert horsewoman, a lovely young woman. And she seems more versed in world affairs than most?"

"Yes. Her father was an avid reader of both the daily papers and liked to discuss news with her." Nicholas paused before voicing a new concern. "There is a ball in a few days. Are you over your nerves? And more, I realized the other evening that having your newly acquired title linked with anyone on the marriage mart might cause you some unwanted attention."

"I had not considered that aspect," Edward mused. "But since I am not planning to marry any time soon, mayhap it will help me ward off others. After she expands her dance card, I could pine for her, adding to her appeal." But even as he said the words, something inside him twisted at the thought of her little frown of concentration and inquiring gaze directed at another man as she debated with him on a morning ride.

Nicholas looked away, tapping his first finger on the arm of his chair. Edward knew that movement from university days. His friend was pondering a problem he had yet to solve.

"Nick? Mayhap I can help solve whatever is concerning you?" He barked a short laugh. "'Twould also make me feel better about asking you for help with all this reading."

Nicholas turned back to meet his gaze and smiled. "No problems on my end, old man. But I have a question for you. Why are you so sure that you'd have to give up your…interests, shall we say, when you marry?"

Edward's head pulled back, and he stared. "Are you suggesting that I enter a society marriage with the plan to betray my vows before I even say them?"

"No, no. But why could you not teach someone what you like?"

Edward scoffed. "Ha. Yes, I cannot see a society princess bending over the settee to be cropped…much less enjoying it." He silently berated himself for the images his overeager mind conjured of Sophia.

Nicholas would kill me. "You know their pleasure in being 'disciplined' is a prerequisite for my enjoyment. I do not think that can be taught."

"What if it could be?"

"That would certainly be...interesting, I suppose." Edward cocked his head, contemplating for a second, then straightened. "No. There is more to it than that, as you're well aware. My illiteracy is not something I'm willing to risk. And there is fun in variety. What is with the repeated questions about marriage? I don't see an urgency here. Is this because you're happy and now you want your friends to all marry and be happy? Have I wandered into a ladies' tea?"

He laughed at his friend, and Nicholas held up his hands in surrender. "Right, then. Moving along, let's talk Parliament."

But as they reviewed yet another infernal bill, Edward's focus wandered to thoughts of teaching Sophia the joys of the crop.

Chapter Five

Engrossed in thought, Sophia sat in Nellie's stall, legs swinging off the hay bale, having done a walkthrough of the stables for any medical needs.

Edward—oops, Lord Peterborough—runs a horse training business and needs veterinary support. It seemed like a perfect fit to her Suitable Husband Attributes list.

Mayhap she could help care for the animals.

She recalled the steel of his arm under his silk dinner jacket. The play of muscles under his riding breeches as he squeezed Ash's sides into a canter. His calloused hands on the reins, then lifting her down from Nellie.

Her body sang, much like when she'd stood at the library door watching her hosts' animalistic mating. That was a positive reaction to a potential husband, wasn't it? Her heart beat faster, and she swore she felt it pulse between her legs under her dress.

Nellie blew a breath through her equine nostrils, and Sophia turned her thoughts to the auction Nicholas had mentioned to Edward at dinner.

"I've got to find out more about that event next Friday. It sounds like heaven. Hundreds of horses being presented for sale and purchase." As Nellie shifted, Sophia jumped down to grab the curry brush. "Not that I am in the market for another horse, my love."

Patting the mare with her left hand where she'd already brushed with her right, Sophia paused when Bobby came by the stall.

She looked up as he leaned over the half door.

"I heard you talking," he said.

Sophia ducked her head, thinking he was going to make fun of her for having ongoing one-sided conversations with Nellie.

"I'm going with a few of the lads from neighboring stables. I can tell you about the Vauxhall sale afterward."

Her head shot up. "Really? May I go?"

"*Well...*it's not really a place for women or gentry," he said. "Mayhap if his lordship was going?"

"Oh." Her heart sank. Edward's talk of different breeds had sparked a desire to learn about them more than ever. The event had sounded like the perfect opportunity to see more than the few in her village.

"You know, though," he said, head cocked, "a lad down the lane gave us all a story a while back about smuggling his girl into a pub. Another stable hand would not be looked at twice." His gaze ran over her stature.

She stared at him questioningly. How did a stable hand and a pub have any relevance to her attending the tradeshow?

"Nate next door is close to your size. Let me see if he has clothes we could borrow. If you can hide your hair and whatever else..." Blushing, he turned his face to the side and gestured blindly up and down her body. "...you could come with me and the boys. They'd love a lark, and I've told them how much you care for Nellie."

"Oh!" Sophia was too excited to be disconcerted by the reference to her breasts. She could not resist a secret adventure. "Oh, that would be wonderful. Do you really think I might?"

"We'll figure it out. Give me a few days to work on the clothes." He smiled and winked before strolling off whistling.

As Sophia entered the main hall from the kitchen, her usual route back from the stables, Roslynn peeked out the doors of the front parlor.

"Sophia, can I have a word?"

Nervous, Sophia nodded and followed Ros into the room. She perched on the edge of a chair as Ros served tea.

"How was your ride with Edward the other day?"

"Lovely, thank you. 'Twas kind of him to make time for his friend's country cousin."

Ros snorted. "If 'twas anything but riding, he would not have volunteered." She waved a hand, dismissing that subject. "I wanted to continue our conversation from the library the other morning. Nicholas and I both wish to help you find your path forward. Your father desired a good marriage for you, but what do you want, Sophia?"

"I am happy enough to marry. I know I want children. And I never minded running the country house, with the help of a housekeeper."

"Hmm. Not exactly the level of enthusiasm I was hoping for. What about love? And romance?"

It was Sophia's turn to snort. "No, thank you. I've had enough love and loss in my life. I'd rather have a place I know will always be my home and Nellie's."

"Fair enough. You want financial independence.

Nicholas can ensure that in any marriage contract he negotiates for you. What else?"

"I don't really know, Roslynn. I regret that I cannot help you more. I wish very much not to be a burden or an impediment to your, er, marital activities." Sophia gasped and covered her mouth as she realized what she'd just said.

Ros smiled gently. "Sophia, you are not a burden. Or an impediment." She chuckled. "It appears I was right when I thought I glimpsed your hair in the library doorway the other night. 'Tis hard to hide such a pale shade of gold in the dark."

"Oh! I beg your pardon."

"'Tis quite all right, dear. We should talk about it. And Nicholas will join us, too. He wants to ensure you understand and answer any questions."

"Ask Nicholas questions?" Sophia yelped.

"Then ask me if you'd prefer. Now or later. First, let me explain a little. I asked you what you were looking for because there is a private school for young ladies, offering a wide variety of skills. Girls can train to become a governess or a housekeeper or any number of other options, or train for marriage. That may sound strange, but not all girls of the Ton have the skills they need for a happy marriage. Some may not read or write well or be familiar with directing staff or managing a household's accounts. Or arranging dinner parties or even sharing a house with a husband."

Ros looked down and fidgeted her hands in her skirt for a moment before looking back up at Sophia. "The school also teaches girls about their own bodies and sexual awareness. To whatever extent the girls and their families are comfortable learning, which brings us to the other evening."

As she took a breath, Sophia jumped in. "Ros, I do apologize. 'Tis none of my business. And I don't need a school. It sounds terribly expensive and not something you and Nicholas should be burdened with."

"Nonsense. Stop worrying about our money, cousin. You are family. Now, as to the other. You saw things you did not understand, and it would not be right to leave them unexplained."

She took a deep breath. "Sophia, Nicholas enjoys spanking, for both play and pleasure. He shared that predilection with me early in our marriage. I was interested enough to try it and found it—er, quite acceptable. I also consented to Nicholas having final say on rules in the house. If I disobey, I submit to a physical punishment of his choice. If I truly hate something or it hurts too much, he will stop. But otherwise, once I have been penalized, all is forgiven, and we start fresh. It has worked very well for our marriage, and frankly, as you saw, I have even come to enjoy some punishments. But we recognize that it is not for everyone. You can learn more about it from us or at the school, but it is entirely optional."

Sophia gaped. "What if you hated it?"

"Nicholas swears he was ready to give it all up, had I not wanted it. But I don't like contemplating how unhappy he would have been."

"But...but...Nicholas listens to you and asks for your opinion. He doesn't sound like a dictator?"

Roslynn laughed long and loud, wiping tears away with her handkerchief. "Please," she gasped. "Never let him hear that word." And she was off into laughter again. Finally, she calmed. "My apologies. I'll explain.

All rules, decisions, and the like are subject to conversation. Any good partnership relies on that, and a marriage should more so. We've even discussed different penalties for him, should he go wildly amiss. But after consultation, even negotiation, Nicholas's vote overrides a tie."

"Oh. I see. Now I realize why you found my question funny." Sophia smiled back at Roslynn.

"You also may have noticed I often use his title in the vernacular—*milord*. That is my private signal of deference. Or, shh, an attempt to flirt my way to a lighter penalty when I know I've misstepped."

"Ah." Sophia returned her friend's grin at the shared secret.

"It seemed as though you lingered for a few minutes. Is there anything you saw that you have questions about? For me or Nicholas?"

Sophia made a face at the repeated reference to asking her cousin questions.

Ros waited. When Sophia remained silent, she asked, "How did you feel when you watched? What were you thinking about?"

Sophia thought of all the changes in her body. Not knowing where to start, she said, "A bit afraid. The strap looked like it hurt."

"It did. But Nicholas eases me into it. He starts lighter. And as we both enjoy that, our bodies react to it as pleasure. Then when he hits harder, my body teeters on a line between pleasure and pain. As I said, if it gets to be too much, I can ask him to stop. There is something simply delectable about riding that edge, knowing that Nicholas almost always keeps me on the right side of it. Any other reactions?"

"I felt warmer, rather strange." Sophia shifted as she recalled the sensations and her discovery of her swollen folds and sensitivity afterward. She leaned in, and her voice dropped to a whisper. "Especially when he, er, reached around you?"

"Ah. Yes. I'd encourage you to explore if you haven't already. 'Tis your body to own, after all. He touched a certain part of me that is very sensitive and becomes more so when I feel sexual pleasure. It sounds like you were excited watching, which is natural," she quickly added when Sophia looked mortified.

"But…"

"Some people enjoy watching others. 'Tis called voyeurism, but that is a different conversation. Keep in mind that watching and doing it yourself are quite different. The *idea* of pain versus real pain, and all that. Should you want to explore, the school can help you do that. What did you think of the other elements of a marriage preparation course?"

"Why do you think it would be a good fit for me? I know how to manage a household."

"For a few reasons. First, you'll learn some skills about advocating for yourself with a husband, as you have seen me do. Secondly, I firmly believe all girls should understand their own sexual pleasure, even more than they need to know how to please a husband. If a woman can be a partner to her husband in all things, it can strengthen a marriage, ensure fidelity, and most times lead to love. And lastly, the fact that you lurked for more than a few seconds the other night shows that you're open-minded to various types of relationships. The more you can learn, the more choices you'll have in husbands."

Sophia's interest increased with every point Ros raised. She liked the idea of marriage being a partnership, even if she was not interested in forming a love bond. Given Edward's threat the first day, she hoped he might offer opportunities to explore spanking. Despite their disparate positions in society, mayhap he would consider her if they fit in this manner.

Ros was watching her closely so Sophia asked, "Even if I learn what I like at the school, how will we know what a prospective husband prefers?"

The older woman grinned. "Leave that to Nicholas and me. We can make discreet inquiries." She sent Sophia a long look. "Given Nicholas's choices, it's inevitable that he'll know others with similar leanings. Why, some of his closest friends may share his tastes." She raised her eyebrows.

Sophia blushed and lowered her gaze to her hands, clutching and unclutching her skirt.

Nicholas knocked on the open door and strolled in. "Ladies, may I join you?"

Sophia's focus remained locked on her lap, her cheeks growing hotter.

"Sophia." Nick's voice was gentle, but he waited until her gaze met his before continuing. "I want you to be comfortable here, and I am very sorry that we caused you any embarrassment."

She rolled her eyes. "I think I am more embarrassed now, cousin."

He laughed before sobering to ask again, "What are your thoughts on what you have learned today?" His gaze was locked on her, demanding an answer, ignoring her nervous fingers.

His expression reminded her of Edward's.

She thought for a long silent moment. Another new place, new people, more unknowns. But weighed against that was an opportunity to learn a variety of subjects and her newfound knowledge that her infatuation with Edward was not only a girlish crush. Her body had reacted to Edward sexually as her mind had reacted to him emotionally. Even if marriage to him was unlikely, she needed to find her own path. She could not rely on her cousin and his wife forever. This would give her options.

She looked at Nicholas. "Thank you, cousin. I appreciate your concern. I wish to be as prepared as possible for marriage. From what Ros says, this might increase my odds at ensuring a happy marriage, which is important to me. I want what you have, mayhap in more ways than I knew." She gave a quick impish grin, turning to Ros to include her in it.

He barked a quick laugh. "Right, then. I'm glad. I think that ultimately you shall enjoy it, despite any uncomfortable moments."

Ros snickered, but he ignored her. "I will write to the headmistress, and we shall see when you can join an introductory course."

****

Sophia fidgeted with the decorative ribbons on her gloves. She had no idea what to expect, but given how crowded and smelly the city was as a whole, she suspected she would not enjoy balls. She'd barely learned the city dances.

Ros had told her that Edward would help smooth her way into society as the fourth in their party. At least after the dinner and their ride, he felt familiar.

She followed Ros down the stairs, her silk gown

whispering against her skin, making her twitch with its very foreignness. She knew the cool pale blue heightened her eye color, but she'd never worn anything near this fancy in her life, and her hands clenched, sweating in her gloves.

The men stepped out of the library to meet them at the base of the steps, and Edward's gaze dipped down her form. Did it linger on her bosom?

I knew these stays are too low. Now I shall be self-conscious all evening. And I need to focus on my Suitable Husband Attributes list, finding men who fit the criteria.

Edward bowed over Ros's hand, then curtsied when he turned to her. As she straightened, she caught his gaze on her neckline.

On second thought, it seems one who fits many of my criteria likes the look of my décolletage. Mayhap it will help my efforts.

His silver and dark-blue diamond-patterned waistcoat, white shirt, and navy cravat with black coat and breeches heightened his dark looks. As she wore sky blue with accents of navy and rose, she tilted her head and considered. They again looked like a matched pair, an idea she found she liked.

Focus on the list. Look for non-titled men with country estates who are looking for a wife.

Ros chattered about the traditional opening balls for the Season and the fact that one duke's wife and one earl's wife had laid claim to first night for the past several years. They were attending the Earl of Carlisle's ball. His wife was one of the two ladies Sophia and Ros had met riding their first morning.

Once announced at the entrance to the ballroom,

they greeted their hosts. As they made their way to one side of the room, Nicholas and Edward saw cronies from the House of Lords.

Sophia lost track of the names and ranks of people she met and who was married to whom. She hoped Ros would help refresh her memory before the next ball so she wouldn't embarrass her cousins. Watching the glitter of jewels and gowns, hearing the noise of countless voices competing, she shrank back, wishing to be in a quiet stall with her best friend rather than here.

As her nerves started to get the best of her, the music swelled with the musicians' preparations for the first dance set. Edward excused himself from the discussion he'd been in and returned to her side. "Are you ready?"

Terror stole her breath and turned her gloved hands damp. Ros and lessons with a dancing instructor had given her more confidence in the past days, but the crush of people kept her anxious.

"How will we keep from bumping into people?"

"Leave that to me," Edward smiled. "You shall be fine. Simply relax and follow my lead."

The first dance went smoothly. Sophia's grip on his coat sleeve went from bruising to gentle as she became comfortable in his lead. An accomplished dancer, he effortlessly glided them about the floor, turning her to protect her from other dancers' elbows or slippers. His face mesmerized her with his dark hair, brows, and eyes, the shadow of beard stubble under his skin, and his firm, full lips, with a hint of his teeth shadowed in the small opening. She recognized his scent now, a hint of leather with an outdoorsy citrus spice that made her think of trees along their ride. Her gloved hand tingled at the memory of muscles being squeezed under her nervous grip, and she bit her lip as heat shot through her core.

She knew she was lucky. Nicholas could have kept her at the townhouse with no chance to ride Nellie or make friends until he married her off. While she didn't think she'd enjoy balls anytime soon, she enjoyed Ros's company and the opportunity to meet other people her age. Late-night library activities aside, Nicholas's warmth and generosity had been unexpected.

More, this friend of Nicholas had also gone out of his way to smooth her transition. Would anyone else make time for their friend's cousin for morning rides? And introduce her to society by dancing the first dance with her? Add to that his enticing scent, good looks, and musculature, and she again wished she could avoid these crowds and simply marry him.

She frowned, angry at her thoughts. Wishes and people led to heartache, and she'd do well to remember that.

Sophia kept her focus on Edward, ready to follow his lead as the second dance, a reel, began. As their turn came and they spun off the line, her grip loosened, and the tightness in her shoulders eased. This was familiar and fun, a country dance.

Several partners later, the crowded dance floor was too much for her. She begged off the next dance and found Ros on the edge of the dance floor. Nicholas had gone to fetch his wife champagne and returned with two. He gallantly offered his to Sophia on finding her there and turned back for a third.

As Ros and Sophia sipped, the crush grew greater

around them. One gentleman standing at Sophia's side with his back to them became more animated in a political discussion. Trying to emphasize his point, he raised his arms, his right arm hitting Sophia's right elbow at the same moment she raised her glass to sip.

Her glass jolted its contents onto her neck and ran down her chest to wet her gown over her right breast, some splashing onto Ros as well.

As the man turned, she glimpsed Edward across the circle, his eyes hot and dark, focused on her décolletage. Looking down, she gasped. Her gown was almost transparent, as was the chemise underneath, her nipple's shape and color visible over the edge of her low-cut stays as it tightened from the sudden dousing. She turned her head, wondering which way to turn.

Ros hadn't noticed yet, concerned with her own dress.

Edward was in front of her in a flash, gripping her arm, prying the now-empty champagne glass from her fingers, and placing it on a server's tray. He kept his body between her and the room and steered her toward a hallway.

Ros was now in front of them. She pointed to the staircase and walked toward it. "The ladies' retiring room upstairs will have cloths to dry our dresses."

Edward veered off through an open doorway and tugged Sophia inside, closing and locking the door.

"What? Why—?" she asked, confused. Why were they in here, and why had he locked the door?

He swallowed noticeably and blinked, keeping his gaze on her face now. "I thought you could use a moment to compose yourself," he said as he extracted a handkerchief.

"Thank you," she replied, turning one shoulder to him for privacy. She peered at her dress and dabbed at it with the linen. Trying to soak up the champagne, she ended up holding the fabric to her gown, effectively cupping her breast.

Hearing a stifled groan, she asked, "Are you sure you're feeling all the thing, my lord?" She glanced around at him, only to realize where his gaze centered.

A strangled, "Yes," came out of him.

As she dabbed, she noticed her nipple had puckered from the waft of air over the damp silk. Looking up, she found Edward had shifted his weight and could see her profile. His eyes were trained on the shadow of rose and the pert tip poking through her garments.

"What on earth do your stays look like if I can see that?" he asked hoarsely.

Sophia gasped and flattened her hand over her breast. "I beg your pardon. That is not your concern."

"Perhaps not before, little one, but that incident made it mine," he ground out. He stepped into her and spun her back toward him. Curving one arm around her back, his other hand came to hers, holding his handkerchief to her damp breast. His breath was hot against her mouth.

Shocked at the heat of his palm and the closeness of his lips, Sophia sucked in a breath. Her eyes fluttered closed, and she leaned into him, tilting her head up in tacit permission.

His lips covered hers on a slant, his tongue swooping in with a lightning touch to hers before withdrawing. He twisted his lips against hers to deepen the kiss, and another moan rumbled from him.

Heat flooded through her, and the flick of his tongue startled Sophia. She reveled in the softness of his lips and strength of his tongue against her own. Her whole body burned, not only her lips or where their bodies touched. His delicious scent invaded her nose even as his tongue invaded her mouth. She leaned toward him, pressing her breast into his hand.

Watching Nicholas and Ros in the library had not prepared Sophia for her body's awakening as he continued to kiss her, teasing her with gentle swipes of his tongue. The indistinct cravings racing through her body mimicked the night she'd watched her host and hostess, but so intensely she barely recognized the similarity. Her tongue chased his, imitating his movements, her lips twisting against those firm lips.

Her conscience clanged in the back of her mind, trying to raise the alarm. She ignored it, craving a few more seconds of this pleasure, unable to think. Awash in sensation, she sagged against this handsome, authoritative stranger.

A knock sounded at the door, and they heard Ros's voice, "Edward? Sophia?"

Stepping back, he gestured for her to turn away from the door and compose herself before he opened it.

"Come now," Ros chided Edward. "You know better than to take an unmarried woman behind closed doors. Really, Edward. I brought our cloaks so we can quietly depart, with none the wiser."

As he stepped back with Sophia's cloak to hold it for her, Ros sent Sophia a quick wink.

Still recovering from the kiss, Sophia raised a hand to her lips in confusion and noticed they were swollen.

Oh. Apparently, Ros approves a match with Edward.

Back at Suffolk House, she lay in bed worrying about the evening. Her mind kept playing the embrace over and over.

No wonder Ros and Nicholas participate in lewd acts!

She had never realized a man's touch on her breast would make all her nerve endings come alive. Amazement at her body's reaction to a virtual stranger muddled her thoughts. She could not summon outrage or regret. Despite her discomfort with Ros's mention of scandal, she understood it. If Ros had not knocked, she might have stayed there all evening, kissing Edward. And his tongue! She had never realized how sensuous a man's tongue might feel in her mouth. She supposed she should have, after watching Ros lick Nicholas's...

As her body flushed hot, she turned over again, punching her pillow to reshape it.

Reaffirming her goal of finding a husband, she tried in vain to ignore the memory of Edward's mouth on hers.

Chapter Six

Edward waited for Sophia in the great hall. He noted distractedly that she wore a new habit that fit her better.

"Sophia, might I have a word with you before we go?" He gestured toward the drawing room.

Turning to her after pushing the door to a sliver short of closed, he found her staring at his lips.

It appears I am not the only one who cannot stop thinking of the kiss.

He had not slept much after the ball. Every time he closed his eyes, he could taste her again, her sweet lips and tongue sliding against his with a hint of champagne. His fingers twitched, recalling the pliancy of her breast framed by the bones of her hand and corset. Finally, he had rolled to his back and stroked his cock with that hand until he gained a few minutes of relief, even as he recognized that he was further wronging an innocent with the act. But now, looking at her anew, his conscience struggled to stay afloat in the sea of his desire. Finally, he found his voice.

"Sophia." He attempted to get her attention quietly.

Her hand raised to her lips and rubbed, and he stifled a groan.

"Sophia." His louder tone snapped her gaze to his, and her hand dropped to clutch her skirt. "My behavior last night was beyond the pale. I must beg your forgiveness."

She looked oddly disappointed.

He tried again. "I assure you it shan't happen again."

Her gaze dropped at that, and her shoulders fell. "Right. We mustn't cause a scandal." Her mouth twisted on the bitter words.

"What?" He reached for her hands, then abruptly stopped, dropping his arms to his sides. 'Twas not a good idea to touch her after their shared intimacy when he was trying to reassure her there would not be a recurrence. "Sophia, 'tis not only about your reputation."

"Did you not like it, then?" She squared her shoulders at him, giving him an arch look. "From my perspective, there is nothing to apologize for, other than the possibility of gossip."

Why, the little hellion. She liked the kiss. That thought nearly undid him. He turned away from her so he wouldn't be tempted to re-enact the embrace. *And the breast fondling. Criminy.*

He paced a few feet away, raking his hand through his hair before pivoting to face her. "Sophia. You must know that is not an appropriate question. 'Tis not about liking it. I should not have taken liberties with your person. No matter how much I liked it—"

He pressed his lips together at that slip.

She smiled and ducked her head as pink rose in her cheeks.

"It should not have happened," he continued. "Especially as I am not courting you. This is the type of thing you need to beware of from young men you meet during your Seasons. Even when courting, they should not take advantage of you like that. And if they do, you should tell Nicholas."

Her eyes went wide. "You want me to tell Nicholas?"

"No!" He ran a hand through his dark mane again and gentled his voice. "I am hoping you will accept my apology and my promise to avoid a repeat and that we can move forward as friends."

Her head lowered again, and when she spoke, her voice sounded defeated. "My lord, 'twas but a kiss. And no one saw." Sophia straightened and waved her hand dismissively. "Oh la, this city. Too many people, too many rules. I shall be happy to be done with it."

"Done with it? Did you have plans to leave, then?" Edward arched a brow.

"Well, I can't stay here with Ros and Nicholas forever. I'd like to find a husband to read and discuss the news with. Someone with a country estate where Nellie and I can have fresh air and space to roam." She nodded once as though to reinforce her goals.

"Right, then. Of course." He bowed. "I should still like to be forgiven. For the kiss and..." He gestured vaguely at her bosom.

"Oh!" Sophia blushed. "Er, yes. Of course, my lord. All is forgiven. Shall we ride?" She spun toward the door.

Edward sighed with relief at finishing the embarrassing scene and her confusing reaction and followed her. Relief, tinged with a disconcerting edge of disappointment that she was so set on a husband who liked to read.

As usual, their chosen time meant the park was quiet, and they cantered side by side for as long as she desired. More than once, out of the corner of his eye, he caught her sidelong glances at his lips, his legs, his hands, but when he turned his head, she blushed and averted her eyes.

He watched her as closely as she seemed to be watching him, thankful she did not know his thoughts. He kept imagining her in an upstairs room at the Spanking Club, waiting on her hands and knees for him, arse bared and ready for his crop.

No. She is beguiling and beautiful, but marriage material and untouchable. He enjoyed her intelligence and their discussions, despite all that.

His conversation with Nicholas about marriage played in Edward's head as he contemplated Sophia's trim posterior swaying in the saddle ahead of him. Again, he pictured her bent forward, her naked bottom raised for punishment. He shifted his crop to rest against his leg rather than Ash's side. Flicking his wrist a few times as though wielding it against her flesh, he was glad for his boot. He'd much rather see a pattern of small red squares on her bare posterior. Ah, if wishes were horses, he'd be more willing to ride.

He shifted uncomfortably in his saddle. A surreptitious glance at the young groom with them reassured him his odd maneuvering had not been noticed.

He could envision Sophia under his control all too well. *I doubt Nicholas had his own cousin in mind when he suggested I teach someone. He'd likely call me out. And why would any woman not complain to her father—or cousin—if I asked her to perform the lewd acts I desire? I'd be dead within a month, still with no heir.*

Maggie Sims

He sighed. The whole concept of marriage had never appealed to him, and he refused to consider it further now. He had enough to contemplate.

He glanced at Sophia's back again, thinking of the number of topics they'd discussed. Her dress melted away in his mind, leaving her back bare. Worse than inconvenient, this continued obsession was downright annoying. Couldn't she be homely? And dull? The girl could carry on a discussion of the pros and cons of the Corn Laws, for heaven's sake.

Sophia turned, looking back as they reached a bend in the path, and he returned to the present, adjusting his seat to try to ease the tightness in his breeches. Squeezing his legs, he trotted alongside her.

"How did your conversation with Nicholas go the other day?" Sophia asked.

Edward stifled a groan as his mind jumped right back to Nicholas's suggestion of teaching. He sifted through the rest of their conversation to come up with, "Rather well, thank you. He is helping me fill a necessary post."

"Oh?" she prompted.

"I am in need of a new steward. Though I have caretakers at most properties, I need one to help me oversee all the properties, sort of a head steward, if you will. Someone who can travel with me when need be."

Sophia hesitated. "My lord, if I may ask, is that not what Ros does? Might it be easier to fill that role with a wife, rather than a head steward?"

For the first time ever, Edward felt a surge of desire at the word *wife* as he pictured Sophia in that role, reading for him and being cropped by him. Distracted, he replied without thinking. "Well, yes. 'Tis

80

simply that a wife comes with many other challenges." Then realized his statement would prompt more questions from this country girl looking to understand his world.

"I am not certain I understand. From a woman's perspective, it does not seem like men have many challenges in a marriage. Is everything not their way? 'Tis the woman who has to follow her husband's rules. What issues could she cause a husband?"

Edward barked a short laugh. "A man must keep his wife happy. He must keep his wife's family happy. There are heirs to beget and then be kept happy. And those are all added responsibilities on top of what a man already has."

"Yes," Sophia countered after a moment of consideration. "But you said the right wife could take on some of those other responsibilities. And not all wives will have extensive families."

He suspected she referred to the fact she had only Nicholas for family. He fervently hoped these questions were rhetorical, much as he had enjoyed imagining her bent over for his lash.

She continued, "I suppose I'm glad to hear you say that you'd wish to keep your wife happy, at least. Sometimes it seems like society expects women to keep the men happy, with little or no regard to their own happiness in a marriage."

"That is true for many, sadly, but I noticed a common thread in my parents' marriage, my brother's, and Nicholas's. If the wife is happy, she is much more amenable to doing what her husband wants, just as the husband does for her. It is a more balanced exchange."

"Isn't that good?" Sophia seemed confused.

"Right now, I hardly have time to meet my current needs. Much less think about anyone's happiness, even my own," Edward replied and frowned. Then more quietly, he said, "And I'm not convinced I could keep a young lady from society happy for long."

Sophia cocked her head as they looped back toward the entrance to the park. "Surely it cannot be that terrible, my lord. You are young and healthy and well-spoken, and your home sounds wonderful."

Uh oh. It seems she is indeed picturing herself in the role of my wife. He understood it. She was new to Town and realized she could not stay with Nicholas and Ros forever. Searching for security and a future made sense, and he was the first man she'd gotten to know. But she'd quickly lose interest if she knew he didn't meet her first requirement in a husband—an affinity for reading. Those thoughts needed to stop here and now. He was not marrying anyone, much less Nicholas's cousin.

"Thank you, Sophia. I appreciate the kind words." Edward offered her a fleeting smile but declined to comment further as they made their way back to the house. He was thankful he would not have time to ride the next few days due to preparations for the Vauxhall event.

At Suffolk House, he dismounted to help her down. He caught her waist to guide her off Nellie as she eased out of the stirrups and slid down. Her better-fitting habit showed off her shape, and he had mere inches between his thumbs.

How tiny, yet strong.

Her fine hair, pinned back under a hat but left down, caught on his jacket, and he quelled the urge to rub it between his fingers, to bring it to his face to sniff.

She turned, starting to say something, and gasped at his proximity.

He attempted to step back and felt a tug. They both looked down, seeing the problem.

A loop of decorative braid from her new riding jacket was caught on one of his waistcoat buttons. The braid hung from her shoulder and looped around her sleeve right next to her left breast. He closed his eyes momentarily. Extracting himself would be tricky. He braced to focus on her apparel and not her curves and opened his eyes.

"We seem to be stuck." She peeped up at him through her lashes.

Edward briefly wondered if the snag had been intentional. She'd been questioning him about marriage, after all. "Er, yes. Ahh, mayhap you'd better try to unsnag it?" If it was a deliberate act, he was not going to encourage it by touching her intimately again.

"I beg your pardon, my lord, I cannot see what it's snagged on." Her reply was muffled as she peered downward. Her hat hit him in the chest, preventing her from bending far enough to examine the tangle.

"Criminy." Edward took a calming breath, only to realize he'd made matters worse. His chest nudged her pert breast, and his head swam as he felt the give of the lush mound.

A hundred times more beguiling than the women at the club.

He raised his hands tentatively. "If you tilted your head?" he asked gently, to remove the hat from his vision. He hoped it could also hide his agitation.

"Oh, of course." Her tone was rueful. She leaned

her head toward her other shoulder. When his hands came between them, she sucked in a breath, causing the same response his inhale had.

Then his knuckles were there against the softness of her bosom, almost kneading her as his fingers worked the snag.

Sophia's breathing accelerated. Her chest rose and fell ever faster against his hand.

Knowing his touch affected her did not help the predicament in his breeches. He tried to focus on the tangle, to release her as quickly as possible. His cock did not seem to care about her motivation or lack thereof. He shifted his right leg forward without conscious thought, pressing into the back of her skirts and sliding behind her left leg, bending a bit to encourage her weight to rest against it.

An almost-silent startled "Oh," at the sensation escaped her. Her backside and leg leaned into his leg. Her nipples peaked and poked through her garments. She sighed, pressing her breast into his knuckles again.

Edward gritted his teeth, wanting to flick his thumb over that protrusion, to lean down and catch it between his teeth and worry it. He wanted to hear more sighs, discover what other sounds she'd make from more direct caresses. His hand ached to turn and weigh her breast as he had at the ball.

He closed his eyes for a moment to refocus. A low groan escaped him as the lack of sight enhanced his other senses, magnifying her delicate floral scent and the press of her curves against his leg and hip.

For all he knew, she was manipulating him into compromising her to force his hand. His eyes flew open, refocusing on the task to extricate them and free himself from this torture.

The loop popped free. His arm circled her back, steadying her. "There, 'tis free. Are you quite all right?" He waited for her nod and her weight to shift before stepping back.

"Thank you, my lord," she replied, breathless, her head down and a bright blush on her cheeks. "I'm very sorry about that. Er, would you like some tea?"

"No, thank you. I think 'tis best I go," Edward replied, hearing his own stiffness.

Speaking of stiffness. I'm not sure how I'm going to ride in this condition. He exhaled through pursed lips. *Criminy, 'tis not like I haven't already done that recently. It likely will not kill me, although it might cause some permanent damage if this keeps up…literally.*

****

Edward desperately needed to focus. Reading correspondence and merchant invoices required every ounce of concentration he could muster. But Sophia's breast, lips, and body pressed against his kept interfering, even a day later.

He kept staring into space, daydreaming of her entering the room. He'd take her to task for wearing lewd undergarments. They'd both know he loved them, but it would be an excuse to give her a playful spanking. She'd apologize and pout, but he'd insist on reinforcing the lesson. She would step around the desk to his side, and he'd shove his chair back, position her over his lap, arse up, and drag her skirts slowly up her legs. Of course, he would not have allowed knickers, for all his complaints about naughty stays. His palm would rub her bare cheeks for a moment before reaching for the crop he kept under the desk. Then...*thwack.*

Ouch. That hurt. He came back to the present at the bite of pain on his thigh with one hand pressing his bulging cock through his breeches, the crop in the other hand having come down on his thigh. Wanting nothing more than to unwrap the hard rod and stroke it to completion, he shook his head and set the crop down. Mayhap after he waded through this pile.

Just as he preferred physical punishment for women's bad behavior, he withheld his own pleasure for thinking of his friend's cousin in an unacceptable manner. She was destined for marriage, and he had no interest in that institution, despite his intense and uncomfortable interest in Sophia.

Edward hunched over the letters again. He had struggled through several, reading each slowly and carefully, and crafted terse responses to his steward at the family estate. At times like this, he empathized with James. Despite instructing the steward to write in large clean letters, Edward cultivated poor penmanship, so at least some of his misspellings would be overlooked or undecipherable.

A knock sounded at the library door, and his butler opened the door. "My lord, there is a runner with a note from your tailor."

"Thank you. Leave it there." Edward pointed to the corner of the desk.

"Sir, he indicated he had been asked to wait for a reply."

Edward thought for a moment. Gesturing at the paperwork in front of him, he said, "I am very busy. Read it to me, and I shall send you off with a verbal reply."

"Certainly, sir." The butler unfolded the foolscap and scanned the note. With a quick bow, he said, "Begging your pardon, sir. It says here that your account is due, and as you placed a significant order recently and you are here in London, he thought he might request payment from you directly rather than sending mail north to Peterborough."

"Humph." Edward had requested a number of new clothes for his new title and even asked them to be rushed. He couldn't blame the man. Thankfully, he had discussed this type of scenario with his new man of business here in London. He wished James could handle everything. The man knew to be brief and could decipher Edward's handwriting, important tools to compensate for the new earl's challenges.

Dragging a fresh piece of foolscap to him, Edward carefully wrote a note to the solicitor with the amount owed and the tailor's name and direction. "Here. Take this to the runner. He shall have to see my solicitor. Do you remember the address?"

The butler made another shallow bow. "Yes, sir. Thank you."

Edward returned to his correspondence, hoping the issue was resolved.

****

Cursing, Edward paced his study, his hand clutching a response from his solicitor about the tailor's bill he'd sent over a few days ago. A pulse ticked in his temple above his clenched jaw. *How dare Charles die so young!*

He must have mixed up the digits in the amount again. *You idiot*, he raged, hearing the echo of his governess's voice in his head. *You must be more careful.*

Insofar as he could read, the note stated that the tailor had returned funds to the solicitor, indicating he had overpaid.

Thank the dickens for the man's honesty. Both men's.

The solicitor's note was very polite, and after struggling through it, Edward thought he understood the message. The solicitor and the tailor would correspond directly in the future, and if Lord Peterborough would be so kind as to send a list of other London establishments, the solicitor would set up accounts with them on the earl's behalf as he had done for the prior earl, etcetera.

But Edward could picture the man's sneer. The laugh he snorted as he wrote to remove Edward from the process because he was too stupid to get a payment correct.

His jaw ached from being clamped so tightly, and the letter crumpled in his fist.

He had spent the last several days vacillating between trying not to think about Sophia and a nagging curiosity about Nicholas's suggestion that an affinity for spanking could be cultivated in a wife.

Sophia only had Nicholas and Roslynn as family, so the risk of broader discovery of his reading capability was low. She liked both the country and horses… But he kept circling back to the risk of ridicule. More, even, than the risk of exposure, this was his sticking point. He had vowed after school that no one would look at him with disdain again, particularly a woman.

Whether or not the solicitor actually had sneered was of no matter. It was too easy to make mistakes and be exposed to someone who would. This proved Edward could not risk a wife. Not even Sophia, as lovely and well-suited to him as she was.

Unable to focus on paperwork, afraid of making any more mistakes, he looked at the brandy decanter, debating. Fresh air would do him much more good, as would one of his beloved horses. Calling his butler, he told the servant he was going for a ride and strode through the back of the house to the stables.

****

Leaning over the half door of Nellie's stall, Sophia felt satisfaction at solving Roslynn's mount's sore hock with a few applications of salve. She'd overheard the hands wondering what to do. When they stepped away, she found what she needed in the kit from the tack room and applied it for two days. The mare no longer favored that leg. While the hands might be confused about the horse's quick recovery, Sophia was accustomed to being unobtrusive, even secretive, given some of her father's clients' tender sensibilities about a woman's work. Old habits were hard to break.

Now, she contemplated her prospects for the future. As usual, her thoughts came in a one-sided conversation.

"I shall bring you up to date, Nellie. After attending a ball and meeting several men, I've discovered a problem with our criteria. Most men with country estates are titled gentlemen. Which means seats in the House of Lords. Which means London for part of the year. I haven't met many others. A few younger sons, but they don't meet our requirements." Her lips twisted. Matchmaking was no simple task.

"I shall keep looking, of course. But oh dear, Lord Peterborough... Nellie, he kissed me! And touched me. 'Twas lovely, Nell. Nay, 'twas scrumptious. Like your favorite dessert with chocolate sauce on it."

The mare shifted.

"You know what I mean. Anyway, I cannot stop thinking about it. It made me all shivery, like I was cold, except I felt hot and flushed." It was Sophia's turn to stir. "If only Edward—I think of him as Edward. Is that terrible? I can't help it after that kiss—was considering marriage. Apparently, he is expected to, given his inherited title and the need for heirs. Think of the fun you and I could have at his estate with the horses he trains. And the kissing. Mmm, and mayhap other things."

She tried to picture her and Edward in the positions in which she'd spied Roslynn and Nicholas. "But he is not interested in marriage." Her sigh gusted the horse's mane, eliciting a turn of the equine head.

She finger-combed the mane back into place absently. A tremor ran through her as she recalled the strength of his arms directing and shielding her as they danced. She preferred him over her other dance partners. "He's an exquisite dancer, Nellie. So big, so hard, but so graceful. And an excellent kisser."

She leaned in, her shoulders drooping. "I can only hope that others' kisses will be as nice. But I must be practical and focus more on our criteria, less on kisses. We shall see who calls on me. I know Ros and Nicholas will vet them, but I haven't discussed my criteria with them yet. If only Father and I had time to plan a bit more. Or simply more time together." Sophia sighed again.

The kiss kept replaying in her mind. Darn.

Frustrated, she frowned and grumbled at Nellie. "I need to stop obsessing about someone who doesn't want me, as handsome and horse-friendly as he may be." She recognized that she was admonishing herself more than asserting her plan.

When she returned to the house, Ros reminded her that they had gentlemen callers that afternoon, following up from meeting her at the ball.

"I am not sure I remember their names and titles."

"Names and titles will be easier as you attend more." Ros patted her hand.

Several young men arrived that afternoon, bearing flowers. She and Ros entertained them in the front parlor, sometimes two at once, which was entertaining to watch. The batch included several viscounts, a baron, and a second son of a duke who did not have his own title.

As two of the young men were leaving, Edward arrived.

Sophia straightened her spine a fraction and smiled at him, thinking he had come to visit her, only to realize her mistake as he handed his hat and coat to Harris, nodded briefly at them through the door of the front parlor, and strode toward Nicholas's study.

Shoulders drooping, she turned away, but not before catching Ros's contemplative look.

Chapter Seven

A group of six boys paused inside the gates of Vauxhall to gaze open-mouthed at the noise and crowds. Even for those accustomed to London markets, the raucous air filled them with awe. Maybe it was due to the crowd's exuberance. Give Londoners an opportunity to haggle over fruits and vegetables, and they were happy. Give them a chance to negotiate the price of a horse, they were ecstatic.

Sophia skipped to keep up when they began walking again. Bobby looked back to make sure the smallest group member was with them.

"Don't skip!" he hissed at her.

"Oh, sorry." Sophia's head swiveled as she tried to take it all in, adrenaline still high from retiring to her room after dinner to change and sneak down the back stairs. She had flattened her breasts with a strip of muslin off an old petticoat, which chafed her skin. But the lack of a corset and skirts was liberating. She wished she had time to ride astride while she had these borrowed clothes. Then thoughts of clothing disappeared as they reached the first stalls. Rows and rows of horses. She skipped twice again in excitement before remembering her surroundings.

"Let's walk the stalls first. Then we can hang back on the edges for the bidding and see what's what," one boy who had attended a prior year said.

Horses lined the length of the Gardens. Some owners had created more formal stalls. Others merely roped off their areas. Many had small signs indicating lineage and measurements. As they wandered, the boys' heads came together to exclaim over the most prime horseflesh. Once in a while, they spotted a poorly cared-for horse. Sophia could hardly bear to leave those. She repressed the urge to climb into the enclosure to put salve on cuts, groom snarled manes, and soothe the animals frightened by the surrounding clamor.

Bobby reached for her hand at one point to pull her, only to recover and give her a warning grin and a gentle shove toward the next stall to keep her with them.

They bought ales to sip as they strolled. Sophia bought one with them, to blend in, but forgot to sip it in her distraction with the horses.

The center of the Gardens remained open for the auctions. As the boys made their way round the stalls, gentlemen in capes and hats pushed and shoved along with them to see the horses they were interested in. Strangers commented to each other on the pros and cons of this or that specimen. Some even had notepads. Others were quizzing the owners, trying to get an idea of what price might be accepted.

Sophia had a hard time keeping the boys in sight, given her stature and the height of the gentlemen and their hats. At one point, she thought she glimpsed Edward, but the crowd jostled her. She glanced at her ale to avoid spilling it, and when she looked back up, she didn't see him.

Bells pealed from the auction stage, signaling its

start. The horde shifted direction toward the open arena, and the boys flowed with it. Owners led their horses onto the platform where the auctioneer facilitated the bids, the better to see the raised hands in the crowd. There seemed to be an unspoken protocol. The seemingly impenetrable wall of men parted to grant passage to gentlemen interested in a particular horse, allowing them to get closer. Each horse caused a shift in the throng.

Bobby hauled her up next to him on the low wall of a raised garden for a better view. He and the other boys bet ha'pennies on each horse's final price, but Sophia simply stared at the proceedings.

The boy who'd attended a prior auction commented that only half the horses would go up for bid tonight. The other half would follow suit the following night. Racers and matched sets went the first night, as they brought the most money. This way, the sensitive purebreds were subjected to only one night of crowds and noise.

Before Sophia knew it, there were only a few horses left to auction. The crowds thinned. The boys needed to return to their households, as their employers expected them at work early the next morning. They made their way along a row of pens, aiming for the exit. Men continued to stroll from stall to stall, examining the working horses planned for auction the following night.

Rather than darting around buyers, the boys ducked between two rows to the back alleyway running between them. In one dark spot along the passage, they came upon two stable hands working with a horse in distress. Its eyes were rolling, nostrils flaring and snorting, and the horse was pulling away from the hand holding its lead. The other had a whip and raised it as Sophia watched. A horse shifted in the adjacent stall, and a ray of light poked through the makeshift pen boards, shining on welts along the frightened horse's flanks.

Sophia could not stand it any longer. She rushed forward and grabbed the whip from the man's hand, only then realizing he was nearly twice her size and older than she or any of the boys with her.

Not caring, she railed at him, "Don't you dare hurt that gorgeous animal. Can you not see he is frightened?"

"How dare you interfere. I'll do as I like, and if ye don't give me back my whip this minute, you'll be feeling its tail as well," he yelled, spittle flying at her.

Bobby arrived and stood next to her, unsure what to do but ready to protect her. None of the other boys were in sight.

The man snatched the whip back and shoved her to the side again. Bobby blocked him and shoved him back.

Switching the whip to his left hand, the stable hand sneered and threw a fist. Bobby flew back to sit hard on the ground. Raising a hand to his eye, he shook his head to clear it.

Snapping her gaze back to the bully, she saw the whip raised again. She threw herself against the horse's side to protect him. The man's eyes bulged, clearly contemplating whether he should let the whip fly. He took one step forward, and his hand flashed out to grab the front of Sophia's shirt, wrenching her away from the horse. She heard a ripping sound, and when she fell, cool air wafted over…her breast.

Sophia glanced down. The stable hand had torn one side of her collar downward, taking the binding from her breasts. She clutched the shirt together with a gasp. But the damage was done. The man's entire focus was on her now. Her hat had also come off, her pale hair hanging half out of the pins.

"Well, well, what have we here? Hey Joe, we've got a little stable *gel* here."

Bobby had gained his feet and tried to step forward to get between them, only to be grabbed by Joe with his arms held behind his back. Struggling, he yelled, "Let her go. Don't touch her!"

The men laughed.

"Oh ho, we'll have some jolly fun now. Touch her? Aye, there'll be a fair bit of that, along with swivin'. Run along, lad. We'll send her back when we're done." The bully cackled and grabbed his crotch, approaching where she sat on the ground, clutching her shirt with her shoulders hunched protectively. One hand grabbed her arm, and the other reached for her torn shirt as she cowered away from him.

A deeper, shockingly familiar voice asked, "What is going on here? And whose horse is this?"

Edward stepped forward into the light, his focus on the mistreated horse at first. But as the stable hand shifted to answer him, Sophia raised her eyes to his pleadingly. His widened for a second before his brows came together into a fierce frown.

Turning to the stable hands, he growled, "What do you think you're doing with the girl?"

"This 'stable girl' thought she'd interfere with how we were handling the beast, but we're going to show her how we handle ornery animals." Sophia's captor smirked insolently, assuming that Edward would concur with her inappropriate interference.

"I think not." Edward spied the owner in the stall's darkness, the man's greedy eyes on Sophia's hand clenching her shirtfront. He strode forward. "How much for the horse?" Snapping a glare at the stable hands, he added, "Don't you move."

The owner named a price, Edward scribbled something on a small notepad, and passed it to him, saying, "Bring him to this address tomorrow, and you shall have your money. But there better not be another mark on him."

From the quality of his clothes and his speech, the stable hands recognized Edward as an aristocrat. As he strode back and grabbed Sophia up from where she still sat on the ground, the man holding her released her and scrambled back. Edward turned to go, a hand at Sophia's back.

"Bobby," Sophia whispered, her feet planted. She turned to her friend and would-be protector, still being held by the other man.

Edward turned back and glowered at the other stable hand. "Release him and step away," he snarled.

The man did, obviously nervous about repercussions from a nabob. Edward gestured with his head for Bobby to take off, saying, "I shall get her home safely."

Bobby tugged his forelock, muttering, "Ta, your lordship," and raced off.

Sophia could not stop shaking, even after Edward shrugged out of his cape and draped it around her. He tied it, and she could swear his hands shook but thought it was likely her quaking.

He grabbed her arm tight enough to leave bruises and hauled her through the crowds to the line of carriages. Sophia had no idea how he found his, but his coachman opened the door in the nick of time. Edward did not wait for the step. He lifted her and tossed her inside on the rear-facing seat, then hopped up and settled across from her. Giving the coachman instructions to take her home first, he sat back and scowled at her.

Miserable, trembling in residual fear, Sophia dreaded what might come next. A vision of Nicholas exiling her flashed, and she mentally recoiled. The last thing she wanted was to be left alone in the world yet again.

"Thank you, my lord." She dared a peek up through her lashes. *Uh oh, still mad.*

"May I ask what you were doing there?" he growled.

"I only wished to see the horses," she near-whispered. Her eyes filled with tears, and she started trembling in earnest, clutching his cloak around her.

Edward stared at her and mumbled an oath. "Do you have any idea what could have happened to you that close to a strange horse?"

When her teeth started chattering, he muttered, "Never mind," and dragged her across to his lap and rubbed her arms. Nestled in his cloak, which already smelled like him, and wrapped in his warmth and strength, Sophia's trembling slowly subsided, and her breath evened out. His leather and citrus spice scent comforted her. His muscular arms surrounding her reminded her of the kiss at the ball.

Taking a deep breath, she looked up at him, eyes lingering on his lips before meeting his gaze. She dared a question. "Are you going to tell Nicholas about this, my lord?"

Edward frowned down at her. "He needs to know so that he keeps you in hand better."

Sophia bit her lip, weighing her next request. Now that she was calmer, she saw the possibilities of these strange circumstances. Ros had said that spanking was not for everyone, and even if she enjoyed watching it, she might not enjoy experiencing it firsthand. Given Edward's threat the first time he met her, and Ros's hints, she wondered if she might talk him into trying it.

Although...he looks so angry. But there are no straps here in the carriage. How bad could it be? And it might convince him not to tell Nicholas if I have already been reprimanded.

Her body was already warming at the idea, her nipples perking up through the thin cloth of the shirt, the strip of muslin having been lost along the way. Her limbs felt heavy, languorous, as though the heat pooling between her legs stripped the energy from the rest of her. She breathed in his scent again, leaning into him.

"Please, my lord? I shan't do anything like this again." Sophia peered up at him.

"Sophia, he is your guardian."

"I am eighteen. I hardly need a guardian. You told me you did not even live at home at eighteen." She heard her voice become a whine.

"Tonight proves unequivocally that you *do*, in fact, need a guardian. What were you thinking?" Edward nearly shouted before taking a deep breath. "There must be consequences. You could have been seriously harmed tonight. I've seen men twice your size be permanently maimed by a rearing horse. Punishment for bad behavior and encouragement for good behavior are the best teachers."

Perfect. Now she could offer consequences she hoped would appeal to him. Especially if she reassured him no one would be the wiser. "Um, mayhap you could punish me now, and we needn't bother Nicholas?"

****

Edward was still shaking from adrenaline as the carriage jolted forward, unable to erase the sight of her in that ruffian's clutches from his brain.

His anger had held until he saw her tears. God save him from innocent young ladies' tears. When he heard her teeth clink, he could not wait any longer to hold her, to reassure himself she was safe as much as to comfort her.

Now, he stared at her in shock. "What?"

His cock rose, making it very clear which punishment it wanted. He ignored it. Surely she hadn't said what he thought she did. Or meant what he hoped.

"I'd prefer to have it over and done with."

Thoughts of baring her and putting her over his knee sprang to mind, and his cock nudged her hip happily. 'Twas perfect for a punishment and would allow him to purge the pent-up emotions coursing through him. But of course, she could not have meant that. Or if she had, was this another set up? No, she had said she did not want Nicholas to know.

It was grossly inappropriate to even contemplate spanking a well-bred young lady, trousers or no. Much less Nicholas's cousin. But he could not banish the image long enough to imagine a more suitable punishment.

Stalling, he framed his words carefully. "What penalty do you think this deserves?"

Her response was tentative. "I am not sure. Growing up, my governess would rap my hands with a short stick she kept in the classroom. Since then, I have not had occasion to be punished." She paused, then added, "Nicholas spanked Roslynn with a leather strap, but that seemed awfully harsh."

Edward sat in stunned silence for a moment. His mind raced. *Nicholas and Roslynn* play*? More to the point, how does Sophia know?* And, being the reprobate he was, *how can I capitalize on this?* His conscience regarding his earlier thoughts took a giant step backward, and he smiled at her slowly.

"Right, then. What was Roslynn's spanking for?"

"Er, she purchased nothing for herself when she took me shopping…" Sophia's voice trailed off as she undoubtedly realized her transgression was more dire.

Edward nodded, unable to believe his luck.

He watched her expression. He'd only ever cropped women for pleasure, never as punishment. How should he proceed? It seemed prudent to get not only consent, but authorship of the choice by the recipient. "So, what do you think your punishment should be?"

"Twelve lashes with the strap, sir." Sophia's gaze dropped, her hand twitching where it held her torn shirt.

His cock leaped at the familiar honorific in lieu of my lord. While she seemed understandably nervous at the thought of being beaten, she did not appear afraid. Interesting. Having grown up isolated with her father

101

for her primary companion in a remote village, she was unfamiliar with London's social norms. With no sexual experience, and no gossip to mold her frame of reference, mayhap she did not see corporal punishment as deviant. And she appeared to have witnessed her hosts engage in similar behavior. Add to that his threat at their first meeting, and her follow up question that second day in the stables, and her temerity in suggesting it made sense. At least to his lust-warped brain.

Ecstatic at the chance to enact his fantasy without repercussions, even as he knew it was wrong, he struggled to keep his voice even. "Well, as 'tis your first offense with me, and I do not have a strap here, mayhap we shall compromise. A ten-count spanking with my hand?" His conscience had faded to a whisper from inside a locked wardrobe as his desire to spank her danced gleefully with the key.

"Aye." She looked half-eager, half-wary, but he did not see fear.

"Right, then, across my lap." Edward wanted to start before she had second thoughts. He kept his hands on her waist, maneuvering her around in the tight confines of the carriage. As she lay face down across his lap, one hand braced on the seat beside his leg for balance in the moving vehicle, he smoothed his hand over her bottom. He feared his cock might burst through his trousers, it was so hard.

Did he dare bare her arse? He had not asked if Nicholas had done so for Ros, but he couldn't imagine his lecherous friend spanking anyone clothed. While this differed vastly from a paddling within marriage or Sarah's club, the beauty of Sophia's innocence was that she did not realize how different.

She squirmed on his legs. Raising her head, she unknowingly solved Edward's internal dilemma by asking, "Must I remove my trousers?"

Edward debated swiftly and silently. His cock pulsed a hearty, "Yes!" but he was still a gentleman and Nicholas's friend. His thoughts ricocheted between the faint echo of his conscience, his relief that she was unharmed, and his anger that she'd put herself in danger. Under it all, his fierce desire pulsed through his veins, unfulfilled this past fortnight while he dealt with the transition of the estate and the distraction of the very girl on his lap.

Ultimately, he knew from childhood that a bare-bottom spanking could improve behavior by cementing consequences without lasting pain—humiliation and discomfort twisted together. And it would give him at least a small outlet for the suppressed desires coursing through him.

Gently, he answered, "You need to feel the full effect of the punishment so you do not put yourself in danger again. This is for your own good."

Ignoring the internal whisper that scorned his excuse, he reached around her tiny waist and plucked open the placket of her borrowed trousers. They were loose, which he was relieved to realize had helped disguise her figure. When he grabbed the fabric at the hips and tugged, they slid down easily.

As the creamy skin of her pale derriere came into view, he sucked in a breath. His palm raised to cup a cheek as the other shifted to the middle of her back. All thoughts of her being his friend's cousin and an innocent flew out of his mind. His entire focus was on her arse, spanking it, and somehow refraining from thrusting into her right there in the carriage afterward.

The carriage drove over a bump, and Edward pressed his hand to her lower spine, pinning her shirt out of the way. He caught flashing glimpses of her satiny muscular posterior from streetlights they passed, saliva pooling in his mouth. His other palm rubbed her cheeks, warming her skin to prepare her.

She wiggled again on his knee, and his hand on her back pressed her into stillness. "Be still. And tell me why you are being punished."

"Because I snuck out to an event dressed as a stable hand and put myself in danger," she replied.

Edward nodded, then spoke as he realized she could not see him. "And? Are you penitent?"

"Yes, my lord, I am very sorry," came her whisper.

"Ten strokes. Do not move. No wriggling or trying to get away, or I shall add more." His hand raised, then struck with a thwack.

He heard her gasp, and before she could catch her breath, he issued another crack on the other cheek. 'Twas best to get it over quickly for a beginner.

He alternated cheeks, moving from top to bottom, and even onto her thighs. He daren't leave visible marks for a maid to see, nor did he desire to severely hurt a novice. The silkiness of her skin and the glow of her arse turning pink distracted him. His cock pulsed against her leg, harder with each impact, even as he worried he was hurting her.

She froze at the first spank and clenched tightly for each of the following ones. Only after six did she squirm even a little. Her weight shifted and her hips pressed forward, pushing against his thigh. Panting, she arched again. When his hand on her back pressed more firmly to hold her still, she calmed, moaning once before cutting the sound off.

Edward's worry turned to wonder. Her obedience, acquiescence, and sensuality astounded him. The fact that she allowed him—indeed, offered the idea for him—to bare and spank her, trusting him not to exceed her pain tolerance, appealed to his intellect as well as his body. He could not tear his eyes away from her cheeks, marked with handprints, as they jiggled after each slap. His breath came in harsh rasps. His hips thrust once into her side to gain friction against his weeping cock.

Wrestling his thoughts back under control, he only hoped the bumps of the ride, her innocence, and the spanks deterred her from noticing. The final two smacks were the hardest, and he placed them directly where the first two landed.

Sophia yelped, and her head raised, arching her back, making it look like she was offering her arse for more.

Distracted by her voice, Edward noted her curved back and heightened breathing and leaned in, reluctant to re-cover her skin. He sucked in a breath and smelled her…arousal? He recognized the musky feminine aroma but could hardly fathom that this innocent was excited after her first spanking.

He paused, hand frozen in the act of reaching for her pants. It dropped to her pinkened globes once again, and he fought the desire to slide it down between her thighs to see if she was as wet as he was hard.

The upside-down girl squirmed, her legs falling open another inch, restricted by her pants around her thighs.

Was that an invitation?

"Ooohh." Not quite a question, but he could hear her curiosity.

"Sophia?" His voice was a rasp.

"Edward." He doubted she realized she had dropped the honorific. "I feel… Your touch soothes me."

"Where do you want me to soothe?"

Her head ducked. He wasn't surprised. She was an innocent. "Everywhere."

With that answer, he was unable to resist. His hand smoothed from her heated cheeks to between her thighs, fingers wrapping around the inside of the leg closest to him. Yanking her tighter against his hard cock was both agony and bliss. He slid his fingers up to her hot wet core, resting them against her to judge her reaction.

She sucked in a breath and quieted, her hand clutching his booted calf for balance in the moving vehicle. She seemed to be waiting to see what he would do, rather than screaming and bucking off his lap. *Interesting, indeed.*

His finger inched up, parting her lips, skimming through her wetness and down to the nub in front of it. He circled that hard raised flesh once.

"Ooohh!" This time it was a shriek, and she arched up.

Pleasure? Pain?

Unsure, he withdrew his hand and helped her back to the other seat. As she struggled to raise her trousers over a sore bottom, he asked, "Sophia? Did I hurt you?"

"No—yes. What do you mean?"

He smiled for a second. "I know the spanking hurt a little. It was meant to. But you shrieked."

"Oh, no." Her voice was breathy. "It felt delicious. So much more than when I touched myself. I was surprised. Is that why you stopped, my lord?" Her lower lip pouted.

She's touched herself? Edward took a minute to refocus. Yes, it was why he'd pulled away, but given her disappointment and the fact that his conscience had escaped from the closet and was yelling at him, he responded only, "I stopped because I should not have touched you there. I must again beg your pardon for taking liberties."

"Is that what sex feels like, then? I feel all hot and itchy."

"You are feeling the friction of your sore bottom against those trousers." But his gaze went to the hard points of her breasts poking through the thin shirt, betraying her arousal, a second before she drew his cloak farther around her.

"'Tis more than that, I think…"

He shrugged. How to explain this to an innocent young lady? "Sex feels like that, only more so. If I had kept rubbing you between your legs, you would have felt an explosion of pleasure. But only a husband should touch you there."

"Hmm. A greater explosion than that? And you would only do that with a wife, then?" She arched a brow at him.

His hand dropped to his lap at her boldness and images their words conjured. Shifting into the darkest corner of his seat, he gripped his hard length for a moment so he did not come in his pants like a novice.

At that moment, the carriage stopped, and they both turned to look at Nicholas's townhome. The coachman climbed down to get the door. Edward regretted that she would not be in his bed that night so he could convert the pain into pleasure for them both, but he shook the thought from his head.

She is marriage material. Not for you. Damned conscience.

Before the door opened, he leaned in and murmured, "You took your punishment very well. We shall skip the ride tomorrow in case you are sore, but I will send a note round to ride in a day or two."

The coachman set the step for her. She appeared dazed as she alighted from the carriage, and he directed the coachman to take her around the mews to get upstairs without detection.

Edward closed the carriage door and slid back into darkness, nursing the most uncomfortable erection of his life. After hours, or perhaps only minutes, the coachman climbed back up and started the ten-minute drive to his home.

He could no longer bear it. Surrounded by her scent, the feel of her soft-yet-firm arse lingering on his hand, he unbuttoned his pants and took a firm grasp of his cock. Momentary relief was quickly replaced with the need to move. His back arched, every inch of his skin sensitized from visions of sex with Sophia. Bringing forth the memory of her skin against the same palm that wrapped around his shaft, he squeezed hard, then smoothed the liquid leaking from the tip down his shaft.

After only a dozen powerful strokes, he exploded, catching his release in his handkerchief, sagging back against the cushions of the still-moving vehicle.

Only then did the cold reality of what he had done become clear. He had compromised his friend's cousin, an innocent, far more so than at the ball. She had been the one to ask him to handle it, he argued with himself. And she seemed to care little for society's rules. But his conscience slapped his excuses down. He knew he ought to tell Nicholas and offer for her.

The snickers of classmates when he was called on to read a passage echoed in his head. The curled lip and rapacious leer of his governess. No. Never again would someone get close enough to realize his deficiency. No woman would call him an idiot again with a sneer on their face. His governess and teachers, they could all go hang. He was an earl now, whether he liked it or not, and by Jove, he'd figure out what he needed to do. No chit was going to derail him or belittle him while he did so. They could simply forget this had ever happened.

He would not wed a young innocent, even one who may be open to corporal punishment…and mayhap even enjoy it. He merely needed to keep his hands off her in the future.

Chapter Eight

Sophia crawled into bed, feeling every shift of the nightrail and bedcovers against her nipples, stomach, and legs. She had pushed Edward, wanting to regain the sensations she'd experienced watching her hosts engage in corporal punishment and more.

Being face down over Edward's lap, his rigid thigh muscles digging into her soft stomach, had started similar flashes of heat through her. The warmth of his hand stroking over her raised backside made her wonder what his skin would feel against hers. She shivered, remembering her inner demon prompting her to ask him about her trousers.

The spanking had hurt, but each flash of hot pain faded to a lingering warmth that curled through her. And as the strikes rained down, they jounced that super-sensitive part of her against his thigh, adding to the spiral of pleasure even before he touched it.

Pain led to pleasure, which led to pain and back again. All somehow wrapped up in the man administering her spanking. She trusted him to punish her without truly harming her and to keep her secrets in exchange.

When he'd stopped, the hot, secret place between her legs throbbed more than her bottom, and she found her hand itching to touch that spot again.

Like Nicholas reaching under Ros, she'd felt

Edward's hand shift and calmed, holding her breath in hope and anticipation. She shouted when his finger found that perfect spot after dipping into her wetness. Only after did she realize she had shouted much like Roslynn had.

He'd stopped then, leaving her body humming, only to explain that there was greater pleasure to be had. The hypocrite had tried to tell her exploration was only acceptable with a husband.

She snickered at the memory, sobering and gasping as she smoothed a hand over her still-smarting bottom and thrust the other under her to find that spot again. Taking a page from Edward's handbook, she dipped her finger in the pool of liquid at her opening before bringing it back to the bundle of nerves and circling.

Ooohh.

Dipping again, then circling, her bottom arched higher, as though reaching for an invisible lover's spanks.

She paused, uncertain how high she'd spiral, but her curiosity about an explosion like the one she'd seen Ros and Nicholas experience kept her finger rubbing. Straining for an unknown end, she imagined she was again over Edward's knee, his scent surrounding her, his hand about to descend on her upturned flesh. Something hard pressing into her hip.

She screamed into her pillow. Her fingers mashed against her pulsing flesh as fire flashed through her. Uncertain if she was trying to hold the sensations longer or protect her from over-stimulation, she panted and pressed as her body throbbed, her pulse beating everywhere from eyelids to toes.

Finally, her bottom sank to the bed, fingers falling

away from her slick folds.

I must remember to check on Bobby in the morning and apologize for rushing in recklessly. She sank closer to the edge of blissful slumber. *Now I have another criterion for my Suitable Attributes list—makes me warm and tingly when he touches me. Edward checks that box as well, darn it.*

But he does not want to wed anyone, much less an untitled country orphan.

****

Nicholas and Edward sipped tea in their usual seats by the fireplace. Nicholas asked about Edward's purchases at Vauxhall.

Debating whether to tell him about his run-in with Sophia and how to raise the question of Nicholas's and Ros's sex life discreetly, Edward's answers were distracted.

Finally, Nicholas commented on his vagueness.

"Hmm? Oh, sorry, I'm stuck on the idea of marriage and heirs." Edward absolutely was not, but he hoped the segue would open the subject.

"Ah, yes. I've given it some thought as well, and I might have a solution for you." Nicholas measured his words.

Edward leaned forward, hoping to hear the solution was Sophia. *Wait, what? He had only known the girl for less than a month.*

"Have you ever heard of the School of Enlightenment?" Nicholas asked.

Frowning, Edward sat back. "No, not at all. Is it here in London? Is it new mayhap?" He laughed. "Is it for recent, unexpected earls?"

"No." Nicholas chuckled with him, then sobered.

"It's a girls' school, two hours outside London. Very private."

"What, a finishing school?"

Nicholas tilted his head. "Well, yes, something like that, actually. It includes a number of programs, young ladies of the Ton married or betrothed, girls training to be governesses or courtesans, or servants. I was thinking of the first in particular. You know Roslynn manages the households for all my holdings, no matter where she is, through correspondence with key staff at the properties?"

Edward nodded.

"This school trains girls whose parents or circumstances did not allow them to learn those skills at home for responsibilities as wives of Peers of the Realm." Nicholas watched him closely. "Maths, reading, money management, correspondence, speech. For the Ton girls, it includes party planning or other choices, at their sponsors' discretion."

Edward understood, having discussed their views of women's education versus society's many times. "Ah, no wonder 'tis private. Half the Ton would be up in arms to hear about women being educated."

"Yes. And there's more." A longer pause.

"Go on." Edward leaned forward again.

"Eh, it would also address your concerns about marriage."

Edward frowned. That was not helpful.

"What do you mean? They train the girls in sexual spankings?" He snickered.

Nicholas flushed. "Well, yes, and other things." As he explained, Edward stared at him open-mouthed and silent. The memory of Sophia suggesting her own punishment was vivid, as was his daydream from their ride of her bent over for spanking play.

"What the devil? I can't even fathom such a place." He was agog. "You are telling me I could find a wife willing to get a crop to the buttocks, who will also help me with the piles of Parliamentary documents and correspondence?"

Nicholas nodded, watching him pace.

"Hmm…" Edward stopped and turned back to him, shaking his head. "No, it shan't work. I can't risk some chit telling her mama that her new husband cannot read and having it spread around the Ton."

Nicholas opened his mouth to respond, when Edward had another thought.

"But how do you know about it? And why did you not use it?"

Nicholas frowned and huffed, looking away. At that moment, a light knock sounded. Ros entered, coming to greet Edward with a kiss on the cheek. As she looked at her husband's discomfort and smiled, Edward stared at her. Turning to look at Nicholas, who wouldn't meet his eyes, then back at Ros, realization dawned.

"Egads, she was right," he breathed.

Nicholas looked sharply at Ros, as though blaming her for telling Edward her background at the school, but she shook her head before they both turned questioning gazes to him.

"Who is 'she' and what was she right about?" Nicholas asked with raised brows.

It was Edward's turn to flush and turn away. This was not how he pictured telling Nicholas about his encounter with Sophia at Vauxhall, after he had intimated he wouldn't. But there was no hope for it after he had voiced his surprise aloud. "Er, Sophia…" he hemmed and hawed. "She may have referred to punishment." He gestured vaguely at them with one hand.

Ros smirked at her husband. Nicholas frowned at her.

Edward turned sharply, opening his mouth to speak.

Before he uttered a word, Ros looked back at him and frowned. "And in what circumstances did that subject arise?"

Edward's shoulders sagged, and Nicholas flashed a grateful look at his wife.

"Hellfi—I beg your pardon, Ros. She did not want me to tell you, although I never agreed to that per se. I discovered her at the Vauxhall event and had to rescue her from a bit of a scrape. I was simply going to deliver her to you for you to handle her as you saw fit, but she raised the idea of punishment."

The couple exchanged a look, obviously surprised to hear of Sophia's stealth. They should have realized the horse event would be irresistible to her.

"Or given what she had seen," Ros mulled aloud, "and not understanding her body's reaction, mayhap she wanted to explore with the dashing gentleman who had squired her to the park and balls this past fortnight." One eyebrow raised, she folded her arms, watching the men.

Edward was taken aback at her bluntness but considered the matter. *The spanking made her wet, and she admitted her shriek was from pleasure.* He had to fight off an erection at the mere thought, not something he wished to explain in Ros's company.

Thankfully, Ros had turned to Nicholas to ask, "Have you discussed my suggestion?"

"Not yet, my dear. We were just getting there." He turned to Edward, "We know that you need a wife. And Sophia was open to the idea of the School when we raised it with her. Now she's explored spanking with you, apparently."

Edward was grateful his friend ignored his repeated flush.

"I was going to ask if you'd contemplate a marriage between you. It would tie our names and form a stronger alliance, together with other associates, and give us more voting power in Parliament. While she is untitled, I planned to settle an amount on her. For you, I'd dower the land her father managed for me, which borders on yours." He shook his head. "But now I must demand you at least consider it. It sounds like she was compromised in the carriage? More than merely being alone with her. Given your reactions to this conversation, I am guessing you spanked her?"

Edward's head dropped forward, and he nodded, not able to meet his friend's gaze. He was well and truly caught between his dread of marrying and respecting his friend by doing the honorable thing.

Nicholas sighed. "Edward, I realize you were a second son, but you know earls are subject to stricter rules."

Edward flashed him a mutinous look.

"Like it or not. Look, you are my closest friend. Nothing would please me more than to have you in the family. I'd also like to see Sophia with someone so well-suited to her. So I admit I am pushing this partly for selfish reasons. But"—he flashed a glance at his wife—"I understand your reluctance. If you believe, after reviewing the situation, that you cannot be happy marrying and cannot commit to taking good care of Sophia, the Vauxhall event will be forgotten."

Edward nodded. *Devil take it. Even before Vauxhall, she tempted me. Nicholas doesn't know about the kiss at the ball, although I think Roslynn suspects. To have her trained for my specific preferences and to help me with this infernal earldom? And she is interested in the work I do in Parliament. But can I risk it?*

Nicholas stood. "I will add one more thing to consider. Sophia's family is all in this room. And she has already proven to be open-minded about corporal punishment. If anyone can help you overcome"—again, he kept the reference oblique, reassuring Edward that Nicholas had not shared his reading challenges even with Roslynn—"your hesitancy, I believe she can. Either way, if Sophia is interested, we will send her to the School of Enlightenment. She does not want to stay with us long term, concerned about overstaying her welcome." He waved a dismissive hand. "And she dislikes London, so she is set on marriage as her solution."

A bolt of anger—he refused to recognize any fear mixed with it—shot through Edward. The thought of her marrying anyone else added a sense of urgency to his considerations.

****

Edward looked around the table at his friends and allies. Lords had just finished, and as usual, the group congregated at White's to discuss next steps for the pieces of legislature they wanted to promote.

One of the more senior Members of Parliament turned to Edward, who held a small leather-bound notebook. "Peterborough, what say you take notes, eh?"

There was a pecking order, and he was the newest member at the table. But that did not stop Edward from sweating. Write notes? That others would have to read? His reading issues extended to writing sometimes, spelling certainly. He tended to spell words how they sounded, rather than the formal spelling, to get information down. But more, he often depicted information with brief sketches, pictures being a quicker way for his brain to record information.

He gulped. There was no help for it. "Certainly, sir."

Hellfire. Nick hadn't arrived to listen and help him supplement his notes later.

Edward did his best, jotting notes and sketching. The conversation centered on the Factory Bill a Welsh textile manufacturer was working with Sir Robert Peel to push through the Commons.

His radical belief in limiting children's hours in factories and an eight-hour workday for adults was controversial even in this progressive group.

Edward sketched a clock with a factory building, a book and a sheep, and a bed denoting the three equal wedges, representing Robert Owen's slogan of eight hours labor, eight hours recreation, and eight hours rest.

As Owen had worked in Sophia's childhood home, only a few miles from Peterborough, Edward was already familiar with some of the tenets of his proposal. *Phew.*

When the debates did not resolve themselves, the

group broke to refresh their drinks and stretch their legs. Nick arrived and made his way around the table toward Edward.

As Edward put his notebook down to rise, the earl who had asked him to record the meeting looked down.

"Peterborough, I thought you were taking notes? All I see are doodles and pictures. Were you even paying attention?" The earl's lip curled.

Edward saw his expression and froze, his governess's, teachers', and headmasters' sneers and contempt echoing in his head.

Nicholas edged in by his side and glanced at the page. "Trust me, sir, you would not want Edward to use words alone. Not even he can read his own handwriting at times, 'tis so atrocious. I know, I had to share notes with him at Cambridge. Now, tell me more of what I missed?" He took the older man's elbow and steered him away, glancing back at his friend and winking.

Edward did not respond. Memories barreled down at him. His hands fisted at his sides, every muscle clenched. He could not move, could not focus on his surroundings as the past overtook him.

He needed to get away before he humiliated himself further. His fingers itched for his mount's reins, his face wanting the wind of a gallop to cool his embarrassment.

But he was an earl now. He must make the best of the situation.

Thank God for Nick. Then his brain turned to the quasi-ultimatum that same friend had proffered. *If a two-hour conversation at the club threatens exposure, how will I ever keep up a front in a marriage? 'Twill be impossible. I cannot risk it.*

Finally, after the meeting had ended, Edward saddled his mount and rode home. Traffic still clogged the streets, particularly in the Mayfair district, but Edward's urgency had lessened. Emotionally wrung out, he could not smother the memories that surfaced whenever his insecurities got the best of him.

Every post on the trotting horse memorialized a birching he'd received. Every flash of the older earl's grimace became another face from his past criticizing him.

No. He would live with the taunts and sneering lips when he had to, but never would he accept that in his own home. Or even the risk of it. And dammit, he was the spanker now. Compromise or not, he had to decline Nicholas's invitation to marry Sophia.

****

As Parliament was now in session, there were fewer mid-week balls. Ros had introduced Sophia to several friends and promised she'd get to know them better when she joined their salon. Sophia had a vague notion of what ladies did at a salon but was about to learn in detail. She trailed down the front stairs in a day dress of palest peach. Several ladies of the Ton had already gathered in Ros's parlor—*or rather, salon*—and were chatting over tea service.

Two of the visitors—one might be a duchess—had sheaves of paper on their laps and had begun discussing them.

Ros patted the settee next to her for Sophia to join her. As everyone sat, Ros re-introduced the group to Sophia. Turning to Sophia, she swept one arm out, saying, "Sophia, I present the Enlightened Salon. Outside these walls, you will not hear that name because we do not reference it beyond our circle. And more to the point, we do not discuss publicly any of the subjects we debate here."

Sophia was perplexed but nodded her accord.

Ros continued, "Are you familiar with the Bastards Act, passed a few years ago?"

"Er, no?" Out of the corner of her eye, Sophia caught the two ladies with papers glance at each other and firm their lips in disappointment.

"What about the Insolvent Debtors Act?" Ros tried.

This one she knew. But would the ladies feel the same about the law? "Yes. I was frustrated when that passed."

The two ladies raised their brows and nodded.

Phew. "But how do Parliamentary Acts relate to this salon? If you don't discuss these with anyone else and none of us has a vote?" Sophia was confused.

Ros and several others smiled. "I knew you would be eager to understand. And as for you two, Elizabeth and Pauline, all of us started somewhere. Have patience." Ros shot the two ladies with paperwork a stern glance.

Ros explained to Sophia, "I never said we did not discuss these subjects with our husbands. But not in public and not always in the manner we discuss them here. You've likely heard of the Blue Stocking Society. They work openly to influence change. This group works more subtly. Our influence on our fathers, brothers, and husbands clarifies for them the need for change, for progress. Helps them envision the long-term effects of laws on women and children, rich and poor, before approving or changing them. We all attended the private school I mentioned to you. Its existence is a closely-held secret, hidden away in the country and funded by our families and a few select others: The School of Enlightenment."

Sophia marveled at these ladies of the Ton, willing to accept her, and Ros's openness and inclusion into this private, secret group. She felt honored and a bit nervous. Despite thinking to remain aloof, she genuinely liked Ros and viewed her as a friend and family member, as she did Nicholas. Returning to the gathering from these distracting reflections, she forced her mind back to the discussion.

Looking at each woman in turn, Ros addressed the group. "Now, ladies, let's give Sophia an idea of how we do things. What is the first topic on the agenda?"

After the salon, Sophia took further reading to her room. She was more excited than ever to ride with Edward, to ask him about these subjects. But she wanted to respect the salon's tenet of privacy so she would need to ask carefully.

****

Sophia watched her hosts and Edward as they journeyed to another ball the next evening. They were assuredly engaged in an unspoken conversation, but she was unable to interpret it.

Nicholas glanced at her, then at Edward. Roslynn smirked and watched the two men. Edward rolled his eyes and looked out the carriage window. Then some variation on that sequence happened again.

Finally, as they waited in the line of carriages to disembark, Roslynn turned to her.

This would be the biggest ball yet, according to Ros. "The Earl of Cheltenham has a larger ballroom than you've seen, but even with that, 'tis a crush."

Nicholas alighted and offered a hand to Ros, then Sophia.

As the two turned up the walk, Edward pulled Sophia aside. "Are you quite all right?"

"Shh." Sophia glanced furtively ahead to her hosts' progress. "Yes, thank you, my lord."

"Sophia, I overstepped. None of what happened in the carriage was acceptable. Please accept my apologies."

Sophia stared at him, trying to hide her devastation. *He regrets the carriage? I've been regretting what he didn't finish, and he is sorry he even began?* Given that she had suggested it, even provoked him into baring her, the rejection came as a slap—an unsexy one. Stung, she struggled to reply. Her hurt twisted into anger. At herself, for caring so much about a reaction from this man who intrigued her. And at him, for ruining her memories of the evening and his rescue.

She turned away to follow her cousin, muttering her response. "Apology accepted, my lord."

He drew her back. "Oh, and do not venture past the veranda into the gardens."

She tilted her head, frowning at the change in subject. "Certainly, my lord. May I ask why not?"

"Some use the gardens for liaisons—Cheltenham's balls cater to a wilder crowd, and—just don't," he said shortly as Nicholas looked back to see where they were.

As was their custom, Edward danced the first dance with Sophia before finding the cluster of allies from the House of Lords. Leather and citrus spice continued to tease her nose as Sophia took turns around the floor with other men. With each, she compared how far around their biceps her hand went compared to

Edward's granite shoulders. The softness of their hands against his callouses. Not a single one measured up.

The candles burned hotly as she spun, catching glimpses of Edward deep in conversation near the hall. As her partner circled her near the veranda doors, the relief of the cool garden air wafted over her heated skin.

After the next dance, the room felt stifling. She looked for Edward before leaving the overcrowded ballroom, but he was engrossed in conversation with other titled lords, his back to her. And suddenly, she didn't care anyway.

Given the activities she'd spied Nicholas and Roslynn engage in, she could handle the gardens of a ball. *I cannot have a liaison if I am alone. And after all, he apologized for kissing me. He regrets having to rescue me. So what will he do if I disobey?* She did not acknowledge the inner voice that said she was testing him to find out.

Chapter Nine

Edward looked up. He'd been immersed in hearing opinions on upcoming bills, ferreting out details of the would-be laws and memorizing them.

Thinking to check for Sophia, he realized how warm the room had become, as the more popular balls often did. And he did not see her pale hair anywhere in the ballroom.

If she is not in the retiring room, she's gone off to a side room with someone or wandered outside despite my warning, and may be in trouble. Hellfire, with Cheltenham, even the ladies' retiring room may not be safe. He snorted.

Excusing himself from the conversation, he waded through the women on the edge of the dance floor. Seeing Roslynn, he asked her if she had seen Sophia. She pointed to an area between the refreshment table and the veranda doors.

He rolled his eyes. He knew if he'd gotten a drink to cool off, he wouldn't have been able to resist the temptation of the cooler air outside. Damned disobedient, inconvenient, distracting chit. Swearing silently, he wended his way to the stone terrace, even as he knew he should convey his concerns to Nicholas and stay away from her.

What are you going to do if she disobeys? Spank her again? Is that why you're looking for her instead of her guardian? But he couldn't seem to stop his forward motion.

Jogging down the steps to the garden, he debated which direction to go when he spotted the back of Sophia strolling along a path.

Catching up to her, he grabbed her arm, his voice a rumble. "What did I tell you?"

She looked up with a gasp, her shoulders relaxing when she realized it was him. "Er, not to go into the gardens."

"And yet, here you are with nary a thought to my directions. Were you trying to get compromised?" he whisper-hissed. *Again. I've already done that twice. I've simply managed to avoid being caught.*

"No! How can you even say that?"

"I can say that because young ladies wandering through dark gardens are asking to be kissed. Are you seeing how many men you can kiss? Is this a game to you?" What was he saying?

She gasped. "No. Why are you being so mean? I have only ever kissed you!"

He growled, almost a groan, relieved.

In the next second, he lost control. The knowledge that he was her only lover and his concern for her innocence at Cheltie's party drove his lips to hers, putting an abrupt end to all thoughts. The kiss was hard and demanding, mashing her lips against her teeth before his tongue snaked into her mouth and played with hers. Her spine arched, flattening her breasts against his front as she sagged into the kiss.

Edward felt more than heard a feminine moan as his arm wrapped around her lower back to support her.

Her fingers crept up his body to his shoulders and

neck to play with the ends of his hair.

A shudder ran through his frame when her fingers tangled in his hair, and he deepened the kiss, probing the edges of her teeth with his tongue, trying to prove a point.

Why did this girl affect him so? He poured his relief and his lust into the kiss.

His inner devil woke up and fanned the spark of his earlier thought. They were at Cheltenham's, after all, known for keeping the garden corners dark for trysts. This was a prime opportunity to indulge in a pastime she'd already accepted. As the girls at Sarah's club hadn't interested him, and he needed to protect this girl from others—and from herself—he might as well get something out of it. She had literally told him she'd rather he punished her than Nicholas, so really, he was doing his friend and her a favor.

Edward gave a mental snort at that last bit of ridiculousness, but it did not deter him from raising his head to say, "You continue to disobey orders."

Sophia groaned in frustration, probably suspecting where his statement was leading. "I'm very sorry." She sucked in a breath. "I shan't do it again. As I came out alone, I thought it would be safe." She sent him a sidelong glance. "Is this a punishable offense, my lord?"

Perfect. She knew she was wrong. She saw what was coming. Her side-eyed glance told him she mayhap even invited it. Who was he to refuse a girl a spanking?

He took a deep breath, wishing… *No. She's not mine to covet. But she* is *mine to punish tonight.*

His eyes shuttered as he considered. Was he taking advantage of her naiveté about Ton rules? He knew she'd enjoyed the last punishment and could not deny either of their desires. He almost heard the turn of the key as his conscience was again locked away.

He pushed, "We have been over this, Sophia. Punishment is an important learning tool. Hopefully, it shall be an incentive for you to obey specific directions in the future."

Frustrated, she crossed her gloved arms. "Darn it. My feet hurt so much. I did not anticipate my bottom becoming sore, too. I shan't be able to sit *or* stand comfortably."

That wasn't a no.

Edward exulted. "You should have thought of that before you wandered out to the gardens against orders. Your discomfort for the rest of the night shall help reinforce the lesson."

He grabbed her hand and led her farther into the garden. Sitting on a bench conveniently under a large apple tree, he checked that it shielded them from the house. He would hear anyone strolling too close.

Discovering them would not shock most of the guests at this particular ball if they did wander by, but he preferred to avoid anyone seeing Sophia bared. And he fully intended to bare her bottom again.

She stood next to him, hand in his, biting her lip. With no warning, she perched on his thighs and pressed her lips to his.

Shocked, Edward was motionless for a moment before his arms snaked around her and his lips twisted on hers, tongue slipping through them to tangle with hers. Less demanding, this kiss was exploratory.

Oh yes. She does want it.

He had already won this round. Now he wanted to

claim her and discover all there was to her. His hand inched up from her thigh to cup a breast and thumb her nipple.

Sophia groaned into his mouth.

The sound brought him back to why they sat there. He jerked his head back. "Sophia. This behavior is unacceptable."

"My lord. You are going to penalize me. I merely decided to make it worthwhile." She stared up at him, her expression mulish.

He stifled a laugh. This was far more entertaining than the girls in Sarah's club.

He managed to frown at her, he hoped severely. "It certainly increased your punishment."

She gulped, eyes wide.

He pushed her up, turned her, and positioned her face down across his lap. She reared up when his hand slid up her stockinged legs.

"What are you doing?" she gasped.

"You'd never be able to feel a spanking through your skirts." Edward's hand shook a little in anticipation, belying his calm tone.

"What if someone sees?" But Sophia's head had already lowered in unconscious submission.

Edward smiled. Her question gave her away. She was more worried someone might see them than the propriety of her dress being raised or the spanking.

"Shh, I shall hear anyone that comes this way, but that means that you must be silent, no squirming or shrieking. Take your punishment like a good girl." Sophia's head nodded, but Edward insisted on a verbal compliance. "Sophia? What are you being punished for?"

"Disobeying orders and going beyond the terrace…" She finished in a breathy whisper. "…and kissing you."

"Minx. I think you were trying to add to this spanking. And will you be quiet for your punishment?"

"Yes, my lord."

Her skirts bunched in the hand that was on her back, Edward's right hand smoothed the thin lawn drawers covering the warm flesh of her arse before dragging them to her upper thighs.

His cock, hard since his lips had first touched hers, pulsed against her hip. He could get used to this. She was delicious.

The first smack landed.

She twitched and a muffled, "Humph," escaped before she fell silent.

Speeding up, he rained smacks across her bottom and thighs.

Edward paused as Sophia arched and inched her legs wider, as some of the submissives in the gentlemen's club he visited did. Leaning in, he was again amazed to smell her arousal.

His breath came in huffs, and the iron rod in his pants tried to punch its way through her thigh to that sweet-smelling cave. His fingers itched to test her wetness, but this was supposed to be a reprimand. *First.*

He resumed the spanking, paying close attention to her body's movements and her breathing. When her arse was hot to the touch, and she began twitching away, he stayed his hand, but could not resist smoothing his hand over the heated flesh again. He paused and centered his middle finger along the seam of her cheeks, sliding his hand down toward her center, hoping she did not scream like she had in the carriage.

"My lord, will you soothe me again? Please?" Her voice sounded hopeful as she stilled.

His breath caught in surprised pleasure, and he began to ease his finger into her wetness. His eyelids lowered as he envisioned stripping her drawers off, ripping his breeches open, and burying himself in her right here on the bench.

Criminy, she's delicious. Marriage seems almost palatable...

And footsteps sounded on the walkway, coming closer.

Sophia was lost to sensation, but Edward yanked her drawers up, smoothed her skirts down, and hissed at her to stand up as he helped her to her feet.

Dizzy, she swayed, and he gripped her arm with one hand as he used the other to fight his cock into submission.

Turning, he drew his handkerchief to wipe her tears and angled his head to see her in the lights from the ballroom. She seemed to think he was leaning to kiss her and surged up, throwing her arms around him.

As their lips met, Edward groaned in helpless pleasure. A throat cleared, and he realized the footsteps had stopped.

Nicholas and Roslynn stared at them.

The reality of marriage, his fears of discovery, all rushed back, and he went cold...and limp. Glancing down, Edward saw Sophia's tear-stained cheeks, swollen lips, the hard points of her nipples poking through her dress. Even without the embrace, she was well and truly compromised.

Never mind Sophia's timeline. He was out of time

and choices.

He bowed to his best friend. "Nich—Suffolk. I shall call on you tomorrow."

****

Edward arrived after breakfast and was ushered into Nicholas's library. There, his friend sat behind the desk rather than in the seating area by the fireplace, relegating him to a guest chair opposite him. Nicholas swiveled his chair and stared out the window, tapping a finger on the armrest. He seemed disinclined to open the conversation.

"Right, then," Edward said. "I feel it only fair to remind you of the reasons this is a bad idea."

Nicholas whipped his head around to shoot him a suspicious look from under lowered brows.

He spread his hands in supplication. "I was up all night. At least let me tell you what I considered. I will absolutely offer for her if that is your wish after listening."

Squinting, Nicholas did not respond but turned back to the window to resume his tapping.

Edward took his silence as permission. "First, my reading impediment—"

Nicholas turned as if to interrupt.

"Let me finish." He spoke over whatever his friend started to say. "'Tis not only my concerns about embarrassment. Sophia wants to spend time with horses. Think about how many hours Roslynn spends on correspondence and household management. And that is without helping with Parliamentary reading, which I'd need Sophia to do." During the long night, many of the worries plaguing him were for Sophia, surprising him.

Nicholas arched a brow.

"Or mayhap Ros does help with that. Anyway, I won't be giving her the life she'd expect. And think about what happened at White's the other night. Even if she doesn't think less of me for my failings, there is the ever-present threat of discovery by my Peers. My wife will be forced to endure the repercussions, should it happen."

"Second is location. Peterborough is two days' ride. And while I will need to be here for Lords votes sometimes, you and I have already discussed doing that through letters where possible, so that I can continue to manage the horse training business. She'll be away from you and Roslynn most of the year, her only family."

Nicholas again looked like he wanted to speak, and Edward held up a hand.

"Third, you know my feelings about women. While I would never abuse her, nor will I ever love her. I don't trust women enough to love one. And let's not forget, you know exactly what I *will* do with her."

"Fourth, what if my ailment is hereditary? Do you really want illiterate nieces or nephews?" He couldn't believe he was divulging all this. He was willing to marry—and he admitted silently—he was more comfortable, if not happier, marrying Sophia than anyone else he'd met to date. But he had concerns for her as well as himself.

Nicholas stopped tapping, turned back to face him, and threw his feet up on his desk. Steepling his hands in front of his chest, elbows on the armrests now, he smiled at his guest.

Edward didn't like the look of that smile.

"Are you quite finished? Or do you have a more ridiculous reason or two?"

Edward slouched in his seat for a moment before standing to pace away and back. "Ridiculous?"

"First, I am willing to wager a rather large sum that Sophia will ensure she gets the life she wants. But either way, that is up to you two. Second," Nicholas ticked off each point on a finger. "I've lived without seeing Sophia for her eighteen years. I suspect I shall manage with holidays and visits. I shall miss her, have no doubt, but Roslynn and I shall be fine. And fourth, you know I don't care about your *ailment*. I've already told you that Sophia won't care. So yes, I really want second cousins, no reading required."

"Ah ha. You missed point three."

Nicholas shrugged. "Of course, I want Sophia to be loved. I suspect she cares for you and that you feel some warmth for her. Happy marriages have started with less. I understand you are not looking for love, but you have much in common. And if she attends the school, mayhap there will be even more. Ros is absolutely sure you are well-paired, and I have learned the hard way not to doubt my very intelligent wife."

Edward stood behind the chair he had occupied, gripping its back. He hung his head momentarily. As he had suspected, no arguments would sway his friend. Raising his head, he straightened to his full height in a formal pose, one hand on his chest, the other fisted by his side.

Damned inconvenient chit. "Lord Suffolk, may I request—"

Nicholas sniggered. "Criminy, Edward, you look like you've a stick up your arse. We shall always be friends. I trust you with Sophia. Now, come sit, and we'll work out the details."

After they had hashed out the marriage contract, they stood and stretched.

Nicholas grinned, came around the desk, and slapped him on the back. "Welcome to the family. I think we've both earned a drink. Your usual?"

Edward nodded and accepted the brandy. He paced the length of the room and back, trying to shake off excess nerves. Why would he be nervous? 'Tis not like he had his heart on the line.

A rejection by Sophia would solve everything...wouldn't it? He rubbed his chest where his heart pounded against his ribs at that thought.

Nicholas opened the library door, but before he could even summon a servant to find Sophia, Edward heard Ros's voice. "We are in here, Nicholas."

"Thank you, Ros, but I only need Sophia."

When she entered, Sophia's gaze found Edward. She curtsied. "My lord, please accept my apologies."

Edward stood by one of the chairs near the hearth. He gestured to the settee after bowing over her hand. Then they both turned to Nicholas as he sat and looked to Edward expectantly.

Still standing, Edward glared at him and gritted out, "Given the circumstances, I think it would not hurt for you to give us a few minutes alone, eh, Nicholas?"

Nicholas grimaced at the reminder the horse was indeed out of the barn.

"Fine, but I shall be right outside." He rose and strode to the door, pulling it over but not closing it behind him.

Sophia gripped her hands together in her skirt,

knuckles white. Her gaze remained on them.

Edward perched on the other end of the settee and turned to Sophia. Unsure how to begin, he blurted out a question. "Why do you feel you need to apologize?"

"If I had stayed inside, none of this would have happened. And if I had not kissed you, the whole thing might have been over with no one the wiser. I know you did not want to marry, and I feel I have placed you in an untenable position." Her hands were unclenching and clenching, crumpling her skirt.

He knew the fault was his as much or more so than hers. He could have stopped the kiss, the spanking, all of it, at any time. Her reference to his forced situation stung, though. Anger roiled under his skin. He took a breath.

Criminy, I don't want a wife! His conscience pushed back. *Not even Sophia? I mean, if you must marry...*

Shaking his head to halt his thoughts, he stood and paced for a moment. He wanted to saddle up and take a gallop to regain his equilibrium. Sighing, he ignored his usual limit and poured a second large brandy, despite the early hour, hoping to drown the panic. He had tried every argument he could think of with Nicholas. Even the pity angle had not worked. He wanted to yell, to pull his hair out, to spank her bottom raw, but most of all, he wished he could run away. He would never betray his family and business and the livelihoods depending on him, but this was too much. The thought of marriage both terrified him with its vulnerability and angered him with its burden of yet more responsibility.

Edward's rage roared to life. At her, at himself, at the situation. It didn't matter. She was in front of him, and he directed it at her. "What exactly are you sorry for, Sophia? Sneaking out and nearly being hurt—or worse—at Vauxhall? Disobeying a direct order last night? Being compromised? Or…"

He clamped his lips shut before *saddling me with another duty* came out. He was blaming her for forcing him to marry her but knew he was equally culpable.

But hellfire and damnation! Fear and frustration made him want to gallop a few laps around Hyde Park. Trapped in this room with this ultimatum, he swigged brandy.

She flinched at his tone, and tears filled her eyes, but she held his gaze. "All of it, my lord."

"You are always sorry after the fact." He shook his head and took another gulp of brandy as he paced back and forth in front of her.

Her spine stiffened. "'Twas not me who dragged us over to that bench in the garden."

He pivoted and glared at her. "Would you have preferred the library? You seem to like those, based on your spying on your generous hosts." Gads, what was he spewing? The country mouse barely understood society's rules. She'd been in London little more than a month, had attended a handful of balls, all after losing everyone she knew and loved.

She gasped and dropped her gaze. "My lord. You needn't offer for me. You were very clear about wanting to avoid marriage. I shall figure something out. Nicholas and Roslynn have been very generous to date…"

Edward sighed, resignation overtaking where anger had burned. "I did not want to wed. But as you stated, I compromised you. Given that you're prepared to handle punishments and the like, I suppose you'll suit as well as anyone."

He turned away to refill his drink, needing the courage. He refused to acknowledge the flash of hurt he had seen in her eyes and the lone tear that had fallen. He knew in ways far beyond spankings she was a good match. Her love of horses and the country alone were more than he could have hoped for.

But the scorn from every person who held power over him resonated through his body every time he considered marriage. Standing at the decanter, he steeled his spine and took another large mouthful of brandy, hoping she'd compose herself before he turned around, and that this infernal throbbing in his chest would go away.

Chapter Ten

Sophia bit her lip and fought back tears. Why was Edward being so mean?

She was beginning to appreciate the idea of domestic discipline as Ros had described it. 'Twas done as close to the misdeed as possible and then was over, so they could move forward. This yelling and pent-up anger was horrible, especially when he shared at least some of the blame.

She had tossed and turned all night, reliving her actions at the ball. Had she subconsciously tried to frame a compromising situation so that he would marry her? *Maybe. I will at least admit excitement at the prospect of his horse training business in the north country.*

In the morning, she had eschewed breakfast for tea in the drawing room with Ros while they kept vigil for Edward's arrival. Her desire to debate her learnings from the Enlightened Salon had been all but forgotten in the turmoil of the past day and night.

Finally, Ros had sighed. "I expected better of Edward. As he wished to avoid marriage, the least he could do was avoid such scandalous behavior."

Sophia cringed. She had forced Edward into a difficult position and had brought shame to Roslynn's house. Now where would she go?

Why was I not more careful? She berated herself

for the thousandth time.

Feeling faintly nauseous from the lack of sleep and terror over her future, she sat and waited for her fate.

Ros seemed to notice her pallor and came to perch next to her on the settee. Putting her arm around Sophia, she said, "My dear. Do not worry. All will be right shortly. Nicholas will make sure of it."

"What? How?"

"'Tis what they referred to last night. Edward is coming to write the betrothal contract."

Sophia stared, shocked. Standing, she wrung her hands and faced her hostess. "But Ros, Edward does not wish to wed."

"That is no longer relevant, Sophia. He compromised you. He must marry you, or you shall be ruined."

"But…but, it was my fault!" It came out as a whisper. *I want to marry him, but I want him to want to marry me. Oh dear, when did that happen? I should not care. I need only secure a home for Nellie and me.*

Ros looked at her archly. "Really? You dragged him to a dark corner of the garden to have your way with him? He weighs double what you do."

"Well, no, not exactly. But…"

"Then he had control over the situation. He knew we trusted him with your care. And he took advantage. 'Tis done."

Sophia fell silent, her mind racing. She was to marry Edward? With the country estate and the horse training with dozens of gorgeous Thoroughbreds and other horses? And those delicious hands and thighs and lips and…cock. Mmm. *If he's coming to write the contract, he must be willing. I can build on that.*

Then Nicholas had called her in and, with no explanation, left her with an angry Edward.

He had yelled at her for being sorry after the fact, which she supposed she deserved. She wanted to shout back and refuse his barely-an-offer. But her pragmatic side shushed her and reminded her that he fit her husband list criteria, and she'd wanted this for weeks.

She had sworn she would not care too deeply again. She had vowed to enter a marriage with her list of priorities and no more expectations. All to no avail, given this pain at Edward's perfunctory declaration.

Her tears turned to frustration. Was she doomed to be shuttled from one house to another? To find people she cared for, only to have them spurn her? Would Edward abandon her in the country and... No, his training business was there. But would he abandon her here in London and go home?

No. She swiped the tears away and straightened her spine. *I'll suit as well as anyone? We shall see about that, my lord. I will be the best darned wife you've ever dreamed—Ugh, whatever.* She focused on the security his commitment would bring and managed to avoid acknowledging her hurt feelings.

She tasted blood and realized she had bitten right through her lip. It refocused her at least.

Right, then. I've had more say in my fate than I ever thought I might. And effectively, I got the husband I desired. Wait until I tell Nellie. In the meantime, despite his attitude, I shall make the best of this situation.

Edward turned from the sideboard to face her. "Do you wish to attend the school?"

"Yes, my lord." Her face on fire, Sophia angled

away from him on the settee. *He regretted punishing me in the carriage. Does he not want me to learn about his likes and dislikes? As if receiving a lukewarm proposal was not humiliating enough, now I must speak of this?*

"Nicholas showed me some curriculum choices. I'd like to have some input on those as I have specific expectations of a wife. Before we finalize the marriage contract, you need to hear them and decide if you can agree to them."

Sophia shifted back to a more neutral angle on the sofa cushions, sucking on her sore lip. She eyed him curiously.

"Ah." Edward cleared his throat.

She thought his cheeks turned a bit pink.

"You've seen Nicholas punish Roslynn. And have, ahem, invited me to punish you in a similar manner." He glanced away, gulped more brandy, and turned back to resume his seat. "I understand Roslynn spoke to you about this when she discussed the school. I expect to rule my house like Nicholas. Punishments will likely involve spankings with my hand, a crop, or other implements. I also demand full access to your body. I would not hurt you—well, not beyond a punishment. But I may stipulate what you wear or require certain activities even beyond the bedroom. And, like Nicholas, sometimes lighter spankings will also be because I enjoy it as part of sex."

He gulped, then sighed, and she blinked at the brandy fumes from his breath. She was even more certain he was uncomfortable discussing this. She was as well. Mayhap she should ask for a brandy.

"We would assess the various implements and

activities together, and I would not use any that were abhorrent to you. And as for the lighter spankings, it seemed you enjoyed them?"

Oh, my. Those were lighter? Must I answer? May I please *have a brandy, too?* "Yes, my lord. And your touch after."

"And are you willing to accept those requirements in a marriage?"

"Yes, my lord." Her voice was breathy as her body remembered his touch.

"Right, then." Edward stood and drew her up. Holding her hands in his, he bowed his head but held her gaze from under his brows. "Sophia Wilkinson, would you do me the honor of marrying me?"

Now the tears that pricked her eyes were of hope. "Oh, Edward. Thank you. I accept. I shall do my best to be a good wife to you."

He leaned in and kissed her. At her gasp, he raised a hand to cup her face and ran a gentle thumb over her bottom lip.

She pulled back, trying to contain her emotions, given his dispassionate demeanor.

He gestured for her to sit again and settled next to her.

"We can discuss the particulars about school later. But for planning, would you prefer to attend before or after we are married?" His tone was softer.

Sophia started to answer that she would defer to his preference when she remembered something Roslynn had mentioned. For girls already married, husbands could join for a few classes. If she wanted to fight for this marriage, and if she wanted him to feel invested in it, the best way to do that was to spend time together.

More, to spend time in pursuits she knew he enjoyed. "After, my lord, if that is acceptable?"

"'Tis fine."

Nicholas knocked on the cracked door and re-entered. Arching a brow at his friend and his rather full glass of brandy, he turned to her. "Sophia? Is all well?"

"Lord Peterborough and I are to be wed, cousin." She needed the reminder of family now more than ever. Much as she hated London, the thought of leaving Nicholas and Ros and the familiarity of their home was daunting given Edward's frustration.

"Right, then. Edward, I shall have the contract finalized. When do you two want your nuptials?"

And so it was done. *No romance, no flowers.* She shook her head. *That wasn't on my list, anyway.*

Edward started to answer, but the door flew open.

Ros came bounding to Sophia to wrap her in a hug, gushing, "Congratulations. I am so happy for both of you." Ignoring the glum expressions on both betrothed faces, she turned to Edward and repeated the hug before plopping to sit across from Sophia. "Now, may we discuss the wedding? I was thinking…"

The men groaned and eyed the liquor decanters again.

****

Edward and Nicholas procured a special license, Ros and Sophia discussed guests, dresses, and menus for the wedding breakfast, and within days, Sophia was walking down the aisle at St. George's on Nicholas's arm. Ros stood at the front opposite Edward. The faces in the pews were a blur. She knew Ros's Salon was present, as were friends and political allies of Nicholas and Edward.

Then Edward turned, and the rest of the church faded away. His black formal coat and trousers matched his boots and hair. Evidently, he had ceded color choices to Ros, as his waistcoat was the same shade of opalescent blue as her overdress, under which a snowy white shirt and cravat provided a perfect contrast to the darkness of his outer layers. His dark visage appeared stern and unreadable but incredibly handsome.

'Twill not be so difficult to look at him over dinner every night.

Sophia squared her shoulders. Ros had ordered her gown as well, but when she donned it this morning, she'd been more than pleased. She would not embarrass him.

From her first glimpse in the mirror, she pictured herself through his eyes. Her gown's frosty white satin underdress shimmered beneath a layer of barely blue tulle that covered the tops of her shoulders but left the sleeves of the underdress exposed. It was caught in the center at the high waistline and draped open, with both skirts edged in blue satin ribbon the color of the overdress. Ros had her maid dress her hair simply. Left down, the blonde mane was held back with a circlet of flowers.

Her mind spun at the speed and strangeness of the steps that brought her to this, her wedding day. Only a few fortnights ago, she had been at her childhood home with simple clothes and a comfortable routine and no concept of London life. Now, she was getting married and going to a third—and then fourth, if she counted the school then Peterborough—place to live.

She had reassured Nellie they'd have a home with space and friends for her, and she found that saying the words soothed her own worries as well. Edward was what she'd hoped for in a husband, aside from his sullenness at their betrothal. Hopefully, school would help her strengthen their relationship from this point.

Standing at the altar, she stifled a giggle, but a small smile escaped. Mayhap a good spanking would help both of them settle into marriage. She felt Edward glance sideways at her and quirk his lips, his arm relaxing under her hand. She guessed she looked a teeny bit less overwhelmed with a smile.

Right, then. They—she and Nellie, at least, but hopefully Edward—would make a go of it. She needn't love him and, in fact, had no intention of doing so, but, she vowed again, she'd be the wife he wanted and ensure security for her and her best friend.

The plan was for her to attend school while Edward made a quick trip to the estate to check on the horse business, as a batch of yearlings was approaching a crucial training point. Then he'd come join her for the hands-on classes for husbands and wives toward the end of the introductory course, after which they'd return to Peterborough for more of the yearling training. Mayhap not the wedding trip every bride wanted, but Sophia was excited.

Sitting quietly in Ros and Nicholas's front parlor at the wedding breakfast, she watched guests mill about. Most knew her hosts better than she, so she sipped champagne and half-listened, distracted by visions of yearlings and meadows.

After two glasses, she lost track of what they were discussing and followed Edward's movements. He brought her a plate and sat next to her to eat. Thoughts of their discussion of the letter from the school's headmistress and class choices made her face warm. Then other parts of her warmed.

As he forked another bite of eggs and mushrooms, she followed the food to his mouth, watching his lips close around the fork and remembering the touch of them. He swallowed, and his powerful throat worked. She ogled the breadth of his shoulders and the size of his hands.

A shiver ran down her spine as she wondered if, or rather when, those hands would again spank her bottom. She had not disobeyed any orders that day, but the day wasn't over yet. And titled gentlemen generally did as they pleased. If it pleased Edward to spank her, she'd be spanked. There were a host of other reasons to look forward to the wedding night as well. Another delicate shiver shook her, drawing his gaze.

Leaning over, he asked quietly, "Are you chilled, my lady?"

"No, thank you, my lord," she replied, not quite meeting his eyes, mesmerized by his hands.

"Look at me."

She looked up from his hands, wide-eyed.

"Mmm, I think that is enough champagne for you," he murmured. "We may leave in a bit. I believe they're setting up the cake in the other room in a few minutes. No more wine until then."

After chatting to the people on his other side, he rose and offered a hand, tucking it into the crook of his arm to progress to the library.

Tea was laid out on a tray, but champagne and wine continued to flow freely. Ros saw Sophia enter and pressed a fresh glass of champagne into her hand. Anticipation turned to nerves as she contemplated their departure, and she took it without thinking. Wandering over to a seating area, she took a distracted sip.

As Edward returned from getting two slices of cake, he noticed the fresh glass of champagne, and his eyes narrowed. Passing her a piece of cake, he commented, "You seem to be looking for another punishment."

She followed his gaze and grimaced in dismay. "Oh! Oh no, I beg your pardon, my lord." She set the glass on a side table.

He shook his head, frowning. "You are always sorry after the fact, but the goal is obedience. Sorry does not escape punishment."

A small bout of defiance—and desire, she admitted—sparked in her. She was nervous, and he was going to punish her anyway. Having already contemplated a spanking, she suddenly could not think of why she shouldn't drain the whole glass. She snatched it back up and guzzled it.

Edward furrowed his brow, lips a flat line, his hand clenched on his fork. He looked as if he was going to either hurl the cake across the room or put it down and drag her somewhere for punishment that very minute.

Staring mutely at him, Sophia waited for his verdict. Belatedly, she realized she should be keeping him malleable and gentle-minded for more important things, like later that night. And recalled her vow to be the best wife possible.

She apologized again, lowering her gaze. "You are right, my lord. I *am* sorry but understand the need for punishment. I await your pleasure."

At the last phrase, Edward sucked in a breath, and his eyes darkened. Taking her cake plate and putting both dishes aside, he tugged her to her feet with him as he rose. The room quieted as guests turned to watch the bride and groom.

He smiled at the gathering and raised his glass, "Lord and Lady Suffolk, please accept our gratitude for being such gracious hosts. Everyone, thank you for attending our celebration. As I'm sure you can understand, I am anxious to start my life with my new bride, so we shall be on our way. Please enjoy the rest of the party."

The guests rose and shared good wishes as Edward and Sophia made their way toward the door. Ros and Nicholas waited there and walked them into the hall.

"We have already sent your trunks to Edward's townhouse, and Bobby personally took Nellie over and is staying with her there. He agreed to move to Peterborough, and is my personal wedding gift to you," Ros said, earning a grateful smile from Sophia. "You needn't be nervous. Edward is a wonderful man. I have fond memories of my honeymoon with Nicholas, and I know you shall do well."

As Sophia settled into the carriage, she realized the last time she'd been in it, she'd been in boys' clothes, and Edward had spanked her for the first time. Her body grew warm and heavy, her eyelids lowered as she replayed the memory. What was ahead? It seemed another spanking might be, given the champagne incident.

****

There were no servants visible when they arrived at Edward's and now her new home. She glanced questioningly at her new husband.

"I've given most staff the day off, as they know 'tis

our wedding night and we are leaving tomorrow. Only your maid is here and my valet and cook. When we travel to Peterborough together later this month, you shall receive a formal bride's welcome there."

She nodded. A bride's welcome? She supposed she'd see. She had bigger things—she smirked at the unintended reference—to worry about now.

Heading for the stairs, Edward tucked her arm through his, saying, "Come. Given the lack of servants and the time of day, it made little sense for someone to light all the lamps and then put them out. I thought we'd be more comfortable in our rooms for the evening."

As they entered a chamber, she saw her trunks. It was a drawing room, erring on the side of feminine in colors and the delicacy of the furniture. A desk stood in front of the window, and a settee and armchairs clustered around the fireplace. To the right was a door leading to a lady's bedchamber where a chaise longue lay by the window. There was a wardrobe as well as a dresser, but a four-poster bed with frilly pillows dominated the room.

At the far end of the room was another door, and Edward led her over. Through the door was a bath and dressing area. They passed through to a bedroom that mirrored hers in size and shape, but was decidedly more masculine, with darker woods and fabrics and somewhat plainer furniture. Rather than a chaise, there was a large wing chair and footstool.

Stripping off his coat and cravat and unbuttoning the starched collar at his neck, he led her back through the trio of rooms to the first drawing room, where a plate of cold meats and cheeses awaited them.

"I arranged for some wine and light refreshments, as I was not sure what you'd eat at the party." He turned to her. "But apparently, we shall skip the wine." Folding his arms, he stared at her.

She gulped. "Yes, my lord." She linked her hands at the base of her spine, trying to appear docile.

Once they'd eaten, Sophia only able to pick at her food, Edward pushed the tray aside and raised her to her feet, then moved them toward the desk.

"As 'tis our wedding night, I shall keep the punishment light," he mused. Dragging out the desk chair, he sat in it and gestured for Sophia to come forward. "If something is too much for you, tell me to stop. I will stop and discuss what is bothering you. If for some reason, you can't speak"—Sophia blinked, biting her lip—"give three taps on my leg or whatever part of me is closest. Does that sound acceptable?"

"Yes, my lord."

His mouth twisted. "I think 'tis acceptable for you to call me Edward now, wife. Do you need help with your dress?"

"My maid…" Sophia looked back toward the door hopefully.

"No, I shall be your maid tonight. Turn around." Edward found the buttons at the back of the gown and undid them, raising his hands to her shoulders and pushing it off to pool at her feet.

Her heart beat so hard it threatened to jump out of her chest. As she turned back to him, she raised her hand to press on it.

His gaze tracked the movement and darkened.

Her nipples pebbled. From cold, anticipation, or worry at a punishment? She wasn't sure, but she wished he would hurry things along, as nerves were creeping in.

He drew her between his thighs and leaned up to kiss her softly. She fell into the kiss, tasting champagne and cake. His leather and citrus spice scent wove around her.

Marriage smells delicious.

His hand skimmed down her arms to her waist and then upward.

Remembering the sheer lacy camisole and petticoat and the low-cut satin stays in the exact color of her gown, she realized his hands would be on her breasts in a second and arched her back toward him without thinking.

He groaned into her mouth at the action, and his hands cupped her mounds, thumbs flicking back and forth over her nipples. Her knees wobbled and she gasped, pulling back from the kiss.

Oh my, his touch is lightning compared to the candle flicker of my own.

Squeezing her eyes shut in shyness, she concentrated on the sparks of pleasure shooting through her body. Her chest rose and fell, swelling into his hands with every breath. With each change of pressure, lightning shot anew. She panted.

He twirled her and made fast work of her laces, dropping the stays and handing her out of the pile of fabric.

When she turned back, his jaw was clenched as his gaze roamed her length, flames behind his eyes. In pleasure or in anger? Nerves rose again.

Before she knew it, he was up, she was in the chair, and he'd removed her shoes and stockings. Recalling that Ros had told her to forsake drawers, she stiffened.

Standing her up, he sat again, and gestured at his lap with one hand. "Right. Time for your punishment. We shall dispense with it quickly, so that we may proceed to more pleasurable parts of the evening."

He hauled her over his lap in one strong tug.

Sophia hung down, one hand braced on the floor and one around his muscular calf in his boot, her toes clinging to the rug. She wanted to ask how many but suspected she knew the answer. As many as he desired.

He patted her bottom through the petticoat. Sighing, she relaxed, enjoying the touches. When she breathed in, the scent of bootblack and leather reawakened her body's response to this position, and she shifted her pelvis against his leg.

"Oh." She jolted as his hand ran up her leg, taking her remaining undergarment with it. The roughness and warmth of his skin raised tingles of awareness on her flesh.

"Shh, take your punishment like a good girl," he murmured. "No sounds, please. This will not be a hard spanking. You can hold your cries. If you do not, then you shall learn quickly what a hard punishment is."

Sophia bit her lip and tensed. *Oh, my. I may not even make a sound?* The very idea of being forced to be silent tormented her, intensifying her nerves.

Edward's hand had arrived at her bare bottom and rubbed a few circles before withdrawing.

She tensed. And waited. Finally, she relaxed her muscles and breathed.

Thwack.

"Mmph." She bit her lip to stop further sound, and her arm tightened around his calf as smacks rained down, alternating between cheeks and upper thighs.

What will happen after this? How will his cock feel in me? Roslynn said the first time might hurt.

Her brain could not stop worrying about what came next, and she remained tense through the spanks, unable to convert them to pleasure. She did not even think to arch her hips forward and try to gain friction against her nub. As her bottom warmed and grew hot and swollen, she sniffled, not enjoying this as she had earlier spankings. Her back remained stiff, but she held still and silent for her new husband.

Best wife, best wife, best wife. Sniff.

Chapter Eleven

As they had entered the master suite of his townhouse, Edward wanted nothing more than to throw her over his shoulder, carry her to his bed, and ravage her. Annoyed at being leg-shackled, his vexation fed his determination to get what he wanted out of this marriage. Lit by frustration, his lust was fueled by her beauty.

But hints of nerves throughout the day and tightness around her mouth and eyes reminded him he must take care for her first time. Her enjoyment of earlier spankings told him such a punishment might aid both their moods for the coming night.

He'd stripped her dress and those distracting stays off her, the candlelight behind her highlighting her curves through the translucent undergarments.

Thank you, Ros.

The hard points of her nipples and her arches toward him encouraged him, and her response to his kisses reassured him.

When he bared her bottom, her floral and lemony scent mingled with the sultry perfume of her arousal, and he relaxed.

She's more excited than nervous. Perfect.

He paused, seeing his dark hand covering almost an entire cheek of her pale flesh. *I must remember our size difference during sex, or I shall hurt her...in unintended ways.*

He wished he had thought to open his pants. Who knew he could do this with a wife?

Obviously Nicholas, the rat. But he couldn't stay mad in this moment of pleasure.

Raising his hand, he watched Sophia tense, and he paused, waiting for her to release that tension before bringing his hand down hard. She lurched from surprise and pain at the first hit, but only a stifled grunt emerged. Her arm tightened around his calf as he angled impacts to avoid spanking the same spot too much. As her rear showed pink hand marks, then became a darker rose, he heard stifled sniffs.

Realizing she was rigid beneath him, he stopped abruptly. "Sophia? Are you all right?"

She sniffled before she replied, "Yes, my lord."

"Right, then. You were very good. Not a peep. 'Tis over, little one." The endearment referencing her petite form slipped out unintentionally. He'd been calling her that in his head since before he'd said it to her at the first ball. Her inner strength and fierce intelligence in such a compact size amazed him. On the other hand, he also used it as a reminder. The difference in their size made him all the more aware that he'd slip past that edge between pleasure and pain if he didn't take care.

Her back sagged, and her knees bent slightly.

He smoothed his hand over her red cheeks and thighs, brushing the sore spots, enjoying the heat. A gasp came from near the floor, bitten off. His hand continued its lazy circles, edging closer to the crease between her legs. Her legs inched apart a fraction as she shifted on his leg. Her hair brushed over his leg and boot.

Edward peered at where his hand stroked and saw her rising arousal glisten between her legs. Her bottom bobbed an inch upward. Toward his hand. He slipped his thumb to the wetly gleaming crease and grazed her center. Rotating his hand to cup her cheek, his thumb gathered her essence, its second pass stretching to skim her hard nub.

Her body jerked taut, and she stopped breathing.

As he had done twice before, he dipped shallowly into her wetness, and then with a slightly firmer touch, he rubbed the exposed bundle of nerves. His other hand shifted from the middle of her back to underneath her, exploring her breast and rubbing her nipple through the lace of her chemise.

Sophia gasped a breath and arched her upper back further. Assuming she was trying to get up, Edward let go and helped her to her feet.

Sophia stood looking dazed, eyes wide on his, as if waiting to see what he would do next.

He stood and brought his hands to his waistcoat and shirt, opening and yanking them off. He led her to the bed, untied her petticoats and chemise, and shoved them off her, before gesturing for her to lie down.

He felt her gaze on him as he turned away to tug off his boots. Then he extinguished the lamps and all but one candle before shedding the rest of his clothes. While he wanted to see her, he did not want to frighten his bride on their wedding night. There would be time enough in the coming years.

Thoughts of the years ahead irritated him again, and he became impatient before reminding himself of their size differences.

Lying next to her, he propped his weight on one

elbow and leaned over to kiss her again. Smoothing his free hand along her length, he kept her mouth occupied with his as his hand returned to her lower curls and threaded through them. Three fingers smoothed downward, the first and third holding her lower lips apart as the middle finger slid into her opening then wetly back up to her sensitized tip. As he teased with light touches, her mouth slackened against his, her hips arching into his hand.

He lowered his head to her breasts and laved a tip with his tongue. Her hands shyly came to his shoulders, then as he sucked on a peak, her fingers clenched fistfuls of his hair. Apparently, she liked that. Her hips made unconscious shallow thrusts, and he heard the wet glide of his finger up and down her folds as he countered her upward movements.

He raised his head, and she groaned. Her gaze flew to his to assess his reaction.

"You may make sounds now. Especially those of pleasure. Your body is preparing itself for me. But first, relax. This is your reward for being quiet for your punishment." His fingers continued to press and retreat.

She ground up against his hand, and as his head lowered to nip at her breasts again, her hands clutched tighter in his hair.

He kept his eyes on her, sucking harder, his hand gaining speed and pressure.

Her head thrashed, her pale hair spread out around her.

When her mouth opened on a soundless cry and her nub hardened further, pulsing against his finger, he stopped sucking. Placing his teeth on her nipple, he tightened them into a gentle bite as his hand sped up.

"Ooohh…" Her cry gained sound, and her eyes popped open again. He watched her, held immobile by her hands in his hair, gripping him to her. Her lower body shuddered and spasmed against his hand. After a moment, he gentled his teeth and his fingers, and her hips lowered to the bed.

Hmm. My bride likes a bite of pain with her pleasure in more ways than spanking. 'Tis not a bad beginning.

She released his hair and smoothed her hands down to his shoulders, her eyes drifting closed.

Edward reached up and brushed her hair back from her face. "Good girl."

Now he was impatient for a different reason. He was not entirely sure he could be careful for her first time after watching her come undone. His cock felt ready to explode, to crush her and pound into her, unleashing the desire that had built since he had first seen her bottom emerge from borrowed breeches. Or perhaps even before.

Gritting his teeth, praying for patience, he rose over her. First on his hands and knees, then lowering his hips slowly so she felt his length flush against her swollen, hyper-sensitive folds.

Her eyes fluttered open, and she clutched his arms.

"Bend your knees for me," he instructed, even as his hips forced hers wider.

Placing her feet on the bed, she did, and he lowered to his elbows over her. Guiding his weeping cock to her opening with one hand, he prodded gently, then thrust just inside her shallowly, re-sparking her desire.

"Mmph."

He glanced at her, reassured when her gaze was

steady on his, her lower lip caught between her teeth in concentration.

Stifling a groan, clinging to control, Edward pushed in an inch more with each foray. As her nipples hardened again, he paused and leaned in to kiss her. Realizing he needed more leverage to not prolong the pain of the first thrust, he drew his knees forward under her hips. He kept kissing her as he withdrew then drove deep.

Her nails scored his triceps, and she clenched around him, breaking off from the kiss and dropping her arms to try to wriggle away from the sharp pain.

"No. Don't pull away. Stay still, and I shall as well," he commanded, holding her head and looking at her. "It shan't hurt any more if you wait a minute, and 'tis the only time you'll have pain, I promise."

She quieted, and they waited a beat, then two. Then she wriggled again, but slowly, and she glanced between them, as if to try to see their joining. Glancing up at him, she bit her lip again, and he felt a rush of wetness flow over his length embedded inside her.

His cock pulsed, eager to slide through that wet warmth, and she wriggled a third time.

He groaned with undisguised pleasure. He moved his hips without conscious knowledge, and he stayed on his knees, knowing he would not last long. Trying to keep his strokes gentle, he rose on one arm to reach the other between them and tap her little nub gently as it re-hardened, making her raise her hips and twist up beneath him, seeking more.

Smiling, he kept tapping and pistoned his hips, unable to hold back his building climax any longer. She used her bent legs to push against his hand, and their hips synced to counterpoint. His eyelids dropped to half-mast. He wished to watch her come, but he could not hold it any more. She was so tight, and he had been hard since her dress dropped.

His bollocks tightened as her hips froze, pressed up against him, and her channel clamped around him, milking him as he pounded into her for long seconds. With two last thrusts that pushed them up the bed, he stilled and exploded inside her.

Rolling over so he did not crush her, he pulled her with him and clasped her to his chest as he dragged a quilt over them and sucked in deep breaths to recover.

"Sophia? How do you feel, little one?"

"Mmm."

"Did I hurt you? Well, beyond that first pinch?"

"You were magnificent," she mumbled. "Like a stallion…"

He thought he felt her nuzzle his breastbone, but then she went slack against him. He grinned, pleased with her analogy.

****

Sophia woke to find herself alone, with lukewarm tea and toast on a table. Noticing she was naked, she scooped her shift off the floor, pulled it on, and climbed back in bed to sit. The only people who might walk in were Jane and Edward, and both knew exactly what she had been doing the night before. Nonetheless, she was not ready to lounge around without clothes.

As she sipped her tea, she wished for Nellie to talk through the events of the prior day. While Edward had punished her for the champagne, it had been her fault for disobeying him. He had been stern but fair, and after the punishment, he had been very attentive in lovemaking, giving her pleasure twice. Her wedding day portended amazing possibilities for their marriage, despite his reluctance.

Shifting slightly, she took a quick inventory of her physique and realized her posterior was a little sore, as well as between her legs. But as her body reacted to her memory of pleasure, lingering warmth replaced the soreness.

Her thoughts drifted back to last night, lying on the bed as Edward strummed her form as though she were a harp, making it sing.

She smoothed the embroidery on the bedcover, remembering its texture reigniting the sore spots on her bottom from her spanking then spinning it to a delicious fire of pleasure where his fingertips rubbed.

So much more than what I expected. More intense, more heat, more pleasure. More.

She recalled the sharp pain of entry, followed by a foreign fullness. Part of him—a big part—was inside her. And oh, the despair when he pulled out, followed by elation when he surged forward, and the climb to another peak of ecstasy.

I only hope he experienced the same intensity, and that it makes him more inclined to view marriage positively.

Edward had said sex wouldn't hurt again. Could they try it again before they left? Throwing back the covers, she leaned over to return her cup to the tea tray.

Jane bustled in. "Oh my lady, thank goodness you are awake. His lordship wanted to let you sleep as long as possible but just sent me up. You'll need to start the trip soon to make the school today." As she spoke, the maid gathered her clothes from the night before, still strewn on the floor, and laid out fresh traveling clothes for her.

Giving up the idea of coaxing her new husband back to bed, Sophia decided she could live with the ache in her private regions but not the stickiness on her thighs. She stood to wash before dressing, daydreaming of the future—waking together every morning, riding over the estate, working in the stables, and discussing Parliamentary actions over dinner in the evening. The nights held their own appeal, despite lacking some specifics.

The best darned wife. She smiled in anticipation.

She found Edward talking to Bobby in the hall. Glancing up, he paused in conversation, calling her over.

"We are riding in the carriage, Sophia," he began. She waited for Bobby to head outside then opened her mouth to argue, but he cut her off. "I thought you might be tender and wished to ensure your comfort today." He brought her hand to his lips and grinned. "I shall ride with you, so we shall suffer together."

Her answering smile was wry as she took his offered arm. He led her outside and handed her up into the carriage before settling opposite her.

After rapping on the roof to start their journey, he asked, "How do you feel? Any soreness? Bleeding?"

"Mmm." Her gaze on her lap, she blushed, not ready to discuss such intimate details with her new husband.

"Come now, as your husband, I need to know these things."

Turning her head to look out the window, she murmured, "Thank you, my lord, I am fine."

Edward sighed. "I'll give you some latitude, as this is so new, so I shall ask again. Before you answer, remember lying leads to punishment."

Another spanking? He'd managed it once in a carriage. Sitting straighter, she raised her gaze to his again, her mouth curling in a small smile.

He shook his head at her and tried again. "How do you feel?"

"A little soreness," she replied. "I don't believe there is, ah, bleeding."

"Thank you, little one. Tell me if you need to stop for any reason before we change the horses. We shall travel several hours today, if it remains comfortable for you."

She nodded, checking out the window to watch Bobby ride Nellie up ahead, as he would set his own pace to get him and the horse safely to the school stables.

As they rode, she and Edward fell into the easy discussion they had found on their daily rides in Town. She asked him about recent Parliamentary sessions to understand the most contentious issues, helping him sift through his thoughts on the matters.

They stopped for a brief lunch and horse change in the afternoon, and she stretched her legs by walking around the yard, feeling good in the fresh air before climbing back into the carriage. But an hour later, stiff and uncomfortable, she needed to shift position every few minutes.

****

Planning for the wedding and school, Edward had been focused on the short term. Now they would be apart for most of a fortnight for her introductory course at the School of Enlightenment. He had that long to come up with a plan for the long term to avoid her discovering his impediment.

As they swayed silently in the carriage, his thoughts became ever tenser. Day-to-day felt less clear-cut with every mile they traveled. Could he really spank her whenever he desired? Every evening, even? What of some of the other sexual games he enjoyed?

He planned to model their marriage like Nicholas and Roslynn's. She'd help James, his steward for the business and the Peterborough estate. James had been struggling to oversee the other properties in Charles and Charlotte's absence. With two of them working and her interest in politics, he anticipated her reading correspondence, then debriefing him on Parliamentary bills, eliminating the need for him to fight through reading them.

That would leave her little time to spend in the stables, where he and the stablemaster would continue to focus on the horse training.

He nodded. It would work. It must. He was stuck with her. While she'd proven last night there were benefits he'd enjoy, he would not risk her scorn. Given Sophia's sneaky outing to Vauxhall, he wondered how much time he needed to give her to ride, to appease her, while ensuring she handled all the correspondence and reading he needed. But he mustn't get comfortable or let down his guard.

With that in mind, he decided the best course of action was to assert his dominance in the relationship from the start. He'd establish the separation of duties: her in the house and him in the stables.

Coming back to the present, he noticed Sophia

fidgeting for the fourth time. "You're not comfortable, Sophia. You should have told me when we stopped."

Upset at himself for not asking again at lunch and her for not telling him, he looked at her grimly. "Now we're halfway between the last inn and the school."

He didn't want this marriage, but neither did he want his new wife to be unnecessarily uncomfortable. He snorted silently. *If she's to be uncomfortable, I want it to be by my hand. At least I planned for this possibility and 'twill introduce her to more of my sexual preferences.*

"I honestly did not realize it until after we were underway again."

"Ah. Well luckily, I have something I think shall help it. Come here." He reached into his jacket and extracted a vial as his other hand patted his lap.

"My lord?" Sophia sounded unsure how to maneuver in the small space.

Reaching over, Edward dragged her onto his lap sideways, propping one of her feet up on the seat she had occupied and the other on the seat alongside him. He leaned her against his arm and the side wall of the carriage.

"Sir, forgive me for saying so, but your leg is not any softer than the seat cushion." Sophia squirmed.

Edward chuckled, even as his body reacted to her squirming and the knowledge of what he planned. "My apologies, little one. But that is not the solution I meant." His arm tightened around her back as his other hand drew up her skirts. With her legs spread, it was a simple task, and his hand came to her thigh.

Clutching it, she gasped, "My lord, what are you doing?"

"I am going to soothe your aches and hopefully take your mind off your sore bottom. Calm yourself and sit still, so I needn't punish you again tonight. I really do want you to be more comfortable in class. And as your husband, this body is mine to touch as I wish. Do not feel embarrassed. I understand it may be distressing now, but the more you can relax, the quicker you shall become accustomed to it."

Her muscles relaxed, her thighs falling open more for him.

Smiling in pleasure at her quick acquiescence, he reached near her waist where his other hand held the vial and opened it, spilling a fragrant oil onto his fingertips. He reached under her skirt and used the outside of his palm to skim up and find her pantaloons' slit. Scooting her so that her lower back and upper thighs rested on his legs, with her bottom in between them, he rubbed the sore spots where she had been spanked, then sat for hours. After massaging the site of her punishment, he dipped one fingertip into the vial, slipped his hand back under her skirt and drawers, and used his thumb to part her folds. Placing one finger at her opening, he eased inside, the oil on his finger smoothing the way.

Given her work with her father, he was mildly surprised Sophia did not recognize the smell of camphor. Of course, she would not have thought to use it just there.

A second finger joined the first, and he rubbed his thumb against his remaining fingers to lubricate it before circling her sensitive nub. Her back arched, hips thrusting into his hand.

"Ah," he sighed near her ear, "you like that. Does it

hurt inside?" As her head shook from side to side and she relaxed back against his arm, he drove both fingers deeper. Arching again, she gasped, and he circled his thumb again.

"Does this help?" he asked.

She nodded but then gulped.

He grinned. Ah, the oil was heating.

Her hips squirmed, rocking against him. He sighed. His cock, already rock-hard, took the rocking as an invitation. But that could not happen today if he wished her to heal and sit comfortably tomorrow.

Sophia bit her lip. "Oh, my lord, the oil, it's tingling." Her nub hardened, and moisture soaked his fingers as her body reacted to his stimulation and tried to flush the oil out.

He eased his fingers in and out, swiveling his thumb and laying his lips next to her ear. "Easy, sweetheart, let your body respond to the heat. 'Twill help your body heal. Concentrate on my thumb."

Keeping his fingers motionless inside her channel, he flicked the hard kernel of flesh from side to side, then pressed and released, judging her reactions. From her breathing, he saw she enjoyed a circular motion the most. He repeated the motion, catching her ear lobe in his teeth and nibbling.

Her hips gyrated. One hand clutched his waistcoat, and the other held his forearm as though she did not know whether to pull it away or hold it to her. Her stomach muscles tightened against his hand. Her breaths became small pants, punctuated by sporadic moans.

His fingers hooked inside her, but he refrained from thrusting them in and out. He was trying to alleviate the soreness. His thumb tapped her faster and faster as his teeth continued to worry her ear lobe.

Keening, Sophia fell over the edge, curling toward him, eyes scrunched closed as her body spasmed in release. Her inner walls milked his fingers.

He petted her, smoothing his hand over her outer folds, avoiding the more sensitive spots as he brought her down, soothing her ear with his tongue and lips.

"Oh, oh…" Sophia gasped for words. "Ah, thank you…my lord."

Chuckling, Edward sat her up but kept his hand cupped around her, unmoving. "'Tis Edward, remember? You are most welcome, my little filly. I rather like you thanking me for giving you pleasure, although 'tis my right to do that as your husband." He shifted to try to ease his cock, which begged to burst through his trousers and shove into her. 'Twould be a long night after he dropped her at the school.

Chapter Twelve

Sophia's head reeled. Marriage, another delicious spanking. And then…nothing had prepared her for Edward being inside her, surrounding her, taking her body to heights she could not have dreamed. Watching Nicholas and Roslynn, the glimpses of animals mating, were like watercolors to an oil painting by a master. *Even the strokes were bolder.*

She snickered. Then the carriage ride… Who would have thought he could do that one-handed? She was eager to see what this school taught.

They had arrived at the school late in the afternoon. Located near London, it appeared to be a gray-stoned country manor with extensive grounds and a few outbuildings. The structures were hidden from the street by copses of trees and were fenced, with a servant at the gate and a sign By Appointment Only. There appeared to be a large gate behind the stables for access to trails around the rest of the property.

The headmistress's comment that "Any friend of Roslynn's was welcome" raised both their eyebrows. Sophia wondered whether her cousin's wife had attended the school.

Edward stayed through the initial interview and discussion of the curriculum.

Mrs. Montague's frank language and calm demeanor alleviated most of Sophia's nervousness.

Edward fidgeted a bit but settled quickly.

The lessons seemed manageable, but some of the course descriptions were vague. Mornings were for estate management lessons or—more likely for her—reading time in the library or garden or riding Nellie on the estate, depending on the particular day's schedule and weather. Mrs. Montague noted that after lunch each day, they'd break into small groups for marriage preparation workshops on various subjects, including anatomy classes.

After ascertaining that Edward preferred domestic discipline as a solution to disagreements or transgressions, Mrs. Montague made a note on Sophia's schedule. "And servants?"

"Ah, no." Edward's reply was matter-of-fact.

"Voyeurism or exhibitionism." She checked down her list.

"Eh." His shoulder went up and down with his noncommittal response.

Sophia was lost. She vaguely remembered Ros mentioning voyeurism. Oh well, she'd learn them in the next few weeks.

"Right, then." The headmistress rattled off two days a fortnight away and indicated Edward should return then for hands-on classes. Despite his indifference to exhibitionism, he did understand they would be monitored, right? He assured her he did.

He may also come a day early to spend time with his bride, if he chose. Edward chose.

Sophia wondered if he agreed because it seemed the gentlemanly thing to do. But did he need to worry about that now she was legally his?

Edward left after dinner, as there was a soiree for

the incoming class for students only, and Sophia would stay in a dormitory for her course.

Before departing, he pulled her aside to check in with her. "Sophia, I know this has all happened quickly. How are you feeling?"

Sophia thought for a moment. "'Tis a little overwhelming. I had barely adapted to London after only having known a small country village. Then there were the layers of trying to understand Roslynn's and Nicholas's relationship, getting to know you, and ball etiquette. Now I must start over again, learning another unfamiliar environment and rules. But I am willing to try this. I want to please you, husband." She put her hand on his sleeve tentatively.

"Good. Then pay close attention. There will be an exam in Peterborough." He gave her a mock leer.

She smiled, not quite relaxed enough to laugh at his teasing.

He leaned in and kissed her. "Keep an open mind. That is all I ask of you. Think of this. You did not know how unusual it was for a husband to spank his wife when you watched Nicholas and Ros. That allowed you to focus on processing your reactions instead of being scandalized because 'twas not to society's standards. So too shall your innocence allow you to learn what rules you *wish to* live by, not what is acceptable."

Sophia followed Mrs. Montague to the after-dinner sherry social. As they walked to the salon to meet the other girls, the headmistress told her, "Everyone you meet tonight is in a position similar to yours. Betrothed or married to a member of the Ton or in one of their first Seasons with matrimony as a goal. You shall see other girls around the school, but they are at different stages of their education or are training for different roles. Some married women return for more advanced courses. But tonight allows the students who will be in class together to get acquainted. All these girls arrived yesterday or today and, like you, are just starting their path to enlightenment."

The evening passed in a whirlwind, with twenty girls in attendance. Afterward, Mrs. Montague led them to the dormitory, a separate building at one end of the large courtyard. When they entered a central hallway, the headmistress turned right and unlocked a door. They entered an enormous room, sectioned into four spaces with partitions. Three bunk beds in each section offered sleeping space for six girls. The sections had three washstands and wardrobes as well, although she did not know how her clothes would fit into half of a wardrobe. Come to think of it, she did not see any trunks.

Mrs. Montague turned to face the new students. "You may pick your own beds. Your trunks are being sorted through and shall arrive shortly."

Several girls shuffled as though to choose a bed or turned to each other to gather friends for a particular shared space. A hand slipped into Sophia's, and a voice asked, "Bunkmates?"

She turned to find Beth, whom she had met at the soiree.

Sophia nodded with a quick smile for her new friend.

Mrs. Montague continued, "Before you find a bed, here is your first lesson. We are all beautiful women. We may be different shapes, colors, and sizes. But the most important lesson you shall learn here is that every woman's body is beautiful, and 'tis up to her to make her mind and personality equally beautiful. Fashion can distract from learning with an open mind, so we shall not focus on it here. Your trunks are being sorted through to remove any clothing you shan't need. For those who ride, you'll have your habit available. But otherwise, you'll wear shifts and pantaloons for all classes and activities. Your classes will be comprised of women only unless we tell you in advance, in which case we can discuss apparel." She paused, as several girls were whispering to each other while others stood in shock. "Are there questions?"

One girl dared ask, "What if we are cold?"

The headmistress smiled. "We shall cross that bridge when we come to it, but as most of your instructors shall wear similar attire, they shall monitor the rooms' temperatures accordingly. The goal is to make you comfortable with your bodies and others', not to get anyone sick."

"Right, then. Remove your dresses and come get the paper with your name on it and a pin here in this basket." She pointed. "And I shall take the dresses with me."

Everyone looked at each other blankly. Undress here? Right now?

Mrs. Montague sighed. "Just once, I should like my orders followed on the first night without me having to lead by example." She turned to the closest student. "A little assistance, if you please, Ingrid."

Ingrid glanced around at the other girls who were still staring and hesitantly reached out to unhook the headmistress's dress.

At that, a few girls began removing their dresses

slowly. Soon the room was a sea of fabric, with heaps of pale colors by the basket on the table.

"Good night then. You'll hear the breakfast bell tomorrow." Mrs. Montague stood calmly in her undergarments, nodded to two assistants who had followed the group of girls into the dormitory. They each grabbed as many dresses as they could hold and carried them out of the dorm.

****

After a one-sided conversation between Sophia and Nellie, so Nellie could learn about the classes being taught as Beth snickered and saddled her own mount, they rode out. Keeping to a leisurely walk to become familiar with the riding path, Sophia and Beth used the time to learn about each other.

They'd had two days of classes. The mornings were for math and reading, which both girls had tested out of. Hence, they had time for this ride.

Sophia had noticed that Beth was one of the few girls here comfortable in her own skin no matter what she was wearing or doing. So she was eager to learn of the other girl's family and how she came to the school.

Beth's parents had died of a fever a few years before, and she was sent to a distant cousin's to live. Her parents had been free spirits, encouraging her to pursue any education or recreation that interested her, to find her passion. Among those interests had been sexual exploration. When her cousin, widowed and attempting to run her dead husband's business, could not balance giving her the freedom she desired without risking her reputation for a future Ton marriage, she had sent Beth here to buy some time to consider a path forward.

Like most of the girls in the class, Beth was not yet married. But after hearing her story, Sophia suspected she could learn a thing or two from the other girl.

Sophia in turn shared her experience as an only child, losing her parents and her best friend, and her love of horses and politics. She provided a brief version of her recent marriage, stating only that she had married her cousin's best friend after a strikingly fast courtship. She sniggered silently at her play on words.

"What did you think of the first day and Juliet's comments?" she asked her new friend, referring to their instructor.

Juliet was their instructor for anatomy and other classes that were scheduled in the afternoons.

She'd given them a warning, couched as an introduction. "Most of the Ton do not have enlightened marriages. Much of what you learn shall feel uncomfortable, like being in dishabille does now. The first set of classes is designed to shock you, to test your continued interest and resolve to learn unconventional methods. There is no shame in deciding you don't wish to remain. We are not condemning the ways of society. We merely offer an alternative for those who desire to explore other choices."

Beth shrugged. "I suspect most girls here are unconventional in one way or another." She glanced at Sophia, who only grinned at her in reply. "'Tis prudent to learn what we like before we must cater to a husband's wishes."

Sophia nodded in agreement as they turned on an alternative path.

The stablemaster had reminded them of the school's rule of mutual respect.

They glimpsed open areas through the small copses of trees. The outer edges of the property were densely forested, and Beth mused aloud that this was likely for privacy. After passing another building similarly sized to their dormitory, the trees gave way to a flat open area the school had turned into a large fruit and vegetable garden, with a greenhouse next to it. Beyond the garden, the path re-entered the trees. The girls shivered in the cooler air as they loosened the reins to let the horses pick their own pace.

After the ride, leaving the barn, Sophia looked back toward the other building they had seen, wondering if it was another dormitory.

Beth leaned in and whispered, "One girl told me there is a separate course here, for courtesans!" She nodded toward the building. "Word is, that is their dormitory."

As Sophia looked at her and glanced back, she spied movement. Squinting, she drew in a shocked breath. The girl entering the other dormitory looked like an older version of her closest childhood friend, Penelope. But the girl slipped inside, and Sophia could not imagine her friend being a courtesan, anyway. Although…

"How does one even become a courtesan?" she asked Beth.

"By being so good at sex that men will buy you a house and pay you for it. I may consider that option yet." She laughed at Sophia's shocked expression.

****

The girls learned how to find common ground with their husbands or suitors. Juliet encouraged them to learn about their husband's hobbies and responsibilities, including Parliament, and to engage their spouses in their own interests where possible.

She reiterated what Roslynn had told Sophia about the Enlightened Salon. "In addition to helping your husband, being aware of the issues being raised to Parliament may help hundreds of women and children who do not have the privileges you have. Our goal is to teach you to influence or support your husband's approach to these issues and move forward protections for those struggling."

Sophia loved that idea, as it gave her a purpose beyond merely reading to acquire knowledge. *Edward already knows I enjoy talking about his Lords duties. I simply need a chance to learn the horse training business.*

In other lessons, the art of negotiations was taught, and in yet others, party planning and more mundane subjects. In anatomy classes, the girls practiced undressing and redressing fully clothed mannequins of women, then men.

Sophia tried to imagine undressing Edward, but she struggled. She knew some of the basics of a man's body. She and her father had once come across village men removing their shirts to bathe in the creek after a hot summer day. But Edward was much bigger, in height and breadth of shoulder. And she hadn't been able to see much in the dark of their wedding night. What would his chest look like? His arse? His cock? *Mmm.*

In the classroom, Juliet instructed, "Yesterday, you dressed and undressed mannequins. Today, you'll practice on a living person. While 'tis not the same as assisting a husband, repetition will provide a level of confidence. Therefore, you shall undress and dress a classmate. Everyone will do this," she added sternly as a few girls crossed their arms defensively and looked dubious. "If you find yourself too uncomfortable with today's lessons, then you need to re-evaluate whether you truly desire this experience that is available to so few women."

She paused to let that sink in before continuing. "Yes, you each will be fully naked at some point. That is likely to happen with your husband, so we are building your courage. And"—she smiled, repeating the school's mantra—"as we are all beautiful and respect each other's beauty, the initial strangeness shall pass. Remember, 'tis important to feel confident in your own skin in a healthy, happy relationship."

She asked everyone to pair with the person on their left. Beth, who had been quite eager to disrobe the male mannequins the class before, sat grinning at her.

"Do you prefer to undress me first or second?" Beth asked, smiling.

"Oh, ah, I do not mind. It sounds like we shall both have our turn anyway."

"In that case, I shall disrobe you first." Beth bounced in her seat, eager as ever. "I cannot wait to see all that pale skin."

Sophia was taken aback at her enthusiasm, but as it was consistent with the girl's zeal the days before, she ignored it. As the girls were only in shifts, drawers, and slippers, it would not take long anyway.

Beth was almost Sophia's height but curvier with rounded breasts, belly, and thighs. Her brown eyes always seemed to have a twinkle, and cinnamon curls bobbed around her shoulders with her energy.

Maggie Sims

Beth stepped close to her, gaze on Sophia's breasts, and asked her to raise her hands. Doing as she was told, Sophia's skin pebbled as her shift lifted from her waist, over her breasts, up along her arms, and stalled... She was blinded by the fabric covering her head, her arms bound in the sleeves.

The other girl stepped in farther, murmuring, "I beg your pardon. You're taller than I, so I'm trying to reach." Before Sophia could bend at the waist to help her, Beth's chest brushed against her bare breasts. Her nipples beaded at the abrasion, and she felt Beth suck in a breath, making the other girl's breasts graze hers before she stepped back with Sophia's top in hand.

The other girl's eyes were bright, her nipples hard. Sophia lowered her arms to her sides, and waited. What would Beth do next? Her friend's reaction was not all that different from her own voyeurism of Ros and Nicholas. But Sophia was too nervous about the group environment to be affected by the contact.

Juliet checked with the pair's progress, and Beth proceeded matter-of-factly to remove the rest of Sophia's clothes. Both women looked at Sophia, who struggled to stand motionless. Gaze darting around the class, her hands fidgeted then fisted, wanting to cover her private areas. Most of the 'models' were in a similar dilemma.

Juliet turned to the classroom, saying, "Great job, ladies. We'll pause here and see if anyone has questions. Or any thoughts they wish to share about today."

Sophia contemplated the feelings evoked by the day's lessons. As she saw Beth's gaze hungrily running up and down her body, she imagined Edward watching her. Her back unconsciously straightened, thrusting her breasts out. Barely noticing her friend's indrawn breath, she was focused on marriage negotiations.

Mayhap a compelling approach to convincing Edward to let me help with the horse care. She smiled. Already she felt secure enough in her marriage to think beyond her desire for a home, to her wish to help with his business.

****

All anyone talked about at lunch was the afternoon's anatomy class. After several increasingly risqué afternoons, they daren't imagine what would follow nudity.

Juliet introduced the day's subject. "Part of being a partner to someone and pleasing them is attending to their needs, as you learned in the clothing lesson. Another part is attending to your own needs or ensuring they attend to yours. To do that, you must understand those needs. Certainly you know what food you like, whether you prefer wine, sherry, or even brandy, and what your favorite color is. Think of it this way," she paused to cite an example. "You are more likely to ensure your husband has pickled herring as a breakfast choice if you also like pickled herring, no?"

The girls tentatively nodded.

"In an advanced class, you would learn how to attend to your partner's physical"—she glanced around the room—"sexual needs, and we shall give a quick introduction to that before you leave at the end of the course. But first, you should appreciate the benefits you can receive." She grinned. "You shall learn about your own body now, to determine some of your likes and dislikes physically."

A couple of the girls squirmed in their seats. From discomfort or eagerness? When Sophia considered her own reaction, she found an odd mix of the two.

Juliet started at the top of the form and talked about various parts of a woman's body and how different women liked different things. From hair brushing to hair pulling, from licking one's neck to sucking or even biting, from tickling the back of the knees, to tying them apart, from a gentle foot massage to sticking pins in them.

Wait, what?

Sophia and a few classmates exchanged wide-eyed glances, and Juliet waved it off. "A more extreme example. Do not worry about that for today."

Juliet reminded the class, "Remember, this school is always about respecting each other, valuing ourselves as women. While society sees some things as taboo or wrong, we believe that any respectful and loving interaction should be valued and embraced."

Some heads nodded, others seemed doubtful, but no one was appalled.

She added, "Note that I include 'respectful and loving' in that description. Today's goal is to discover physical sensations that are pleasurable for each of you. However, emotion and care enhance the physical. So while I want you to find what feels good today, intimacy with your husband will ideally be better."

She turned, looking each student in the eye. "There is more than one lesson here. First, as we discussed, you see that different things excite different people." Here her voice rose, her lips firm. "*All* of them are acceptable. There is naught to be ashamed of about how you become aroused. It is more a question of finding someone who shares those pleasures. And that is why your sponsors sent you here." She let that sink in. "Secondly, even for one person, arousal levels can differ, and those may change, whether due to mood, your monthly flows, or other factors. Be comfortable with those changes, both for yourself and your partner."

"Before we continue, everyone, touch your own breasts. Try various touches, discover what feels good for you." As many of the students remained frozen, she tapped her foot. "Girls, your bodies are beautiful, but how do you expect your husband to know what brings you pleasure if you don't? We shall wait for everyone's participation to do this."

Sophia's hands crept up to her breasts. She touched an extended tip softly, a curl of sensation tingling low in her belly when she did. Then she grasped her other nipple and plucked. The twinge became stronger. Remembering Edward's touch, his teeth tightening and sending her over the edge on their wedding night, she pinched.

Oh! She felt a rush of wetness below. *I am open to many touches, but by only one person.* Then, a stern internal voice said, *No falling in love!*

"Good. Thank you, class. Does anyone have questions before we continue?"

Juliet returned to the forms. "We women have a compact bundle of nerves toward the front of our sex that helps make sex pleasurable for us. 'Tis important you know where this is…" Her expression turned wry as she added the last comment. "Especially as not all men do."

Sophia smirked. *Mine does. And with incendiary results.*

"Knowing how your body likes to be touched is important. By knowing this, you may choose sexual positions that suit you or even encourage your husband to help you enjoy sexual encounters with him. Now, I'll ask everyone to do one more thing, then we shall break. Touch yourself between your legs. Find the small swelling there, not even the size of a knuckle, that is raised and very sensitive."

Looking around the room, Sophia saw Beth with her hand eagerly in her drawers. Other girls had left one hand on a breast, kneading or squeezing it. Others were looking around as she was, not quite ready to commit.

Unwilling to admit to already having found it or sharing that her husband did not need tutoring, she slid her hand down. Following Edward's approach, her first and third finger slid between her lower lips and pressed outward, allowing her middle finger to explore the ridges and bumps. Her middle finger pressed in through the inner folds and gathered wetness. Inching back, she circled the hard nub. She closed her eyes and imagined being bottom up over Edward's knee, this nub rocking against his granite thigh muscles at each spank, until he smoothed his hand over and found her center.

Her eyes flew open. She was not going to explode from pleasure in a classroom full of women. While she had learned more about exhibitionism during her stay here, she was not ready to explore her own predilections.

Coming back to the room, she found herself leaning back in her seat, with her legs spread to provide better access. Her nipples poked through her camisole, and she was panting quietly. Sitting upright in her chair and bringing her hands to the desk, she refocused on her surroundings.

Several girls were turned, looking past her. Following their line of sight, she found Beth, hand wiggling in her bloomers, eyes scrunched in concentration as her face flushed. More of the class noticed and stared as well, until most students watched the girl.

"Oh," Beth moaned under her breath, eyes closed. "Oh...oh, oh, oh...." She grew louder. Her face went scarlet, her hips shot forward in her chair, and her eyes popped open. The loudest "Ooooohhhhh!" sounded, going almost to a scream at the end. Her eyelids slid half-closed, unfocused, and her body sagged in her seat.

Whipping around in embarrassment, the girls found Juliet nodding calmly. "Thank you for the demonstration, Beth. Each of you should think about trying to attain that sexual pinnacle, an orgasm. I shan't force it here with an audience, as some prefer privacy. But every woman should know what arouses them to that level of pleasure, as 'tis excellent motivation to educate your husband."

Sophia smiled at her friend in a show of support and reached out and squeezed Beth's hand, the one that hadn't been in her knickers.

Chapter Thirteen

Edward arrived to ride with Sophia, and they hurried to the stables. Sophia greeted Ash as Edward petted Nellie and saddled her for his wife. Her palms were sweaty, and she remained quiet, uncertain how to act with her new husband. The whirlwind of the wedding, their intimate wedding night, then two weeks apart left her off balance.

Once they were away from the barn and school, they let the horses meander through the forest trails. Edward told her a bit about the yearlings' next stage of training until they entered a clearing. After a quick canter to give the horses some exercise, the couple rode abreast, walking their mounts through a meadow aimlessly.

They had planned to discuss her thoughts on her classes, but Sophia was also eager to understand the other aspects of the school.

"There seems to be a number of levels of classes here," she began tentatively, unsure how to phrase the questions she had.

"Yes," Edward agreed, nodding. "The itinerary you are following of course, then advanced classes, and curricula for different roles."

"Different roles? Are all the students here with marriage in mind?"

"No, little one. Some shall work in households as

servants, for instance."

"Servants? Oh, dear. How does that happen? Where shall they be placed then?" Given her station in life, as a poor relation of a Peer with no dowry, she had not had many alternatives. But servants had even less choice than she did.

"Well, imagine Nicholas before he met Roslynn. He needed an outlet for his need for spanking and dominance. There are of course places that cater to those needs, but some men prefer, shall we say, the convenience of availability within their own household, especially if they do not live in London."

Sophia nodded tentatively but remained concerned. Even the short while between her father's death and Nicholas's letter calling her to London was fraught with anxiety about her future and lack of choices. She could not imagine living with that one's entire life. But just as she had not minded being spanked, she recognized a household might run smoother if the servant was trained and understood the environment in which she'd work. *And the house would be even cleaner*, she thought, giggling internally, *if servants knew their brooms could be used on their bottoms if they did not wield them properly*. "How does the school match households with servants?"

"I don't know all the details, but from what Mrs. Montague and Nicholas told me, they are careful." Edward seemed to understand her concern. "The Peers of the Realm belong to a few select clubs—White's, Brooks', and the like. More gossip is exchanged there than in all the ladies' drawing rooms combined, I suspect. Mrs. Montague, or an alumna of the school who is not well known in London, approaches the men discreetly. She shares some general information, no specifics, to protect the school. If they are interested or have friends who are, they must share their specific inclinations or preferences, and she sends one or more girls to interview. The roles they hire into depend on the household's needs—both for day and night."

"What other roles are trained here?"

"Ah…"

"My lord—Edward, are you embarrassed?" Sophia asked as his cheeks grew ruddy. "This is the School of Enlightenment. You shan't last long here if you embarrass easily. But fine, I shall make it easier. Are girls trained here to become courtesans?" She'd learned enough from both her short time in London and the girls at the school to at least know the term and the general idea.

"Yes. Everyone, gentlemen and ladies alike, enjoys different appetites. You've likely already begun to learn that in your classes." At Sophia's nod, he continued, "So like servants, 'tis better for both to pair courtesans with men with similar tastes. In addition, courtesans and mistresses must learn to manage their own household and money, and most don't have family to teach them. The school educates them on how to attract an advantageous match, keep that man, and ensure their financial future without a marriage contract."

"How does their training differ from that of being a wife? As far as I can tell, that is what I am learning."

"Exactly right. It is largely the same. However, etiquette requires that ladies do not recognize women of the demi-monde, so they are in separate classes. Also, given their role in society, courtesans are expected to be more, shall we say, flexible and amenable in their dealings with men, so their course includes several topics offered in advanced courses for wives. In fact, if you'll remember, we signed you up for one such class, which is tomorrow, timed to my arrival."

****

Edward walked into Training Room P, too engrossed in his own thoughts to immediately notice that it was furnished as a small parlor.

He wasn't sure he'd ever been as uncomfortable as he had for the conversation he'd just had. Not even the bare bottom canings he'd received as a boy or the hard-eyed glares by professors when he missed questions on reading assignments had felt like this.

The headmistress had sat him down and discussed what Sophia had learned in the classroom and what was expected of him, here and beyond. She outlined what she called standard rules of the school, put in place for everyone's safety. His "class" or review with his wife would be monitored from outside the training room. They'd have privacy for the most part, but the door would be cracked, and a monitor would be in the hall to come in and assist or intervene as needed.

As he'd signed Sophia up for training on spanking, both pleasurable and for punishment, there was even more guidance on that subject. He was not to break the skin. That could be covered in a different class if he chose. *What?* He was to stop if Sophia said stop. He was not to punish already-marked skin. He was to ensure the implement of choice was agreed upon in advance…and so on. As if he was a novice.

By the time he walked out, he was grinding his teeth in irritation. Damned condescending woman, assuming he hadn't known what he was doing, hadn't been doing it for years. It was almost as bad as being asked to read aloud. He should have provided a letter of referral from Sarah Potter, the owner of his spanking club. But criminy, he would not have even known what to ask her to write.

Oh, she said these were standard rules, but he didn't trust her, and he didn't like her tone. It reminded him too much of his governesses. His conscience whispered at him that he wasn't being fair. *Not every woman is like your governess. After all, you're starting to trust Sophia, at least with your sexual preferences.*

Now he looked around the training room, one hand holding his crop, which tapped against his leg to help refocus him and clear his mind.

There was a comfortable settee and two chairs by the fireplace as well as a desk and a small table and chairs for a light repast, similar to many parlors.

Sophia waited for him, standing by the desk in a forest green dress.

"Hello." Supremely conscious of ears outside the door, he was at a loss for words.

"My lord—Edward. Come in. Shall I ring for tea?"

"Er—no, thank you. Unless you would like some. Come, sit here with me?" He stepped toward the seating area and paused near a chair, dropping the crop onto the floor so his wife's focus would remain on him.

As she perched on the other chair, he came around and settled across from her.

Get her to talk. "Tell me more about your classes, Sophia."

"We learned about finding common interests with our husbands and rewarding good behavior."

"Hmm. I can be convinced to reward good

behavior, too." He grinned.

Smiling back, she added, "And we learned about our bodies' pleasure points."

"Oh? Do go on." The grin slid into a smirk.

"And this morning, we learned about spanking, some of the implements that might be used, and some of the situations in which husbands might choose to spank us. But..." She looked down at her hands in her lap.

"Yes?" Mayhap he had not been the only person embarrassed by this learning curve, for all her teasing yesterday.

"They said we should discuss that with our husbands."

"And you should. You and I have already covered some of this, as I thought it only fair that you knew what you were choosing by marrying me. But we should and will cover it in more detail. Would you like to do that now, little one?"

"If that is your wish, my lord."

"Such an obedient wife." He quirked a brow, seesawing between being entertained and annoyed at her response.

Since when would that be an annoyance? I should be delighted. But part of him missed the riding partner who challenged him about the Seed Laws and even punishments. He shook his head at his thoughts in irritation.

Right, then. Given the presence of a chaperone, even unseen, he wanted a different approach. "Here is what I wish. I would like to hear more of what you learned about spanking and to give my preferences. But I would prefer today be about pleasure. The satisfaction of your company, the enjoyment of learning more about each other, and mayhap some sensual delight as well. Spanking does not need to be a component of every sexual interaction between us."

"Even if it is pleasurable?" she asked with a grin.

He chuckled. "I would not want you to become bored. Even your favorite food would become tasteless if you ate it every night."

She considered this, head tilted. "I suppose."

"Right, then. Tell me what spanking implements they discussed with you. Wait. Did they have actual objects there to show you?"

"Oh, yes. We passed them around so we might test them on our arms or legs. I have a new appreciation for the nuances of spanking, Edward!"

"So you said you saw Nicholas with a leather strap. And I spanked you with my hand. What else did they show you?"

"Belts, wooden paddles, and"—Sophia shivered—"birch bundles."

A quiver passed through him. He hoped it wasn't perceivable.

"What about a crop?"

"No." Her voice sounded interested, her head cocked.

He picked up his riding crop from beside the chair. "This is my instrument of choice. 'Tis my tool by day and by night, which creates a beautiful symmetry, to my thinking." He passed it to her. "Here, try it as you did the others."

Sophia's mouth dropped open when he first picked it up. Apparently, she had not noticed it in his hand when he first entered the room. She slowly reached to pull it from his proffered hand.

Drawing her skirts halfway up her shin, she sent him a sidelong glance. He suspected the girls had learned flirting as well and suppressed a smile. Flirting wasn't a bad thing in a marriage if 'twas directed at one's spouse.

"Oh." Sophia's voice held wonder as she snapped it a second time a few inches above the knob of her ankle. "I see. Well chosen, my lord."

"Thank you." He took the thin rod with a folded flap of leather at the end. "Now, what did you learn about your body?"

Sophia flushed, looking away, then whipping back to him with a tentative smile. "Nothing you don't already know, actually."

He smiled. *Ah...my wife enjoyed her first sexual experiences. We really should have taken two nights after the wedding before I left her here. If only I'd been able to procure the special license a day or two quicker.*

"Thank you, little one. That is a very generous compliment. But women's bodies are unique, and I've barely started to learn yours. I'd appreciate all the help you can provide."

With the trainer lurking outside the room, Edward was not going to be caught naked and rutting, even on his wife. All it would take is a noise from Sophia to be misheard, and some over-protective woman would come in ready to defend her against him. He did not trust any woman enough to be that vulnerable in this scenario.

But there were other ways, without repeating their wedding night.

"We, er, did something like what you did with your hand."

"You touched yourself? Your breasts? Belly? Your little button?"

Sophia was a bright pink from her chest up to her hairline, but she answered readily enough. "Yes." At his questioning look, she clarified. "All three."

"Mmm." Edward adjusted his suddenly tight breeches and stood, holding out a hand for his wife, where she sat staring up at him. "Come over here."

He directed her to the settee and held her hips as she sat so she was against the corner of one end.

Then he knelt on the floor in front of her.

"It would bring me great pleasure to see what you learned. While you orgasmed on our wedding night and in the carriage, I want to know what other acts we might enjoy together."

His hands lifted her hem, gathering her petticoat with it, and raised it slowly to her lap. The fragrance of her arousal reached his nose and his cock, making both twitch with eagerness. Spy outside the door or not, he wanted to satisfy his wife and mayhap be satisfied by her.

"Now, wife. What was next?"

****

Sophia clutched her skirt for a moment, feeling shy. She had not seen or been seen by her husband in the light of day. Or a lit room.

Edward smiled and squeezed her hand before gently lifting one leg and laying it out along the seat cushion. Clearly amused at her persistent shyness, he shook his head in mock regret. "I was looking forward to learning how to reward you."

Hmm. Well, if he might then use the technique in the future... Not that he really needs help, but there really is no need to be shy, given that.

Sophia took a deep breath. The school had taught courage as well as flirting and that both enhanced sexual play. "If you really desire it..."

She drew her skirts up and smoothed her hand down her belly, finding the slit in her drawers.

Edward's gaze broke from hers to scan down to her puckered nipples. He reached out and tweaked one with a knuckle, and her head dropped back for a moment.

His touch feels so different than mine. I know Beth says 'tis another person's involvement, but I could not do this with anyone else. If only he cared for me.

His gaze followed her hand to the open slit, where her fingers threaded through her curls.

Right, then. Best darned wife. Be bold.

She pushed his firm chest so he would kneel back on his heels.

'Tis to secure a home for Nellie and me. To bind him to us, mayhap enough that he'll give me time with the horse business.

Edward's eyebrow rose as he settled in to enjoy the start of her performance.

Sophia was excited as well as nervous, and her nipples pebbled. Thinking of what he had shown her, the concerns he'd allayed, and how much pleasure he had given her, relaxed her a degree. Even if she appeared slightly awkward, she knew he'd enjoy the show.

And she suspected he wouldn't have patience for long before he stepped in to take charge. That thought sent another frisson of excitement through her, and she quivered as she assumed a pose.

Keeping her leg pressed along the back of the seat cushion, she let her other leg drift apart. Edward's gaze followed her hands, so running her hands out to her knees, she then ran them up her body to cup her breasts before one continued up to her mouth.

Licking her fingers, Sophia then lowered them, not touching her skin, to her lap, where she shyly drew them between her legs. Closing her eyes, she hid her embarrassment, unable to look at Edward in case he was appalled.

A masculine groan shot her eyelids up, however, to find her husband seemingly enthralled. His gaze was intent on her right hand between her legs.

Her other hand stroked her nipple before pinching it. Her wet fingers found her nub, already swollen with need. She rubbed slowly, the sensation causing her to shift against the velvet sofa cushion. Dipping farther down, she gathered more moisture from her opening and returned to rub that hypersensitive bundle of nerves that she had learned brought so much pleasure.

Watching her husband intently, she admired his dark countenance, full lips parted in concentration, eyes fierce and hot flicking between her hand movements. His shoulder rolled, and she looked down to see his hand pressed hard against the bulge in his breeches. It kept pressing and retreating, as though he was trying to maintain some decorum.

Sophia could think of nothing better than to see his enjoyment of her actions. She would also feel much less self-conscious if they shared this experience.

And, yes, I want to see that part of him he's clutching, that was so huge but fit inside me on our wedding night. "My lord. This feels delicious, almost as wonderful as when you touch me. They taught us to understand our bodies and what best excites them, to share with our husbands. Will you not do the same for me?" She nodded to his lap.

Edward's focus on her hands remained unbroken for a beat. Then, without looking away from her, his hands rushed to undo his breeches and draw out his member.

Sophia heard herself moan. Licking her lips, she arched against her touch and her fingers plucked the concerto of her pleasure, faster and faster. She watched Edward's actions, intent on learning his body as well.

He wrapped his hand around his cock and stroked hard up and down, pausing to squeeze the base. His voice guttural, he demanded, "Bend your leg, so I may see more."

As she raised her leg, a wave of shyness hit. Distracted, her hands stilled for a moment. Then, his hand, slick with the wetness seeping from his cock, moving faster and faster, drew her gaze, and her fingers began moving again of their own accord.

His voice still rough, Edward issued his next instruction. "Slide one finger inside."

Someone grunted. She thought it was him but wasn't entirely sure. *Ah, ah.* The explosion built, so much quicker with him directing her and watching.

"Use your thumb on that hard bud."

Her other hand was tugging her nipple, and her finger slid out then in again, her thumb circling the knot of nerves just above.

As her finger slid home, Edward gasped, leaning back and thrusting his hips up and forward. He'd pulled his handkerchief out at some point, and she watched his seed spurt into it, his other hand milking more pulses of liquid from his jerking cock.

Sophia pressed her finger in once, twice, more, then her hips mimicked his as they raised, her stomach contracting and teeth clenching as she moaned her climax.

Edward did not even fasten his breeches. He knelt up and leaned in over her, kissing her first, then praising her. "Little one, that was delightful. You are gorgeous. I could watch you do that every night. Thank you. Thank you." Kissing her neck and shoulder, he then put her fingers in his mouth to suck them clean before wiping them with a clean corner of his handkerchief. He smiled, rewarding her vulnerability and trust.

His actions and words sent a pang through Sophia, not of pleasure but of wistfulness. She let her lids drop over her eyes, hiding her fear.

So magnificent, and kind too. 'Twould be too easy to love him. But no, that path leads to pain.

****

One of the last optional classes offered was an overview to Parliamentary procedure and bills reviewed in past years in which the school's alumnae had taken an interest. Sophia and a few others who read well attended that.

The other final class was on marriage and included a discussion of monthly cycles and pregnancy. It covered the basic facts. Men deposited their seed inside a woman's womb. If she was impregnated, she would miss her monthly cycle and, in nine months, would bear a child. Sophia was surprised not all girls knew this, but then again, most had not helped with their fathers' veterinary practice. The students were encouraged to discuss children with their husbands, both number and timing. And as pregnancies were dangerous to women's health, they discussed precautions.

Edward had not mentioned children either in his betrothal speech or after. But as an earl, he'd need them. She only hoped she'd have a bit of time to know her husband better before children became their focus.

Finally, the last day of the introductory course arrived. Juliet gathered them in her classroom, which Sophia had come to associate with unsettling subjects. *What is left...or rather, what is next?*

"Class, I am so pleased with your growth this past fortnight. You all kept your minds open to learning and overcame any discomfort or embarrassment you felt. I hope you shall continue your quest for learning and exploring beyond the boundaries of society." Juliet paused. "As you do, and as you grow into marriage and a new home, mayhap a new town, remember there shall always be awkwardness and time needed for adaptation. But respect for others will do much to mitigate that."

She paused before continuing, "Some of you are already married or betrothed while others are new to the Ton. As you progress further in your relationships, consider whether it would help you to return here. For that purpose, I shall review some of the advanced classes with you now."

"There is an entire advanced series. However, you can also return for one or two days if you wish to attend a specific class. There are lessons to expand your knowledge of society and for furthering your knowledge of sexual relations with your husband. For instance, if someone marries a duke, stricter societal protocols must be observed, and we can help you with that."

"What about the sex classes?" someone in the back bravely asked.

"Ah yes, I love to wait for that question. It never fails to arise. I am glad to see your curiosity now exceeds your reserve," Juliet responded with a grin. "There are several, but I shall outline a few of the more popular ones. For the first example, which a few of you have already finished—when negotiations fail, or you disobey a direct order from your husband, some men prefer corporal punishment. Boys are publicly birched for bad behavior in grammar school, and some decide to then practice it in marriage, either as the spanker or the spankee. We can help you navigate either scenario. In addition, when done right and for the right person— again, everyone's bodies process pleasure differently— it may even become play. And just as some men enjoy that, some of you may as well. A second option is to learn about role playing as a sexual preference. Sometimes, husbands prefer to join private lessons with their wives. In another class, we review advanced foreplay—stimulation of each other's bodies before engaging in intercourse."

"And last, we have discussed oral sex. Putting your husband's penis, or cock in the vernacular, in your mouth to bring him to orgasm. Or perhaps, hopefully, your husband puts his mouth on your sex to bring you to orgasm. There is an advanced class on that, but for now, you'll remember last week I told you I would share a few tips on pleasing a man sexually?"

The students nodded.

Sophia's Schooling

Juliet grinned. "Here it is, my parting gift to you." Taking a basket with a cloth thrown over it, she started to the first row of students. "How many of you have seen a naked man? You needn't share details. Simply raise your hand."

A third of the class raised their hands, including both Beth and Sophia.

Sophia rolled her eyes at her friend, knowing by then that Beth had seen more than one.

Juliet continued, "For the rest of you, you've likely seen a horse or a hound, no?"

She folded back the cloth and started handing an item to each student, circling the room.

They looked like...*cucumbers*? Sophia frowned, as that was not a usual snack—a whole, unsliced cucumber. *How odd...oh. It seems a decent replica of an aroused cock, although Edward's looked thicker and longer.*

"Keep in mind when a man is aroused, his member will grow. Men differ in size or shape, or even straightness." At this, Juliet held up a curved cucumber. "Sorry, Beth," she added as she handed Beth that vegetable.

Sophia snickered at Beth, despite having a hard time envisioning a curved penis.

"Right, then. Now, ladies, those of you who practiced touching yourself will understand this next part better than the shier ones," she said, smiling. "You should start with gentle touches, by either your fingers or your mouth. As your husband's penis gets harder, closer to the size and consistency of a cucumber, you may have a firmer grip. However," she said, her voice rising on that word to emphasize it, "men almost universally dislike teeth."

Juliet scored the skin of one cucumber with her fingernail. "That is why these are great practice tools. If you do not cover your teeth with your lips enough, a mark or tear in the skin shall result."

Sophia remembered Ros's punishment in the library, kneeling before Nicholas, taking him in her mouth. She'd wondered if they'd learn about that, as she hadn't been able to fathom forming such a question to her new husband. Ros had even licked beyond the shaft. It seemed awkward and so…intimate. *Oh, but a man's fingers and cock inside me aren't intimate?* She snorted.

Juliet was speaking again. "Ladies, enjoy these as something to occupy you the next few days when you are home and missing me. Thank you for being such wonderful students. I hope to see you again!"

Clapping twice and smiling, the instructor made her way around the room again to hug each student.

Sophia pictured Edward's fingers in her, then him kneeling before her, his tongue where her fingers had been the night before, her pleasure cresting with his touch. Him urging her to her knees, telling her to wet his cock as he stood over her. Her tongue flicked over her lips.

How will it feel? Taste? She squirmed in her seat as warmth shot through her, her nipples peaking in her camisole.

Sophia's Schooling

Chapter Fourteen

Edward had warned his bride that the carriage ride to his estate in Peterborough would take a day and a half. He'd made it in one long day before by changing mounts but wanted to give Sophia a softer introduction to his home, in the daylight.

For the first few hours, she pestered him with questions about the estate, the horses, and the training. Finally, he threw up his hands. "You shall see it soon enough and can judge for yourself. 'Tis always been my home, so I am biased, but I think you will find it more than acceptable."

She smiled and subsided.

Given her focus on the business, he asked her more about her experience helping her father. "'Twas frustrating sometimes, as the townspeople sometimes did not find it acceptable for a young unmarried girl to help. I learned to quietly anticipate what would be needed and slip into the barn while my father asked questions of the animal owners."

Like she'd slipped into Ash's stall, spied on her hosts, snuck out to the Vauxhall event, and slunk away from parties. He'd have to keep a close eye on things and keep her occupied indoors.

Since she had summarized her school experience for him on their ride, he asked, "Given what you learned in school, do you have any questions for me?"

Please ask me something sexual. He arched a brow, unsure whether it was at his own begging or to lead her to ask what he wished. Either way, he was ready to explore more of the benefits of being married. He could hardly wait to get to the inn they'd stay at overnight.

"You haven't said—I mean, I know you need heirs—" She stopped, flustered.

Edward cocked his head, confused for a moment. Understanding dawned. "Ah, you mean children? Do I want them?"

She nodded, pink-cheeked.

"I do. I should have stated that earlier. Is there a problem with that?" He frowned. *Bah, he hadn't thought about that. What if she discovered his lack of reading skills before he had an heir?*

"Not at all, my lord. I merely wondered if you wanted them straight away. Otherwise, there are…" She waved a vague hand.

"School covered many subjects, I see. While I hope we have some time before they arrive, I don't think we need to worry about precautions, do you?" *Children would bind her to me. She can't spurn me and run off to Nicholas in London if she has babies to care for.* A jolt of warmth suffused him at the idea of tying her to him further.

"No."

It took him a minute to recall what he'd asked her. She was already moving to a new line of inquiry.

"What is your typical day like, my lord?"

He nearly groaned but answered her. "We keep country hours for the light, not London society hours. So breakfast is early, then I either check in with my steward about correspondence or go straight to the training ring. I usually eat lunch with the training staff so we can trade off working with the horses and eat in shifts. Or use the time to work with cantankerous or sensitive horses. I return to bathe the stable smell off me before dinner."

"And what do you see me doing?" She gulped, appearing a little nervous.

"With all the additional paperwork for Lords, you know that both James, my steward, and I are overwhelmed. That is where I need your help. And I think it is something you enjoy?"

"Yes, I do. I am happy to help you, husband."

"Excellent, then that is how we shall proceed." He nodded with a smile.

At the inn, they ate a light dinner in a private room and strolled the inn yard. After nipping into the stables to check on Nellie and Ash, they retired to their room.

Again, Edward offered to play lady's maid, drawing her to him and helping her out of her gown and stays. He found this uninterrupted time with Sophia felt easier than expected, like their rides. Probably due to the absence of servant interference and the demands of Town reminding him of the risks of exposure in his role.

As she turned toward the bed in only petticoat, drawers, and chemise, her floral scent and enticing figure had him on edge. He had been hard for most of dinner, contemplating their second night sleeping in a bed together and...*benefits*.

Pausing near the candle on the bedside table, Sophia turned to him and drew in an audible breath. Peering up at him through her lashes, she admitted, "I have another question if you please."

"Yes, little one?" The invitation was husky, and he gritted his teeth to find patience.

"You have touched me from head to toe. I have not touched you without clothes. I would like to know how you feel. Please, Edward?" By the end, her voice was almost a whisper.

"Absolutely. In fact, I insist." His fingers moved down his waistcoat buttons, stilling when she laid her hand over his.

"May I?"

He thought he might explode from the idea of her undressing him, unable even to wait for the reality. Gulping, he nodded.

She pushed the waistcoat off his shoulders and pulled his shirt free of his trousers.

He stopped her hands when they moved to the laces of his trousers. "Carefully."

"Yes, sir." Her eager hands slowed. He had removed his boots and placed them in the hall to be shined when they first gained the room. With that obstacle out of the way, she carefully peeled the fabric away from his cock. She knelt to strip off his stockings and smallclothes and sat back on her heels to await further direction.

Pushing aside the thought that first came to mind with her on her knees before him, he held a hand out to help her up. Lying back against the pillows, he spread his arms, palms up and smiled at her. "I am at your disposal, wife."

Sophia put a knee on the bed, but Edward stopped her.

"Uh uh. You are not allowed to wear any clothes for this exploration." *Benefits*.

"Oh." She scrambled back and shed her undergarments, throwing them on the pile of his clothing. Climbing back on the bed, she knelt next to him, hesitating as if unsure where to begin.

Edward raised his hand to cup a breast.

That seemed to spur her into action. She swatted his hand away, saying, "No, my turn—" before gasping and looking to him with a hint of nerves.

"Right, then. I was merely trying to provide inspiration." He laced his hands behind his head, his arm muscles bulging, unintentionally drawing her gaze.

She smoothed fingertips from his elbow toward his chest.

He twitched. "Mayhap a firmer touch if you please, Sophia? I admit to being ticklish."

"Hmm." She looked intrigued but did as he asked, her hand then following the planes of his chest and stomach to his hip. She leaned over him to try to reach his other side.

Edward touched her closest leg. "May I?"

Tilting her head, she nodded.

He hauled it over him so she was astride his thighs.

She leaned in, running both hands over him.

He breathed in citrus and flowers, mixed with her arousal. His eyes nearly rolled back in his head. Under his head, his laced fingers tightened in an effort not to grab her hips and thrust up into her.

She grazed his nipples, pinching them as he had hers, her fingernails adding an exquisite point of pain.

His hips shoved upward an inch, and he grunted. Every muscle tensed to refrain from flipping them and driving into her over and over until they both exploded.

"My lord, I beg your pardon. Did I hurt you?" She

had drawn her hands back, sitting up on his legs.

He felt her wet heat against him and wanted to writhe. He gritted out, "No, Sophia. I liked it, as you do."

His cock added its thoughts, pulsing up.

She looked down, shocked.

"It does that when I feel a spike of pleasure. Would you like to touch it?" *Touch it!* Criminy, he was begging again. At least it was silent—she couldn't hear his vulnerability.

Before his thoughts derailed him, Sophia's fingers curled tentatively around his shaft, bringing his pleasure back into sharp focus.

She grasped the base of his cock, pulling it up away from his body, her expression rapt. Her tongue came out to lick her lips, and he pulsed in her hand again, making her jump, then grin with pride.

"Now slide your hand up until your thumb goes over the ridge and is at the tip, then slide it back down. Like what I did at your school." His grin slid away as she followed his instructions, and his neck arched back as lightning shot up his spine from her stroke.

She repeated the movement. The moisture leaking from the slit allowed her hand to glide easily up and down. Exploring, she lingered at the round helmeted head, circling it, then squeezed the base when her hand met his groin. She glanced up to watch his expressions as she changed her caress. "What else should I do?"

"Give me your other hand." He guided her to his sac, curling her fingers around it.

She weighed it in her palm, watching as it shifted. Her hand on his cock slowed.

He tapped one wrist. "Gentle here." The other, on

his shaft. "Firm here."

"Oh, hmm. And you went faster." She sped up her pull and push.

"Yesss, that. Perfect, little one," he gasped out, throwing his head back.

But he did not want to spill in her hand. Unable to wait a moment longer, his hands shot out from behind his head. Grabbing her waist, he lifted them both and twisted, flipping her under him.

Sophia gasped, a look of surprise trickling into a smile of satisfaction. "You like my touch, husband."

"Yes. And you'll like this touch." He lined himself up at her wet warmth and thrust halfway inside. Back, and then he shoved all the way in.

"Mmm. Yes, I love this touch." Her eyes were half-shut as she wiggled once beneath him.

One arm held his weight off her. The other skimmed down, brushing her nipple, skimming her belly then hip before curling around a feminine thigh. Lifting it up to almost his shoulder, he thrust again.

Her eyes widened, her mouth dropping open.

He smirked and thrust. And kept thrusting.

Sophia's hips lifted to his in counterpoint.

The School of Enlightenment did not deserve all the credit for these benefits. This was Sophia being a perfect fit for him. Not physically, although there was that. But her open mind to let him show her the many paths to pleasure, her desire to explore him, and her smart brain she was willing to use to help him with his Parliamentary duties.

No! I cannot let down my guard, must not care too much for her. Then spending the rest of my days with someone who looks at me with disdain would be more than I can bear. And what if my child cannot read, too?

He frowned at that sudden thought and thrust harder, faster.

His wife, thankfully unaware of his thoughts, moaned in pleasure and thrust back against him. Her moan escalated through clenched teeth.

"Oh, oh, ooohh." Her channel clenched around him, her fingers digging into his biceps where she clutched him.

His fears at the top of his mind, Edward scrabbled backward onto his knees, yanking himself out of her, and fisting his cock. His hand pumped only twice before his seed spurted onto her belly, her legs, and his hand and thighs.

Sophia lay in ignorant bliss of his turmoil, staring up at him with a hazy smile. Looking down, she said, "'Tis much messier than when you pleasure me with your hand." She sent him an arch look.

He threw himself down beside her on his back with a bark of surprised laughter. "Imp." He rolled his head to look at her. "For that, you may fetch a damp cloth from the washstand and clean us."

As she rose to do that, she trailed a finger through the evidence of his orgasm. "We learned that sometimes we might also taste it." She raised her finger to her mouth. "Hmm. Oh, salty."

Edward groaned, and his cock jumped a little at her actions, although he would have sworn a minute ago that he was sated for the night. *Good to know she is open to other ways to avoid a child without me being overt. I owe Nick some good Scotch for that school idea.*

She returned with the cloth and wiped the liquid

from him. Then she crawled into the bed and curled next to him as though seeking his warmth.

He knew he needed to think more about children or preventing them. The wedding night already created the possibility of a child, but he was sated and sleepy. He let go of the day, his worries along with the discoveries they had made. Wrapping his arm around her, he sank into a dreamless slumber for the first time since he had learned of Charles's death.

****

They arrived at Peterborough mid-afternoon. Sophia bit her lip when Edward mentioned tea, reminding herself of the need for patience. She was almost levitating off the seat in her excitement to see the stables and training yards, not to mention checking on Nellie. Both would have to wait, as the staff had already assembled to greet them.

After meeting the members of the household, she turned to Edward. "May we check on Nellie, my lord?"

He tucked her hand into the crook of his elbow and steered her back down the front steps toward the side of the house.

"Come along, then. You know any other woman would have wished to go through each room in the house, unpack her bags, and rest, do you not?" he asked as they strolled toward the stables.

"I beg your pardon, my lord. We can return and do a formal tour." Sophia stopped walking, resolved to do her best to act like a wife, whatever that meant, starting with meeting Edward's expectations.

"No, let us begin as we shall go on. I spend most of my time here, and we have spoken so much about my work, I am flattered you wish to see it. The staff will not mind waiting, as long as we do not delay dinner. They shall have done something special to impress you," he warned.

The two large stables and a glimpse of a training yard lay ahead, but much of it wasn't visible past the hedge. The stables faced away from the road, and the training yard stretched out beyond them. Pastures flanked the buildings on both sides, with large sections fenced to give the animals grass to eat and space to roam in mild weather. Several had horses in them, seemingly grouped by age, if she had to guess based on size.

Bobby popped out of the stables and grinned when he spied her. Waving, he ran over. Edward looked at him sharply, and he skidded to a halt and tugged his forelock, bobbing his head to them both. "Felicitations, my lady, and welcome home, my lord."

"Oh, Bobby, please, 'tis me. Call me Sophia, as you have. Anyone I trust with Nellie's care, I trust with my first name," she retorted, smiling.

Bobby ignored that request, sliding a glance at her husband. But grinning, he gave her what she was waiting for. "Nellie was a complete lady the whole trip. She enjoyed the trip as much as I did riding her. We stopped for water and a bit of sweet grass and flowers a few times and came in this morning. She's been resting since, looking for you, no doubt."

Knowing the mare would not fully settle until she saw her mistress, Sophia asked where to find her and made her way to the stall. Even as her eyes adjusted to the dimness of the stables, she heard the telltale whicker.

"Hello, girl, how was your trip?" she murmured

into the horse's nose as she hugged her.

Nellie snuffled at her, looking for treats, and Sophia laughed. "No, sorry, not right now, my girl. But get accustomed to this place. We shall be living here. I hope you like it." Then, under her breath, "I hope I like it…"

After giving her another minute to check out Nellie's accommodations, Edward strolled over to begin her tour of the training endeavors. Before they left, Edward asked Bobby, "Did you go through Nellie's routine with Russell?" At the boy's nod, he added, "And did he cover the rules of the stables with you?"

"Yes, sir." Bobby gave a deferential nod.

"Excellent. Sophia, you need to know these, too. All equine care must be approved by the stablemaster or directed by him. He knows Nellie's routine, so she'll receive the food and care you expect. Any changes for her or any of the horses require his involvement."

Sophia chafed at the restriction, given her veterinary knowledge, but she was determined to make the best of this marriage and not annoy her new husband.

Outside, a lean man nearly as tall as Edward, in a dusty shirt and breeches, circled the oval training area with a bay on a long lead. The horse kept tossing its head, but the man's firm grip stayed steady, and the whip in his other hand trailed in the dust.

"That is our stablemaster, Stephen Russell." Edward nodded toward the ring. "He is midway through training Barkley, one of our yearlings. Barkley accepts the bridle now, and we have started working with the saddle and the carriage shafts."

"Did you help break him to bridle?" Sophia asked.

"No, they were just starting with him as I left for Town. He comes from excellent stock so we did not expect any problems, nor were there based on Russell's letter while I was away."

They walked along the fenced ring. The land appeared to have been built up to make it flat enough for the training ring and buildings. At the end of the oval, the earth dropped away, and they looked out over rolling hills with pasture fences creating rectangular frames for them.

Edward pointed to the far right. "Our yearling group. Only a half dozen now. As I told you, we only started that program a few years ago." Pivoting left, he indicated the next group. "Those are the more mature horses. They were our first test group and are ready for sale, but until then, we must keep them accustomed to both the carts and the saddle. The rest," he said, nodding to the larger group even further left, "are the Thoroughbreds we've bred for the last hundred years. Beyond the pastures are various riding paths around the grounds and toward the village."

Sophia loved it already. She was eager to see more of the training process.

****

Edward turned them toward the house. "Right, then. I need tea, mayhap some brandy," he commented. "Then I shall show you the house."

As they turned back, Russell approached, having handed off Barkley to a stable hand.

Edward introduced them, noting, "Russell, Sophia likes to take part in Nellie's care, and Bobby is familiar with their preferences, as you know. I also informed her of the rules. You are in charge of all matters regarding the stables and horses."

Sophia nodded to the stablemaster. "Lovely to meet you, Mr. Russell."

They entered through the kitchen, nodding to the staff. Sophia guessed from their lack of surprise that Edward came and went this way often. He had said that he spent most of his days working with the horses. She wondered how much that would change now he was the earl. While they had discussed it during their morning rides in Town, she suspected Edward did not know what to expect either, so they would learn together.

"Tea in my study, please, Mrs. Barton," Edward said.

The housekeeper smiled. "I have the kettle already on, my lord."

"Good woman." He smiled as they left the kitchen to enter the main hall of the house. "Conservatory, music room, and," he paused at the third door on the left. "My study—or the library, as we don't have a separate library. My parents always ended up here after dinner while my mother was alive. I guess it was more a shared space then. My brother and his wife spent most of their time in Town."

The room pleasantly surprised Sophia. Most libraries and men's studies had dark paneling and floor to ceiling books. She could see why Edward's parents were so comfortable here together.

The walls had neutral silvery-blue coverings that offset the dark wood bookshelves and furniture frames beautifully. The bookshelves around the room had spaces between them, so the lighter-colored walls provided a break to the eye. Chairs and a settee clustered to one side of the massive fireplace were upholstered in a deep sapphire blue, and the jewel-toned Persian rug was lush beneath her feet and covered almost every inch of floor. On the far side, an enormous desk sat diagonal to the room to catch both the warmth of the fireplace and the light of the windows. The top of the desk was mostly clear, with a few ledgers and correspondence in a pile on one end. In the center was an inkwell and a beautiful faceted amethyst wax seal.

Edward turned toward the sitting area. Waiting for her to sit, he hovered near one of the wing chairs as a servant rolled in the tea tray. As Sophia poured, he disappeared behind her and returned with a snifter of brandy, setting it down to accept a cup of tea first.

"Let me show you around, then we can change for dinner. I shall arrange for a bath for us."

"May I explore this room a little first, my lord?"

"Certainly." Edward stood as she did. Having finished his tea quickly, he cradled his brandy in one large hand as he followed her circuit of the room.

"Who are the people in the paintings?"

"The large one over the fireplace is my great-grandmother." The elegant woman was almost life-sized in an ivory gown. "Others are various ancestors and relatives. We keep the more formal portraits of the earls in the front hall, upstairs hall, and drawing room, for public consumption. This was my grandfather's and father's favorite, so they hung it here."

Items on a shelf behind the desk captured Sophia's interest. A collection of what she assumed were desk seals with elaborate and unique handles was displayed there. Most desk seals she had seen had a wider top to fit in a man's palm, narrowing at the base where their fingers would grasp. These shapes were unique. Some were cylindrical, some had carvings in them, and a couple curved in a shallow arch almost like a feather. Two were teardrop shaped, polished to a deep shine, narrowing again just above the seal itself, one of them larger than the other. The materials varied widely as well. While the desktop amethyst was faceted, most on the shelf were made of highly polished materials, although she was not sure what. One might have been ivory.

"What is this?" she asked, reaching one finger toward the narrow teardrop one. It was in a smooth wood-like material, if wood grains were multi-colored.

"Ah, so you like my wax seal collection, hmm?" Edward asked with a huge grin. "That one I call my day-to-day seal. 'Tis striated agate. Feel its smoothness."

She glided her fingers up and down. Turning to agree with him, she found his eyes hot and focused on her hands.

"We can return and examine them and the room more after dinner."

Dropping her hands, she came forward to take his offered arm and continue the tour.

Upstairs, the family rooms were in the west wing, and guest rooms in the east wing, with the staircase rising from the main hall on the ground floor to the perpendicular main hall on the second floor that ran between the wings. Halls in each wing completed the "H" pattern, with narrower staircases at the back of each wing to the kitchen below and the servants' quarters above.

The house she'd grown up in had been smaller. But

Sophia did not worry about managing an estate this size, especially with a steward, a housekeeper, and servants. No, her concerns centered around the man at her side. Had she found someone who would value her equine knowledge as her father had? Or would she have to sneak around for the rest of her life? Or worse, live with less time helping animals?

She supposed children would eventually take her time up. Thinking back on her lessons, she recalled the coaching for patience. *Win his support and trust first. Then negotiate from a position of strength.* There was much to like about Edward, after all, including his love of horses. And she could prove her merit through helping him with secretarial matters.

The master's suite and mistress's suite had a similar layout to the London townhouse, although they were on a grander scale. Colorings of the furnishings were also similar to Edward's townhouse. She found them warm and comfortable and reassuringly familiar at this point with everything else being so new. The grandeur of the house and the amount of land belonging to her husband were intimidating. These rooms felt safe, like a haven. The rest she would grow to love over time.

Sophia's Schooling

Chapter Fifteen

After helping her maid unpack, Sophia realized it was time to dress for dinner.

There was a permanent bathtub in a bathing chamber between the two suites, and servants were filling it with hot water. Eagerly anticipating a bath, she stripped out of her clothes and donned a dressing gown.

Coming to an abrupt halt inside the door, she gaped at her naked husband in the bath.

"No, don't leave. This is part of your wifely responsibilities," Edward said as she turned to flee. "It is good you changed. I would not want you to get your dress wet."

Sophia drew closer, curious about the opportunity to study him—his muscle-padded shoulders and chest, the trail of dark hair from his chest down to his groin. That cock, even now standing upright.

"This is how we shall bathe, my dear. I shall take first bath, only because I prefer not to smell of that lavender foam you put in yours." At her stare, he added mildly, "I checked with Jane. I have not been spying on your baths. You shall wash me, then I'll get out and dry off and refresh the water and help you with your bath…if you do well enough at helping with mine."

She looked at him, uncertain. This was not something she had learned, but she was willing to try. Only she wasn't sure where to begin.

"Come, take the cloth and soap off the stool and sit, and I shall guide you. We are married. There is no reason to feel shy. Did you not tell me your school taught you that?" he asked gently.

That is all true. And I like touching him. "But what will the servants say?"

Edward snorted. "They know better than to discuss either of our bathing habits, and frankly, I hope they have better things to talk about. I try to give them personal time, unlike some of my peers."

Slowly, she turned, dipping the cloth and soap as she did so before raising them. "Shall I wash your hair, my lord?"

"Yes, please, top to bottom."

She worked in silence, concentrating on not getting soap in his eyes and swinging back and forth between shyness and pleasure at the textures of his soft hair and firm, furred body. As she slid the cloth down his upper body, she felt the play of thick muscles, the same as when she curried Nellie and smoothed her hand after the brush. Without thinking, her hands followed the same motion, continuing down his flanks and along the length of his legs.

She parted her lips in concentration, her gaze followed her hands, and she shifted to kneel by the tub to reach all of him. Her tongue darted out to lick her lips as her hand pressed his bulky thigh muscles, built from years of horse riding and training. She wrapped her fingers around his leg and squeezed, testing the firmness, her breaths now little pants from arousal.

He is so sleek and powerful, like a stallion. I should like to run my hands and eyes over his naked form without water again soon. Mayhap my lips. Her nipples tightened and beaded. Was there time for an intimate interlude before dinner? She was not quite comfortable enough yet to initiate such a request, though, and wondered if it was even acceptable to do so.

After finishing both legs, she leaned back, peering up at him. Lips wet, she swallowed and made to hand him back the cloth. While she wanted to touch him everywhere, she craved his direction to know how to best arouse him.

"You missed some, Sophia," his voice was matter-of-fact. He leaned back and spread his arms along the rim of the tub, his erection bobbing in the water between his bent legs.

She reached down with the cloth. "For this, use your hand, not the cloth."

"Oh." She withdrew and wrung out the cloth before draping it at the end of the tub. Reaching forward again with a soapy hand, she placed the other on his arm and leaned in.

Edward's eyes fluttered closed, and she heard a soft groan.

"Yes, like that," he huffed as her fingers fondled his testicles.

She slid her hand along the length of his cock as she had at the inn.

His spine arched, and she paused.

"Make sure 'tis clean," he rasped.

She glanced at him, surprised at the gravel in his voice. His eyes remained closed, his head thrown back. She admired the arch of his throat and the strength of his jaw. *Mine. I am so glad I can excite him.*

Several strokes later, he stayed her hand. "Thank

you, Sophia, that was a lovely first bath. Let me dry off a bit and refresh the water for you."

As he stood, she retreated onto the stool, feeling the cool air against her wet front. Edward stared as she plucked at her dressing gown, which had dampened to the point of transparency. Her nipples were dark shadowy points against the fabric, the lightness of her globes a contrast. She cupped her hands around them to warm herself.

Stepping out to fetch buckets of water left by the fire, he drew out water from the tub and added the hotter ones for her, along with her bath oil.

"Your turn, little one." He turned to her, holding out his hands for her robe.

A flash of happiness at the repeated endearment brightened her gaze. She shrugged out of the gown, handing it to him then scrambling into the water without waiting for help.

He dipped the cloth and soap and leaned in, starting down her front.

Already stimulated from touching him, she gasped and arched forward as his hands smoothed from her neck down to her breasts.

The contrast of the slick soap and his palm on one side and the cloth's abrasion on the other made her eyes want to cross with pleasure.

"Hmm, do you prefer the cloth or my hand?" he asked.

"I…I…I'm not sure, my lord," she squirmed. *Both! More.*

But shyness and the novelty of this intimacy prevented her from asking for anything. No matter what confidence the School of Enlightenment had instilled, it was still very different with one's new husband in a brightly lit bathing chamber. But she'd learn.

"Right, then. Let's try the other way around then, shall we?" He switched the cloth to his other hand and reapplied both hands to her nipples. Drawing them out, he tugged gently as her body followed. Then he soothed them before lowering his hands to cup her breasts as she had earlier. "Now, do you prefer the cloth or my hand?"

"Oh, I like both, sir. I love your hands, but the cloth adds a bit of abrasion that makes me shiver."

His eyes gleamed, clearly liking that answer.

Oh good. He must enjoy the firmer touch, too. A shiver of heat ran through her, and she unconsciously pressed her breasts further into his hands. *'Tis sweet of him to ask. From Juliet's comments, it seems many husbands do not. But I trust him with my pleasure already.* She renewed her vow. *I will be the best wife ever.*

His hands stroked over her shoulders and back, down her arms, then skipped to her toes to work back up toward her center.

She had to lean back when he pulled her legs forward and outward, spreading her for his view. As his hands circled ever higher on her outer legs then inner thighs, she instinctively drove her hips forward, mutely begging him to hurry to touch her most sensitive places.

Watching his face, she saw him smile at her hip movement, relieved it hadn't been too forward.

Finally, his hands met at her lower curls. Parting her with one hand, he smoothed his other over her inner folds, pressing with his middle finger against her bundle of nerves and pausing there to press and release.

Her hips mimicked his motion, pushing forward to meet his finger each time.

He stopped, and she moaned.

"Ah, but you are quite clean now here." He slipped his finger out and down to swiftly circle her rear hole. "And here, now, too." He pressed once, without penetrating but leaving his finger at her entrance.

Sophia gasped, clamping her legs closed around his arms. "My lord!"

"What did I tell you about shyness, Sophia?"

"But…but—"

"Open. I shall touch you everywhere. I shall kiss you everywhere. And I shall come inside you everywhere." His finger flexed against her, and her rear muscles, firm from riding, clenched.

"What?" she squealed.

"Did they not teach you about that in school? Ah well, no matter. I shall teach you. We shan't rush it, but it *shall* happen, Sophia." He prodded a thigh outward with one elbow. "Now open up, let me finish, and we shall go to dinner."

Finish? Well, for the delicious feelings like in the carriage yesterday, mayhap I can handle him touching me there. Her legs dropped open a few inches.

His finger swirled quickly around, followed by the cloth rubbing first her curls and the nub still poking out, then down to brush at her bottom. Then he was gone.

"But, my lord…" She wasn't sure how to word her question or if it was indeed a request.

Edward seemed to understand her reaction. "Oh no, little one. Finishing meant touching you where I desired and getting you clean and ready for dinner." He grinned. "You do not get orgasms when you want them.

You receive them when I give them to you."

****

Edward's mind had raced as they toured the house. When he had reconciled himself to marriage, he had focused on the most important aspect—determining how to hide his difficulty reading. He also decided to get his own benefits out of the marriage but had not spent time considering how.

The wedding night, school visit, and trip had sharpened his focus on those benefits. He had new hope he could push for perks sooner than he might with an innocent without the benefit of training.

And spying. He smirked at the memory.

Getting her comfortable with his nudity and her own—or mayhap seeing her comfort level, given the school—was a good start, and pre-dinner baths would bring them together each evening. Her obvious enjoyment of bathing him aroused him unbearably, as did her final cleaning caresses of his cock. But anticipation was key in foreplay, and he wanted to reinforce his control in their marriage, including her access to orgasms.

Mayhap that will occupy her focus, so she does not question our separation during the day. I need her handling correspondence rather than pestering me for time with the horses as I suspect she wants. Hmm...a reward and punishment system. Yes. This will be perfect.

A tiny part of him admitted that Sophia might be what made the arrangement perfect, but he ignored it, focusing on the physical. Children would be another good way to keep her in the house. And as he needed heirs, he was going to risk his affliction being hereditary and not worry about prevention…another benefit.

Given her openness to all aspects of sex so far, he'd even pressed her bottom hole, testing the edges of her comfort. Pleased with how quickly she acquiesced, he barely refrained from throwing her on the bed for a quick toss before dinner. He shook his head and tried to keep his goal of quid pro quo in mind.

Sophia squirmed through the first dinner course, stilling when Edward reprimanded her with a look.

By dessert, she was worked up into such a state that Edward commented. "My dear, 'tis obvious you have concerns, and as I said, I want us both to be open with each other. About the bath mayhap?"

"Er…do your climaxes feel like mine?" she asked.

Edward laughed. "I suspect so, but I really have no way of knowing, do I?" He smiled. "The pleasure builds and builds, almost like pressure, and it keeps climbing until it explodes. Does that sound about right?"

She nodded, blushing. "Thank you. So, if it feels that good, why did you not wish to finish earlier?"

This girl. She is not only eager but inquisitive. If I must have a wife, Sophia will… He remembered his sullen words to her at their betrothal. *Suit better than I could have hoped,* he amended with a wince. He'd regretted those words almost as soon as he'd said them. And the more he learned about his petite wife, the more potential he saw. But his fear of his secret being discovered ratcheted higher the more he liked the way the future looked.

Returning to the present, he answered her question. "You've only had a few orgasms to date. Orgasms come in many forms, with different ways to get there and even varying intensities. I want to explore all of those with you, my dear. Not all at once, of course, but as we move forward. One way to increase the intensity is to build anticipation. That is what I was doing earlier. I wished you to contemplate touching me, and me touching you, throughout dinner. Obviously, that did not work as I had intended this time, but 'twas my intent."

She absorbed this for a moment. "Oh. I am certainly thinking about touching, or the lack thereof. I suppose without understanding the goal of anticipation, it felt frustrating. I beg your pardon, Edward."

"There is naught to be sorry for, little one. Hopefully it will work better next time," he replied with a quick grin. "However, since we're on the subject, shall we build some more excitement?" He rose, holding his hand out to her.

"Oh, aye, my lord." She bit her lip and put her hand in his. "Where are we going?"

"Let's return to the study, shall we?" He tucked her hand in his arm and strolled them across the hall. Moving to the set of decanters, he offered, "Sherry or brandy?"

"Nothing, thank you, my lord. Wine with dinner was enough, mayhap a spot of tea later." She wandered along the bookcases, eyeing the offerings. He wondered if her tastes in reading ran similarly to his and she'd find the books on horse training engaging. Most books she'd find on the first several shelves were around the business of the estate. That was the only subject he'd suffer through trying to read.

Brandy in hand, he turned to where she had paused,

watching him. Realizing this was really their first night together at home as man and wife, he worried about how to proceed. He wished to set the tone for evenings to come but also wanted to be solicitous of her comfort.

"Would you care to read for a bit, then? Or talk by the fire? Or we may stroll the gallery," he offered.

"Whatever pleases you, my lord."

He decided to plow ahead. *Benefits.* He smirked at his pretty partner. "Right, then. If 'tis what pleases me, we shall move directly to the entertainment portion of the evening."

After a last sip of brandy, he placed the snifter on the desk and opened the cabinet beneath the seal collection, displaying a collection of hunting whips and crops, as well as a few horse brushes and combs.

"Why keep those in your study, rather than the stables?" She tilted her head in curiosity.

"These are for indoor use only. Remember what we talked about at the school?" He selected two crops, one with a very narrow leather strip on the end, the second with a tab the width of his thumb.

Sophia straightened a fraction, her unblinking gaze on the crops.

Edward came around the desk and put his hand to her lower back, guiding her to stand behind the settee.

"See the difference in the width of the leather?" He showed them in one hand.

"Yes," she replied, licking her lips.

I bet she's already wet. I'm glad. I want her to be happy in this marriage. He tried to cover his surprise at his sudden thought. "These shall feel quite different against your skin, pet."

"This is meant for pleasure, not punishment, so if

'tis not enjoyable, tell me, and I shall try something different. But I shall endeavor to ensure your enjoyment."

Sophia watched, wide-eyed, as he reached over the back to lay them on the sofa seat. Turning her to face the sofa, he directed her, "Widen your stance, my dear, and bend at the waist. Put your hands on the seat cushion. Can you reach comfortably?"

He helped her into position and as she bent, she nodded.

He squatted behind her and put his hands on her ankles. Sliding his hands up her legs, he carried her dress and petticoat on his forearms as he straightened, then flipped her dress over her back. He fondled the cotton-clad globes of her rear. "Hmm. We need another rule. I did not have time to discuss this with you before dinner. No pantaloons in the house. I am happy to keep the house as warm as possible for you to be comfortable, but I desire access to your body at all times."

Sophia was shocked. "I beg your pardon. That is—is—"

Edward chuckled. "Impolite? Scandalous?" He suspected she was searching for excuses. "If you wear them again, I shall punish you. After which, I shall remove them from the house. Riding Nellie in the winter might be chilly without drawers."

She gasped and shifted as though to stand and argue with him.

He kept a hand on her lower back to hold her in place and drew the offending garment off her, helping her step out of it.

Smoothing his hands back up her legs, skin to skin,

he rose and focused on rubbing her hindquarters for a few moments. She remained stiff, and he patted her hip. "Relax, little one."

"What if someone comes in?"

"No one will. All the staff here are discreet. The spankings in London hurt, but I know you enjoyed them, too. Now relax." He slapped her flank a little harder to bring her back to the present.

Her breath let out with a whoosh, and her back dropped a fraction as she deflated.

He leaned over her to grab the crop with the broader end, and she tensed again.

"Try not to tense, little one. Relaxing your muscles makes it hurt less." He rubbed her bottom again, and her muscles untensed. Immediately, as his hand slid to one hip, he swung, and the crop left a small red square on the opposite cheek.

She jumped but relaxed into the pose again docilely.

He swung faster, enjoying the sharp smacking sounds, the little rectangular red marks on her bottom, and her quiet gasps for breath. He watched her closely, wanting to ensure this was pleasurable for her as well as him. Her hips wiggled, then—*ahh, there 'tis*—her stance widened. *Criminy, who knew a wife would offer this—and like it? Could I but let down my guard, this might be the perfect partnership...*

Sophia's Schooling

Chapter Sixteen

Sophia was ready to beg. Edward's touch in the bath had begun a fire in her belly that had smoldered through dinner. Watching his muscles shift under his clothing and along his jaw reminded her of the feel of them naked under her hand in the bath, and she'd eaten little in her distraction.

She had not dared an after-dinner drink, wanting to keep her wits about her and not beg right there and then. But his crop had a stronger effect than any drink.

Squirming her hips, she widened her stance and arched her back, panting, no longer caring about the threat of servants or her bare bottom in the air. She needed more. More of the crop, his touch on her bottom, his fingers on her center. Ideally, his cock. Soon.

"You're doing so well. Exquisite," he murmured as his hand passed over her warm flesh again.

The crop came harder now, and she gasped once, but the sting faded quickly each time, becoming a spear of warmth that spread from her bottom directly to her core, swelling her breasts and the lips of her womanhood further. Her heart pounded, her breaths harsh in her ears. Every inhale chafed the hard tips of her hyper-sensitive breasts against her chemise, every smack of the crop doubling the effect. Her desire leaked out onto her inner thighs. She debated touching herself,

231

but that might earn her harder spanks.

Then he solved that dilemma, running a hand over her again before skimming it between her legs to where she was wet and aching. Sliding his fingers between her lips, he ducked one into her moisture then circled her hard nub. She went up on tiptoes, pushing her backside toward him again.

"Ah, so much more than I dared hope for, the first time. You obviously enjoyed that. Let's see what you think of the other one."

Gads, I had forgotten there was a second one. She bit her lip, contemplating begging again but wanting to understand his comment about anticipation and different orgasms.

Switching the crops, he didn't pause and was not as gentle as with the first. The narrower strip of leather created more of a burn, and it took longer to fade. He spanked over the mounds of her rear and down to her upper thighs.

With the lingering heat, she felt several stings at once. The urgency in her core built along with the simmer on her bottom.

Her nether cheeks heated further, and her nub pulsed, craving his touch again. Her breasts hung heavier, fuller, and her belly tightened with each impact. She *needed* his fingers or his cock back at her entrance and on her pleasure spot.

"Please, please," she whispered, indeed begging aloud.

He paused. "What do you want, Sophia?"

"Please, my lord," was all she could manage. She may have learned to advocate for her desires, but no one had warned her how hard it would be to form thoughts, never mind words, in the heat of the moment.

"You'll need to be more specific."

"Touch me," she begged.

"Here?" His hand came to rest on her hot bottom.

"Lower."

The hand slid between her cheeks to her rear hole. "Here?"

"Uh, lower, please. My lord, where you touched me in the carriage. *Please*," she drew out her plea, thrusting her bottom at him.

"Well, that was prettily done, although you shall need to learn to use the words as I do, Sophia." His hand slid lower, wetting his finger and circling her sensitive flesh.

She raised on her toes again at the sensation, panting, her hips pistoning back and forward. "Uh, uh…"

"Stay still." His fingers withdrew, and a sharp swat on her sore bottom had her planting her feet again.

"Now, little one, 'tis time for what I desire." Edward came around the settee, keeping one hand on her back so she knew he was near. "Push up with your hands. Lift your head." He slid his hand up her back and closed his fist around her hair piled on her head.

Her head raised, and she found herself face to face with his other hand opening his breeches and lifting out his cock.

"Wet it nicely with your lips and tongue."

Through a fog of desire, Sophia dimly understood he was asking her to suck him. Sophia's shoulders stiffened in anxiety as she tried to recall the techniques she had worked on with the cucumber. She leaned forward, licking her lips, worried about how to get her mouth around his girth.

Edward tightened his grip on her hair and rumbled, "Relax, Sophia. I shall tell you if I wish you to do something other than what you're doing."

As her mouth dropped open, he leaned forward, putting one knee next to her hand on the seat cushions so she needn't strain forward. Resting his cockhead on her bottom lip, he pressed forward. She sucked him in, and her tongue darted around the ridge at the head, making him groan.

"So good, sweetheart," he murmured as he watched her.

She licked the length of him, swirling around to wet all sides. Then dragging her tongue up, she found her head held by his fist in her hair as he slid forward until he hit the back of her throat. Her eyes watered, but she remembered the vegetables from class. Keeping her teeth sheathed as best she could, she swallowed against him.

He groaned, and his cock pulsed in her mouth.

Ah, he likes that. I can do this. I can submit to his needs and ensure security and a good home for Nellie and me. But goodness, if I like everything he does as much as I liked the crops, he'll have me begging all the time. Then all thoughts flew away as he moved.

She focused on sucking, even as he withdrew. Her cheeks hollowed, and her tongue flicked the underside of him as he retreated. He surged again, pressing forward toward her almost before she drew a breath.

Again, she relaxed her throat as she tightened her lips, and her nose ended up buried in the dark curls at the base of his length. His hands loosened, and her lips dragged up him. Able to breathe again, her nose assimilated his unique scent of leather, outdoors, and something uniquely him.

A waft of brandy was added as he leaned forward to watch and exhaled roughly. "I'll tell you when you may stop."

Sophia relaxed into his guidance. Her skin felt hot, her chemise chafing the hard points of her breasts. Her bottom blazed against the coolness of the room, and a pulse beat between her legs.

Echoes of watching Ros and Nicholas, the School of Enlightenment, and her wedding night ran through her thoughts. This was so far beyond any of those experiences she wanted to rip her clothes from her body for relief. If her mouth was not busy, she'd be pleading with him nonstop. Through her haze of pleasure, she realized part of why she was more excited was his grip on her, his commands. She was not in control, nor did she want to be. His comments about anticipation were dust in the fire of his grip on her head. She trusted this man to see to her pleasure. More than that, to take care of her.

But I cannot fall in love. I can't bear to become attached to another person and have them send me away or leave me. I must concentrate on what gives him pleasure more than what I want.

Refocusing, ignoring her body's cravings for her own release, she followed his hands' push and pull as they sped up and worked to satisfy him. His hand directing her head was the same as she had seen Nicholas do to Ros, and she relaxed into it, confident he would lead her to his liking.

Edward gasped and withdrew. "I wish to come inside your sweet channel, not your mouth."

"Yes," she panted.

He smiled as he circled back around her, releasing her hair.

One of his hands went to her hip, and the other came between them, then his cock nudged against her opening.

"Hold on," he gritted out.

She threw a hand out to the settee arm as he slammed into her.

"Aaaahhh!" she wailed at the sudden impalement.

He froze. "Sophia? Did I hurt you?" he growled.

"No, my lord, no. It was simply…" She groped for the word through the fog of craving. "…intense."

He sighed with relief. "That was merely the start," he gritted through clenched teeth before pulling out, slapping her reddened bottom hard, then shoving in again.

"Ah, ah," she panted. Her inner muscles twitched around him in pleasure every time he drove into her, building in force with each surge. He was hitting a place inside that made her see spots. She shuddered in ecstasy as he drove and drove, afraid of where or even if it would end.

His hips plunged faster, hand alternating cheeks for spanking as he retreated each time.

Sophia's thoughts fuzzed, her body acting of its own accord, shoving back against him. Her blood throbbed through her veins, eddying from her swollen bud that his bollocks bumped on each thrust. The lingering sweet-salty taste of him ratcheted her desire higher, and she licked her lips. Heat coiled in her belly, edging toward a conflagration.

Each snap of his hips brought unintelligible words

from her.

On one thrust, he reached around and flicked her hard nub.

She froze, then curled forward as every muscle inside and out contracted. Everything from her fingertips and toes to her core burned. Her nipples inside her dress were stiff points. Her whole body flushed with fire as her muscles spasmed and milked him endlessly.

He drove once, twice more through the tightness, and then his cock jerked and jetted into her, extending the intense sensations.

Wilting onto the sofa, she found her legs were not ready to support her. Her nerves still buzzed, and her stomach muscles hurt from being contracted so long in the pursuit of pleasure. Faint echoes of throbbing still wracked her. She wanted nothing so much as to slither onto the settee and take a nap.

He leaned over her, panting, then seized his handkerchief and held it to where they were joined as he withdrew. When he cleaned her gently, aftershocks of pleasure rippled through her. He cleaned himself up, put his clothes to rights, and smoothed her skirts down. Helping her upright, he led her around to the front of the sofa and sat, drawing her onto his lap.

"I am seeing more and more what Nicholas meant as the benefits of marriage," he murmured into her hair.

Sagging against him, she lacked the energy to voice her thoughts. *I agree, although sitting on my bottom right now is not comfortable. But I'm willing to pay that price if I can experience that explosion every night.*

Too tired to worry about her future or her heart, she

subsided against him as he rang for tea.

By the tea cart's arrival, she was feeling more lively and shifted off his lap to pour. He rose, grabbed his brandy snifter, and returned to drag her back onto his lap with her tea in hand.

"So which crop did you prefer?" he asked, glancing down to his left.

Sophia realized the crops had been out when the servant delivered tea. "Oh no, my lord, what if the maid saw those?"

"She could not have known what we used them for." He grinned. "Although as loud as you were, they might have heard you in the kitchen. Now, answer my question."

She pondered, distracted by the thought of servants knowing their activities with crops. "The first one seemed gentler. But I wonder, if you began softer with the second one as you did with the wider one, it might have the same effect?"

"I like the way you think. We shall try it that way next time then." Edward smiled at her. "But I shall tell you I suspect the overall effect shall be different."

"Shall we do this every night then, my lord?" Sophia asked, attempting neutrality despite her eagerness.

"Many nights, little one. I have so much to show you and do to you. You shan't be bored, I promise you that."

She could hardly wait for her first full day on the estate she'd call home, as Edward's wife.

****

Sophia finished her breakfast and poured more tea.

"You said you handled the accounts for your

father's household, right?" Edward asked. "And most of his correspondence?"

"Yes, my lord."

"Then I'd like to review the estate management with you, as 'twill be your responsibility along with the steward. My brother hired James to help, as I need as much time as possible with the horses and trainers. But he is struggling to keep up with the earldom's various holdings and the business, given the number of horses we now have. After our ride, we shall spend a bit of time in the study before I head out to train. James shall join us when he arrives."

She ventured a quick offer. "Edward, you know I helped my father with veterinary work. Let me know if I can help you."

He frowned, shaking his head. "I have people who can help with horse care, both on the estate and the vet in the village. My steward cannot keep up with the demands of my estates, the business, and Parliamentary correspondence, so that is where I need the help. But thank you." His tone did not invite debate.

Sophia's shoulders sank, but remembering Juliet's guidance, she chose to pick her battles. She needed to be careful if she wanted this to be a permanent home. "Of course, my lord, I am happy to help." Besides, 'twas not that she found reviewing the Parliamentary bills boring. It simply was not a passion like her love of all things equine.

In the library, Edward briefly outlined the household accounts and the correspondence waiting. When James arrived, they reviewed the business accounts, kept separate so that Edward could measure the payoff of the new direction he was taking with the horses. After a brief overview, Edward excused himself to check on the drills in the training ring.

"Would you like tea or lunch, James?" Sophia asked.

James's head did not raise from the ledger he was focused on. "Mmph," was all Sophia heard.

Frowning for a moment, Sophia nodded once and decided to proceed, ringing the bell and requesting a light lunch and tea when the servant arrived.

James continued to scratch notes and figures in the ledger before him, keeping his focus on the desktop.

Sophia wandered over. "Shall I start with the correspondence then?"

A low grunt was the only reply. When she approached the desk, he handed over the packet of letters without a word.

Reading through each, Sophia separated them into piles for personal notes to Edward, Parliamentary-related documents, business correspondence, and various estate questions. She saw one personal note to Edward came from Nicholas, attached to the Parliament summaries. As it referenced the bills, she kept it with them. She remembered Edward telling her he and Nicholas were working with others to vote in unity on bills that interested them. Mayhap reading and summarizing that first for her new husband would impress him.

When lunch arrived, James reluctantly emerged from behind the desk to join her at the sitting area. Attempting to bridge the awkward gap, Sophia asked, "Do you know Nicholas—ah, the Earl of Suffolk, Edward's friend?"

At his nod, she continued, "I am Nicholas's cousin.

Two months ago, I had never even been to London. Then Nicholas brought me there, and now I am here in Peterborough, married. 'Tis been a bit of a shock to my senses, honestly. But I helped my father keep his accounts for the house and his practice, as he was a vet who was often traveling around the county." She paused. "So I do hope I'll be a help to you rather than a hindrance."

His brow furrowed, and he gulped his tea, continuing to stare into the cup as he muttered, "I do not need any help."

Aahh. There was the issue. He either thought his competence was being questioned or his job was being threatened.

"Would you tell me about yourself, James? Have you lived here all your life?"

James was a thin man, just over average height, with the typical pale skin brought on by British weather and indoor work, topped by fair hair. He was around Edward's age, so she wondered if he was married but could not find a polite way to ask.

"Mmm…Mum and Da still live in the village. Da used to help here at the stables, so I played with Charles and Edward. The family was kind enough to invite me to attend the schoolroom with the earl's sons as well." He fell silent, eating a small sandwich from the tray.

"Have you been to London then?" Sophia asked, desperate to find common ground.

"Apprenticeship. Quite a shock, I agree." His focus remained on his sandwich.

Ah-ha, something in common. "I love it here. My old home is not far, so this feels comfortable and somewhat familiar."

A softening around his eyes was all Sophia got before he tensed again. Putting his teacup on the tray, he rose to return to work.

Sophia deferred further review of any ledgers and spent the next hour responding to a note Nicholas had sent to her, checking on her well-being as a newlywed, until James rose, indicating he needed to get home.

"Will I see you tomorrow then?" she asked as she followed him out to the hall to retrieve his hat and gloves.

A curt nod, tip of the hat, and "Good day, my lady," was all she received in reply.

Undeterred, Sophia returned to the library and decided to start with the simpler household accounts. They were mostly in order. She noted a question for the housekeeper on sugar costs that seemed high, then returned to the Parliamentary correspondence.

Given James's distrust, she feared this marriage might be a very lonely affair. She'd need to win both James and Edward over to change that.

****

Sophia set about learning the costs and management of the horse training business, as well as the cadence, hoping she might participate. Learning that Edward usually ate lunch at the stables with the trainers, she ate in silence at the library table most days. Missing the intellectual debates she'd always had with him and yearning to learn from him directly, she watched the activity at the stables through the window as James ignored her from the desk.

Occasionally, she would make a quiet trip down to check on Nellie and wander areas of the stables away from the tack room and hay bales where the men congregated on their lunch break. Schooling herself to bide her time went only so far after years of sneaking around villagers' unfair notions regarding a young lady's role in horse care.

Within a sennight, she was caught up on the business books and correspondence. She and James had reached a tentative détente. She had learned that he had a wife and three daughters in the village, and the reason he left mid-afternoon was to make dinner. She found that fact surprising, although decorum and their fragile relationship forbade her from questioning him further about it.

In the evenings, she and Edward discussed Parliamentary bills under consideration, the affairs of his estates, and the horse training. And they tested several more of the crops and whips in the cabinet.

Sophia enjoyed their evenings of exploration and soaked in details of the business from Edward. They had gone riding together a few mornings, and she visited Nellie almost every evening as work wrapped up.

But she was afraid. Edward respected her opinions, thanked her for her help, and turned her into a rag doll every evening with sexual pleasure. She feared she was very much in love with her husband, and that wouldn't do. She was bound to mess up, to give him reason to send her back to London or worse. When she wasn't itching to check each of the horses and make notes on their health conditions, she was wondering how to make him care for her. She slept poorly, despite the orgasms, and was exhausted after a fortnight.

When Edward made his excuses after dinner to discuss some business matter with Russell, she sighed with relief.

What now?

Deciding that talking it over with Nellie would help, she made her way down to the mares' stable.

"So, Nellie. What do I do?" Scratching her friend's forehead and around her ears, Sophia hummed under her breath as she considered options. "I know, I know. Patience. And yes, I also know that we have more than we hoped for here, and I should not risk it to pursue what can only be a hobby."

She sulked as she checked that Nellie's hooves and forelocks were dry and healthy.

"I haven't seen him address the personal missives I've put aside. See? If I helped here more, he'd have more time for his own desk work."

Nellie bucked her head.

Bobby's head popped over the half door of the stall. "Oh, thank heavens, my lady," he panted as though he'd been running.

Sophia frowned at the urgency in his voice. "What is wrong?"

"Remember that poultice you gave Nellie when she got a stone in her hoof, in Town?" he asked.

"Yes, of course." Where was this leading?

"Well, one of the mares has done the same."

"Aahh…" Sophia thought about what herbs and supplies she had in the house. "I can create something that will help. I'll bring it down within the hour." Shaking the loose straw off her skirt, she stood and patted Nellie good night before striding out of the stables.

She quickly created the poultice and grabbed a mug of hot water from the kitchen, bringing them to the stables. She directed Bobby to pour the water over the poultice to warm it and flatten it before placing it under the hoof, tying it around the mare's leg to hold it there with the tail ends of the poultice wrap that she had left long.

"You can reuse this for the next few days, too, by pouring fresh hot water on it."

From there, she wandered over to the yearling stables, looking for Barkley. He'd had outstanding training performances recently, according to Edward. Checking on him and a few others she had befriended in her spare time, she meandered to the next building.

The double doors were open. As she approached, she heard the murmur of voices, interspersed with a repeated rhythmic swish and thump. Frowning, she tried to imagine what would make that sound.

Peering through the doors, she saw Russell and her husband in a pool of light at the far end of the wide aisle between stalls. Their backs were to her as they faced a bulky object hanging on the wall.

Edward poked his finger at it, and she realized there were strips cut in it. She saw that the dense, fabric-covered object was a mattress. And Russell held a whip handle in his hand, the tail snaked on the floor beside him.

As she watched, he passed her husband the whip and took several steps back.

Edward shook the whip out, hefting the weight. Then his arm canted, his wrist snapped, and swish and thump. The new rip was near the one he had poked but was thicker and angled. And as the men poked at it, their fingers pushed deeper into the ticking.

The men murmured again, Russell gesturing,

Edward nodding. The stablemaster stepped back again, and Edward let fly.

Sophia took another step, strangely entranced. She envisioned standing against the mattress, Edward asking her about her thoughts on the whip versus a crop.

Abruptly, the stablemaster turned and looked at Sophia, and she gasped. Her action had betrayed her presence.

Turning, Edward frowned. "Sophia." His tone demanded obedience.

She stepped toward the light. "Yes, my lord?"

He stalked toward her and hissed, "You should not be here at night. Go back to the house at once." He was flushed, and she wondered if he was embarrassed at her catching him practicing.

"But, my lord…"

His eyebrows raised at her, but his voice remained low to avoid Russell hearing his words. "You have earned a punishment for spying on people. 'Tis a bad habit of yours. We will discuss it tomorrow."

Tears pricked her eyes, and her heart twisted. He'd kept her at arm's length by day, and while most of their evenings had been beyond satisfying, she had hoped for more. Now he was sending her away without even a good night and threatening an unknown punishment he knew would keep her thinking all night.

Just as she had feared, while she was in love with Edward, his feelings were nowhere near as strong. She was merely convenient for Parliamentary reading and for sex. But could she make him love her?

She turned, disheartened. But by the time she entered her bedroom, she was repeating her mantra under her breath. *Best darned wife. I shall earn his love. And mayhap even time with the horses...and the whip.*

Chapter Seventeen

Striding into the library the following afternoon, Edward's mouth was dryer than dust. His heart raced. He was sweating through his coat.

So that is how fear tastes.

When he had first found the poultice, he'd been angry. He'd discovered the poultice wrapped around a mare's front hoof. Confused, because the stablemaster usually kept him apprised when a horse needed any veterinary care, he had found Russell and quizzed the stable hands. No one recognized it, but one boy mentioned that Bobby had been in charge of the mare's care the night before. He and Russell had shared a look, realizing Bobby was unlikely to have made such a poultice but probably knew Sophia's skills with equine care.

Then he considered the ramifications—Sophia finding time to spend out in the stables—and the anger turned to cold dread. *Hellfire, she'll ask to see records of the horses' health or training. She'll realize I track most of it in my head, and Russell keeps the notes, and wonder. Then she might start to question the personal correspondence I keep avoiding.*

He'd planned a mild punishment for Sophia that they'd both enjoy, for her spying, but now he had in mind a more serious penalty. He'd ask questions first, of course, but in his heart, he knew Sophia had made the poultice he'd discovered. She cared so much, particularly about horses.

He gritted his teeth. *Interferes. I meant interferes.* He ignored the voice that whispered *and cares* in his head.

Throughout the day, he had striven for calm. Visions flashed through him over and over, replacing the calm with terror. Sophia with her arm in a sling, unable to ride for months. Or laying prone on the floor after a horse reared and caught her with a hoof—in the leg, in the ribs. All things he'd seen happen to his men in a horse training business. But none of those incidents had frightened him like the very idea of Sophia being hurt did.

Because you care about her the way she does about the horses.

No. Please, no.

'Twould make it unbearable if she learned his secret and left him. At that thought, he'd circle back to searching for ways to ensure she stayed in the library with the paperwork, ignoring the voice that told him his reason had changed.

Sophia turned from her seat at the table to exclaim, "My lord. You're back early." She rose to greet him.

Shooting her a grim look, Edward nodded to James as the man closed the ledger, grabbed his coat, and departed the library.

"Edward?"

"Russell will be here in a minute. We need to have a word," he ground out. He felt a muscle in his cheek ticking, his jaw clenched so tight.

Taking the chair vacated by James behind the desk, he pointed to a spot in front of the desk. "Come over here."

A knock sounded.

At his command, the stablemaster entered, closing the door behind him and striding forward to stand beside Sophia.

Edward threw the poultice on the desk, watching his wife. "What is this?"

He noted that Sophia did not appear confused, but neither was she forthcoming about the item.

"Sophia?"

"My lord, 'tis a poultice. I noticed a mare came up lame. This reduces the swelling and the pain."

Edward noticed she did not betray Bobby's confidence, protecting him. *Because she cares, about people as well as animals.*

"Stephen, when I found it and asked you, you said you were not aware this was being administered?" Edward turned back to the stablemaster.

"No, sir." Stephen hung his head, very familiar with Edward's rules about the stables, access to the horses, and approvals for medicines or food.

"And are you or are you not required to approve all care for ailments?"

"Yes, sir," was the quiet response.

"And were the stable hands aware of this requirement?"

"Yes, sir," Stephen said again.

"Sophia, did you not remember this rule that we went over upon our arrival from London?" Edward shifted again.

"Ah, yes sir, I mean, no, sir." Sophia paused and inhaled shakily. "I did not remember."

"This leaves me in a difficult position. It was

Stephen's duty to oversee care of the horses, and he neglected to do so. But that appears in most part because you did not follow the stable rules. Those protocols are for everyone's safety. You may not know what other treatments Stephen has given a particular horse. Or that one is more cantankerous than you recall and may not be safe to approach. Do you understand, Sophia?"

Even saying that out loud sent a shiver of fear through him again. He frowned. *Confound it, 'tis more than her protection. I feared losing her respect, but more and more I fear losing her company. And the possibility of more—of her love.*

"Yes, my lord."

"I've told you before, I've seen strong men permanently disabled by taking risks with horses. I know I sound overly strict, but it's for everyone's safety."

"I know how to handle horses."

"So did those men. You follow the rules, young lady."

"Yes, my lord."

"Then you spied on activities in the stable that were not your concern."

"'Tis not as if the stables are private—" She clamped her mouth shut then tried again. "Yes, Edward."

Out of the corner of his eye, Edward saw Russell cough, obviously grinning behind his hand.

"Stephen, that will be all, thank you. Wait in the hall if you please. And I expect you to keep a closer eye on Sophia's activities in the stables."

"Sir." The stablemaster made a hasty retreat.

"Right, then. Sophia, fetch the birch." He gestured to the cabinet where the crops and brushes were.

Her shoulders dropped. "Yes, sir."

Edward had only swatted her with it once, and she had yelped, grabbing her bottom in pain. That had prompted a conversation about the difference between spankings for sensual pleasure and punishment. They had agreed the birch would be an implement of punishment. He had staged that to prepare for a moment like this. The mere request for the birch was designed to heighten her awareness of incurring discipline. And ideally, its application would increase penitence and help her avoid future transgressions, particularly as he'd made it clear that a birching would not exempt her from her marital duties. They would simply be carried out with a sore bottom.

He did not want to really hurt his wife beyond a few lingering marks, and he much preferred to whip or spank her for pleasure. "Bend over the desk."

As she bent and gripped the far edge of the desk, Edward flipped her skirts.

Edward stepped back. "Sophia, you shall count. You shall receive at least six swats, after which you may beg your apologies to both of us."

The branches of the birch whistled before a resounding thwack sounded.

"Ooohh." She clutched the desk hard, squirming a bit, her arse jiggling. "One."

Edward adjusted his rising cock in his pants as he stared at her creamy skin striped with pink. He watched as she tensed momentarily before remembering to relax her muscles.

Thwack!

Her breath wheezed out between clenched teeth, then she inhaled sharply. "Two."

Thwack!

She panted a few times, shaking her bottom a bit with each breath. Edward ran his hand over the raised red marks, his moan covered by her loud gasp.

"Three."

Thwack—"Four."

He heard her sniffling. Her feet shifted in a clear but evidently vain effort to distribute the pain emanating from her hot striped backside. His erection flagged. There was no joy in administering pain with no pleasure. While he regretted causing it, he'd rather control it than have her seriously injured in a stables accident. He'd seen too many of those. *And I don't care for the hands as I do Soph—*

He stopped his thoughts, gritting his teeth and landing the fifth and sixth swats quickly. "Now, Sophia, stand up, and I will call Russell back in for his apology."

She stood and shook her skirts, flinching, probably because they rubbed against her sore buttocks.

As Russell entered and hovered just inside the door, Edward watched her. "Wife, what do you have to say?" Then, quieter, for her ears only, "If 'tis inadequate, you shall likely not sit comfortably for a sennight."

"My lord. Stephen, er, Mr. Russell." She bowed her head awkwardly to each of them. "I beg your pardon. Truly, I am very sorry. I did not mean to cause any disruption or get anyone in trouble. I only wished to help the horse."

Edward frowned. He did not appreciate her attempt

at gaining sympathy, for her or the horse. He stiffened with another bolt of fear. His hand holding the birch tightened, rattling the branches as he again conjured a recalcitrant horse kicking her as she tried to apply a poultice.

She twisted at the scuttling sound, looked up at him, and hurriedly continued her apology. "Mr. Russell, I apologize for putting you in an awkward situation, and I shan't give anything to the horses without your permission in future." She paused. "Edward, please, my lord. I am sorry."

"Very well, Sophia. You are dismissed." Edward ran his hand over her arse through the dress to light the pain again before stepping back.

Sophia's tear-clogged eyes were wide, and her mouth opened and closed while she searched for how to respond.

After a long moment, she nodded. She curtsied with a sharp breath accompanying it and took mincing steps to the door, hands hovering by her side as though trying to keep from inelegantly holding her skirts away from her bottom.

Edward nodded to his friend. "Thank you, Stephen. You can return to the stables. I shall see you later."

He sat heavily as the stablemaster left the library. He wondered when and if the pain would abate to be tinged with pleasure as so often happened for his wife. No matter. He'd warned her that part of her punishment would be serving his needs with a sore arse.

****

Baths that evening were painful. On edge from punishing her, Edward could hardly bear her hands traveling over him, and her discomfort sitting on her striped posterior was visible, although he wondered how much of it was edged with arousal. Afterward, she fidgeted through dinner until Edward's patience ran out.

He bade the servants enjoy the pudding and dragged Sophia upstairs by the hand. Entering her room, he led her to the end of her four-poster bed, bent her forward over it, and flipped her skirts.

"Sophia, this is the second half of your punishment. I will take you for my pleasure. Tell me if I hurt you, but otherwise, you will lie still. Understood?"

"Yes, my lord."

He ran his hand over the stripes visible from earlier and tapped them, then quickly undid his breeches and fit his cock to her opening, only to hesitate.

Punishment was one thing, but he needed to ensure her body was prepared.

Before he touched his fingers to her nub, she shivered from head to toe. She twitched her arse against his other hand where it sat on her still-hot backside. A rush of moisture coated his cockhead, causing it to leap against her.

Ah, as I hoped. My wife reacts well to pain. She may not have enjoyed the punishment. In fact, I hope she didn't. I don't think I could bear to hit her lovely little rear any harder. But that itch of fabric against the reddened skin and my plan to use her for my own pleasure appear to hold an appeal. She is—would be—easy to love. Bah.

Shutting his thoughts off, he refocused on pleasure and slid inward easily. With no waiting needed, he shot his hips forward, impaling her on his cock. He leaned down to imprison her between his still-clothed chest and the bed, much as a stallion might a mare.

As her hands scrabbled for purchase, he reared his hips back and thrust again, dragging out slowly to drive in, over and over. His open breeches rubbed the birch marks on her bottom, and one hand held her hip, the other bracing his weight on the bed beside her.

Sighing, Sophia went limp under him.

Plunging hard, Edward grabbed her hair, leaning forward to growl in her ear, not realizing until too late how his words betrayed his greatest concern. "Blast it, Sophia—you're mine. You will take care of *my wife*." He ground his teeth.

The angle of his cock changed as he leaned those last inches, and she writhed and gasped.

Ah, there. Despite himself, he wanted her to climax along with him, rather than merely take the punishment. He kept his pace steady and deep, fighting his orgasm to give hers time to build.

Feeling her internal muscles clench around his length, he straightened. Holding her hair, he tugged her head back, arching her so her arse tipped up farther.

His hips pounded even harder, once, twice, releasing her hair to hold both hips. He shot his release with a series of quick thrusts and a long groan.

She whimpered, and her internal muscles tightened around him again, spasming as his hips dragged over her raw skin. Finally, she lay prone, hands relaxed on the bed, hips twitching in sensitivity as his pulses slowed, then stopped, and he leaned over her again to catch his breath.

Moments later, as he withdrew slowly, abrading her sensitized flesh one last time, she whimpered again.

Concerned, he bent his head to look at her.

"Sophia? Did I hurt you?"

"No, my lord, that was delicious." She gave another small shiver. "Well, except for the birching part," she added with a quick grin.

Smiling while he was out of her sight, he smacked her sore bottom lightly as he stood. "That part was not meant to be delicious. Otherwise 'twould not be a punishment."

Even punishments bring us closer. If only I did not need to hide my weakness, if only I could trust her completely, it might become as great a partnership as Nicholas has with Ros. As great a love. The last thought chased his smile away.

****

Rain had driven Edward indoors. He had avoided the library, instead taking one item off the pile of personal correspondence Sophia had set aside for him and withdrawing to his sitting room.

The letter was only one page from Nicholas, with several pages of drawings and diagrams attached, to help Edward understand the concerns of the upcoming bill.

Edward had pored over the letter, following the number references to the numbers on the pages of sketches. He was hot and tired and irritable and more than ready for his bath, but he had one last paragraph to wade through.

Working through it letter by letter, word by word, to painstakingly build the sentence, he was so intent he did not hear Sophia in the bathing chamber until she came through into his room calling for him.

Snapping upright in the chair from his hunch, he scrambled to pile the papers and hide them away.

She glided toward him. "So this is where you've been working. James and I would have been glad for your company, husband."

In his haste, Edward turned partially toward her to put her off and managed to drag the papers he'd been gathering off the desk, scattering them on the floor.

She bent to help him pick them up.

"Don't!" His voice held panic, and he schooled it as best he could when she popped her head up to stare at him in surprise. "I've got it. 'Twas my clumsiness."

"I am happy to help. Here— Oh, what is this?" She turned a sketch toward her. "Is that the bill—"

Edward snatched the paper out of her hand and tucked it into the pile.

"Edward?"

"'Tis personal correspondence, Sophia. I told you I'd handle those."

"I am sorry. I was only trying to help."

"Yes, well, don't."

"All right," Sophia said slowly. "I shan't. I am not sure I understand your concern, but I shall respect your request. Don't you know I would never betray your confidence or someone else's shared with you?"

He barked a laugh.

Her chin jerked back, and she stared at him as though she did not recognize him.

"In my experience," he hissed, "women's ability to keep secrets is limited to how juicy the gossip is." He knew he was not being fair, but he could not help his gut reaction. This was his worst fear, come to life.

She gasped in outrage. "That is not fair at all. When have I ever been fond of gossip? Or, for that matter, had friends I'd want to gossip with?" She laid a hand on his arm. "Edward, I love you. I would not reveal information you wished to remain between us."

She gulped and stared at him, not blinking, her hand frozen on his arm.

Edward imagined his expression matched hers for a fleeting second. *She loves me? Oh, damn, and I... But can she really?* Hope flared for a moment.

Then an image flashed in his mind of him telling her he struggled to read, only to be greeted with derisive laughter and her packing to leave as her response. He shoved the hope down, yanking his protective walls back up and tensing his shoulders. *She cannot love me without understanding my greatest flaw.*

"Love? You have only known me for a month. And what is love? A silly notion created by women to add drama to their gossip. No, you cannot love me."

Sophia shook her head, mouth opening, then closing, eyes filling with tears.

Her theoretical abandonment still echoing in his mind, Edward was unable to find the desire to console her or apologize. He shoved her hand off him and strode out the door, clutching the letter and drawings in one hand, the other rubbing his chest. On his way out to the stables, he told the housekeeper he would not be in for dinner, and the lady of the house might wish to dine in her room this evening.

Criminy. I do love her. Why else would the thought of her leaving hurt so much?

He knew what love was, no matter what nonsense he said to her. And he knew her well enough to love her after a month. But she didn't have a secret like he did.

What if— No. I can't. I want her to be happy here. Here. With me. I'd rather keep her at a distance, both physically—her indoors and me training—and emotionally, to ensure she remains here.

He was terrified at how happy he was to hear her say she loved him. How much it hurt to push her away. And at the realization he cared for her happiness more than he did his own.

****

A whicker greeted Sophia, even before Nellie's head poked over the half door of her stall early the next day.

"Good morning, my love," Sophia crooned as she hugged and scratched the enormous head.

Slipping into the stall, she eschewed her usual perch on a straw bale, opting for the soothing repetitive motions of brushing Nellie.

"Oh, Nellie girl. I don't know what to do. First, I got myself in trouble. I was simply trying to help, but I forgot the rules. But then..." She sighed. "I told Edward I love him, and he denied it. Was it because of the poultice? Or am I so unlovable? Oh, no. What if he makes me leave? I love it here, almost as much as I love him. I don't know if I could live back in London...or really, anywhere without Edward."

She leaned her head against the mare's chest, tears wetting Nellie's coat. "What do I do? I've tried so hard to be a good wife to Edward. I have hardly spent any time with the other horses, and I only asked if I might help once."

Nellie reset a foot, turning her head to sniff at her mistress.

"I'd even live without ever helping down here, if only Edward would accept my love. And mayhap in time come to care for me."

Nellie snorted.

"Ah. You know me too well. I'll reword. I can live with only sneaking down to check on horses as I can get away. This place—Edward really—has made me happier than I ever imagined, despite my vow to avoid caring too deeply for anyone. I must focus on that joy and hope for the best."

Leaning her head against her best friend's massive chest, she took a deep breath and changed the subject. "Right, girl. Let's give you some time outside, even if 'tis not a ride." She led the horse out to a nearby pasture designated for the mares.

She returned to the house to find Juliet waiting for her. Showing her into the music room, she exclaimed, "Oh! Welcome to our home. Let me ring for tea." Flustered at first, she quickly realized this was a perfect opportunity to obtain guidance in confidence without waiting for the post to and from Roslynn. "'Tis lovely to see you."

She sat opposite Juliet and clasped her hands together in her lap, leaning forward. "Is this the follow-up visit we were told would happen?"

The instructor laughed. "Indeed it is, my lady. We find 'tis best to do them with little or no notice. If there is anything amiss in a marriage, we are more apt to see it and be able to address it."

Sophia supposed it made sense. Given the wide range of activities taught, there was an unfortunate possibility of women coming to physical harm, despite the school's thorough vetting of candidates. After all, the marriage contracts for young ladies of noble birth were subject to the whims of their fathers or custodians.

"Thank you, Juliet. I am delighted to report that my

marriage is a happy one." She sighed. "But I am struggling with one aspect and would welcome your advice."

The instructor nodded, accepting a cup of tea.

"As you know, I like to stay abreast of our country's news, laws, and challenges. Edward has been generous in allowing me to handle correspondence for his Lords duties."

"Ah, yes. I was amazed Lady Suffolk was able to join such a well-matched couple."

Sophia's eyebrows rose. Juliet knew Roslynn? And thought that Roslynn had paired her with Edward? Had her marriage been framed that way intentionally to protect her reputation, or had Roslynn really had a hand in it? She remembered her cousin's wife's attitude after the first ball when Edward whisked her away without a chaperone. *Hmm.*

Juliet continued. "But I detected a hint of wistfulness. What is as yet unsettled between you and the earl?"

Still not willing to discuss the one-sided declaration of love, Sophia blurted, "I want to spend more time helping with veterinary care."

Realizing Juliet might not know her history, she started to mumble about her father.

Juliet held up a hand. "Remember, we are all beautiful. And worthy of love."

Sophia flinched at the last sentence.

Juliet continued. "There is no need to justify your dreams." She smiled at her host. "The question is, what is the best way to attain them? What have you tried?"

It all came pouring out. Sneaking to the stables, her requests to help rebuffed, her attempts to learn the horse business via watching, his long hours away from the house for the work, and her general frustration.

"Right, then. Let's review the idea of negotiation. Women have fewer tools of leverage, so we need to use them wisely. Consider men's thinking—or what we know of it." Juliet paused for Sophia's snicker, clearly in teaching mode. "We talked in class about offering incentives through provocative posture or clothing. Men not only admire seeing more of the female form, they often may be distracted or sexually aroused by it." The instructor looked at her pointedly. "If you're aware of that, you can give them that, either to please them or as a negotiating tactic. Mayhap letting him find you in the bath..."

Sophia giggled again. He'd pre-empted her on that one, hadn't he? No, if he found her now, he'd be annoyed at smelling like lavender after his own. But she recalled Edward's face and tone when confronted with her damp bodice at the ball. *"What on earth do your stays look like if I can see that?"* She'd have to review her gowns and stays.

"There are other options, too. Have you learned his favorite things? A food or drink or cigar. When is he most relaxed? When is he happiest? And when are you happiest and most relaxed? Marriage will always require negotiations. Which of two conflicting invitations shall you accept? Whose parents shall you visit at the holidays? At what age shall you allow your child to have a pony? Conversations such as the one you desire will be more successful when you are both more relaxed. Ultimately, as we know, men get the final decision. However, we may influence that."

Sophia nodded, remembering how easy it had been

to talk to Edward while they rode together. Mayhap breakfast, when he was focused on the work ahead, had not been the right time. *And mayhap I rushed it, as I hadn't shown him I could handle helping James and the horse care.*

Sophia nodded. Mayhap she'd ask again after a spanking in the library when they were both sated.

"And remember, these steps may also work in reverse. Imagine that your husband buys you a beautiful necklace," Juliet started.

I'd rather have riding boots. The thought was accompanied with a tiny smile.

"You might have his favorite dessert made the next day as a thank you. The basic principle is to encourage good behavior. But..." She flashed Sophia a look of solidarity. "There will be times when you've done what you can to influence your husband to your way of thinking and have not been successful in swaying him. If you escalate every disagreement into an argument, you shall not have a happy marriage. You must determine the issues most important to you."

Sophia considered the shared interests in horse training, Parliament, *and spanking.* Two out of three was a good start to a happy marriage. And she *was* happy, darn it. She'd just said as much to her instructor. *Have patience. Best darned wife.*

Chapter Eighteen

Sophia found a column of figures in the business ledger that did not tally. Dreading a confrontation, she delayed raising the question with James, checking and rechecking her work. The last thing she needed was Edward seeing conflict between her and James. He'd blame her. While they'd both pretended the sitting room scene had not occurred, there was a fragile détente between them these past days, and she did not want to disturb it.

She and James had taken to working on separate holdings of Edward's, with data from other stewards coming in the mail. James's role as head steward was to consolidate all personal holdings, allowing him and Edward to compare costs of maintaining each property, as well as total costs per annum. The business records were kept separate for Edward to track its profitability. He used that information to judge what to reinvest into new stock and new training before channeling the rest into the estate or investments.

As Sophia was still learning the various properties of the earldom and the many layers of costs needed to breed and train horses, she reviewed past ledgers before entering new data. The page with the error was recent, dated within a sennight of her arrival.

After reviewing it several times, she reluctantly rose from the table with the ledger. She carried it over to James where he worked in silence, as usual.

Waiting until he finished entering a note next to a ledger column, she slid the ledger toward him.

James looked up from his work, eyebrows raised in inquiry.

Sophia pointed to the column she'd been reviewing, her voice hoarse with nerves. "Would you recheck this total, please? I've added it a few times, but it keeps coming up ten guineas different."

Frowning, James pulled the ledger closer to him. Adding the column once, he frowned again and added it a second time. Straightening from the ledger, he sat rigidly, his spine inches from the desk chair back, saying stiffly, "You are correct. It is wrong. Now what?"

"I shall merely make a note on that page and add the ten guineas back into the running tally on today's date, referencing that date, no?" Noting his stiffness, Sophia attempted to ease his mind. "That is what I always did when I found errors—often my own—in my father's ledger." She smiled.

James narrowed his eyes.

She wondered if he was judging her sincerity.

"And what if you find another error? What then?"

Sophia shrugged. "We do the same. You may find errors I make."

"Yes, but I am not the earl's wife. It seems he wishes you to take over my role, given your daily presence and the fact that you're reviewing my work. Why not simply be rid of me and have done with it?" James asked bitterly, throwing down his pen, spattering ink onto the ledger.

"No, James, I assure you—"

A knock sounded at the door, and a servant entered without waiting for a summons.

"Sir, you are needed in the village."

James seemed to understand why immediately. He grabbed his coat from the servant, rushing out the door as he donned it.

Sophia reached the hall as he took his hat from the butler, looking grim.

Catching sight of her as he placed it on his head, his lips flattened further. Tipping his hat, he nodded curtly. "My lady, if you'll pardon me." Not waiting for a reply, he raced out to his mount being held by a stable hand.

Sophia frowned, confused at the coordination among the servants to facilitate his exit. It seemed they had knowledge that she did not. "What is wrong?" she asked the butler.

"His wife is sickly. She has had a cough and an intermittent fever for over a fortnight. When she takes a turn for the worse, it helps soothe her if he is near, and the children need minding."

"Oh, how awful. Do you know if her cough is a sharp bark or more phlegmy?" she asked, thinking of the difference between any number of lesser illnesses and the dreaded consumption.

The butler looked askance at her, so Sophia demurred from further questions and went upstairs to find her herbal kit.

Selecting horehound and ginger, she ventured to the kitchen to ask the chef for honey and chicken stock and a small pot. Mixing them over the stove, so the roots infused the liquid, she placed them into a lidded jar to carry. Writing a note with dosage suggestions and

267

the recommendation to put a hot compress on his wife's chest as well, she dispatched a servant to James's home. As much as she'd like to meet his wife and children and hear the cough, she did not want to intrude, given where they had left their conversation that morning.

****

The next morning, James arrived later than usual with a small bowl holding a scented candle.

Sophia was already seated at the table with a ledger open before her when he entered.

Moving to stand by the table, James bowed deeply. "Madam, the tonic you provided worked wonders. My wife is already feeling better." Placing the candle on the table before her, he bowed again. "You have our eternal gratitude for your efforts and generosity. My wife made these when she was stronger. We'd like you to have that as a token of our thanks."

Sophia rose, sniffing the candle. "'Tis lovely, James, and I shall treasure it. I do hope she uses the whole jar over the next sennight. If 'tis croup and she rests and takes that, the cough should disappear." She didn't want to consider consumption, as the syrup would only be a temporary salve for that.

James inclined his head. "Yes, the doctor gave her a similar elixir once before, but she would not let me call him this time. She was afraid it was consumption and naught would help." His lips twisted as he admitted, "She said she did not want to waste the money. It has been difficult to accede to her wishes. I'd spend any amount of time and money to have her healthy, but with three children, she worries about money for their ailments and their future." His voice caught as he finished, his gaze skittering to the side.

"Oh, James. I have more herbs, and chef always has honey for Edward's sweet tooth, so never fear if you need more. Please don't hesitate to ask." She did not quite dare pat his hand, but her heart turned over for his family.

James closed his eyes and swallowed, taking two deep breaths to get his emotions under control, then nodded once and moved around the desk.

Sophia sat again. Thinking of his situation, she considered her training from the School of Enlightenment. Negotiations need not be limited to a husband. She wished for more time in the stable yard with Edward and the horse training. James needed time with his wife and children to ensure her ongoing health. They could help each other.

Leaning forward, she explained her goals. "James, I not only helped my father with his books, I also rode with him and helped him minister to animals sometimes. I am particularly fond of horses. 'Tis part of what brought Edward and me together."

Well, and spanking. She suppressed her chuckle and thought of that fateful night at Vauxhall and the carriage ride back.

"I love helping Edward—and you—with the books and his correspondence, but I want to spend more time out learning his business." Her voice went soft. "It appears we might help each other. I don't want to do this all day, nor do you want to carry the burden of it alone, given your family's needs. Perhaps you'd feel less torn between your duties here and at home if I assist with a few things. And I could reserve time to learn from Edward and Mr. Russell by not taking on too much."

He focused intently as she spoke, as if weighing her words. His face visibly brightened over her last words, hopefully understanding that she was offering a partnership with him, not a rout.

Breathing a sigh of relief, he nodded vigorously. "Madam, I would like nothing better. Again, I cannot thank you enough for your generosity."

"You are most welcome, sir. Come, let us continue to catch up on these, so we may pursue our other duties." Sophia smiled before bending to the ledger she was reviewing.

****

Sophia was determined to win her husband's respect and trust, if not love. She forged ahead, hoping she'd regain lost ground by bringing him current on paperwork and following his lead in the bedroom. *In essence, be the best darned wife.*

She focused on learning about Edward's various holdings from James, the ledgers, and correspondence from the various households. At dinners, she shared her new knowledge with Edward, asking him to paint a picture of each property so it was not only names and numbers to her.

She interspersed the conversations with seemingly casual questions about training, continuing to learn the business indirectly.

When packets of correspondence and Parliamentary business arrived, she read and reread them, digesting issues and laws, forming her thoughts on them to review at dinner.

One night, Edward returned to the house distracted.

As Sophia bathed him, she asked him about his day, as was their habit. Another yearling they'd been cart training on the roads had come up lame. "Newfangled roads, I do not know what that Scot was thinking or Parliament," he grumbled, referring to the engineer John McAdam, whose innovative crushed stone roads on a few main routes had already expedited travel, alleviating the fear of breakdowns and injuries to horses. When the stones used were not small enough, horses sometimes came up lame from pointed rocks. Smaller rocks shifted and compacted better, and wore down quicker from traffic to make a smoother path. Despite the risk of bruised hooves, these smoother roads with drainage alleviated many more serious injuries and carriage axle breakages versus the old dirt lanes.

She had read that bill and Nicholas's thoughts on it, and she had her own, knowing horses' injuries as she did.

She ran her hands down his legs to finish his bath before holding a towel for him. "How bad was the bruise?"

"Not terrible. Russell said it should heal in a day or two, thankfully."

Sophia climbed into the tub for her turn. "Ah, good. Did the horses ever get infections from slogging through the mud and their hooves not being dry for days at a time on the old roads?"

"We did our best to keep the stable straw dry to avoid that, but once in a while, yes."

"How long did horses typically need to recover?"

Edward pondered. "It depended on how long it rained, but if we kept the stable as dry as possible and had enough dry straw to change out regularly, then four or five days."

She stood, stepped into the towel Edward held distractedly, and held his shoulder as he scrubbed it roughly down her to capture the droplets of bathwater. As he straightened, she replied, "Right, then. The new road construction drains the rain off, so that is less likely now. A one- or two-day delay in training is better than a four- to five-day delay, is it not?"

He looked at her pensively. After a long pause, he cocked his head, and one side of his mouth twisted up. "Yes, well, perhaps you are correct, madam, but I'm still annoyed with the macadam road." His eyes twinkling, he added, "And with your lack of appreciation for my bathing skills this evening."

They both laughed. Sophia's held a note of relief at the return to normalcy between them.

"Understood," she replied contritely. Taking her instructor's advice, she had laid out a gown that she'd asked her maid to lower the neckline on and wore her stays extra tight that evening. She dressed quickly to get back to their discussion.

After they sat to eat dinner, she raised the subject again. "How might the issues with the roads be solved?"

"Parliament reviews all funding for road improvements. I was thinking to vote against any such bill, but your point is valid. Now, I'm unsure," he replied, forking beef tips in a wine gravy. He squinted into space, which Sophia knew by now was a sign of concentration.

"What if you amended the bill to specify standards for new roads," she asked, "mayhap require inspections?"

"That might work." Edward's brows lifted. "We'd

need to decide what standards would make sense and what is even measurable in an inspection, to write our request for Nicholas and the others."

Sophia placed her fork on her plate to stare at him. His pondering of pros and cons, which was largely done out loud, always fascinated her. But this was the first time he had used "we" in reference to reaching a solution.

She considered the instructors at the school, the women in Ros's salon, and the little she had learned of other noblemen in her time on the London circuit. Other than perhaps Nicholas—she did not know enough about the other salon members' husbands—she could not fathom a nobleman casually including his wife's participation in such a decision. Of course, she had helped and nudged on other Parliamentary reviews these past weeks, but those had been at her instigation.

She sighed with happiness. Considering the similarities in Edward's behavior to Nicholas's and knowing that Nicholas loved Ros beyond reason, she hoped this was a sign Edward cared for her more than he let on. And for all his penchant for punishment and his over-protectiveness of her despite her equine knowledge, she was very lucky. She felt safe to be herself. Despite her best intentions of self-protection, she not only had a cousin and friend she cared for, she had fallen in love with her new husband. And she suspected he loved her.

If only he'd trust her. *Patience.*

She'd been content to remain isolated, making the best of her situation after her father's death. Then she'd had to adjust to Nicholas and Ros, London, school, and most recently Edward. Somewhere in all that, along with the enlightenment that classes and Edward offered, she had lowered her walls and let people in. She had family again, and she could not find it in her to regret that, even if losing any of them would tear her apart.

****

Edward was determined to ignore the fact that his wife thought she loved him. *Silliness. Romantic drivel.*

But it had been a sennight of near-silent baths and stilted dinner conversations. Then tonight of all nights, when he was preoccupied with the health of a horse, they rediscovered their previous comfortable routine.

Hopefully, that will be the end of misguided admissions. And of her pressing. He shook these thoughts off and resolved to enjoy their deliberations on a solution to road conditions.

Having discovered his wife enjoyed wine more than sherry or tea after dinner, he topped up her glass and carried it to the study for her. Pouring a brandy for himself, he sat to hash out details of road inspections scope and frequency with her.

He doodled on a pad as they talked, sketching roads with drainage, various sizes of rocks and other related notes he tracked pictorially.

Sophia nodded and listened closely, meandering in circles around the sitting area, holding her wineglass.

Finally, he sat back, satisfied, and picked up his brandy snifter to sip. "Thank you, Sophia. You will write that up to send back, tomorrow?" He looked up, not finding her in sight.

She spoke from behind him. "Oh! I thought you were taking notes, but those sketches are even better. You are quite the artist, husband."

He jerked to his feet, clutching the notebook,

274

unable to form a coherent thought.

"Did you happen to write down any of the timing details we discussed?" She leaned in as though to look again.

"No." Holding the notebook to his chest like a child, Edward shuddered in fear. An insidious idea inched its way into his consciousness. *Tell her. She says she loves you, and you are falling in love with her. Let her prove it.*

"No!" he shouted.

She stepped back, eyes wide.

"I beg your pardon, Sophia." He blinked, attempting to recover. "I was upset I hadn't thought of it."

"'Tis quite all right, my lord." She smiled again, reassured. "I remember them. May I borrow the sketches, and I'll note them right now, so I can reference it all tomorrow when I write the reply?" She extended her hand tentatively.

"Of course." He ripped the pages out of the notebook, stifling another tremor at her riffling through the pages of sketches and poorly spelled notes from the past months. Picturing her sneer at his spelling, his way of recording information. *No. I can't tell her. At least not now.*

Road discussion done, his attention turned to his wife...and an unusually low décolletage. Her hair was how he liked it best, swept back but left loose down her back.

Hmm. Delicious. He may not fully trust her, but he always desired her. He licked his lips. Reaching out, he trailed one finger along the neckline of her dress, causing her to shiver and her nipples to peak beneath the bodice.

He wished he had more time to spend with her. Her brain was as appealing as the package it came in, and he suspected she'd have useful suggestions for the training business. He could ill afford her taking that time away and then expecting his help with correspondence or proposing an idea like documentation of training techniques, but he could reinforce good behavior—and please himself while doing so.

"Such an excellent idea deserves a reward," he murmured as he captured her hand and drew her sideways onto his lap. "Can you think of something suitable?"

Sophia's hand lay on his chest, the other holding her wine glass. She turned her head to look up at him. "Well, James and I caught up on the books, and I've finished responding to the correspondence we've received. Perhaps allowing me to help with the horses occasionally, my lord?" Her voice was tentative.

Edward froze, fear shooting through him. "Are you sure? I saw a pile of letters on the corner of the desk only yesterday."

"Those are your personal correspondence that you said you wished to handle."

"Hmm. I've changed my mind. I'd like you to open those, too. And summarize, as with the other missives."

She groaned.

He stifled a grin. That pile had grown because of his neglect. But a frown chased away the smile. *She will not let this go. This risk is only going to escalate. What then? I already care for her more than I should.*

His early plan of separate by day and exploring each other sexually by night had quickly buckled under his desire to be with Sophia whenever possible. He enjoyed his wife's company far more than he had expected and valued discussions like the one they had just completed. He couldn't have it both ways. Separate was safe, but together was more than pleasant. It felt like home.

Tonight, though, their discussion had gone so well, he wanted to celebrate, not brood. He put the conundrum aside.

Sophia's thoughts obviously aligned with his. She glanced at his mouth, then up to meet his eyes, licking her own lips.

"Hmm, mayhap a kiss," Edward considered aloud, contemplating another nuance of lovemaking he had yet to show her.

That spark of inquisitive arousal that lit Sophia's eyes each time she discovered another layer of sensuality encouraged him to be creative. He strove to keep her curiosity sated, finding it increased his own pleasure to see her master new skills.

"Oh, yes, my lord, I always like those."

His hand slid up her back to grasp her hair and tilt her head at the angle he desired. Leaning down, his gaze remained on hers as he tugged her head back. He passed her mouth to trail kisses along the rise of her breasts above her dress before dragging his lips up her neck.

She groped to put the wineglass on the table, then slid her hands around his shoulders.

Finally reaching her mouth, he whispered against it, "I do not believe one kiss is enough."

Twisting his lips against hers, he sipped on her. His tongue swept along hers as he increased the pressure of the kiss, his signal that more delicious acts would follow.

Then he handed her to her feet and straightened off the sofa. Recapturing her hand, he ignored her wine and his brandy and dragged her toward the door.

"Edward?" Sophia begged from behind him. "Where are we going?"

"Upstairs. I need more room for the kisses I wish to give you," was his cryptic answer as they ascended the staircase.

Out of breath from keeping up with his pace, Sophia gasped, "You need more space to kiss me?"

Edward stopped as he reached the second-floor hallway and turned to her. Pulling her into him, he leaned in to kiss her hard again. "I mean to kiss you everywhere, my wife. Every inch of you."

Sophia's mouth dropped open in startled wonder. She smiled dreamily up at him for the second before he yanked her into motion again, bypassing her room to head to his.

Chapter Nineteen

While they almost always slept together in one room or another, they maintained the traditional two rooms for changing and, he had offered, for the time during her monthly courses if she wished.

Edward chose his room for the bed with sturdy carved posts hidden behind the bed hangings.

He twirled her around to quickly undo the buttons of her gown. Shortly after their arrival at the estate, Edward had informed his valet and her maid that they should not wait in the rooms, but remain on call from the servants' quarters should they be needed.

Gesturing for her to disrobe, he threw his coat and waistcoat aside and loosened his cravat. Crossing to his wardrobe, he pulled out a few things in one fist and threw them on the bed before sitting to remove his boots.

Sophia's gaze followed him as she dropped her last article of clothing, then darted to the bed, her brows lifting when she discovered the neck ties he'd tossed there.

Edward tilted his head at the bed, commanding, "On the bed, Sophia, on your stomach."

Lying down, she gathered her hair to one side and turned to face him.

She's learned to obey without questioning. Perfect. Hellfire, I am desperately in love with my wife. If only…

He liked spanking and tying her because it reinforced his control in the relationship. Sharing his weakness would shift that balance of control to her. Could he trust her with that?

But now was not the time to worry about that, with this delectable feast before him. He shook his head and refocused on the beauty waiting for him.

Having removed his clothes except his breeches, he stood, unfastening his pants. Crossing to the bed, he gathered a cravat and one of her wrists. He tied the neckcloth around her wrist and stretched it to the closest post of the four-poster bed. After repeating the action with her other wrist, he turned to her ankles, leaving her spread-eagled and vulnerable, with him behind her.

Sophia strained against her ties, twisting her head to try to see what he would do next.

"Relax, little one."

She calmed, and he gathered her hair away from her face. His hand grasped one ankle. "Hmm, where to start…"

Kneeling on the bed behind her, he trailed his lips over the ankle he held, slowly skimming up her leg. He knew from experience that she enjoyed the contrast of his hot mouth and the cool air over it. Her skin pebbled in the wake of his lips, and her back arched, her nipples hardening to points as though he had licked them, too.

Reaching the crease where her leg met her arse, he started over at the right ankle. She uttered a moan of pleasure, and her limbs relaxed even more. Pausing again at the top of her leg, he blew over her bottom and watched her cheeks clench in anticipation.

Delicious. He nuzzled her satiny skin in the crease

of her leg, inhaling her floral perfume mixed with a hint of her arousal.

He shifted to butterfly kisses along her shoulder and down one side to her waist, then the other side. Feathered open-mouthed kisses across her shoulder blades and down her spine followed, so his tongue could taste her, sweet from her pre-dinner bath. He trailed a hand behind his lips to ease the shivers they caused.

Finally, his teeth nipped at the muscle and flesh of her backside before his tongue came to soothe the sting. He traced swirls on her other cheek, followed by a long wet deep lick along the seam of her arse to between her legs but not quite to her center.

She arched her back and panted. "Edward?" Barely more than a breath of sound.

He pressed his full length along hers for a moment as he shifted atop her, a knee between hers and a hand bracing his weight by her head, and stretched to untie a wrist. The rest of the ties followed, and he knelt astride her and twisted her hips to turn her over to face him. Retying her, he surveyed her from head to toe.

He stepped to the foot of the bed, hand trailing along her leg, to start over.

Sophia squirmed. "Edward, please…"

"Still rewarding you, shh."

Starting again at her ankles, his lips skimmed up each leg until his breath disturbed the curls at the vee of her thighs, but neither lips nor tongue touched there.

Then he concentrated on the sensitive underside of her upper arms, making her shiver and her skin pebble again. He kissed across her collarbone and along her sternum before slowly, gaze on hers, going left then

8

Maggie Sims

right to kiss and lick each breast thoroughly and suck each nipple in turn.

Sophia's back arched over and over, the only action her ties allowed. The scent of her arousal was stronger.

Edward scooted lower on the bed, his lips now on her stomach. Looking up at her as he laved her skin with his tongue, he thought keeping her tied to his bed and naked every night was the best idea he'd had in…ever.

He lowered his gaze to stare at her glistening sex. His hands held her hips, thumbs dropping to pull her lower lips apart.

"Edward? My lord?"

"Yes, wife? You kissed me here several times already, did you not?" He knew where her question was going.

"Yes, but—"

"But naught. We are shaped differently, but everything you did to me can be done to you. I am sure they included that concept at school."

"Yes, but I could not imagine it," she whispered, her whole body tremoring as his mouth nibbled on one swollen lip, then the other.

****

"Well, now you shall not have to imagine." Edward's breath gusted against Sophia's flesh.

Fire danced from her fingers and toes, racing inward to her breasts and her core. She wasn't sure she even had skin left—it might have burned off. Only Edward's mouth cooled the flames inside her, even as it stoked them higher. And his tongue…

Her body arched off the bed as his breath wafted

over her most sensitive spot. She tried to thrust her hips toward him, only to realize her ties would not allow it, which somehow heightened her sensitivity further.

Why does being at Edward's mercy excite me this much? Mayhap because I trust him. I trust him with my body, my future...and my heart. She sighed in acceptance as well as pleasure.

Her head dropped back, eyes closing, yielding to his stimulation and the fire he licked into her. Moaning, she tried to angle toward him again as his lips and tongue teased her opening and the taut bundle of nerves just above. The restriction of her ties, the knowledge that he would do what he liked to her and she was helpless to stop him spiraled the sensation into a vortex of pleasure.

He toyed with her nub back and forth, his tongue nudging it in a quick flicking motion. When she gasped and arched further, he changed to her favorite circular motion.

She considered his attention to her pleasure. *I wish he'd do the same about helping with the horses. But oh!*

A thumb teased her opening, swirling in the wetness there before pushing in and out shallowly.

Sophia squirmed, struggling to process the intense sensations. "Ooohh, Edward. That is…"

Again words failed her as his mouth returned to her hardened button with his thumb breaching her. Inserting his thumb farther into her channel and making tiny forays in and out, he tongued her sensitive bundle of nerves faster and more firmly, not giving her any pauses.

Sophia's muscles clenched, tighter and tighter, her back arched, her head tossed to one side, and her teeth clenched. A keening sound came from her as the climax built. Her entire focus was on the wet, hot press of his tongue as it flicked back and forth, as his thumb teased her with the promise of fullness. Her core spasmed, wanting more than a digit, craving his cock. The flames licked at her, suffusing her in heat, inside and out. She yanked at her ties, torn between wanting to pull away and impale herself on his cock and locking her knees around his head to gain more pressure. School had not prepared her for these wonders, this incredible intimacy.

He removed his hand, and her eyes shot open in dismay. "*No...*"

He smiled, licked his middle finger, and slid his hand back to where her body pulsed, craving the crest of the climb he'd just propelled it up.

His hand slid over her wetness. What felt like his thumb re-entered her channel, and his lips landed on her hard, swollen bundle of nerves.

Why, then, had he wet his finger?

Delirious with pleasure, her mouth worked but could not form the words. She gaped when his finger slid back from where his thumb entered her to press against her bottom hole.

"Unh," she grunted, squirming as his finger drove slowly but surely into her rear passage. It felt foreign, more so even than when his cock had first slid into her on their wedding night. And so full, with his thumb in her also. Tendrils of heat curled ever higher from all three touches. Her body tightened around his digits rhythmically.

He warned me about this. But why did he not mention how delicious it was? I would have begged for it.

He slid both digits deeper, and her thoughts stalled. Overcome with pleasure from all ends, she was fascinated, confused, and could not even clench her muscles against such a foreign invasion. Her heels dug into the bed, and her hips punched the air, little motions all that the ties allowed. Even that prompted his fingers to shift inside her, front and back, and fan the flames further.

Each shift of his hand and tongue ricocheted the pleasure between the places he touched her. The fiery vortex of pleasure coiled inside her, tighter, higher than ever before. She wasn't sure where it would take her. His thumb dragged against a spot in her he had found and exploited regularly. His finger probed a fraction deeper on the next thrust, in tandem with his thumb.

Whimpering, she held her breath. Her hips raised, her back arching off the bed. He latched on to her firm button with his mouth, sucking hard as his thumb and finger pumped faster, making wet sounds with each thrust.

With one last thrust of her hips, she exploded, keening through clenched teeth. Her internal muscles squeezed him rhythmically, her bundle of nerves pulsing between his lips. The fire raged and raged, so hot her fingertips burned with it. Then, suddenly, it was all too much, and she tried to squirm away.

His mouth and fingers stilled, his lips loosening, tongue sweeping around her softening nub, not touching it directly.

She relaxed muscle by muscle, lowering her hips to the bed, cognizant of his fingers inside her. Then, prone, she went limp with a gusty sigh.

Edward withdrew and untied her ankles and wrists before skimming his breeches off. Returning, he crawled up her body and eased his cock into her swollen, slick folds.

"Mmm, mmph," Sophia squirmed more now she was free, oversensitive.

"Shh, I shall stay still a moment," he whispered, soothing her with his hands.

She felt like a skittish mare being petted. Widening her legs, she stared blearily up at him. "Does it feel like that when I kiss you there?"

"Mmm, probably," came his reply, with a slight shrug that made her twitch when he rubbed against her sensitized skin.

"I am surprised you do not ask me to do it every night then," she murmured, only half aware of what she was saying.

Edward's laughter barked out, then he stared down at her.

"I've never laughed during sex before." There was wonder in his voice.

"Neither have I, but it feels good." She smiled up at her husband.

Bracing on his hands, he surged in and out of her, ratcheting her arousal back up to another quick orgasm as he reached his.

****

Edward was up and gone when Sophia awoke. She lounged in bed, replaying the night before and reveling in her satisfaction with life. Well, other than being allowed to help with the horses.

She was caught up on correspondence until a new packet arrived, but she helped James with the ledgers until lunchtime.

Reading a book on horse breeding after James left, she heard a commotion in the hall and rushed out of the study, book still in hand.

She found two trainers carrying her husband between them in a seat made of their linked arms, his arms around each man's shoulders. The stablemaster trailed behind with one of her husband's boots and a compress he must have gotten from the housekeeper.

"Edward! You're hurt. What happened? Where? How?" *Let him be all right. He is the most important part of my world. I want many years with him hale and hearty.*

"Put me down," Edward snarled at them. "I can walk, damn you." When they ignored him. "Well then, take me to the study. I don't want to be upstairs in my bed like an invalid all day."

Hmm, he sounds more angry than hurt. I hope that means 'tis not serious.

Turning to her, he grumbled, "I am fine, Sophia. A minor mishap. I shall be right as rain in no time. But"— he shot her a look—"this is why I worry for your safety. Injuries are all too likely even with the utmost care, strength, and experience."

Her breath had whooshed out in relief at his first statement, only to be sucked in again at his second. But now was not the time to debate with her stubborn husband.

The two hands looked to the stablemaster, who gestured to continue toward the stairs. He retorted, "My lord, you know what the physician says. You must stay off it for a fortnight in order for it to heal. You keep re-injuring yourself because you do not rest long enough."

The men went quiet as they negotiated the stairs. While they worked with horses all day, Edward was not a small man, and his weight and the full flight were enough to take their breath.

Sophia called for tea and ale to be waiting for the men when they returned, then hurried after the entourage.

"What happened, Edward?" When she had first seen him being carried, she feared he had done irreparable harm to his leg, her heart beating double time. Russell's comments downstairs had calmed her enough to help settle him before trying to understand the problem. Still, she could not shake the anxiety. Helping her father had exposed her to a number of very serious horse-related injuries, like Edward's experience had.

"That devil Fury will not take a bridle, blasted horse. I landed wrong on my ankle. It shall be fine in a day or two."

The stablemaster caught her eye and firmed his lips, shaking his head quickly once.

"Well, won't it be lovely to be up here? You'll have all the comforts you need, staff and me to bring you food and a view of the stables to keep an eye on things?" She kept her tone light, trying to make the grumbling stop for the servants' sakes.

And stop it did. He raised his head. "Excellent idea. Take me to my lady's drawing room and put me on the window seat, men."

They hastened to do so, Sophia running ahead to open the door, then finding a stool to prop his foot on. His legs were too long for the padded seat, so he sat angled and looked sideways out the window.

There goes my ability to watch and learn more of the training process.

But if it would keep Edward resting for longer to help him heal, it was worth it. Having admitted she loved him, she was more determined than ever to ensure her future here and be the best darned wife to him. Then one day he might return her affections.

****

After two hours of compresses, including one of Sophia's, Edward's valet helped him to a wingback chair with a footstool in his drawing room. He'd refused an elixir she offered, opting for spirits, and was on his second glass of brandy. As dusk brought the shadows out of hiding, servants dragged a table close and served dinner there. The staff seemed familiar with the routine, which Sophia was grateful for, else she might have worried about the degree of the injury.

"So you've done this before, my lord?" she asked as they ate.

"Once or twice a year, unfortunately. 'Tis always the same one. I think the ankle is weakened."

"Is it always when you are performing the same task?" She angled her head to one side as she considered similar recurring injuries she'd seen in animals.

"Hmm." He considered the question. "I am not sure. Why do you ask?"

"If 'tis a particular task and we can find another person or another way to accomplish that, you might avoid similar injuries."

'Twill also preserve you, my love. Only privately would she admit how far her walls had fallen and how precious he was to her.

"I shall think about that and ask Russell if he recollects anything along those lines. Today, I was walking backward, trying to coax Fury to take a bridle, and fumbled the reins when he acted up, and my feet got tangled. When I went down, I knew right away I'd re-injured it."

Sophia stood to walk toward her own rooms. "I am going to ring for them to remove the supper trays and help you to your bed. Shall I find a book for you to read or that you'd like me to read to you?"

Edward replied quickly, looking strangely fearful. "Thank you, my dear. I would enjoy you reading to me. No need to call servants with you here. Come, we can make do."

Sophia arrived at his side next to his injured leg as he levered out of the chair with his arm strength and one leg, holding his injured ankle out in front of himself. Slipping his arm around her shoulders, he lowered the foot gingerly to the floor. Wincing, he picked it up again and took a small hop, leaning heavily on her.

"Will I hurt you if we maneuver this way?" he asked, judging the distance around furniture to the bedroom.

"No, Edward, I am fine. Come, let's get you off that leg." Sophia slid her arm around his waist and lifted her outside hand to hold his wrist where it rested on her shoulder.

By the time they gained the rug at the side of his bed, they were both winded. He turned and held the bedpost at the foot of the bed and fumbled at his shirt with his other hand.

"Oh, dear. Let me help you with that." Sophia

brushed his hands away, smiling as she considered how comfortable she was with handling his form.

Glancing down, she noticed his trousers had a rather large bulge in them and looked up accusingly. "You are injured!"

He shrugged.

"You cannot possibly…" She cocked her head, reviewing the various positions they had explored, but none seemed appropriate for his leg.

"Sex would be a welcome distraction. Now, finish removing my breeches. I cannot do the work, so you must. You did not get a ride in today, did you? I think we can remedy that now."

Staring at him quizzically, she took a moment to resume her task. Unlacing him and pushing the fabric down, she gestured for him to sit on the bed so she could remove his trousers. As she leaned forward, the scooped neckline of her dress gaped.

His hand raised, slipping in the gap, and swept to the side to cup her breast and thumb her nipple.

She arched into his hand, flicking her gaze up to his as she wet her lips, and a memory from a class about sexual positions enlightened her. "I do not wish to hurt you, my lord. Mayhap a gentle ride…"

His eyes gleamed. As her dress slipped away, he admonished, "Leave the stays on."

Swinging his legs onto the bed, he lay back against the pillows and held her hand with his. She climbed on and, being careful not to jar his ankle, swung her other leg over his hips to straddle him. Her stays kept her sitting upright.

"Put your hands on the bed, raise your bottom, and come kiss me."

She searched his countenance for signs of pain before closing her eyes and touching her lips to his. *Ah, brandy. It must have helped dull his pain.*

He cupped a hand at the back of her head and deepened the kiss, plunging his tongue into her mouth. His other hand curled around her breast and ribcage, his elbow and upper arm braced on the bed to help maintain her balance.

Again and again, his thumb brushed over her nipple through the stays with exactly the pressure she liked, making her hips twist a bit. The hand behind her head yanked her chemise down under her breasts and tucked it in her stays, then settled on the other side of her ribs. He drew her upper body toward him, reaching for the top of one breast with his mouth. Laving back and forth with his tongue, he got closer and closer to where her nipple peeked over the shelf of her stays.

Sophia arched, her breasts swelling with desire, and that was all it took for them to pop over the edge.

He did not waste a second and sucked one peak into his mouth and then the other, using his arms to keep her over him.

Her hips sank, her core seeking his. After both nipples were hard and she was twitching in his hands, he pushed her chest back a bit, allowing her hips to drop. His long fingers dropped to dip into her wetness and swirl around her nub.

"I love how responsive you are," he murmured as he watched her face and her body react to his touch. "You are wet, my love. Are you ready to ride?"

She nodded eagerly.

"Relax and let me direct you for a minute."

She braced her hands on his chest as he raised her

hips. One hand left her, and then his tip was at her opening, swirling in her wetness. As his cock nudged into her an inch, his hand returned to her hip, and he urged her down onto him.

She sank her bottom to his thighs, and his hardness thrust farther into her. Her head fell back, and she gasped at the exquisite fullness. His cock bottomed out inside her with a small jolt, and she realized this angle was even better than when he had tied her to the bed. His fingers tweaked her hard knot one more time, and she squirmed, moving her hips forward and backward then around in a circle, reveling in her control of the pace and pleasure for a change.

His hands rested loosely on her hips. "Now, imagine yourself riding astride as I know you sometimes have. Think about trotting. Posting…" His hands urged her up, almost to his tip, then down. "Start slow and see what feels best. Let your body set a comfortable pace."

Self-conscious with him watching her attempt this for the first time, Sophia slid her eyes closed to experiment. At first, she was clumsy, the slide of his cock against her nerve endings disconcerting even to an expert rider. But she quickly found her rhythm, rocking up and down, arching forward on the way up to scrape her sensitive flesh against his pubic bone and the crisp hair at the base of his cock. Her breath stuttered as pressure built.

Fingers touched the hard points of her breasts again, and her eyes flew open. She stared at her hands on his chest and his hands on hers above her stays, the vision adding to her excitement. Given the angle of penetration and her stays keeping her upright, he was hitting a spot that sent shocks of pleasure through her each time she sank onto him.

Faster and faster, she rode him.

He arched up at one point but bit back a sound of pain and lay still beneath her. Before she could argue against continuing, he grabbed her hips again to help her with his upper body strength and increased the pace.

As he grew harder and harder within her, she strained toward that irresistible explosion. His grasp tightened, and one hand left her hip to slip between them again, rubbing at the hard nub, taking her over the edge.

Once, twice, she raised and slammed down before everything contracted. Her head curled forward, eyes closed, and her hips swiveled of their own accord, grinding that bundle of nerves against his fingers and groin.

His back arched again at the swivel, and he burst within her, his hips making small pumps hampered by only having one foot for leverage against the bed.

As she sat, replete and curling forward, he reached behind her, untied her stays, and unwrapped and loosened them enough for her to fall forward to lie on him. She sighed, reveling in the small pulses of him inside her where they were attached. "I am so glad I could ride today, my love."

He stiffened, and she froze, realizing her slip, but his muscles loosened after a moment, and he chuckled.

She smiled against his chest and breathed a sigh of relief.

Hearing soft snores, she gazed unseeing into the darkness and replayed his description of his injury, trying to talk herself out of visiting Fury in the stables.

She hated to risk the budding trust between them, but she might be able to help, darn it.

Chapter Twenty

Sophia's focus bounced between the training below and her husband's frustration. The past few days had centered around the window seat of her sitting room. The servants had retrieved a cane from the attic for Edward to use to maneuver around his rooms as needed, and Sophia had dragged her chair and eventually her desk over next to him.

She read correspondence to him during breaks in the training and ran up and down the stairs regularly to check in with James. Most of the time, their focus was on the yard below. The stablemaster was the only person other than Edward willing to work with Fury.

Each day at midday, the trainers cleared the ring and took a lunch break. Then Russell would put a halter with a lead line over the stallion's head and lead him out to the training enclosure. Trainers took turns staying ringside in case Russell needed help.

Every day, the horse circled the ring on the lead docilely until Russell tried to put the bit of the bridle in his teeth. Each time the bit neared his mouth, Fury tossed his head, pulling away, sometimes rearing up. The horse was decidedly stubborn. While all the trainers were experts at handling stallions, after several failures, Edward was itching to help. Sophia was as well and was increasingly agitated at not being allowed to do so. She knew her husband would not allow her to examine an untamed stallion, given his fear of injuries.

Grinding his teeth, Edward grabbed his cane and pushed to his feet. "I cannot watch this any longer," he declared, hobbling across the room. "Bring me my boots, Sophia."

"But, my lord, I thought the doctor said it needed at least a fortnight?"

"Fury does not have a fortnight," Edward bit out. "In order to get him saddle-trained for the auction and keep him on schedule with his age group, he needs to already be in a bridle. I need my boots, and I need to get down to the ring."

Sophia mentally scrambled for ways to stop him, running through school classes. Negotiations. Rewarding good behavior. Directing behavior subtly. *Ah, yes, that.* Aggravating his injury might do permanent harm. He'd be miserable without the ability to train and ride, and she wanted to prevent that even if it meant angering him.

She recalled from the past few days that his ankle swelled by the end of the day, from even the small amount of walking he had done on the upper level. If he was unable to get his boot on, he could not go out and damage it further. And he sounded impatient, something she was counting on with her next question. "Certainly, my lord. I believe your valet took them to polish for you, and they may be downstairs. Do you prefer that I bring them up, or may I meet you at the base of the stairs with them?"

"Downstairs is fine. I shall need time to navigate the stairs, and I do not want to delay any longer than necessary."

Sophia bit her lip and walked to the door of her

sitting room. "Do you need help on the stairs?"

"No, thank you. I'll be fine. Just find those boots!"

"Yes, my lord," she replied, scurrying out to the hallway. She thought she remembered his boots in his wardrobe, but she turned as though heading to the back stairs. Nipping in through the hall door to his bedroom, she left the door open a crack and grabbed the boots. She watched through the crack as Edward slowly made his way to the top of the stairs. He held the rail tightly, placed the cane on the first step with his sore leg, and lowered his strong side, trying to put as much weight as possible on his hands.

He made it a third of the way down before he started grimacing. At two-thirds, he paused and surreptitiously wiped his brow with his handkerchief before tucking it away.

She scampered down the back stairs, boots in hand. Circling to come forward, past the darkened abandoned dining room on her right, the echoingly quiet music room on her left, she made her way to the grand entryway and the base of the front stairs.

Edward's grip on the banister was white-knuckled, his nostrils were flared, and lines of pain bracketed his mouth.

Knowing that the ache likely would not stop him, she waited as he navigated the last few steps and sat back heavily on the third stair.

"Would you like help with these, my lord?" Sophia knelt in front of him, boots in hand.

"Yes, please."

As slowly as she dared, Sophia started with Edward's healthy left leg, pulling the boot onto his foot, then tugging it upward until he took it. Then she turned to his sore foot. She had placed her hand under his ankle for directing the foot into the left boot, but when he managed to lift his right leg, and she touched the underside of his ankle, he hissed in pain. She quickly let go, and he held his leg right below his knee, stubbornly expecting her to pull the boot on.

Sophia dragged the boot onto his foot, but when the mouth got to his ankle, she daren't pull.

Edward looked up at her hesitation and reached with one hand to do it himself. His face whitened, and he swayed a little when the boot forced his toes to point as it came up to his ankle. He set his jaw and tugged more, but the boot did not budge.

Sophia sat back on her heels, hoping he'd reach the same conclusion she had.

"Hellfire," Edward swore. Yanking harder, he whitened again and let go of the boot in a hurry. Leaning forward, Sophia saw how swollen the ankle was.

"My lord, if you do get that boot on, you shall do irreparable damage to your ankle walking any further on it, and we shall need to cut the boots off you."

He glared at her.

"I am simply stating a fact." She remained calm. "I understand your frustration. Do you wish to sit a spell in the study with a compress to see if the swelling decreases?"

He nodded shortly, his jaw clamped shut in pain. Between them, they got him to his feet and across the hall to the study, where he collapsed onto the settee. She lifted his leg onto the seat and called for tea and another of the compresses she had made.

"Brandy for me, never mind tea." Edward let a

long breath out between pursed lips.

She thought she heard a muttered curse.

Once Edward was settled and had finished his brandy, he drifted into a doze to escape the pain.

Sophia placed the book she had been reading to him nearby and tiptoed out of the study. After a quick trip upstairs, she used the rear entrance to head to the stables. It was nearing the end of the training day, and she grabbed some vegetable greenery from the chef's waste bin to take to the horses. Her patience was as frayed as Edward's, and she wasn't incapacitated.

Slipping into the mares' stable, she headed first to Nellie.

"Hiya, girl." She rubbed the sweet nose that had popped over the stable door the minute she entered. "I'll be out to ride you tomorrow, one way or another, I promise. Is Bobby taking good care of you?" A quiet nicker and roll of the gigantic head into her hand was a positive response. "Right, then. I'll be back soon then. Sorry, girl." Sophia offered her half the greens before continuing to the other stables buildings.

Worried about the injured horse from the macadam road, as well as Fury's refusal to take a bridle, she walked slowly down the yearling's boisterous aisle, giving each accessible nose a pat or a scratch and greeting them by name. Checking the young stallion's hoof, she replaced the poultice on it with one she'd secreted in her pocket before leaving her room.

She knew she was disobeying the stable rules. It was hard to break the habit of stealth from when she helped her father. She also recognized she had an ulterior motive now. She wanted to help these horses, to prove herself to Edward and win her husband's affection, mayhap even his love.

Coming to Fury's stall, she made a quiet double click with her tongue against her teeth to get his attention. His head raised from his hay supper, and he turned to see who it was. She watched him chew and contemplate her. Clicking again, she raised her hand with the remaining greenery, switching hands deliberately and keeping a few vegetables in her left hand below the door level.

Sauntering over, the stallion flared his nostrils, checking her scent and scouting for the greens. As he neared, she held her right hand with the greens out along the top of the half door, away from her body. He came closer than he had the past few times she had visited, bringing his body almost parallel to the door to take the treat from her. She cocked her head, remembering that Nellie had come straight on at the door, giving Sophia her nose and ears to rub, rather than turning her body where she could not see the human clearly.

Sophia stroked Fury's neck as he nibbled the treat from her palm. Running both hands along his side, she clicked again and shoved his right rear haunch to see if he would turn toward her. He sidestepped and brought his head around. Switching the greens to her other hand, she petted to the right of his nose with her left hand, keeping him centered on her. Pushing against her hand, he raised his head and knickered. Slowly, she drew her right hand toward the left side of his mouth to see if he would take the rest of the greenery.

Fury pulled his head away and stepped back.

"Shh," Sophia crooned to him. "Let me see your mouth."

With one hand holding the halter's nose strap, she touched the left side of his head gently. The young horse did not shy away. Then she ran her thumb under his top lip at the front of his mouth and slid it around to the left, raising it a little away from his teeth. The top teeth looked fine, but his gums were swollen around one lower tooth in particular, and the swelling had spread along several teeth. The horse did not want to chew soft greens on that side, much less take a bit.

"Stay calm, sweeting," she continued to soothe him. "I shan't hurt you. Let me come in for a minute."

Slipping into his stall, she quickly poured a vial of liquid into his water. Hoping he would not mind the taste, she encouraged him to drink it by rubbing a small amount on his upper left gum, letting it drip down to the swollen area below to avoid hurting him.

She praised him for being so docile when she put her fingers in his mouth. "You simply have a toothache with no way to tell us, Fury."

Scratching his nose, she made sure he enjoyed the last of the kitchen greenery and stepped out.

Returning to the house, she debated whether or not to tell Edward. She'd need to check on Fury and discuss care with the stablemaster the next day, so he would find out at some point. Would it be better to have progress to show or to be upfront?

****

The sofa in the music room was oversized, but to Sophia, it fit Edward perfectly. Longer than most, it also had a deeper seat cushion. When she'd asked him, he admitted that he'd bought it after an earlier injury, so he could sleep there and avoid the stairs. He used it as a temporary bedroom and had easy access to the study for managing the estate by day.

It also provided him a view of the training ring. Thankfully, no rooms on the lower floor had a view of the stables since Sophia had not told him her suspicions about Fury's ailment yet.

Bringing correspondence in to keep him company as she worked, she noticed he had not read any of the books she'd left. When she asked if he would prefer a different one, he declined. What did he do when she wasn't there to read to him?

Edward slept in the music room that night and returned there after breakfast. She slipped out, telling him she desired a quick ride on Nellie, as the horse was not getting enough exercise. With another vial pocketed and more treats from the kitchen, Sophia stopped at Fury's stall first.

At her tongue click, the stallion came right over to the half door, nodding his head at her in recognition. Giving him greens, she stroked behind his ears while he chewed. He was still chewing on the right side. When he nudged her arm for more goodies, she held the halter and lifted his lip gently. The swelling was down, although not gone. Rubbing a bit of liquid on the inside of his lip—she avoided touching the irritated gums—she unlatched the door and added the rest to his water again.

As she stepped back, sliding the empty vial into the pocket of her gown, the stablemaster's voice growled low from the half door. "What exactly are you doing in there? What did you give him?"

Clearly suspicious, Russell frowned at her, seeming not to notice she'd ventured into the stallion's stall when most stable hands would not even reach over the threshold.

Sophia started but quickly calmed for the horse's sake. She walked back to the door and slipped out to the main corridor next to him. "Tincture of myrrh. He has a toothache. I included cloves and peppermint to add to his feed for pain relief and taste, but myrrh will reduce the swelling."

Russell gaped. "How did you know he had a toothache?"

"I suspected after watching him act up only when you wanted to give him the bit. I checked last night before giving him the first dose of myrrh."

Russell appeared dazed. Hoping to make a quick escape before the stablemaster remembered she had again broken the stable rules, Sophia rewarded Fury with another bunch of greens and pivoted away from the man toward the mares' stable and Nellie.

As she walked away, she called over her shoulder, "I'm off for a quick ride on Nellie. You may want to check his mouth later, or I can tomorrow morning. Hopefully, by then he shall be ready for the bit. If he is not, that tooth may need to be pulled."

"Nellie girl! Time to play!" Sophia rushed through saddling Nellie, impatient to ride. The mare seemed to share her enthusiasm, prancing in place once or twice, holding still only for the blanket and saddle.

Then they were out and flying across the rolling green hills, wind streaming through her hair and Nellie's tail.

Sophia chatted the whole while to her confidant. "I am so bored with the books and correspondence. And now we're caught up with the bookkeeping. I am trying to convince Edward to give me more time with you and

Fury and the rest of the brood. That is my one last wish."

Well, one of two, really. I wish he would love me. I think he cares for me, but I'd worry less about him leaving me if he loved me as Nicholas loves Ros.

Shrugging it off for the moment, she continued. "Edward is teaching me so much about marriage. I am amazed at all the activities for husbands and wives. I mean, I have seen some of your brethren, but 'tis different. Do you know I rode *him* the other night, Nellie? But the deuced man hurt himself. And I cannot lose him. I've lost too many people. I promised myself I would not love again, but I cannot seem to help it. Edward has encouraged me and taught me so much, and is so kind. Well, in a spanking sort of way, I suppose..."

****

Edward stood at the music room window, ignoring the lunch that had been brought in and his wife, who hovered near him, watching him and the training ring alternately. Her handwringing in the corner of his vision was distracting, but he'd find out why she was upset after he saw if today would be the day Fury accepted the bit.

Motion in the yard drew his focus. The stablemaster led Fury out and walked him around the yard several times. A hand passed Russell the bridle and bit, and he held Fury's lead, moving the bridle up toward the horse's mouth.

Edward held his breath, hearing Sophia's indrawn breath as well.

Fury tossed his head and pulled away a little but did not rear or back up.

305

Soothing him with words and the hand holding the lead, Russell raised the bridle again slowly and smoothly.

This time, the horse allowed the straps to glide over his nose, taking the bit in his mouth. His ears flicked as the top straps settled behind them. Quivering, nostrils flaring, he tossed his head once more but stood while the trainer praised him and petted him.

Edward sighed his breath out in a gust and leaned forward. "He did it."

Collapsing onto the settee, Edward bounced once in excitement. "Hellfire, that was in the nick of time. Stephen deserves a bonus for that. I cannot imagine how he managed it." Ringing for a servant, he asked the maid to send someone to ask the stablemaster to come to the house after he finished with Fury. He wanted to celebrate this step forward in training Fury with his friend. He turned back to watch Stephen take the bridle off and on, leading the horse around the yard with it on for longer each time.

Reaching out and squeezing his wife's hand, he smiled at her momentarily before his smile faded to a frown. *She still looks worried.*

****

"She *what*?" Edward yelled.

By all that is holy, what if the beast had reared and stomped her? Losing her would destroy me. Where in hellfire *had Russell been? And why did neither of them tell me?* Edward fumed, channeling his frightful imaginations of his wife being hurt or killed by an unruly stallion into his anger. *I don't care how angry I was at her for disobeying before—Sophia needs to trust me.*

An internal voice niggled at him. *You did not trust her with your secrets.*

He shoved the logic back, focusing on the fact that Russell had also not told him.

Standing to one side, Sophia cringed. Russell faced Edward, who sat in an armchair with his foot elevated on the matching ottoman in the study.

"Begging your lordship's pardon, but she *did* solve the issue," Russell dared to reply.

Sophia's head whipped toward the stablemaster.

Ignoring his wife's obvious surprise, Edward glared at him, shock and anger warring inside at his friend taking his wife's side. The man clearly had no care for his job or his life. He would have forfeited one or both if Sophia had been injured.

"You and I have seen too many injuries," he gritted out, "from hands trying to take the initiative without full knowledge of a horse's situation. Hellfire, I injured myself walking backward with a lead. Those rules are in place for a reason!" He was roaring by the time he finished, leaning forward over his propped leg.

As he escalated to a shout, Sophia squared her shoulders and turned to him. "My lord, 'tis not the stablemaster's fault. I went there after he had left. Do not blame him." Under her breath, she added, "Particularly as no one was hurt, and the horse is better."

Edward glared at her. "You, madam, best watch your tongue. You are already in more trouble than you can handle."

"Edward, I was perfectly safe. I have worked with horses for almost as long as you have. You're being ridiculous."

Too late, she realized how that sounded. She'd never truly argued with her husband, and now she'd diminished him in front of a servant. She bit her lip.

Sending her an icy stare, Edward turned to Russell and decreed, "Stephen, let the hands know. Sophia is not allowed in the stables without you or me accompanying her, other than to fetch Nellie." He knew it was extreme, but he was so angry he couldn't think of anything else.

"What? No! You cannot do that. You know I helped my father—" Sophia snapped her mouth closed as Edward turned back to glare at her again.

Without moving his gaze, he bit out, "Thank you, Stephen. That will be all tonight. We shall speak tomorrow. Plan to come up here for lunch."

The stablemaster nodded and withdrew, seeming grateful for the reprieve.

Sophia stood, putting one foot down hard in an almost-stomp. "My lord!"

Edward growled. "Sophia, you put yourself in danger. You went into a stallion's stall with no one around, one who is not fully broken yet. You might have been seriously hurt. That is not acceptable, and you *shall* be punished." His mouth firmed.

She bowed her head, mumbling like a recalcitrant child. "So did you. You've repeatedly hurt your ankle. And I helped…"

"You put yourself at risk. Not. Acceptable." His teeth were clenched, a muscle ticking in his jaw.

He needed to bind her to him, ensure her happiness with him other than the reading. 'Twas the worst time to require punishment, but she had snuck around again, breaking the rules even after a birching. More, she had risked her life, and he could not bear to contemplate that.

He observed his wife. Based on her slumped shoulders and lowered head, she was well and truly cowed.

Finally, her voice small, she responded, "Yes, my lord. I am sorry."

Shaking his head, he realized he was too angry to consider punishing her now. Sarah had taught him that early on. "I am going out." He dared her to say one word about his damned injury. "You are going to stay inside and think about your transgression. The rules are in place for a reason."

His anger drained, to be replaced by fatigue. Fighting to keep her from discovering his secret, banning her from something she clearly loved, was exhausting.

Chapter Twenty-One

After taking a page from Sophia's book and hiding in Ash's stall to talk things over with him, Edward returned to the house, still tired, scared, and befuddled as to the next step. He was limping slightly from the walk to and from the stables but had known better than to ride or try to help with the training. He'd kept the foot elevated on his hay bale perch.

Ash had not clarified anything for him, and Edward had the fleeting thought that mayhap he should have asked Nellie. *No, she would have sided with Sophia.*

He snorted. He might have lost his mind along with his heart.

Realizing he had left his notebook in the library where anyone might find it, he headed there...and found Sophia sitting at the table reading it.

"What are you doing?" His tone was flat.

"I was trying to determine what paperwork you'd already handled and what I could help with. I found this." She held the notebook up. "And these." She held up a letter from Nicholas, covered in sketches and arrows, large block letters making up short words between them.

"Why do you and Nicholas use pictures so much?" A small furrow in her brow belied her confusion.

He stared at her, grim-faced, jaw clenched. Sweat broke out under his clothes. This was it, then. He'd banned her from the stables, and now she'd learn of his incompetence with the written word, and she'd leave him. Hell, he'd even rejected her declaration of love, even if it was in self-defense. She may as well take his right arm. 'Twould hurt that much.

'Twas past time to come clean. He couldn't fathom how he'd keep this secret much longer. His wife was far too smart.

His heavy sigh bespoke his surrender to the inevitable. He was so tired of fighting with words. Tired of being afraid. He loved Sophia so much. He had no idea how he'd cope if she scorned his intellect, but he would rather find out now than in another month or year when he could no longer envisage his life without her. Hellfire and damnation, he was almost there now. He had just enough memory of his loneliness before her to know it would be horrible.

That thought made his exhaustion and frustration emerge as defensive anger. "I hadn't handled any of it."

Blinking at his tone, she gestured. "Would you prefer that I leave it?"

"No, blast it. If you must know, I cannot read those! Are you happy now? You have a dullard for a husband." He threw his hand out at the letters, only to rake it through his hair in agitation. "Well, I could read them, but it would take me a day to get through the one letter. Why do you think Nicholas draws pictures for me like I'm a child? And why else do I keep you in here doing all this drudgery? Bah, I never wanted you to know this. I wished for your respect, your lo—care for me." He slumped down on the sofa, dropping his head into his hands, unwilling to meet her eyes.

****

Sophia had gone up to her room for a good cry when Edward banned her from the stables. But after her tears had dried, she was determined to get back into her husband's good graces. She loved him and was determined to make this a home and a partnership.

As he was not available, she could only do that through actions. Such as obeying his rules. She sighed. As interesting as Parliamentary law was, she was bored with only correspondence and paperwork.

Sitting at the study table where she usually worked, she riffled through the personal correspondence that had accumulated. Edward had apparently started to sort it, as it was in several piles. Looking under one, she spied his notebook.

Wanting to see what he might have already addressed and what she should focus on next, she opened it to the latest entries. And found sketches. Scribbled, sometimes illegible notes in the margins, but mostly sketches. Roads with drainage, an eye, and clocks and calendars from their discussion of the macadam roads. Bags of money and workhouses and an old person with a cane from their debate about the Insolvent Debtors Act. And so on.

She struggled to understand his notes, having to sound out some words to even know what he referred to. He seemed to write words phonetically rather than anything resembling a standard spelling.

Confused by it all, she flipped pages backward, engrossed.

An hour later, Edward found her there, only to become angry at her again.

Tears welled in her eyes as she slumped. She felt as though she could not do anything right, could not please him.

She barely understood what he was saying, staring at him through watery eyes. He was... What? Illiterate? Why was he so angry about it? And why hadn't he told her? She would have had more patience being stuck inside at a desk every day if she knew she was supporting him in a way he needed.

You did *know that. You simply didn't know the reason behind it. Mayhap you should trust your husband more.*

Sophia thought back to their discussions of Parliament during their rides in London. His meetings with Nicholas.

Might his reluctance to consider marriage have been for this, not his love of the crop?

The pile of personal correspondence on his desk came to mind. His debates about laws after dinner, having her draft the proposal for the macadam roads. All performed seamlessly to avoid having to read or write.

Why did he think she'd condemn him for this? Had his family? Had Nicholas?

She frowned. She could not imagine family or Nicholas not supporting someone they cared about, but she knew there were all sorts of families, and the Ton had proven itself closed-minded and rule-driven.

As she sat there reviewing the past in light of this new information, she realized she hadn't responded to him or reassured him.

Belatedly, she made an attempt. "Edward! Why would you believe I—"

"Just go, Sophia. If you're going to leave me, go. I'll ensure you have safe passage to London."

"What? No! I—"

Glaring at her, he made a shooing motion. "Go! I cannot bear to see you look at me with disdain like the others."

She shook her head. "Edward, I—"

"*Go!* Please. I'm begging you," his voice broke, and he threw himself backward on the sofa, arm over his eyes to avoid her.

Shocked at her husband, always strong and in command, sounding so broken, she left the room. She needed time to think, to determine how to reassure him.

Sophia hardly slept that night. She had been told that her husband had taken dinner in his room and was not to be disturbed. Shoulders slumped, she picked at the cold dinner she'd requested to save the kitchen some work and went to bed, only to lay staring at the bed canopy, alternating between fear he'd send her away and elaborate ideas on how repair her marriage.

What would she do if he sent her away? Where would she go? She supposed she might return to Nicholas's house. Or mayhap Edward's townhouse in London. But she hated London. Really, though, the issue wasn't where to live—it was how to live without Edward. She loved him, reading or no. She would not lose another person she loved, and she loved him desperately, more so than she'd ever cared for anyone. What could she do to make him love her? Or at the very least, keep her. As she lay with too many questions and not enough answers, wishing for Ros or Juliet or Penelope to talk to, she had only one thought. Being the best wife ever remained her primary goal.

As she lay there, she grew angry. She knew she had helped Fury. Even the stablemaster had stood up for her, despite her blatant misstep of not including him in her treatment of Fury. While she had circumvented the rules, she'd spent too many years slipping around people's disapproval of a woman working with horses to lose the habit that easily.

Frustration at not being able to work through this with Edward fueled her anger. Admittedly, this was a bigger disagreement than they'd ever had, or rather, the biggest two arguments they'd ever had. Her diagnosis and treatment of Fury—she refused to call it anything else—followed by her discovery of Edward's notebook and, therefore, his secret. But she'd never ended up wallowing in uncertainty overnight.

With a start, she remembered what Ros had told her when she was describing the School of Enlightenment and her own marriage. She did not mind, mayhap even preferred spanking as a resolution to transgressions because then it was over, penance was paid, and they returned to normal. Edward had always provided that, too, until this time.

He'd promised a punishment but then left her stewing for the whole afternoon and evening and overnight.

So what now?

She snorted. She knew what now. She very definitely deserved a punishment for breaking the rules. He sort of did as well, for not trusting her to support him, but she suspected she'd need to let that pass.

He was not being fair, stringing her along. Either punish her or send her away, but she could not deal with this purgatory.

She would have to demand her punishment.

****

Having fallen asleep as dawn lightened the horizon, Sophia missed breakfast.

She checked his rooms, the dining room, and the music room. No Edward. Even the study, where she'd found the notebook, held only James. She mumbled a greeting and returned to the music room, hoping she would not find her husband in the training ring. His ankle was not fully healed yet, and no matter how angry she was with him, she still loved him and wanted him hale and hearty again.

She did not see him, but Russell was there with another yearling, as well as two other trainers. He kept turning his head to speak to someone out of view in the direction of the stables. One of the other trainers carried a hay bale into the ring. Her husband walked over, limp almost gone thankfully, and sat on the bale, propping his leg straight along the makeshift seat.

She sighed. 'Twas better than walking around the ring. And his boots were not his usual tight-fitting ones, so she hoped he'd be able to remove them if the leg swelled.

But it meant he wouldn't walk back and forth to the house for lunch. 'Twould be a long day of more stewing, damn him.

An hour later, her frustration had reached a peak. How dared the blasted man go back to work as though nothing was amiss? She could not read more than four words without losing her train of thought. And while that should have made her more empathetic to Edward's daily plight, she was in no mood to be considerate. He needed to resolve his threats, and she was tired of waiting for him to pick one or the opportunity to pick her own.

Finally, she sent a servant down to the training area with the message that James wished to speak with him over tea that afternoon.

Turning to James, she kept her tone bright. "I'm finally making headway through this pile of personal correspondence Edward handed me. There are several items I need to review with him, and 'tis a rare dry day. Why don't you finish early and spend some time with your family?"

He smiled. "If you're sure, my lady?"

"Very." She smiled back.

She was alone with the tea tray when Edward entered the room an hour later, shoulders back and jaw set, ready for a fight.

He scowled at her. "Where is James?"

"I sent him home early."

"But he said—"

"I sent that message, Edward."

"What? Why? Never mind. I can only guess. You're packed, then? When do you wish to leave?" His shoulders slumped, the scowl still in place.

"I am not packed. Nor do I plan on leaving." Growing more agitated with every word, she practically growled by the end. How dare he assume? What about their vows? Even if he didn't trust her, did he not hear her when she told him she loved him? He did not get to throw her away. "We have unfinished business."

His voice was weary. "You know everything. No more secrets." He spread his hands wide.

Tea forgotten, she stood, chest out, ready to take him on despite the near-foot difference in heights. "You owe me..." She faltered at his eyebrows raised in question but carried on. "...a punishment."

****

Edward gaped at his wife for a moment. He'd been so sure she was packed and ready to demand her return to London.

He hadn't slept much the night before, agonizing over whether he should beg her to stay or let her go. Loving someone was so much harder than he'd expected. Ultimately, he'd decided the decision had to be hers, as the most important outcome was her happiness.

Staying out of her way to give her space, he'd had a hay bale pricking his arse all morning, as his stablemaster would not allow him in his own training ring otherwise. It seemed his wife had even won his stablemaster's loyalty. The hay bale had given him interesting ideas for future punishments, until he realized he'd told Sophia to leave him and she would not be here to tease and torture.

Now she was asking—no demanding, by Jove—that he punish her. Did that mean what he thought it did? Did he dare hope?

Despite the questions he still entertained, most of his blood drained from his head to his cock. Having enough wits to ask one last question, he asked, "That is your choice? Stay and be punished?"

She could change her mind any time, but if he loved her, he had to trust her to stay. He needed to hear it in her words, though.

"Yes. 'Twas unfair of you to let this remain unresolved for a day and night, my lord."

"You are quite right, wife. Letting a punishment linger in your mind is not fair." He was getting into the spirit of the thing. "Much better to let it linger on your lovely form." He was also starting to remember his terror when he'd discovered she'd been alone in Fury's stall with her hands in his mouth.

She sucked in a breath. He wasn't sure if it was in fear or anticipation, but he hoped it was both.

Leading her to the library, he released her hand and went to his desk chair. "Go to the cabinet and fetch the brush and the agate wax seal from the shelf and come to my desk." He could have easily grabbed either item on his path, but part of the punishment was making her select the implements.

Frowning askance, Sophia opened her mouth.

Edward was watching for an argument. "And you may not speak. I shall gag you with my handkerchief if you make a sound." He deliberately did not choose the birch in order to ensure she couldn't judge the severity or style of a penalty, thus keeping the risks of disobedience higher.

I shall have to remember this when I have children. He gulped. *Children? Yes. I want that.* Especially as she seemed ready to stay, despite his reading limitations. But he had more immediate concerns.

He pictured her hands and face near Fury's teeth, and flames of fear and anger were reignited. Imagining her prone beneath the stallion's hooves was a bellows, fanning the feelings higher.

"Sophia, if I have to get them myself, you'll be sorry." His voice was steel.

She brought the items to him at the desk. They had played with the brush in the first weeks of their time there, with him brushing her skin to sensitize it. She had liked it, but when he asked what her favorite toys were, this was not one of them. But nor had she disliked it, as

319

she did the birch.

He gestured her around to his right, behind the desk. "Stand here next to my chair, bend over the desk, and raise your skirts to your waist." When she stood for a minute, still frowning at the tools he'd chosen, he gritted out, "*Now.*"

Sophia gathered her skirt and petticoats in hand and raised the back of them as she bent forward over the desk. Per his rules, she had nothing on beneath them.

Edward placed her arms out in front of her and curled her fingers around the far edge of the desk. "Do not move from there."

As he straightened, he gathered the double ink well and seal rest from the desk and slid it closer to him.

Opening one inkwell, he dipped a finger in. His finger came out coated not with ink but with a rather thick orange-tinted oil. He placed it against her rear hole and smoothed it around the entrance, rubbing then pressing only the tip of his finger inward.

Gasping, she stiffened, starting to straighten, and Edward slapped his hand on her back. "Wife, tell me now if you cannot endure this punishment. Otherwise, you will stay in place. Make your decision."

Chapter Twenty-Two

Sophia stilled, holding her breath as well as her body motionless. She trusted Edward absolutely. Here was another opportunity to show him. "I will accept whatever you deem appropriate, husband."

His hand clenched on her back before flattening again. "You know the rules by now. Repeat them for me, then you will be silent again."

He gathered more oil and pressed his finger in again, moving it in and out and angling it differently, stretching her rear passage.

She shifted from side to side, distracted by the sensations. The prickling heat of an intrusion in her most private place without the sexual stimulation of the first time felt wrong, but the oil prevented it from hurting.

His hand left, and fire exploded on her left bottom cheek.

"Humph. I, uh, am not to move while being punished."

"And? Why are you being punished?"

"Be-because I did not check with Russell before helping Fury."

She squirmed. He had two oil-slicked fingers in her now, and as he scissored them and sawed them in and out, she felt less discomfort. Instead, she found she didn't mind the invasion. It drew her attention to the proximity of his fingers to more pleasurable areas. Tendrils of desire curled forward from her bottom.

"Sophia, during your first bath I told you I would have you everywhere. Your body is mine, for pleasure and punishment. Do you recall that?"

"Yes, Edward."

"I shan't take you here now, but you will take this punishment and feel it for the evening. Hopefully, you will think about your actions and reconsider in the future." His fingers withdrew. "My goal is to punish you but not to hurt you…much. Tell me if 'tis too painful."

His fingers dipped into the inkwell again, and he rubbed oil onto the agate seal, from the top of the teardrop over the widest bit, perhaps an inch and a half diameter, to the narrow neck above the base that held the seal itself. Confused, she watched as it disappeared toward the back of the desk.

Something hard pressed at her rear entrance.

That is not a finger! She gasped and tensed, raising her head. 'Twas the seal, and the pear shape's width ballooned in her imagination.

Edward tightened his hand holding one of her bottom cheeks and eased it open. "It shall be easier and less painful if you do not clench, but either way this is going inside you, Sophia."

"It—"

Belatedly, she remembered she was not allowed to speak.

Too late, though, as his hand released her cheek only to return in an excruciatingly hard slap.

"Eeep!" escaped before she pressed her lips closed and lay her head flat on the desk, signaling surrender.

Being spanked felt very different when he hadn't stroked her flesh first and started with light swats. This plain stung.

Tears pricked her eyes.

But it had also distracted her, so when he tugged her bottom cheek out again and positioned the tip of the wax seal at her opening, it slid in an inch before she realized it. She tensed again, but he stretched her carefully, working the seal in and out, going farther each time. When it was almost to the widest part, he held it there, jiggling it, to allow her ring of muscle to become accustomed to the intrusion. Then one last short pull back, a firm push, and it was in, her head jerking off the desk again with a gasp.

He tapped on the end a few times.

The jostles of the desk instrument sent darts through her, part fear of pain, part...pleasure. Was that allowed?

Her hips wiggled on the desk. The thing felt huge, and it had pinched going in, but now the burn was subsiding to a simmer. She kept wiggling, thinking to dislodge it somehow, but it did not budge, other than to hit already-sensitized nerve endings.

It absolutely did not belong, but it was well and truly wedged in there. *For how long? Oh no. He had said "for the evening."*

"Stop wriggling," he growled. "If you had squirmed like that in Fury's stall, he'd likely have bitten you. This is nowhere near as painful as that."

She watched sideways, prone, as he reached for the brush.

Thwack!

"Ooowww," she cried.

Now she understood his request. He had turned the brush around, bristles to his palm, the hard wood back to her. The heavy weight of the brush added to the impact, and the implement in her bottom shifted each time, causing her to clench and sending tendrils of discomfort—and a dark edge of pleasure—through her.

Thwack!

"Ooohh!"

"Be quiet. You will take this punishment in silence, Sophia, or it will be much longer," Edward said roughly as he continued to spank her with the brushback. "Do you have any idea how scared I was when I heard about your disobedience from Russell? If you had fallen or Fury had bitten you...I would have been devastated."

The strain in his voice and his confession of fear warmed her heart and clarified the reason for severity of the punishment.

Meaning to reassure him, she started to speak, "Mmph." Quickly, she caught herself and bit her lip to stay quiet.

Without the release of even a yelp, the burn of pleasure-filled pain built hotter as more smacks rained down. Every blow jiggled the giant object in her bottom, lighting up nerve endings and making her clench and squirm.

His free hand went to her lower back, and his lower leg braced against hers to stop her movements.

She was trapped, surrounded, and all that coalesced in her brain. He was again controlling her, out of care for her safety.

Dare I hope it's more? Suddenly, his reaction the day before made sense. *He was embarrassed, yes. That had been obvious. But mayhap he was also scared I will not return his affections with my new knowledge?*

Her frame went limp as she relaxed. Her adoration and admiration for her husband swelled hotly inside as her bottom burned from the outside, igniting in a burst of love.

She admitted silently that while she'd keep trying to help, she could live without participating in the horse training, but not without Edward's affection. Now she needed to make him believe that.

Thwack! Thwack, thwack, thwack! Her bottom burned, inside and out, as the curry brush continued to descend, moving from cheek to cheek and down to her thighs.

"Now, stand up."

Oh, will he take that horrible object out?

But no, he set the brush aside and drew her up, flipping her skirts down.

Sophia's breath caught as she stood, and her eyes sheened with unshed tears, both from how much she loved him and from the pain in her bottom. The seal plugging her shifted again as she straightened, and she inadvertently clenched again, causing her bottom to sting more from the spanking.

"Come. You shall sit with me now, then go in to dinner like that. You will think about what you did, so you do not easily forget to keep yourself safe again."

Sophia followed him back to the settee, and as he stood waiting, she gingerly lowered to perch on the edge of the settee. She gasped and bit her lip as she sank onto the cushion, only to realize her mistake at choosing that piece of furniture when he dropped unabashedly, causing the cushion to bounce under her.

She moaned. "My lord—Edward," she whined.

"Shh." He smiled grimly, watching her face. "You can bear it. You *shall* bear it, for me. I need to know you are safe."

Hmm, when he words it like that, she thought with a quick tilt of her lips at his admission. "Yes, my lord."

A servant announced dinner, and she had to navigate standing, walking, then sitting again, on the far-less-cushioned dining room chair.

Sophia fidgeted on her chair. This was not how she pictured having this conversation.

However, communication was more important than her discomfort. She needed to assuage her husband's fears. She forced her focus away from the heat in her bottom and the throbbing in her swollen folds.

"My lord—Edward," she started firmly.

Edward sat back, his shoulders stiff, placing his utensils down. He took a deep breath, seeming to brace for her next words. *Why, he is as afraid as I am.*

"Husband, I respect you. I've told you I love you, and I meant it, no matter what you believe. I do not care that you read slowly or even if you did not read at all. I am happy to help you, like you help me with things."

He watched her through narrowed eyes, skeptical.

"How could you believe that I would think less of you because you have trouble reading?" Sophia was building a full head of steam now she had begun.

"Aaahh, I beg your pardon?" He looked at her blankly.

"Edward, you are my husband. I would not think less of you if you were permanently injured training horses. I never treated any of the townspeople my father cared for differently, including those with mental or physical disabilities. And I would not scorn someone for struggling in a particular area, only if they were deliberately cruel."

"What do I help you with?" He contested, frowning. "You do not need help to read. You know as much about the laws I am voting on as I do. You need no assistance with horses. You know as much about their care as I do."

"Look!" Waving her arm around again, she gestured at the room, the house. "Look at the beautiful home you have given me and Nellie. I suppose I could live anywhere, but Nellie can't. And neither of us would want to. You give us the space we want even beyond the house."

She knocked the side of her fist on the table twice, and her words came faster now. "Consider how many other husbands would not only allow their wife to read the paper but invite them to engage in discussion on news and government. And..." She lowered her voice. "...I know you look out for my safety, even when I don't follow your rules. I accept my punishments because I know you are taking care of me. It seems only fair that I handle things that help you."

Edward slumped back in his chair, food forgotten. His eyes were wide on hers. "I-I never thought of it that way."

He was quiet for several moments, staring down at his lap, before continuing. "Sophia, I beg your pardon. I should not have kept my reading impairment from you. I had several bad experiences with women discovering it during my younger years, and it became a habit to keep it secret. 'Twas especially hard to trust a woman with it again."

She was curious about those experiences, but this

was not the time to ask probing questions. "I accept your apology, husband. I hope now you feel you can trust me in all things."

"I do." He nodded in emphasis. "And I hope to prove worthy of your trust."

She barely registered that his statement implied moving forward together. She shifted. "Can my punishment be over now, then?"

He shook his head, although she thought his cheek quirked in a quick smile. "Absolutely not. 'Tis my job to protect my wife, even from herself. I hope this lesson will be thorough enough to convince you of that."

She sighed.

After that, Edward kept the dinner conversation light and did most of the talking, for which Sophia was grateful. With things right between them again, her focus moved to the parts of her pressed against the chair seat. She could not have carried on a discussion and struggled to follow his.

By the main course, she was shifting almost nonstop and her nipples were hard. She tried to focus. She really did. The heat in her bottom had spread through her body, making her feel every inch of fabric shifting against her. The hard chair under her, the metal utensils in her hand, the warmth of the wine threading through the sexual heat and fanning the flames.

Her nostrils flared, seeking his scent over that of the beef before her. She caught a whiff of leather and nearly moaned.

Mixing with the sensory overload was a heady layer of emotions. She remembered her earlier punishment for wandering the stables. She wondered if Edward realized he had commanded her then to "take care of my wife." And his reaction this time seemed to also focus on worry for her.

I knew it. I know he cares. And I suspect that, in addition to risk of injury, he wouldn't let me help in the stables because if I spent more time there, I might need him to handle more correspondence.

"Sophia," he said sharply, eyes on her twitching bottom. "You shall sit through dinner and pudding, silent and still, and contemplate what you should have done. Or I shall bend you over the table and spank you more, servants be damned."

Eyes wide, she glanced around to check if anyone had heard him. Two footmen stood near the door in case Edward or she wanted anything and to hold the door for servants bearing more food. They were far enough away they likely had not heard, but she scrutinized their expressions in case.

"Yes, my lord," she subsided.

He took longer to eat his berry tart than she ever remembered. When his attention was on his plate or his wine, she'd make a minuscule shift, but his focus snapped to her every time. And her wriggling seemed to slow him further.

She was panting by the time he pushed back his chair. "Shall we?"

Sophia had given up trying to eat eons ago and had fought for calm since, gulping shallow breaths as she processed the sensations ricocheting from the seal through her. She nodded and rose, taking his proffered hand.

He tucked her arm through his and strolled toward the library, his limp from the strained ankle hardly noticeable.

329

Gulping at the pace and resulting shifts in her bottom, she clenched to keep pace with him.

Leading her back to the desk, Edward left her standing where she had for her punishment earlier and poured them each a snifter of brandy.

He chose this rather than her usual wine when their play was going to be new or more extreme. Her eyes widened, given that she already had a foreign object in her bottom.

Handing her one for a sip, he then took it over to place it by the settee, sipping his as he strolled back to the desk.

"I am in a bit of a quandary, little one," he said. "I wish to ensure this punishment resonates with you. I do not want to muddy the waters with pleasure, but watching you through dinner, knowing you have my plug in you and are likely so wet you've stained your petticoat, I feel the need to enjoy you."

Oh, thank goodness. He's using his pet name for me and will mayhap offer some relief.

Glancing down, she saw his need outlined through his breeches. She licked her lips and returned her gaze to his.

"I shall let this be the end of your punishment now, but if it happens again, know that you shall go to bed without an orgasm. *And…*" He strolled over to the shelf with the other seals on it. "…note the sizes and shapes of these. Not all shall be as comfortable as the plug you're currently wearing."

Her eyes widened. *Some were curved…and carved!*

"All of these—and I do mean all—may be used for either pleasure or punishment," he continued. "I'm sure you'll experience every version of that in our marriage, but I am also guessing from your expression, you aren't in a hurry to try all of them. Good. Hopefully, there shall be no more repeats of putting yourself in danger with unbroken stallions." He raised his eyebrows at her.

Sophia breathed a sigh of relief at this second reference to a future together. Knowing he expected her to remain silent until given leave to speak, she nodded. Her body took over in reaction to the rest of his words, and she barely refrained from rubbing her legs together around her swollen nether lips and nub.

"Now then, let's see if I was correct." Edward turned her and bent her over the desk again.

As he flipped up her dress and petticoats, she felt cool air waft over wetness between her legs and even on her thighs.

His fingers slid through her folds, the moisture preventing enough pressure for her pleasure. He slid them up to the flange of the plug and grasped it, rotating and tugging on it. Her body resisted for a moment, but then the flare was out, only to be pushed back in again.

Her hips shimmied, her feet widened, and her back arched in supplication for him to do more.

He groaned, and she heard him fumble with what she hoped was the fall of his breeches.

"Please, my lord," she whispered. She was not certain she was allowed to speak, and somehow her brain ended up with a whisper being a compromise.

"Soon, Sophia, soon." Edward pistoned the plug several more times, leaving it in her and moving to stand between her legs when she tried to close them to get friction where she desired it most. His cock probed her entrance, sliding up and down through her wetness, setting off sparks from that sensitive bundle of nerves that made her want to twist toward him. She daren't, but was rewarded for her stillness when he notched it to her and shoved inside in one long, decisive thrust.

"Aaahhh," she cried. She felt stretched and tight and full with him in her front hole and the seal in her rear hole. Her nerve endings waffled between pleasure and pain, even more than when he had inserted the plug. While he usually eased into her, his aggressive claiming told her his focus remained on showing her who was in charge. She panted, completely willing to be at his mercy, to accept whatever he did to her.

He grunted. "Hold the desk," he gritted out before arching his hips back and pressing on the plug, then shoving into her as he pulled it partially out of her.

In and out, out and in, she could hardly process the sensations. Writhing on the desk, she moaned and gasped, struggling to keep up with the upward spiral. Before she gained a purchase on it, everything burst, every muscle clenched, her back bowing up off the desk, her fists and toes curling as her channel clamped around him. Suspended there for two more thrusts of his cock and the plug, her body fought him for possession of both, spasming around him and the seal over and over. Her stomach flipped, and her head swam in a whole-body orgasm, more intense than any she had experienced.

She finally sagged, her knees weakening so that all that held her on the desk were her hands on the far edge and his hips as he surged in one more time and held her down, his cock pulsing, his seed pumping into her.

Sophia barely noticed as Edward removed the seal, wrapped it in a cloth from a desk drawer, smoothed her skirts over her, and picked her up to sit in his desk chair with her in his lap, her head tucked under his chin.

Does he not see how perfect we are together?

After a few minutes and two sips of his brandy when he offered it to share, she raised her head.

Edward had a lopsided smile, accompanied by a furrowed brow of concern. "Sophia? Did I hurt you? I hope I was not too rough with you. I lost control a bit there. You had me so on edge from everything."

She shook her head and smiled sleepily, laying her head back against his chest. She was sure she wanted to ask him something—*about trust? love?*—but she was exhausted and overcome with sensation and emotion, content to be held in her husband's arms.

****

Edward took his time walking down to the stables after breakfast, still in awe over his wife's reaction—or lack of one—to his struggles. She was right. He had not trusted her, and he should have. She had done nothing to make him think she would spurn him. He had let his fears from his past cloud his thinking.

Sophia had agreed to do everything he asked—moving away from her only remaining family, attending the School of Enlightenment, being further isolated to handle correspondence rather than horses, his sexual proclivities, and even punishment.

He shrugged at his last thoughts with a smile. Given her shared interest in those, he marveled anew.

Nicholas and Charles did not care how well you read. Why did you think she would?

Because she was bearing the weight of his ineptitude. Thinking back to the examples he had thrown at her the day before, they still rang true. This all felt very one-sided, but he could not bear to think of her leaving him.

He would bribe her with all the horse time in the world if she'd agree to safety protocols. She would never have to read another bit of Parliamentary drudgery. And whatever other requests she might have. Except letting her go.

He had no intention of barring her from the stables long term, but it had seemed an apt punishment to enforce the rules that were for everyone's safety.

Considering her reaction to his other disciplinary action, he smiled. *Well, well, well, the little filly does not mind being plugged. Even with a sore arse.*

He was glad his gamble had paid off. Like having her suck him, he wanted her to enjoy anal penetration, rather than it being only a punishment. 'Twas all in how he handled it, but something about prodding a young lady's bottom seemed to keep her focused on who was in charge. *Reading be damned.*

His smile became an outright grin.

And her wide-eyed reaction to his proclamation about the other seals had nearly made him laugh out loud.

When he had bared her arse a second time and seen exactly how aroused she was, nether lips all puffy and begging for his cock, he had only just refrained from slamming into her. Taking the time to wet his cock so he didn't hurt her was torture, but then he could not hold back. He needed the forceful connection, her under him and bared to his dominance, to reaffirm life and banish his lingering fear for her safety.

But now he needed to focus. She said she loved him, but he needed to make sure she did not change her mind. More than that, after his unfounded tirade, she deserved a sign of his love.

Children.

For the first time since the night at the inn, he let his mind envision it. If they had his disability, he'd teach them the tricks he had learned to cope. He imagined himself, older and grayer, a grown son beside him as they navigated the rough waters of White's to pull out details of news and laws.

Finally having realized how nurturing his wife was, he knew children would bring them closer, but that would take time. He needed something immediate.

After some time contemplating a plan, he found Russell. James would have to wait until the afternoon, but he could put part of the strategy into action.

Later that day, after speaking to both men, he searched for his wife. When she was not in the study, Edward glanced out the window to see her streaking over the last hill toward the stables as rain spattered the windows. She must have ducked out to try to fit a ride in between the almost never-ending showers this summer.

By the time she got to the house, the rain had become a cold deluge, and her hair and habit were plastered to her. *Criminy, she looks so fragile yet is so strong.*

Her boots squeaked on the gleaming stone of the great hall as she crossed from the kitchen toward the stairs.

"Sophia, come in here if you please," he requested, shaking his head with a smile at her wet hair and habit.

"My lord, may I change first?" Sophia asked.

"No, but this shall be quick." Edward gestured her

into the study. Seizing a throw off the settee, he placed it around her shoulders to stop her from getting chilled and gestured to chairs, and they sat.

****

At a loss, Sophia leaned on her school training, "How may I serve you, my lord?"

"Sophia," Edward said. "James informed me that you are both up-to-date on the ledgers, and you've been a tremendous help with the bookkeeping and correspondence."

"Thank you. Yes, we seem to be," she replied. Inwardly, she thrilled. *Thank you, James.* She barely refrained from wiggling in her chair.

"He said the ledgers were so caught up that he only needs your help for half days now." He paused, and Sophia sat forward in her chair. "And he told me about the tonic you sent for his wife's cough."

Sophia bit her lip, afraid she was in trouble for helping a human with medicine now, as well as the horses.

Edward's face offered no hint of the goal of this recitation as he continued. "I was also speaking to Stephen, and he has been lauding your praises. Apparently, the poultice you made for sore hooves works miracles, and he's worn it out. He'd like a few more."

Her heart jolted once in hope. "My lord?"

She frowned in confusion as her husband rose and went to the door, returning with the stablemaster.

"Mr. Russell." Sophia's voice quivered. Despite his defense of her actions with Fury to Edward and his apparent request for more poultices, she was nervous.

He sketched a shallow bow in return.

She spared the stablemaster another quick glance as he sat beside her, and he lifted one side of his mouth in a half smile for her.

"Russell would also like your help with a few other horses," Edward informed her, "given how you won Fury over and found a toothache none of us had thought of." He firmed his lips briefly in regret. "Sophia, you know I value your knowledge. We spoke of that yesterday. I also want you safe. My anger over Fury was borne of fear for your safety." He gave her a stern look. "Which is why there are rules in place for the stables. Untrained stallions and even yearlings are difficult to manage, particularly for someone as petite as you."

"I understand, husband."

"Stephen and I have discussed having you advise on horse care."

Her eyes flared, and she bounced in her seat. *Yes!*

"*But*…there will be rules, which Stephen and I have already agreed on. We shall discuss those later. For now, I wanted you to hear this with Stephen present. Can you make him another poultice or two by day's end?"

"Oh, yes, certainly. Thank you, Edward. Thank you, Stephen." She clumsily bowed a half curtsy to each from her seat.

"Thank you, Stephen. That will be all. I shall see you later."

"Thank you, oh thank you, husband!" Sophia flew out of her chair even as the stablemaster departed. Plopping herself on her husband's lap, she pressed kisses all over his face. "Oh, I love you so. You shan't be sorry."

337

Edward pulled back. "Darn it, Sophia. Now you've beaten me to it."

"Wh-what?" Her smile dropped as she stared at him in consternation. What had she done wrong now?

He smiled. "I brought you here not only to tell you I was wrong to hide my disability from you and wrong to keep you locked in the library, but that I love you. I want you safe, and I want you happy. And…I just want *you*." He gave a quick shrug.

"I knew it." She gloated for a second before saying, "Goodness, I've been waiting to hear you say it, though. Oh, my love. We are a pair. Afraid of love." She bounced again in happiness. "Oh, Edward. I am so happy. Thank you, my love." She peppered kisses over his face again.

Grinning, he sighed. He stroked her damp hair. "Ah, but what a perfect pair we make. What other wife would actually want to read Parliamentary bills and debate with me about macadam roads? And who else's bottom would I crop until she was twitching and begging for my cock?"

She squirmed on his lap, her blood rushing, a blush spreading up her chest and face. She felt his blood rising too, against her hip.

"I believe now 'tis a perfect time for a reward, little one. What would you like?"

She bit her lower lip, then shrugged. "I trust your judgment."

"Mmm. Not this time. I should like to see what you choose."

She glanced around the room for inspiration. Her gaze lit on the wax seal collection and an idea formed.

"Um…Edward," she whispered, "mayhap another

seal? But without the spanking? You said they could all be used for pleasure…"

His eyes flared, and his muscles stiffened around her, the length of him hardening against her hip. He grinned and dropped a quick kiss on her smiling lips.

"My wife, I love you more every minute!"

Epilogue

Edward leaned back against the chaise longue in his wife's bedroom.

Sophia sat with her legs curled to one side on the end between his shins, book in hand. Reading, or rather being read to, had become one of his favorite pastimes in recent months, particularly now Parliament had finished, summer was waning, and he had more time.

"What are we reading tonight, my love?"

"I chose poetry from the library, my lord, as I was punished for finding other works." She bristled slightly as she recalled being penalized.

The minx had written to Roslynn and requested help in finding books to entertain her husband. A few evenings ago, she had started the penny dreadful that had arrived that day and had them both squirming with sexual tension within a few chapters.

Who knew how she had phrased the request, or if 'twas Roslynn's idea, but the chaise had proved useful. He had grabbed her and bent her over the tall end to spank her for using naughty words, only to pound into her immediately after, bringing them both to pleasure.

Come to think of it, he needed to struggle through writing a note to his friend to get Ros a spanking for that. A pleasurable one.

"Right, then. Read on." He settled in to listen. How would he have managed the loneliness, never mind the correspondence? He couldn't imagine being happy here, even with his horse training, without her. She was his life.

They had agreed on her spending mornings with James. Afternoons depended on the amount of correspondence or review of laws needed. When she had free time, she would report to Stephen or Edward to see if they needed any help with equine care. If not, someone would accompany her to the village where James's wife acted as agent for messages from villagers needing help with ailments. Or she and Bobby would ride out to gather herbs grown locally.

Occasionally, she would call him up to the office to get through a pile of paperwork that required his thoughts.

And more often than not, they found time for a quick ride together.

He had only one other wish, which they'd discussed. He was relieved to find she shared it. Children.

Coming back to the poetry, he decided that was enough reading. 'Twas time to work on that final wish.

Maggie Sims

A word about the author...

Maggie Sims began her love affair with romance before her teen years, drawn to the Regency by her mum's British influence. In her twenties, she did her best to live the Carrie Bradshaw life in New York City, albeit with less expensive shoes and more books.

Despite reading hundreds of romance novels in her life, she was still blown away when she met the love of her life, an ex-Marine cinnamon roll with creative culinary skills.

They live in Central Texas and are parents to a varying number of dogs and cats. When not writing, Maggie is a wine enthusiast and a travel junkie and crochets sporadically for Knots of Love.

~*~

Contact Maggie at
www.MaggieSims.com
and sign up for her newsletter
to get Roslynn's & Nicholas's
story in a free novella.

Coming Soon
from The Wild Rose Press, Inc.
and major retailers.

Penelope's Passion
School of Enlightenment Book Two
By Maggie Sims

1816 London

After her mother's death, Penelope Wood's hope of opening a bakery falls victim to the real need to support herself. When four retired courtesans present her with a temporary yet lucrative path back to her dream, she wants to hear more. Attending the School of Enlightenment, participating in a Virgin Auction, and becoming a courtesan all sound feasible. The most important rule—do not fall in love.

Lord Michael Slade, heir to the Earl of Mansfield, loves his family above all else, cooks for relaxation, and revels in his membership to a discreet spanking club. But his father is ill, and his mother is pushing him to marry. Even so, when he meets a dark-haired beauty who doesn't mind a good spanking and discovers she's up for auction, he can't let her go to another man. He has to have her...at least until he finds a wife.

With an inevitable marriage looming and a vow to remain faithful to his hypothetical bride once he's engaged, both Penelope and Michael must protect their hearts, even as they find a connection they cannot deny.

A Matter of Manners

Shades of Sin Book One

By Terry Graham

Jeremy Wyles believes himself sterile. He's also a sadist and fears no lady would agree to marry him. When a woman shows up on his doorstep, pregnant and claiming to be his wife, he'll do whatever is necessary to ensure his dukedom has an heir. A loveless marriage in name only seems the perfect solution, but his disobedient duchess stirs his desire for discipline...and something more.

Irish rebel Kathleen "Katy" Brennan only seeks recompense from the husband whose cousin married her by proxy and left her with child. The bargain he offers is tempting. He'll claim her baby as his own, and she can become the grand lady she's always imagined. There's just one condition she's not sure she can live with. The delicious-looking duke refuses to touch her...ever.

Can Jeremy put aside the wicked urges that rule his life, or will Katy's rebellious spirit destroy his tenuous control?

Thank you for purchasing
this publication of The Wild Rose Press, Inc.

For questions or more information
contact us at
info@thewildrosepress.com.

Lightning Source UK Ltd.
Milton Keynes UK
UKHW020652290822
408013UK00009B/833